TEAM TRIAD

Fernando Ugarte
I wish you the
best,

Joe

TEAM TRIAD

A NUCLEAR SPY HUNT:
IRAN

J. E. HARB, JR.

HABU PRESS
覇武
プレス
LAKEWOOD RANCH

Team Triad is a work of fiction. The events described in this tale are all products of my imagination.

The views expressed are entirely my own, not those of NSA or any other intelligence agency.

Copyright © 2017 by Joseph E. Harb, Jr.

ISBN: 978-0-9991428-0-6

Cover photograph is public domain. All other photographs are by author and family members.
All diagrams, maps, and cryptograms created by author

Published by

Team Triad is dedicated to current and former civilian and military members of the U.S. Intelligence Community, who have focused their professional lives on ensuring the security of our nation and protecting the rights of all Americans. Among them are those who have selflessly given their lives, often anonymously, to protect us.

Contents

Acknowledgements

I deeply appreciate the invaluable advice and assistance that a number of people - particularly my wife, Linda, and friends and exceptionally talented former colleagues Les Myers, Dolores Powers, Kathleen Rahal, and Ivan Pressman - provided to help improve the quality of *Team Triad*. I am very thankful for Jose M. Troche, and his wife and daughter for their invaluable assistance with creating the front cover. Thank you all very much!

I am very grateful to the Naval Security Group and to the National Security Agency for the training and opportunities they provided me over the years. The knowledge I gained is reflected in *Team Triad*.

I am very thankful for the timely prepublication review of my manuscript by the responsible NSA office.

Introduction

The prospect of a nuclear-armed Iran raised deep concerns in the international community in 2002, when an Iranian dissident group revealed the existence of two nuclear-weapons-related facilities hidden from the International Atomic Energy Agency (IAEA). Those most alarmed were the U.S., Israel, and Iran's Sunni Arab neighbors such as Saudi Arabia. The Israeli Government considered an Iranian nuclear capability an existential threat because of Iran's oft-stated objective of "Death to Israel." By early 2015, experts believed Iran was within a few months to a year of producing enough fissile material for one nuclear weapon.

In 2006, the UN Security Council imposed harsh sanctions on Iran for refusing to comply with the Nuclear Non-Proliferation Treaty. By 2013, the sanctions were taking a heavy toll on the Iranian economy. Iran, with a new, more-moderate president, entered into negotiations with the P5+1 – the five permanent members of the UN Security Council (China, France, Russia, the United Kingdom, and the United States), plus Germany, a key Iranian trading partner which provided many products and services to the Iranian nuclear program. Despite the damaging sanctions, some conservatives in Iran were adamantly opposed to Iran ending its nuclear weapons program.

On April 2, 2015 the P5+1 reached agreement on a framework for a final agreement, which was to be completed by July 1, 2015, but was not finalized until July 14.

3

The Prime Minister of Israel and many in the U.S. believed Iran could not be trusted or that the Iranian program could be stopped by harsher sanctions or military action. Others believed that any agreement should cover Iran's nuclear, ballistic missile, terrorist, and external military activities. They wanted to hold off on attacking the stage four cancer until they could cure the stage one and stage two cancers at the same time.

Military action against Iran's deeply buried, bomb-resistant enrichment facilities might have produced temporary results at best and might have prompted bloody Iranian responses. In the Iran-Iraq War, Iran demonstrated its unwillingness to surrender despite massive losses of at least 125,000 killed in action, 320,000 wounded, and 60,000 missing.

The bottom line was that Iran's imminent acquisition of nuclear weapons posed a grave threat to international security and stability in the Middle East and South Asia.

Team Triad illustrates how the dynamics of such a major contentious international issue can pose complex analytic challenges with major historic consequences to the analysts of our Intelligence Community (IC). As is the case with many complex endeavors, successful intelligence depends on a combination of many factors, including access, talent, education, experience, dedication, teamwork, hardware, software, management, organization, and luck. Absent any one critical element, an entire effort can fail.

This tale depicts the high value of interagency cooperation that combines different analytic disciplines and types of information, including Human Intelligence (HUMINT), Signals Intelligence (SIGINT), Imagery Intelligence (IMINT), Cyber Intelligence, and publicly available information.

Team Triad describes the importance of timeliness, a sine qua non of intelligence reporting. It does no good to produce intelligence about an impending attack after the attack has started. The intelligence must be delivered in time to thwart the attack.

The unfolding of events in this story demonstrates the

importance of keeping an open mind while analyzing intelligence information. What might at first appear to be a logical conclusion could be proven totally wrong with more complete information. I expect this is similar to what police detectives encounter in their crime-solving analysis.

It is also important to understand that each intelligence agency in the IC has a unique mission or set of missions.

IC professionals are taught from the beginning that one of their two most important responsibilities is to honor and protect the sacred constitutional rights of fellow Americans. There are strong penalties for violating those rights. In the rare instances when violations are discovered, agencies develop new processes and procedures to prevent recurrences. The other most important responsibility is to produce timely, accurate, unbiased intelligence that meets the needs of the U.S. Government and is untainted by politics.

The specific analytic endeavors in this story are pure fiction, but they represent the art of the possible.

Team Triad represents the very best in interagency and intraagency cooperation and collaboration. The reader will also note references to tensions within and between agencies. Like any other human endeavor, intelligence organizations experience frictions, even between the most dedicated and well-intentioned individuals.

Many of the names of the characters in this tale are takeoffs on the names of real people whom I have known and admired throughout my career, and a few of the characters bear strong or moderate resemblance to real individuals. There are far more whom I have admired and would love to have included.

I have created a number of foreign-language chapter titles for several reasons. First, language can play a critical role in intelligence analysis. Second, each foreign-language title feels more meaningful and powerful to me in the language I chose. Third, language connects us to foreign cultures and helps us understand them. And finally, I take great pleasure in playing with language because it is such an essential ingredient in our lives. Most of the foreign-language titles are in Italian because so much of this story takes place in Italy.

I have included three simple cryptograms because cryptanalysis can play a critical role in SIGINT. English is the underlying text of these cryptograms. Their solution should be fairly simple for those with cryptanalytic experience. I have provided some clues in the text of the story, and have explained the solutions in end notes.

Every profession has its own lexicon, which can include unique words or can use certain words differently than they are used in normal discourse or writing. SIGINT is no exception. In this story, I have sprinkled in a bit of SIGINT spice by using words like "probable" rather than "likely," or "unspecified" rather than "that wasn't mentioned."

I have flavored this tale with food and wine because food, at least, is critical to any human activity; and because our lives can be greatly enriched if we are fortunate enough to experience many cuisines.

I have provided URLs for the web sites of many eateries and hotels mentioned in this novel, so that the reader who wishes can have a fuller sense of the atmosphere of these pleasant places. A few URLs have been omitted because security software suggests those web pages may be unsafe. A few of the businesses I have mentioned do not have their own web sites. I have enjoyed dining at many of the eateries and staying at some of the hotels I have mentioned.

I have provided translations for only those Italian sights, street names, and menu items that I thought might interest the reader.

The National Security Agency (NSA) has reviewed this novel to ensure it contains no classified information. The views and opinions expressed are entirely my own.

One

In Khorasan, sweet Khorasan,

Where Seljuks brought their hearts and souls,
The sun shines bright
On those who seek the truth.[1]

Monday April 6, 2015

The first Monday in April - an early morning of blue skies + smallish waves of warmth = spring/بهار[2]/printemps/primavera/春[3]/Frühling/ άνοιξη[4] = blossoming cherry trees + dogwood trees + tree-filling leaves + azaleas + carpets of grass = new beginnings.

And then the mind of Javad "Josh" Shirazi returned to its favored universe - the worlds of cultures and languages and analysis and cuisines and love of life and landscapes sublime.

His brown eyes scanned southwest out of his office window across a cluster of NSA parking lots toward the Baltimore-Washington Parkway and Maryland Route 32. He watched a small Monday-morning tsunami of vehicles surging across the asphalt and concrete into the lots, disgorging streams of people pouring into work.

---

[1] In the eleventh century, the Turkish Seljuk clan, which had converted to Islam, moved into Khorasan in Northern Persia and established the Seljuk Empire. They mixed with the local population and adopted the Persian culture and language. "Khorasan" means, "land where the sun rises."
[2] baehar - Persian
[3] haru - Japanese
[4] aneeksee - Greek

J. E. HARB, JR.

Gazing out the window, he did what he most enjoyed - contemplating the unique attributes of groups of people that had some major connection or set of connections in common, like ethnicity, profession, hobby, religion, passion for a particular sports team – or intelligence analysis. He wondered what kind of hidden dots he could connect between these colleagues if only he could have access to complex data sets about them. There were the simpler dots, like age, gender, politics, and religion. They often provided interesting connections, but he really wished he could see a much broader set of data, including types and environments of upbringing, like parental occupation, ethnic mix, and childhood milieu, for example, military brats with extensive overseas living - on base or off, free-range or protected. Analysis was his passion, his addiction, his life.

Another aspect of group analysis that he found equally interesting was *Group Discovery and Affiliation Analysis*. It was a set of techniques he was developing to help discover members or prospective members of any group, even when there was only minimal data available about the group, and no information about its communications. He felt these techniques would prove invaluable in uncovering activities of high-interest foreign groups such as terrorists, narcotraffickers, and clandestine intelligence agents.

He thought it ironic that while NSA's primary focus was on a broad range of analytic endeavors, it could perform only limited Human Resources analysis of its own work force, rather than the comprehensive substantive analysis that could identify attributes likely to develop the most successful analysts for its varied analytic disciplines.

He appreciated the important reasons for these limitations - the Constitutional protections, and the Federal Civil Service laws and regulations designed to ensure a high-quality, professional, ethical civil service free of political pressure. These controls prohibited government agencies from hiring and promoting on the basis of religion, political affiliation, or family connections. They also prohibited keeping records of employees' religious beliefs and political affiliations. Josh knew that many Americans, including politicians and government employees, did not appreciate the insidious political pressures on the civil service prior to the Civil Service Reform Act of 1883, which changed the Civil Service from a *spoils system* to a *merit system,* and the Hatch Act of 1939 and subsequent amendments, which removed some of the remaining political influences. Most Americans didn't appreciate how fortunate they were to be served by one of the world's best civil services.

While some U.S. Government organizations, such as intelligence agencies and the FBI had more flexible and streamlined hiring and promotion, they still had strict prohibitions against political favoritism, discrimination, and nepotism, and protected employees' religious and political freedoms.

Josh was troubled by politicians who'd become fond of demeaning government and civil service by contrasting alleged government incompetence to private sector superiority, despite demonstrations of incredible stupidity, crassness, and incompetence by the likes of Enron, WorldCom, and many others.

As myriad possibilities streamed through his mind about the interesting potential of connecting a sea of dots about his colleagues, he heard soft steps approaching from behind, and turned to find his boss, Megan Volker, coming toward him.

"Sob bekheir Khanom-e Volker[5]. Hal-e-shomah che tor?" (Good morning Miss Volker. How're you doing?), he greeted her with a Persian phrase he'd taught her.

"Besiar khub, Aghaye Shirazi, vae shomah?" (Fine, Mr. Shirazi, and you?), she answered with the warm smile that characterized her outlook toward her colleagues, whom she considered part of her extended family.

"Besiar khub aem, mersi." (I'm fine thanks.)

---

[5] While they were on a first-name basis, the proper Persian etiquette was to use last names.

"Are you ready?" she asked.

"Ready for what?"

"The meeting at ten."

He was puzzled. He couldn't remember any meeting that he'd been scheduled to attend, and he never forgot meetings. In fact, he rarely ever forgot anything. "What meeting?"

"The meeting with the Director."

"What?" he exclaimed softly. "I don't remember any meeting with the Director."

"I'm surprised! I can't remember you ever forgetting anything, especially something that important."

"I can't believe it! I'd never forget a meeting with the Director. Are you sure?"

"I'm absolutely positive, but I'm just pulling your chain about it being scheduled. I was just called, and asked if you could come to chat with the Director. I said I was pretty sure, but I'd check. Are you available?"

"Sure. But what's the subject?"

"I don't really know. I was only told that he wants to ask you to undertake some project, but the caller wouldn't give me any information about the project."

"That's a bit strange. I assume the meeting's in the Director's office."

"It is."

"Is there anything I should prepare?"

"Nothing other than your name, rank, and serial number," she joked.

"Ha, ha! Do you know if anyone else will be there?"

"I don't know that either. Sorry!"

"We're in the intel business, and I need intel from you about what's going on here!"

"Well, I guess I'm guilty of an intelligence failure. Perhaps there'll be a congressional inquiry into my failure."

"There should be. Well this is really strange. We're always told the topic in advance. I can't imagine what he wants me to do."

"I don't know, but I'm sure you'll do a superb job at whatever it is. Best of luck, Josh. Please let me know how it goes."

"Will do."

Megan turned and left.

"Great!" he thought. "Now I've got two hours to wait before I find out what's going on." As he'd told Megan, he couldn't imagine why the Director wanted to meet with him. He wasn't working on anything particularly sensitive or interesting at the moment.

Josh reflected on a couple of earlier encounters with the Director, Admiral Charles Saunders, when Josh briefed him on complex, high-value intel. Josh found him very easy to talk to. In fact, on the first occasion, the Director surprised him by greeting him in proper, perfectly pronounced Persian. Josh learned that when the Director was a young officer supervising a unit with a focus on Iran, he'd studied a bit of Persian on his own to get a sense for the linguistic and learning challenges his sailors faced, and to learn more about Iran. When Josh researched the Director's background prior to the first briefing, he'd found nothing about Persian-language skills.

(While many in the IC called the language "Farsi" rather than Persian, Josh preferred the English word. Using the foreign word was analogous to saying, "I speak Deutsch" or "Français" instead of "I speak German" or "French.")

Josh could appreciate an officer like the Director because of his own Navy experiences. When he graduated from university in the spring of 2001, he joined the Navy, as he'd been planning to do since he was a junior in high school. Behrouz Shirazi, a cousin whom he admired and who was in the Naval Security Group (NSG), discussed with Josh, to the extent he could, his Navy experiences. Josh was impressed, and decided to follow his cousin's example.

With a university degree, he could have applied to go to Officer Candidate School to become an officer. However, he decided to enlist and become a Communications Technician (CT), the Navy *rating* (professional specialization) that dealt with SIGINT, the intelligence that exploits a broad range of electronic communications, radar transmissions, etc. His reason for becoming a CT was to get hands-on collection, language analysis, and intelligence analysis experience. His specialty within the CT profession was *I Branch*, which was the field of foreign-language-based SIGINT operations.

He completed Navy *boot camp* at Great Lakes Naval Station just north of Chicago in Mid-August, 2001. When he later learned how cold the winter weather could be at Great Lakes, he felt fortunate to have gone there during the summer.

Following boot camp, he was sent to an intensive course in Pashto, a language spoken by 14 million Pashtuns in Afghanistan and 29 million in Pakistan. The timing was extremely fortuitous - starting two weeks prior to the horrific events of 9/11. The language became critically important to U.S. military operations in the Afghan war because the Taliban enemy were primarily Pashtun. Josh would have worked hard to master the language under any circumstance, but its importance to warfighters drove him to spare no effort.

He initially thought Pashto wouldn't be that difficult because it was from the Northeastern Iranian Group of Indo-European Languages, with much of its vocabulary of Persian origin; and he was very fluent in Persian.

He soon discovered he was mistaken. It was very tough. Developing a strong foundation in Pashto required more than eight hours a day of intense classroom study. So he devoted a significant amount of his free time to learning it.

There were two major variants of Pashto - northern and southern; and those were further divided into some twenty dialects.[6] He also discovered that the language and ethnic mixes in Afghanistan were very complex. Pashto was one of two official languages of

---

Dialects develop when geographic, political, tribal, or sectarian barriers impede travel and communication, as in Germany where mutually unintelligible variants of German developed in kingdoms like Prussia, Bavaria, and Saxony.

Afghanistan; the other was Dari, which was closely related to Persian, and was also known as Afghan Persian. It was more prestigious than Pashto and served as the lingua franca of Afghanistan. When Josh spoke with an educated Afghan Dari speaker or read a Dari newspaper, he found Dari so close to Persian that he could understand it. However, he couldn't comprehend the Dari of uneducated speakers.

In addition to the two official languages, there were about forty other native tongues in Afghanistan, including Uzbek, Turkmen, Balochi, Pashayi, and Nuristani.

Ali, one of his Pashto teachers, was superb. He was a highly educated Pashtun lawyer who fled Afghanistan at the time of the 1979 Soviet invasion. He was a natural-born teacher with a profound understanding of both American English and Pashto. He knew exactly how to guide a good student along the fastest learning path. He was more than a language teacher. He provided Josh with a deep understanding of Afghan society and culture - both critical dimensions to understanding the real meaning of any language. Josh would always consider him one of his two best language teachers.

Once Josh came to know the Pashtun people and their culture, he believed they should have their own separate country of Pashtunistan, incorporating the principal Pashtun areas of Pakistan and Afghanistan. Instead, like most countries in the world, national borders were determined not by logical demographic factors, but by power - colonial or other.

Following graduation in the spring of 2002, he was immediately deployed to Afghanistan. After a year in Afghanistan, he was assigned to sea duty. A year later, he returned to Afghanistan for another year. His experiences in direct support of military operations against terrorists and insurgents gave him a great appreciation for the critical and decisive value that timely and accurate SIGINT could play in operational success and saving lives. In many cases, a critical determinant in the accuracy of the intel was the skill of the linguist. Linguistic incompetence could lead to the loss of friendly lives, operational failure, and missed opportunities.

He also learned the importance of considering all types of intel and open-source info. There were instances in which the SIGINT couldn't be understood without knowing the HUMINT or the IMINT, and vice versa. In one case, he and his colleagues had been trying to identify a Taliban military leader whose code name was "The Shepherd." One day, they intercepted a message in which the sender informed the recipient that "The Shepherd cannot come until tomorrow because of his father." A HUMINT source reported that the father of a named Taliban military leader had passed away that day. In reviewing drone video footage from the same day, an imagery analyst saw what appeared to be a funeral in a suspected Taliban area. That allowed them to determine the probable identity and location of the leader. From that point on, they developed the capability to track The Shepherd, and were able to provide intel to a Special Forces unit, which captured him.

While at sea in the Persian Gulf[7], Josh found it interesting that he could sometimes see Iran in the distance, but couldn't go there. When he knew there were Iranian naval vessels nearby, he wondered if some distant relative might be serving aboard one of those ships.

When his four-year enlistment ended, he decided to leave the Navy and apply for civilian employment at NSA, where he felt he could experience a wider range of complex challenges. With his Navy experiences, skills, and security clearance, he was quickly hired by NSA. He would always be grateful to the Navy for the training and experiences it had given him.

---

[6] Also known as the Arabian Gulf. U.S. forces cooperating with Arab countries in the region generally use this alternate name.

Two

Missions from the Bridge[8]

Josh arrived at the Director's office a few minutes before ten, and introduced himself to the Director's secretary.

"Good morning, my name's Javad Shirazi, and I've been told to come here for a ten o'clock meeting with the Director," he said.

"Yes," she replied. "I've been expecting you. Please come with me."

She led him to a small conference room; offered him a seat; and told him the Director would be there shortly. She then turned and left.

A few minutes later, the Director, who was also the Director of U.S. Cyber Command, walked in with a man whom Josh recognized as the Director of NSA's Cyber Operations.

Once again, the Director greeted him in Persian, and then added. "It's nice to see you again. Thanks for coming."

Josh could tell from the Director's tone of voice and body language that the meeting had nothing to do with any problem Josh might have created. He couldn't imagine any problem, but he was relieved to have this phonemic and visual confirmation.

"It's my pleasure, Admiral Saunders."

"Great. I'd like to introduce you to Mac Roberts, our Director of Cyber Ops."

---

[8] In the naval sense of the word.

"It's a pleasure to meet you, sir."

"The feeling is mutual, Javad. I've heard a lot of great things about you, particularly from my chief of staff, Bill Bergmann. You can call me Mac."

"Bill loves working with you and has a very high opinion of you, too, Josh commented. "He's not easily impressed. You can call me Josh if you'd like. Javad is my given name, but I've gone by Josh since grade school when one of my classmates coined the nickname using the initial consonants of my first and last names."

"Then we'll both call you Josh from now on," the Admiral said. "Since you're probably very anxious to know why I've asked you here, I won't waste time with small talk. I'd like your help in dealing with a major national security threat that has surfaced in the past week. We believe you have an exceptional mix of skills that make you uniquely equipped to help us understand and hopefully identify the source of this threat. This matter is extremely sensitive, and you can only discuss it with me, Mac, and a few other people we'll identify. This will be a full-time job. It may require lots of extra hours of work, and has some potential to put you at risk. Before I explain the threat, I'd like to know if we can count on you to help us. I'd also like to make sure there are no family issues that would keep you from working long hours if need be."

"Sir, there's no way I'd pass up the chance to help," Josh replied. "I don't know if you're aware, but my wife's an Agency Chinese linguist and analyst who is as dedicated to her job as I am to mine, so each of us is very understanding when the other has special work requirements. We have no children and have no travel or other outside commitments."

"Great! I didn't realize your wife was an Agency employee. I'd love to meet her."

"I know she'd love to meet you as well."

"Do be careful though, Josh. Too many times during my career, I've seen relationships permanently damaged due to complete focus on work. I'd hate to see that happen with you and your wife."

"Thanks for your concern, Admiral. We try to carve out special time for each other, even during intensive work commitments. When those commitments are finished, we try to get away for a few days and just focus on each other."

"I'm happy to hear that. Your management informed us that you're not in the midst of any special project at the moment, and that you're available to start work immediately."

"That's correct, sir."

"To help provide cover for this effort, we have a high-value project that we'll openly assign to you. I'll explain the threat, then describe the cover project; then discuss some of the mechanics.

"You know and appreciate the intense and critical negotiations that are currently under way with Iran with the objective of stopping its nuclear weapons program. A successful outcome of those negotiations would eliminate a major national security threat and the strong possibility of significant military action."

"I understand and know," Josh commented", that events of the next couple of months will likely determine the success or failure of those negotiations."

"That's even truer than you realize. We've learned that the Iranian intelligence service, the MOIS (Ministry of Intelligence and Security), which you know very well, has at least one and possibly several U.S. Government sources at a very high-level. We're not sure if the Iranian asset or assets are in the Executive Branch, the Legislative Branch, or both; and we're not sure if the person or persons involved are senior officials, senior staff, or both.

"The reason we think the Iranian penetration is at a senior level is because of the types of information that seem to have been compromised. The information appears to have come from the kinds of briefings typically presented at the senior level, for example to senior Defense Department, State Department, or National Security Council members, or Congressional intelligence oversight committees, rather than from the sorts of information that specialists at the technical level would provide. Among the potential Iranian source or sources, are staff members of high-level officials, who often sit in on such briefings.

"We have discovered three types of indicators, all of which popped up within the space of two weeks. The indicators were connected by Delia A. Kraft, the Director of National Intelligence (DNI). She learned of the first indicator from Adam Rolph, the CIA Director. He informed her that two of the best human assets the CIA had within the Iranian Government had disappeared, probably after being identified. One was a senior administrator within their nuclear program and one was a high-level Foreign Ministry official who'd been playing a key support role on the Iranian side of the negotiations. Other important assets within the Foreign Ministry do not appear to have been identified. An NSA SIGINT report suggested that the Foreign Ministry official's cooperation with the CIA had been discovered.

"The Foreign Ministry asset did not show up for a planned meeting with his CIA handler at Ribeauvillé in Alsace, France. Additionally, someone broke into the CIA officer's hotel room, and planted a micro monitoring device within the officer's personal laptop. The device was detected immediately, and analysis revealed it was an Iranian device.

"Several days after learning of the disappearance of the CIA assets, DNI Kraft learned from the Secretary of State that our most experienced negotiators at the nuclear talks with the Iranians had the sense that the Iranians had access to insider knowledge of our minimum acceptable end-state, and of our tactics and strategies in the negotiations.

"A week later, I informed her that the Iranians had completely changed one of their technical capabilities that had been giving us key insights into their objectives, intentions, tactics, and strategies in the negotiations."

"Do you think the Snowden compromises had anything to do with the technical change?" Josh asked. Like all of his colleagues, Josh was pained by the immense national security damage done by

Edward Snowden, the NSA contractor who'd been working at an NSA field site and who'd downloaded massive amounts of classified information, which he'd turned over to journalists. While Snowden claimed to be a whistleblower whose only purpose was to protect the rights of his fellow Americans, the duplicity of his claims was evidenced by his revelations about critical capabilities against America's greatest threats. Furthermore, substantive analysis of his claims about purported violations of Americans' civil rights would easily demonstrate the falseness of his allegations. Josh hoped that Snowden would be "privileged" to spend the rest of his life in Russia.

"Snowden's painfully treasonous betrayals have caused our country immeasurable harm," the Admiral replied. "However, we believe this particular change is not due to his actions because it has just occurred. In this case, we believe the Iranians have analyzed the information they've been getting from their asset or assets in our government, and then determined the most likely source of that information.

"Not surprisingly, it appears that the MOIS sides with conservative Iranian elements, such as the Revolutionary Guard, who vehemently oppose any agreement with the P5+1 that would make it difficult for Iran to acquire nuclear weapons.

"When the DNI recognized the likely magnitude of the problem, she first discussed it with James Pasquali, Director of the FBI, because of the FBI's lead role in counterespionage on U.S. soil[9]. The DNI and the FBI Director then briefed the President because of the gravity of the problem and because of the potential political implications if the Congress was involved. The President directed them to inform the Senate Majority Leader and the Speaker of the House to obtain their approval for the part of the investigation

---

[9] The FBI's Counterintelligence Division is the U.S. Government's lead organization responsible for exposing, preventing, and investigating domestic-based espionage. The FBI has been the principal player in this activity since 1917.

involving the Congress. Both leaders agreed, with the proviso that they be kept constantly informed of any developments relating to the Congress.

"The FBI Director, the DNI, the CIA Director, and I then met to discuss the investigation. The Bureau is taking the lead, and has formed a team of two experts from the FBI and two from the CIA. I suggested to FBI Director Pasquali that we involve you because of your exceptional SIGINT analytic and linguistic skills. He agreed, but said he'd first like to have his folks look into your background a bit because of your ethnicity. I agreed, but also reflected to myself on the typical background of America's most damaging spies - almost all have been Christian Caucasian males whose families have been U.S. citizens for at least several generations. First-generation Americans tend to appreciate their great good fortune at living in the U.S. rather than in some country with religious persecution, ethnic atrocities, abysmal economic opportunities, rigid class structure, or other intractable problems.

"The Bureau examined your security bona fides, and gave its blessing to your joining the team.

"This sealed envelope has the names, roles, and contact information for the key FBI and CIA officers involved in this mission."

"Could I ask why you've chosen me for this effort?" Josh inquired.

"Certainly. It's your exceptional combined skill set - your extraordinary analytic talents and your profound linguistic capabilities in Persian, Arabic, and Pashtun. Your analytic accomplishments based on out-of-the-box thinking are really impressive. We have many very talented analysts and linguists at the Agency. However, there are none who couple your particular language skills with your ability to analyze problems in unconventional ways that lead to exceptional results.

"One of the great examples of your analytic skills was how you solved the al-Qaeda cipher system that had defied solution by some very skilled cryptanalysts. Your success allowed the U.S. to eliminate an important al-Qaeda capability in the Arabian Peninsula. That was a terrific accomplishment. We hope you can achieve similar results in this case."

The Director was referring to a cryptographic system that two Palestinians operating an al-Qaeda logistics network had been using to encrypt the texts of the messages they'd been exchanging with each other.

Josh recalled the experience well, not only because of its impact on al-Qaeda operations, but also because it had underscored for him the importance of expanding his analytic solutions toolbox to include looking for unconventional possibilities.

Prior to Josh's effort to solve that al-Qaeda encryption system, everyone had assumed that the underlying plaintext was in Arabic, and a few had tried English. Josh decided to study the backgrounds of the two communicants to look for alternative possibilities. He learned that one of them had studied Hebrew intensively when he was in high school. Josh then examined the background of the other communicant to see if he might have some connection to Hebrew. He learned that the second communicant's wife was an Israeli Jewish woman who had converted to Islam, and had become a fervent believer. After that discovery, Josh correctly guessed that the messages were in Hebrew, and that the Jewish wife was translating messages to and from Arabic for her husband. Like others who'd examined the encrypted messages, Josh noticed that the first six cipher letters of each encrypted message were the same as the last six. He agreed with others that this was a key to how the cipher for each message was generated. He decided to test whether these letters might represent numbers that equated to book, chapter, and verse of the Hebrew Bible, and that the cited verse might be the starting point for a running key additive cipher system[i]. Although Josh knew very little Hebrew, he was able to test his hypothesis, and it was proven correct.

Once the system had been solved, a joint CIA-Special Forces

team was created to use the SIGINT to locate and neutralize al-Qaeda elements which the network was supporting in Saudi Arabia and Yemen. The team was also able to identify and neutralize several key suppliers of the network.

What Josh loved about being an American and working in the IC was that his ethnic and religious background had no effect on his career advancement. The only thing that seemed to matter was his competence.

"We're going to ask one other person to join you on this project. He's a senior technical expert in our special technical solutions organization. Involving him is a bit unconventional because he has no SIGINT analytic experience. However, I believe it's sometimes helpful to attack a problem by using creative thinkers from outside the disciplines normally applied to that problem.

"We're confident he'll accept because he loves tough challenges. He combines exceptionally innovative thinking with advanced degrees in math, physics, computer science, electrical engineering, and chemistry. He uses that combination to develop quick and pragmatic solutions. To him, barriers are opportunities, and borders between disciplines are artificial constructs that he ignores. The more complex the challenge, the more he delights in pursuing solutions. He has achieved many mind-boggling successes. He also has certain types of exceptional cyber skills that will compliment your SIGINT skills.

"My sense from examining his background and yours is that you are both exceptionally creative, but that the two of you think very differently. I think you'll make a great team. His name is Daniel Dechado. He's the one who developed the hack-proof computer you'll be using to browse the Internet. Once he has agreed, I'll ask him to get in touch with you.

"There are two reasons I've asked Mac to be involved. The first is that I may not always be available when you need me, so I wanted another senior person to be available for guidance and assistance. The second is to provide you with a way to obtain communications collection in a way that will not be connected to you. Whenever you'd like any type of communications collected, let Mac know, and he'll make the necessary arrangements. In that way, there'll be no direct connection between you and the collection.

"One part of my guidance to you is that you are to inform me and Mac immediately if and when you detect or do anything relating to the Congress. There is no indication that any member of Congress has ever been involved in espionage. If someone in the Congress is involved, the implications could be far greater than what we encounter in the typical espionage case. There are two reasons for this. The first is the extraordinary congressional opposition to these negotiations. The second is that both houses of the Congress are controlled by the President's opponents. We do our very best to keep politics out of intelligence issues, but there are a few instances in which this is unusually difficult.

"Hopefully, no one in the Congress is involved. My experience throughout my career has been that most espionage cases involve technical civilian or military employees of the Executive Branch or contractors.

"The only people in the Agency whom we have informed about your counterespionage task are the head of SIGINT Services and the head of Security.

"We've prepared for you a separate small office on this floor. You, Daniel, and I will be the only ones with keys to your office. There will also be an electronic keypad on the door. Entering the room will require use of both a key and the keypad. You and Daniel cannot let anyone else use your keys without my permission.

"We've equipped your office with three separate computers. The first is a computer that is connected to the NSA, secure "high-side" network, which like all such networks, is not connected to the Internet. You can use that computer to perform SIGINT and other classified research. The second is a secure, stand-alone, high-side computer. You can use that computer to perform your analysis and store the results, and to prepare any reports to me and Mac. We will return reports to you for storage in the safe in your office. The third is a computer that is connected to the Internet. You can use that computer to browse the Internet anonymously. It has no microphone or camera. It's a special machine that is invulnerable to viruses and hacking. You will learn why shortly.

"You are to preserve all correspondence and reports you create relating to this project. Retention of government records is always a requirement, but given the importance and sensitivity of this case, I want to reemphasize that need.

"Most NSA linguists and analysts are only permitted to access the limited types of intercepted foreign communications that relate to their geographical or topical responsibilities. However, we're giving you very broad access to foreign intercept because there's no telling where you might find helpful clues and insights. Needless to say, you will have no access to the communications of U.S. citizens except in a very rare instance when we're able to get approval from the FISA (Foreign Intelligence Surveillance Act) Court. Despite the false impressions created by Snowden and the media, we all know how much effort we take to protect the constitutional rights of our fellow citizens, how difficult it is to make a case for Court approval, and how few approvals the court grants us each year."

Josh indeed knew the efforts the Agency had taken to create a culture and processes designed to protect the rights of American citizens. Each year, he and every other NSA employee with access to SIGINT was required to take Agency on-line courses that described in great detail the protections of the 4th Amendment rights of U.S. Persons. (U.S. Persons included not only U.S. citizens, but even non-citizen Permanent Residents, known as Green Card Holders, and foreigners visiting the U.S.) SIGINT linguists and analysts even had to report instances in which they accidentally listened to the communications of U.S. Persons before realizing who they were. There were a few very rare exceptions, such as discovering that someone planned to commit murder or a terrorist attack. Otherwise, the linguists and analysts had to immediately cease and delete the

U.S. communications. Any NSA employee who was discovered to be deliberately targeting U.S. persons faced severe penalties.

"Now, I'd like to discuss the project that will be both a cover project for your counterespionage detective work, and a high-value project in its own right. It's something I've been thinking about for a while, and have been trying to figure out the best way to do it. You might find it of value because it could provide you with new tactics and strategies to use in your detective work.

"I'd like you to find and interview the most exceptional analysts and problem solvers throughout the cryptologic and cyber communities, including:

- Offense - the SIGINT system
- Defense - the Information Security[10] system, and
- Cyber.

"I want you to include not only civilian and military analysts at NSA HQ, but those throughout the SIGINT system.

"In the course of your research, I'd like you to see if there are unique capabilities of those analysts who've worked in two or more of those systems, as well as those who've had experiences in other types of intelligence such as HUMINT and imagery.

"I have a sense that the time may have come to combine our operations across offense and defense because capabilities and behaviors of our opponents and foreign societies at large have changed so dramatically due to technological change.

"Our military services understand that we cannot conduct warfare effectively without training our forces in both offense and defense. But they also understand that specialization is critical, which is why, for example, we have fighter pilots, bomber pilots, cargo pilots, helo pilots, etc.

"There are always pros and cons of major organizational changes. While rationale for the change may seem intellectually sound, the reality may be quite different."

---

[10] Responsible for protecting U.S. Government communications.

(Many with long SIGINT experience recalled how the Army lost capability through a 1976 reorganization in which it merged its SIGINT organization, the Army Security Agency (ASA), with its HUMINT arm to form the Army Intelligence and Security Command (INSCOM). A key driver was to develop officers who were skilled across a variety of intelligence types. Many who observed Army cryptologic efforts before and after the change concluded that this had hurt the Army because newer officers lacked the cryptologic skills of their predecessors. The newer officers had greater breadth, but they lost critical depth - jack of all trades and master of none. The Navy never made that change, and consequently, maintained its corps of skilled cryptologic officers.)

"If I make changes," the Admiral continued, "I want to do my best to understand all the implications before I make the changes and to evaluate the results afterwards to see if the changes have had a positive impact, need to be adjusted, or even need to be reversed. I realize there are major political and perception obstacles to overcome if we move in that direction, but I first want to understand the operational implications. I also know that what can seem to be a more effective way of doing business can have the opposite impact.

"Your objectives will be to try to identify the unique attributes, skill sets, high-value training, mind-sets, partnerships, and experiences which contribute to the success of these individuals. I'd also like you to identify any important impediments they face. I'm convinced that Daniel will be very helpful to you by bringing a creative outside perspective that may help us add new tactics, methodologies, and strategies to the existing analytic processes. In the end, I'd like you to publish your findings for the benefit of management, the analytic community, Agency educators, recruiters, and any other relevant group. I'd also like you to make recommendations to me about changes we might implement. What do you think?"

"It's incredibly fortuitous that you should ask me to do that Admiral Saunders," Josh replied. "Just a couple of hours ago, before

I was informed of this meeting, I was looking out the window at people coming into work, and I thought how interesting it would be to be able to study various types of Agency analysts to understand them better. I could not have imagined that I would have an opportunity like this.

"Under normal circumstances, there's no way I would have been able to gather and consider data critical to making meaningful assessments. In this case, I'll be able to ask many of the great ones questions that might allow me to analyze a vital segment of the analytic community. This will give me the challenge of trying to connect the dots between the dot connecters, and potentially have a broader impact on the SIGINT System. Thank you very much for the opportunity. I really appreciate your confidence in me, and hope I can justify that confidence."

"I'm pleased that this is something of high interest to you," the admiral responded. "I'll announce this project to my executive team this afternoon and to the workforce tomorrow. I'll ask that they assist you in every possible way, to include letting you know about exceptional analysts and analytic successes, and making any suggestions they might have.

"I'd like you to keep your notes and findings from this project on the stand-alone secure computer because the compilation of information from exceptional analytic successes is likely to be extremely sensitive.

"I want to emphasize that you should feel free to consult me or Mac at any time on either project, and immediately inform us of any serious impediment you encounter. I'd like you to update us at least once a week on the status of both projects. You can do the update by email unless it involves an issue you feel requires in-person discussion. I'll let you be the judge. Don't hesitate to arrange an in-person meeting if you believe it's necessary. At the top of the text of any emails you send to me or Mac on the Iran issue, put the words, "EYES ONLY" in large, bold font at the beginning of the text.

"I'll direct my executive assistant, Sofie Ingenios, to have you immediately reassigned to my staff. I'll also instruct Marilyn Carter, a senior secretary on my staff, to provide you with any administrative support you need. She's terrific."

"Thank you, sir."

"I know this is a lot to take on board out of the blue. Do you have any initial questions?"

"I have an initial reaction to both projects, and a couple of questions about the cover project. I'm certain I'll have more after I've had a little time to think about the projects."

"What's your initial reaction to the counterespionage project, Josh?"

"Well sir, I think it's a huge challenge - the most difficult I've ever faced. There are two major components to this challenge. First, the likelihood of discovering this sort of espionage activity in normal Iranian communications is very slim unless I have incredible luck. I'll have to find some other vulnerability.

"Second, success or failure has enormous implications for our national security. If I'm successful, I'll be thrilled. If I fail, I'll be deeply disappointed."

"I realize the difficulty," the Admiral responded, "but I'm hoping you'll find some approach that will work. What's your reaction to the cover project beyond your immediate expression of surprise and delight when I described it?"

"That seems much more straightforward. It will involve a lot of work, and will take at least six months, and more likely, a year. I'll have a better idea after I develop a plan, and after I spend the first month considering the dimensions of the effort and doing the first interviews. Would that be acceptable to you, sir?"

"That would be fine. In fact, my thoughts about the duration were similar to yours. I think we're on the same wave length. What's your next question?"

"I wonder if I might invite exceptional retired analysts in for classified interviews."

"You can invite them in for interviews relating to the cover project, but you can't discuss the counterespionage project."

"One reason I ask is that there's an incredible retired Persian language analyst who may be the greatest Iran expert the IC has known. I might be able to ask him about his experiences for the cover project in a way that could provide insights for the counterespionage project."

"Great idea, Josh. Just provide the names to Marilyn, and she'll make the necessary arrangements with security.

"Do you have any additional questions?"

"My only other question is whether I might ask our British SIGINT partners from GCHQ (the Government Communications HQ) if I could interview their exceptional analysts. I'm aware of some extraordinary successes they've achieved."

"I like the idea because people from different cultures and subcultures have different approaches to problem solving. In fact, we might want to consider a follow-on project in which we talk to analysts in other government organizations and in the private sector. Mac, would you please ask the senior GCHQ representative if Josh could interview some of their exceptional analysts. You can tell him we'd be happy to share the results of our findings."

"Certainly, Admiral," Mac replied. "I'll let Josh know as soon as I have a response. I can't imagine any reason they wouldn't agree."

"Josh," said the Admiral, "if those are your only questions at the moment, I'd like to reiterate a couple of very important points."

"The only NSA people who know about the counterespionage project now are the Director of SIGINT Services, the head of Security, Mac and me. We hope to have Daniel Dechado on board by the end of the day. I'll have him contact you if he agrees.

"Do not inform anyone else without prior approval from me or Mac.

"You will be limited by the usual restrictions against monitoring or analyzing the communications of U.S. persons. You cannot listen to the communications of any U.S. person without FISA Court approval.

"If you discover any hint of Congressional involvement in espionage, you are to inform me immediately. That includes not only members of Congress, but also Congressional staff.

"I've informed your senior management that I would be asking you to undertake the cover project. All of them except the Chief of SIGINT Services believe it will be your only project. Now I'll let them know you've accepted. In the meantime, you can inform your immediate management. Then, come back here and chat with Sofie. She'll show you your room and give you the keys and pass code. She'll also introduce you to Marilyn."

"Thanks again for your confidence in me, Admiral. I can't begin to tell you how honored I am, especially given the number of superb linguists and analysts I've known here during my career. I'll do my very best to identify the Iranian source or sources. I'll devote the same effort to providing you with a comprehensive picture of exceptional analysis, and a set of recommendations to expand those analytic skills."

"One other point I'd like to add, Josh. I'll know immediately and pass on to you any SIGINT report that anyone in the Agency is about to publish that may relate to the counterespionage project. That's because I already have in place standing instructions for all the Agency's reporting staffs to bring to my immediate attention prior to publication any report involving espionage against the U.S. on certain high-priority topics, such as the Iran nuclear negotiations."

"That's great."

"That's it for now, Josh. We'll talk to you soon," said the Admiral, as he rose. He shook hands with Josh, and said "Khoda hafez" - good-bye - in Persian.

"Khoda hafez e Shomah (Good-bye to you)," Josh replied.

"Good luck, Josh. I look forward to working with you. Here's my secure phone number," said Mac, as he handed Josh a small slip of paper. He too shook hands, and left.

Three

Musing & Moving Out

Josh sat back down to reflect on the tasks he'd just accepted. He was a bit stunned at the sudden interesting turn his life had taken. These were the types of challenges he loved. He would have been thrilled with either one, but to be offered both at the same time was amazing. He was confident he'd produce great results with the analytic project, and those results could have a significant influence on analytic disciplines and outcomes, with resultant advances in national security and saving American lives.

The counterespionage project was a different story. Its outcome was unpredictable and the implications for success or failure were huge. Success could have a significant positive affect on the course of history; while failure could have the opposite impact. Success would improve the likelihood of halting the Iranian nuclear weapons effort for at least a decade – perhaps much longer, as was the case with South Africa, which dismantled its nuclear weapons program in 1989. An agreement with Iran would obviate the need for any U.S. and/or Israeli military action against Iran and could save American lives. Failure would give the upper hand to the hardliners in Iran and would increase the probability that military action might be necessary. He believed that the type of military operation needed to take out the hardened, dispersed Iranian nuclear infrastructure would be much larger, more complex, and more dangerous than the straightforward 1981 Israeli takeout of the Iraqi Osirak reactor that was under construction and that had no nuclear materials.

31

He knew that his success in helping uncover the Iranian spy or spies would require a combination of luck and skill. He felt he had the skills and would spare no effort to apply those skills, but he could only hope for the luck. It was a heavy burden and an exciting challenge. He'd been very lucky with previous complex analytic endeavors, and hoped his luck would continue.

He reflected on his first analytic success - a combination of luck and simple, straightforward analysis. He was able to uncover a small Taliban network in Kandahar Province in southeastern Afghanistan. The province shared a border with Pakistan. Its capital was the city of Kandahar, and it was overwhelmingly inhabited by Pashtuns. One day, as he and others often did, he stayed beyond his normal shift in the SIGINT analysis and collection center to which he was assigned as a collector. His objective was to improve his skills in dealing with Pashto Language comms (communications). This was his first assignment out of language school, and he'd only been on the job about four months.

He tuned through the VHF (very high frequency) portion of the radio frequency spectrum, which is used for short-range comms by a variety of governmental, commercial, insurgent, and other tactical organizations such as tactical military forces, police, and firefighters.

On one freq, he found three or four communicants discussing tire deliveries. As he listened, his suspicions were aroused by how they conversed. They sounded more disciplined and less relaxed than communicants he normally found in commercial comms. He could usually distinguish between commercial, insurgent, military, police, and other comms not just by words, but by distinctly different discipline and procedures.

His suspicions were further aroused by his analysis of the content. The communicants referred to the sizes of tires they said were about to be delivered to an unspecified location. However, the numbers did not match any tire sizes he knew. He immediately started recording the comms and noted the freq.

One communicant mentioned that the delivery would arrive in

fifteen minutes. Ten minutes later, a second communicant said they would arrive in five minutes. Six minutes later, a third communicant stated the tires had just arrived, and had been unloaded. He ended his transmission by softly saying, "Allahu Akbar." (God is great.) The comms immediately ceased. The final fact that seemed to confirm his suspicions was the last communicant's statement that the tires had already been unloaded. That could not have happened within a minute of arrival.

Josh noted the time - 0930. He immediately used a secure phone to contact one of his colleagues on the J3 staff, the Joint Operations Staff. He asked the J3 colleague to let him know if he was aware now or discovered later that anything unusual had occurred at about 0930. The colleague mentioned that the J3 staff had just been notified that a Humvee in a convoy that departed Kandahar a short while earlier had been destroyed by an IED (Improvised Explosive Device) at about 0930.

When the J3 colleague asked the reason for the question, Josh explained what he'd heard and that he believed he might have discovered a Taliban network. He said he'd work with his coworkers to develop the network and locate its stations. Concurrently, they'd tip off the J3 staff to any future talk of tire deliveries so that the operations staff could alert nearby tactical forces to potential IED attacks.

During the next three weeks, the SIGINT support staff informed the J3 staff of five possible impending IED events.

By the end of the third week, the SIGINT staff had identified and located all six stations on the Taliban network. Josh wrote a detailed report for the J2 staff, the intelligence staff. That report was briefed to the J3 -- the Chief of Operations -- who then directed action to disrupt the Taliban effort. U.S. Special Operations Forces captured several of the Taliban and killed others.

It was only luck that Josh had stumbled onto this network and that he had listened long enough to realize they were not who they pretended to be. As he would see over and over in his career, luck was often a critical component to success.

Josh left the Director's suite of offices and returned to his own office. He immediately walked to the office of his boss, Megan Volker. It was a small room within the larger office where he worked. He told Megan's secretary it was important that he talk to her as soon as possible to inform her about his meeting with the Director. The secretary checked with Megan, and then told Josh he could go in.

"Well," Megan started, "what's going on?"

"The Director has promoted me to replace you as chief of this division. Now, I'm going to be your boss."

"Wow! That's incredible! I can't believe it!" she responded with a bit of a shocked expression on her face.

"You have good reason not to believe me. It's not true. Actually, the Director asked me to immediately take on an analytic project that could take up to a year."

"Whew! Glad to hear I'm not being demoted," she chuckled. "What sort of project did he ask you to undertake?"

Josh explained the project.

"On the one hand, I'm happy for you and the Agency," Megan reacted. "You're certainly the perfect person for that sort of project. On the other hand, your loss will be very painful for us. I've often told you how critical you are to our success. I wish you the very best, and hope we'll see you back here in less than a year."

"I'll keep in touch and let you know how the project is progressing. I'd also be grateful for your suggestions. You have very broad SIGINT experience from both your military and civilian careers. I'd also appreciate any names of exceptional analysts you can give me."

"You can count on me Josh. I'll let my boss know about your assignment. I know he'll be supportive. He think's your great."

"Flawed judgment on his part," Josh joked.

He left Megan's office and then called the Director's suite to see if Sofie was available to show him his new office. She told him she'd be available for the next hour. After that, she had to support the Director, who'd be meeting with a visiting Senator from the Senate Select Committee on Intelligence (SSCI).

Josh returned to the Director's suite and introduced himself to Sofie, who was very pleasant and extremely sharp. People who were chosen to be executive assistants to the Director were always very smart, but some were not pleasant.

Sofie emphasized that Josh should not hesitate to come to her for assistance if he encountered any impediments in dealing with the analytic project the Admiral had given him. It was clear she didn't know about the counterespionage project.

They chatted for a few minutes; and then she took him and introduced him to Marilyn, the secretary, who was also very nice and who said she looked forward to helping him in any way she could.

While he was talking to them, he mentioned there might be occasions when he'd need to meet with the Director on very short notice. He asked which one of them he should contact. They both said he should start with Sofie. If she wasn't available, he should call Marilyn.

Sofie then led Josh the short distance down the hall to his new office. She gave him a sealed envelope with his key and the combination for the electronic key pad. He tested the key and combination and confirmed that they worked. Sofie left him to check out the office.

He found it completely set up with everything he might need. It was large enough to accommodate him and a second person, and to allow them to interview several people at the same time.

Josh returned to the office where he'd been working. He chatted with the linguists and analysts whose desks were near his, and explained the analytic project he was starting. They thought it was great that one of their own had been given such a neat project – one that could improve their world. They wished him the best.

Megan's secretary found him a couple of empty cardboard boxes, which he used to move his belongings to the new office.

Four

2 x ((Innovation + Analytic Skill + Open Mind + Passion) +Top Support) = Mega Potential

As he brought the last box into the new office, the secure phone rang. It was Daniel Dechado. He introduced himself and told Josh he'd agreed to the Director's request. He was very excited and couldn't wait to get started, so Josh invited him to come up as soon as he wanted. Daniel said he'd be there in a heartbeat – or two.

Within a couple of minutes, there was a knock on the door. Josh opened it and saw a guy who was about six feet tall, fair-skinned, and thin, with dark brown hair and blue eyes. He had a genuinely friendly and impish smile that seemed to be as wide as he was tall. He appeared to be in his early forties, and seemed infused with a high level of energy.

"Hey Josh! Great to meet you! Sounds like we've got a couple of really fun projects. I can't wait. I've had lots of great challenges, but nothing like either of these. I'm ready to go."

"Great to meet you too. The Dir had lots of great things to say about you."

"I certainly deserve every compliment he gave and lots more. My skills and accomplishments require a supercomputer to catalogue," Daniel joked. "It probably took him a couple of hours to tell you how sharp I am."

"Actually, it took him about a nanosecond," Josh joked back. "He spent most of the time telling me how smart I am, and how much you might be able to learn under my tutelage and mentoring."

"I can only imagine. Perhaps I should write a suite of software with some advanced algorithms to calculate the extent of your greatness. Moving back to reality, I think it would be great to get to know something about each other before we start talking about our new projects. That way, we'll have some sense for how we see things from our different perspectives. If it's ok with you, we could talk about our backgrounds, including the jobs we've had, our education, the challenges we've faced, the solutions we've developed, our philosophies, and our methodologies. Then we can discuss the two projects. How does that sound?"

"I completely agree," Josh responded. "How 'bout if you start?"

"Well, as you can tell from my name, my origin is Hispanic. My great grandparents on both sides were from Toledo in Spain. My paternal great grandfather was a Spanish Army officer in Cuba at the time of the Spanish-American War. My maternal great grandfather was a Spanish civil servant there at the same time. When Spain lost the war, they both opted to remain in Cuba rather than returning to Spain. After a few years, they moved to Miami. My family lived there from that time on.

"I grew up in a bilingual family, where both English and Spanish were spoken. However, I've never had any formal education in Spanish. From the time I started elementary school, I was always interested in math and science. I was heavily influenced by my father. Although he worked in the Dade County building permitting department, his first love and hobbies involved technology and science. He looked at everything he saw from the perspective of how it could be improved with some innovation or invention. While he turned many of his ideas into functioning creations, he never pursued converting them into patents and commercial products. It's a shame because some of them were incredible. He taught me how to rework my toys in ways that would have them perform functions they weren't designed to do. One very simple example involves the model train set he bought me - a large, pre-World War II, standard-gauge Lionel set. He showed me how to configure the tracks in many different ways that were not part of the track setup. For a couple of weeks, we'd reconfigure the tracks every day or two. Each time I thought we'd done everything possible, he'd show me a new approach.

"My undergraduate major was math and my minor was physics. My master's degrees are in math, physics, computer science, electrical engineering, and chemistry; and my PhD is in math. I didn't study all those disciplines for their own sake, but because I thought that combination would help me create more effective cross-disciplinary solutions.

"I love technology, and am addicted to buying the latest devices. My wife says I should buy a warehouse to store the gadgets that I've bought and that I keep replacing with newer models. If you're not careful, I'll addict you to buying the latest technology"

"I'd love that," Josh interjected.

"I've had some experience flying aircraft," Daniel continued, "and I've studied cooking under a master chef. At one point, I even had a catering business on the side.

"Most of my experiences at the Agency have involved finding technical solutions to problems. The solutions are generally focused on developing hardware, software, or combinations of both for many purposes - from collection through cyber warfare. I've also done some cryptanalysis (CA)[11]. I have no experience with analyzing intercepted communications.

"I become frustrated with people who spend their time either looking for the most elegant solutions or trying to figure out why proposed solutions can't succeed. The history of innovation is full of examples of so-called 'experts' who are blind to the potential of new ideas, and devote their energies to blocking them."

"What a background!" Josh responded. "Our educational and experiential backgrounds are completely different. However, I think

---

[11] Analysis to solve codes and ciphers.

that in some ways, we're very similar. We love problem solving, analysis, and technology.

"I'm convinced that, in order to achieve solutions," Josh remarked, "you have to be great at analyzing problems, and then opening your mind to applying existing capabilities in creative ways. Among my favorite examples is the evolution of pullable, wheeled suitcases. The technology was long available to make the fantastic 4-wheel spinners we have today, but it took over forty years and four major changes to evolve to this point. The innovation began in the 1960s, with suitcases strapped to foldable wheeled carts; followed by affixing four casters to suitcases laying horizontally; then standing them up vertically with only two casters and telescoping handles; and finally attaching four spinning casters so the suitcases could be easily maneuvered in different situations. It was all a matter of coming up with the right concept, not developing new technology. I could give lots more examples and I'm sure you could too.

"I can't wait to hear about some of your creations," Josh continued. "I love analysis; and I also love technology, but more from a user standpoint than from a developer perspective. I've owned most generations of Internet-capable cell phones and their successor smart phones.

"I have no substantive background in any of your areas of specialization.

"My parents are from Iran. As my last name suggests, our family origins are in the city of Shiraz, the capital of the province of Fars, in southeastern Iran. The city is at least four thousand years old and is famous for its culture and gardens. In the late 1960s, my paternal grandparents sent my father to UCLA, where he majored in business. That's where he met my mother, who was a premed student. She became a doctor - a pediatrician. When they finished their studies and returned to Iran, my father went to work for an American defense company with operations in Iran. He rose to the company's top management position in the country.

"When he realized in the fall of 1978 that the demise of the

Shah's regime was likely imminent, he convinced my mother to go to the U.S. for a long "visit." He also convinced his company to begin reducing its operations in Iran. By the time the Shah went into exile in mid-January 1979, the firm's operations had been closed and all of its American employees had been evacuated. Many of its Iranian employees had also been transferred to the U.S.

"The firm transferred my father to its headquarters in Massachusetts, where he continued to work for them until he retired as a senior executive. My mother obtained a medical license and went to work at Mass General.

"I was born there about a year after my father had been transferred to the U.S. My brother was born a year later, and my sister was born one year after that.

"At home, we spoke both English and Persian. My parents were equally comfortable in both, and they made every effort to ensure that we were bilingual. They hired a Persian tutor for us to make sure we were very literate in Persian, and well educated in Persian history, culture, the arts, etc.

"Our tutor was a renaissance man who inspired me to become passionate about language and the study of foreign cultures, particularly those of the Middle East. In high school, I studied Classical Greek, Latin, and French.

"As an undergraduate, I majored in Arabic, and minored in Middle Eastern studies.

"After college, I joined the Navy and became an NSG Communications Technician with a focus on language analysis. The Navy sent me to language school, where I learned Pashto, a language used in Afghanistan and Pakistan. I had two tours in Afghanistan and one at sea aboard Navy ships of the 5th Fleet in the Persian Gulf. During those tours, I provided support to U.S. military operations by intercepting and analyzing foreign-language comms, primarily Arabic, Persian, and Pashto. In some cases, I collected comms in foreign languages that I didn't know.

"In the latter experiences, I learned something very interesting -

that a linguist who is collecting and listening to a language he doesn't know can sometimes make important discoveries that have eluded linguists who know the language. That's because the linguist who knows the language focuses on the meaning of the words that are being said, while the person who doesn't know the language may focus on how the words are spoken. Perhaps it's analogous to how blind people can develop acute senses of hearing, feeling, and/or smell that are better than those of people who can see.

"For example, at one point during my second tour in Afghanistan, I was tasked with collecting comms in Urdu[12], the national language of Pakistan, on a particular HF freq. Those comms had recently been discovered, but hadn't been identified. I knew only a few words of Urdu. I occasionally heard two of the five communicants on this freq exchange a few words of Pashto, spoken in a way that indicated both speakers were native Pashto speakers, with Pakistani Pashto accents. With direction finding equipment, we determined that the five communicants were located at two stations. Two of the communicants were at a location in the city of Peshawar in the Pakistani Province of Khyber-Pakhtunkhwam, which used to be called the North-West Frontier Province. The other three were at a site located in the Afghan city of Jalalabad, just west of the Afghanistan-Pakistan border.

"One of my fellow collectors, who was an Urdu linguist, told me these communicants seemed to be discussing business issues, and that collection would probably be dropped in a few days if there was no indication they weren't business comms.

"As I listened to them, I tried to analyze the way they talked to see if I could figure out who they might be. I noticed a number of attributes in the way they talked. They sounded too disciplined to be either commercial or corporate. Their comms were not formatted or procedure-oriented like those of military or police organizations.

---

[12] Standard Urdu is mutually intelligible with the Indian language, Standard Hindi.

They did not sound 'furtive' like insurgents. They sounded a bit bureaucratic, like certain governmental communicants. They also seemed very guarded in their discussions, like they were concerned about letting something slip, or making a mistake.

"When I thought about everything I'd observed, I came to the conclusion that the communicants were members of some intel service. Since they were using Urdu, the official governmental language of Pakistan, and were Pakistani Pashtuns, I thought they might belong to Pakistan's principal intelligence service, the military Inter-Services Intelligence Directorate (ISI).

"I informed my supervisor, who was initially skeptical because I was not an Urdu linguist. Nonetheless, I made enough of a case that he had our most skilled Urdu linguist and analyst spend some time trying to figure out the nature of these comms. That linguist was normally so occupied with handling high-priority target[13] comms that he wouldn't have been asked to devote time to analyzing a new target unless there was a strong probability it had high value. It was fortunate that he was both a superb linguist and an extraordinarily talented analyst. There are some linguists who are only skilled at language processing, and others who are great intelligence analysts, but not outstanding linguists.

"After several weeks, he developed a solid basis for concluding that these were ISI comms. A small team of collectors focused on further development of the comms, and discovered that the Jalalabad station used other freqs for communicating with stations in various Pashtun areas of Afghanistan. The CIA then used its assets to determine that ISI agents at these stations were conducting liaison with Taliban forces.

"Drone surveillance was used to follow some of the Taliban to pinpoint Taliban sites. In some instances, Taliban were captured. In other cases, they were killed. The ISI never realized its operation had

---

[13] The word "target," when referring to communications in this story, refers to desired communications or communicants, not to military targets.

been compromised.

"So that gives you some sense for how a person who doesn't know a particular language can use general linguistic skills and analysis to make interesting discoveries."

"That's fascinating," Daniel replied. "It completely changes my view of the talents needed to derive value from language analysis. Interestingly, I've seen similar phenomena in technology development. Sometimes techies who are too close to a given technology are blind to how different uses of that technology or slight changes to it can result in revolutionary new capabilities.

"Screw heads are a good example. Screw devices were invented a couple of thousand years ago. It wasn't until the late eighteenth century that screws could be mass-produced. It took another hundred years for the invention of the square head screw to prevent slippage that occurs with a slotted head screw. It took another thirty years for the simple invention of the Phillips head screw. There was massive resistance from the American screw industry to the Phillips head. It took an open-minded owner of a small company to order his employees to manufacture it. Its use immediately went viral with auto manufacturers because it worked much better with machines.

"Another example is the use of aircraft in warfare. The first military use of aircraft was in World War I. Initially, they were only used for reconnaissance. The military and the aircraft manufacturers didn't conceive of them for use in air-to-air combat or air-to-ground attacks. Those capabilities only happened because pilots realized the potential.

"I'll give you an example from my own experience. One day, I was examining a software program that was created a few years earlier to help solve manual polyalphabetic cryptographic systems. It occurred to me that if I simply changed a couple of lines of code, the software could also be very helpful in solving additive systems. I made the changes in a couple of minutes, and then asked a friend who was working on solving an additive system to see if it would work. It did. That program had been used over and over, but it had never occurred to anyone that a few minor changes could make a big difference," said Daniel, finishing the innovation exchange that interrupted Josh's discussion about his background.

"After four years," Josh continued, "I left the Navy and came to work at NSA. My focus here has always been on language analysis - both voice and graphic. I've also learned how to perform CA of manual cryptographic systems. Although most of my assignments at the Agency have involved the Middle East and South Asia, I did spend six months working against Chinese espionage efforts in the U.S. I did that to broaden my analytic skills. However, there was an unexpected side benefit because that's where I met my wife. My bottom line is that I absolutely love SIGINT because of what it means for our national security. I find it extremely rewarding to have a job that can affect the course of history.

"Now that we know a bit about each other, perhaps we can discuss the challenges the Director has given us," Josh said.

"Yeah," Daniel answered. "I'd like to start with the counterespionage task, because that's the most time critical."

"That's the really tough one. The other project involves a lot of work, but it's one that ought to be pretty straightforward," Josh replied.

"Let's begin by giving each project a nickname. That's especially important for the counterespionage project so that we avoid any risk of compromising our efforts. If we give them very similar names, it'll sound like we're discussing a single project. What do you think about "Metanalysis" for the cover project, and "Meta" for the counterespionage project?"

"Sounds like a plan. We could ask someone on the Director's staff to spread the word about what we're calling the analysis improvement project."

"Ok. I'll mention that to Sofie Ingenios, the Director's executive assistant, whom he's asked to help us," Josh said. "How much has the Director told you about Meta?"

"He gave me a rough outline, but didn't go into a lot of detail. He said you'd do that for me."

"There isn't a lot of detail, but let me tell you what he told me." Josh proceeded to describe the information he'd been given by the Director, and then added some of his own thoughts. "Since you're not a collection and analysis guy, and don't know the Iran target, I'd like to explain what makes this task really tough.

"The first is that, even though one or more Americans appear to be involved, we can't search or examine any American comms without specific court orders. Since you haven't been involved in SIGINT analysis, you might not realize how difficult it is to get court approval. Consequently, we have to focus entirely on Iranian or other foreign comms until and if we find some information about specific Americans. If we find something about an American, we have to work with Agency lawyers to try to obtain court approval to monitor that American's communications with individuals outside the U.S. We would also work with the FBI, which would be responsible for monitoring and analyzing the suspect's comms within the U.S. NSA is never given authorization to monitor comms between Americans inside the U.S. The whole process is very painful and time consuming."

"I knew there were a lot of constraints, but I didn't know the specifics. I can understand why, but I'm glad I haven't had to deal with that," Daniel commented. "I hate bureaucracy."

"It's definitely a headache, but it's the only way to ensure that we protect constitutional rights, which is, after all, a key driver for protecting American national security. By the way," Josh continued, "from now on, when I say 'source,' that means one or more sources. I think the espionage is most likely only being carried out by a single individual, but there have been past cases of several Americans working together, such as the two NSA mathematicians, Martin and Mitchell, and the John Walker U.S. Navy spy ring.

"To continue with the challenges, the second problem has to do with the Iranians. There are probably only five to ten Iranians who know the true identity of the source. Most of those are likely to be members of Iran's Ministry of Intelligence and Security, the MOIS, which is the principal Iranian intelligence organization. The ones who probably know are:

"The 'handler' or 'case officer' who deals with the source,

"The case officer's supervisor,

"The head of the MOIS department that deals with operations involving nuclear espionage,

"The MOIS director of human espionage, and

"The head of the MOIS.

"One additional MOIS person who might know is the head of counterespionage. He might be tasked with ensuring that the source is not a double agent.

"Outside the MOIS, there's a strong possibility that the source's identity is known to the two most senior figures in the country - the Supreme Leader of Iran, the Ayatollah Ali Khamenei, and the President, Hassan Rouhani. It's also possible that the Ayatollah or the President have confided in one or two very close confidants.

"The third problem also has to do with Iranian security. Their comms, especially vis-à-vis their intelligence operations, are extremely sophisticated and encrypted with very powerful encryption systems. Moreover, if the MOIS members discuss the source in formal comms, they would probably always refer to him by a cover name, never by his real name.

"The source has to have some way of passing information to the Iranians in a timely way. Otherwise, the information is of little value. There are a number of ways a source can convey information to a foreign government contact - his case officer. The case officer could be based in a diplomatic facility as a diplomat. Alternatively, he could be living on the economy under deep cover. In this case, the deep cover option is the most likely because the nearest Iranian diplomatic facility is its UN Mission in New York. So for this situation, the Iranians would have to have a handler operating under deep cover. One clever way would be to have an Iranian immigrant employed by the U.S. Postal Service. That postman could make occasional deliveries or pick up priority or express mail from the source's residence. I can think of lots of other approaches they could use for human-to-human transfer."

Josh recounted for Daniel some of the methods that the Soviets, the Russians, and others had effectively used to pass information from the source to the intelligence service. The source could drop the information off at an agreed-upon drop point and on a schedule known only to the source and his case officer. Another method was for the source to use some form of covert electronic comms. Properly done, such comms were very difficult to uncover. A third was to set up encrypted wireless contact between laptops or tablets when the source and contact were relatively close to each other, but not in direct contact, for example, when they were in different vehicles in the same shopping center parking lot. That method was used by a Russian network uncovered in the U.S. in 2010.

"Once the MOIS has the intelligence, it has to distribute it to those who need the information, for example, Iranian negotiators in Switzerland and Vienna, Austria. That information could be sent via courier from Tehran or via encrypted electronic comms.

"That means that we have to look for Iranian vulnerabilities, for example, personal comms between individuals.

"We also have to keep our minds open to other possibilities as to which parties might be involved in this espionage," Josh mentioned.

"One possibility that occurs to me is that another country or someone from another country could be providing the information to the Iranians," Daniel offered.

"Exactly!" Josh said. "Another possibility is that the Iranians have penetrated and are exploiting the comms or the bureaucracy or the computer networks of one of our allies or one of our partners in the nuclear negotiations.

"If the source or the MOIS ever needed to meet with each other," Josh continued, "the meeting would probably happen outside the U.S. One reason for such a meeting would be if the source wanted to change the terms of his relationship, such as the amount of money he was receiving. Another would be if the MOIS wanted to discuss some special requirement it had. Such meetings would be very rare."

"I've just thought of a couple of interesting cyber tactics we could try," said Daniel. "Instead of searching for the proverbial needle in a haystack, we could tempt the needle to search for us. I'll give my ideas some thought, and then explain them to see what you think. So what do you feel we should do next?"

"I can think of several things. I'll mention some of the first steps I see, but in no particular order. Feel free to interrupt when you have any questions or thoughts."

"Great. By the way, thought I'd let you know that I've got very few outside demands on my time. I'm married, but have no children, so I can spend as much time as necessary on both of these projects. My wife is super understanding about the demands of my job," Daniel advised. "Either that, or she's happy to see me out of the house."

"We don't have any children either," Josh explained, "and since my wife and I have similar jobs, we both end up in these kinds of situations from time to time. So we understand the pressures of work. Nonetheless, we work hard not to take each other for granted. We've seen too many situations where work stresses have destroyed relationships. That happened to a couple who were our best friends, and so we try to carve out time to dedicate to each other. We even have a type of special home dining experience, which I call by the Italian name, 'Intervallo di Sapori,' which means, 'A Flavors Break.' In those flavors breaks, we prepare special meals together. When one of us finishes a time-intensive project, we try to get away for a few days and just spend time focusing on each other. The great thing about living in this area is that it's really easy to head up to Philly or New York, or to head west to the Shenandoah or east to Cape May or Ocean City - lots of choices."

"Sounds like a great way of keeping a close relationship."

"Seems to work for us. Now, I'd like to suggest that you do a quick study of the major U.S. espionage cases so you gain some insights into espionage motives, mechanics, techniques, methodologies, etc."

"Ok Josh. I'll review the major espionage cases of the last fifty to sixty years."

Josh knew that Daniel would discover some very interesting facts if he carefully analyzed previous major espionage cases.

First, he'd find that most major spies were white males. There were very few females, even though there were roughly even numbers of males and females in at least the civilian segment of the IC.

Second, he'd learn that most spies were not identified by the government's counterespionage efforts, but by defectors from the nations for whom they were spying or by family members.

Third, he'd discover that their basic motivation was often some perfect storm of personal crisis rather than simply ideology, money, or other motivations that might appear to be the primary driver. For example, a person could feel crushed by a divorce while at the same time not being recognized at work for his professional contributions.

"Daniel, did the Director discuss with you the subject of retirees?"

"He didn't. That sounds like it might relate to Metanalysis rather than Meta."

"You're mostly right, but with one exception. I asked the Admiral if I could invite brilliant retired analysts for interviews here. He said that I could, but that we could not discuss Meta with them.

"I mentioned to him that there's a retiree who's an incredibly talented Persian linguist and who's also an extraordinary analyst with a profound understanding of Iranian society and culture. He's a genius with respect to Iran. He's marvelously articulate at explaining the complexities of Iran in concise and easily understandable ways.

"On top of that, he has a warm personality. A reflection of his caring personality is the way he devoted much of his time to mentoring other linguists. He was never jealous of the success of others. Rather, he enjoyed helping others master skills and analyze complex language challenges, and reveled in their accomplishments. His view was that the deeper our talent base, the more we could contribute to the well-being of our nation.

"We call him 'Baeradaer Bishtaer.' It's a takeoff on his name - Herman Moore. Baeradaer is the Persian word for brother. His first name, Herman, is like the Spanish word, 'Hermano,' which means, 'brother.' 'Bishtaer,' means, 'more,' which sounds like his last name Moore. The Persian linguist who coined the name rightly thought that Baeradaer Bishtaer was 'more' accomplished than anyone else, and was like an older brother.

"He worked on issues relating to Iran for something like fifty years. Iran was more than a day job for him. It was a part of his life. He loved its ancient vibrant culture, art, music, and literature in contrast to the dark world created by the clerics, the Revolutionary Guard, and other creatures of the '79 revolution. He had no particular love for the regime of the Shah and its SAVAK intelligence service, but he felt that there were more individual freedoms under that regime.

"Although he grew up in a small northeastern town and had no exposure to foreign languages until high school, his wife felt he was born speaking Persian. You and I can call him "BB" for short.

"I told the Director that I'd like to invite BB in for Metanalysis, in order to see if we could get some insights that would help with Meta. The Director thought that was a great idea. So one of the first actions I'll take is to phone BB and ask if we could interview him."

"He sounds very interesting. I can't wait to meet him."

"One thing I've got to focus on right away is figuring out which Iranian and other comms are most likely to yield clues as to the identity of the source. I can then concentrate on those comms.

"Since Iran is a large country, it has a large comms environment. Fortunately, there are many types of comms I can pretty much rule out, for example, military and police comms."

"I'm beginning to understand why Meta will be very challenging," Daniel replied. "If it's OK, I'd like to take a couple of minutes to discuss equipment for our work."

"Sure. Please do."

"You'll notice that there are three computers, one secure phone and one nonsecure phone. When the Director told me how this office would be set up, I explained that we'd need double the number of computers and an additional secure phone if I'm to work with you. For example, there are times we may both need to do Internet research or high-side research at the same time. The Director agreed. I've made all the arrangements; and the other equipment will be installed tomorrow."

"Fantastic! The Director told me that the Internet research computer is something that you invented and that is invulnerable to hacking. Can you explain the concept?"

"Yes. It's a concept I developed a couple of years ago, but had trouble getting anyone to accept. When I gave the Director a briefing on another subject about six months ago, I mentioned it to him. He loved the idea and asked how fast I could develop it. I told him I could show him a working model in a couple of months if I could get a couple of talented programmers to work with me and a couple of thousand bucks to buy some publicly-available equipment. He gave me the go ahead, and I delivered. He loved it and directed that ten of them be produced and that experts not connected to me test it aggressively. They did, and no one was able to penetrate it. The Director then ordered that one hundred of them, including fifty laptops, be produced and made available to other Defense Department and IC organizations. Some of those organizations made further efforts to compromise the machines, but none succeeded.

"It's ideal for certain situations like ours, and for certain types of sensitive travelers. The main limitation is that it takes two people to install software at the same time - the user and an IT support tech. I'll explain how it works."

Daniel stood at a white board in the room, drew the hardware components, and explained how special hardware and software worked together.

"Wow!" Josh exclaimed, "I can't believe how simple this concept is; and I'm really amazed that you met with resistance to creating this jewel."

"I could understand the resistance if the concept was difficult to understand or the capability wasn't needed, or the costs were high," Daniel responded, "but none of those factors apply. This is another example of the kind of innovation blindness we discussed earlier. One irony is that a key basis for our Agency's success is innovation. It drives me crazy that so many can be so blind to simple innovation. I envy people like Steve Jobs who've had not only the vision, but also the power to push their innovative ideas."

"Well," said Josh, "We've discussed a lot and have a lot to think about. Shall we call it a day?"

"Sounds good to me."

"What time do you like to start your day, Daniel?"

"I'm an early bird. I typically start about six a.m. What about you?"

"I'm the same, out of necessity. Because of the time difference between here and Iran, if I get in at six in the morning, it's already two-thirty in the afternoon there, and lots has happened. There are many times I've been called in to work in the middle of the night. During some periods of high tension or crisis I've started my workday at eleven in the evening.

"That's true for many linguists, analysts, and others who deal with high-priority efforts involving the Middle East, South Asia, East Asia, Africa, and elsewhere. In fact, the only analysts who don't have to deal with significant time differences are those who are involved in efforts in our Western Hemisphere - for example, against Cuba or narcotraffickers."

"I think engineers and computer scientists who work on long-term projects don't appreciate those aspects of jobs on your side of the house," commented Daniel. "By the way, where do you live?"

"My wife and I live in Davidsonville, just outside Annapolis. It's nice and peaceful. We love it. What about you?"

"We live in a planet on the other side of the NSA sun – Columbia. You mentioned earlier that your wife is a Chinese linguist?"

"Yes, she's very talented and is ethnically Chinese. Her name is Meihui, which means 'Beautiful Wisdom.' I jokingly pronounce it like the French, 'Mais, oui!,' which means something like, 'Of course!' - 'Will you take out the garbage?' 'Mais oui!' 'Do you like the way I look?' 'Mais oui, Meihui!' And what about your wife?"

"Her name is Gabriela, and she's a bank manager at a bank near our house."

"Well, say hello to Gabriela, and we'll continue in the morning."

"Give my regards to your wife. See you tomorrow."

"Mai oui!"

Five

Initial Analysis - Pondering the Possibilities

Josh walked out to his silver Miata MX-5, got in, started the engine, and immediately turned off the music. He wanted silence to allow him to think on the way home. He found that he developed some of his best ideas when he was driving alone. He tended to do one of three things when driving alone. If he'd been trying to figure out some analytic challenge at work, he found it could be helpful to drive home in silence and try to solve the problem. He also liked to work on his language skills by using an app on his Galaxy S5 to listen to live streaming audio from foreign radio stations. If he just felt like relaxing, he'd listen to one of the music genres he most enjoyed - Persian, Afghan (especially Farzana Naz[14]), Arabic, French, Italian, Cajun, Country, or Blues.

Josh and Meihui rarely commuted to work together because they felt they needed to be very flexible about staying at work longer if an opportunity or requirement suddenly popped up.

On this drive home, he thought about the two challenges the Director had just given him.

He followed his usual route home - down Piney Orchard Parkway, along Conway Rd., and down Route 424 to Davidsonville. Traffic was relatively light and he had time to think about both projects, but particularly Meta.

He decided he'd have to openly devote about four hours per day

---

[14] A famous Afghan female singer who sings mostly Pashto songs.

to Metanalysis, the cover project, so no one would suspect it wasn't his primary assignment. He worked out a strategy and a rough timeline. He'd flesh it out on a computer at work in the morning, and then discuss it with Daniel.

He had a couple of quick thoughts about how to begin Meta. First, after dinner, he'd think through a couple of possible espionage scenarios.

In the morning, he'd give Daniel background and context on Iran. After that, he'd call Baeradaer Bishtaer to try to arrange an interview as soon as possible. Then, he'd phone the FBI and CIA counterespionage reps whose contact info the Director had given him.

When Josh walked into the house, he found Meihui seated on the living room couch reading something on her iPad, and sipping a glass of Zenato Lugana white wine from the Veneto in Italy.

"Hey, Josh, anything exciting going on?" she greeted him, not expecting much of an answer.

"Mais oui, Meihui, there's a lot going on. It's been a strange day."

"I hope it's all good,"

"In fact, yes." He knew he couldn't tell her anything about Meta, but the Metanalysis project was pretty straightforward, and he could describe it completely. One of the great things about having a spouse who worked at NSA was that he could discuss some unclassified topics at home and some classified items at work. Meta was an exception. One of the great frustrations for employees without spouses or other family members at the Agency or in the IC was that they could discuss nothing of substance with their families or friends. Everyone knew and understood why, and accepted that as a downside of working in the intel world. Most people love to discuss the challenges and successes of their work; and others like to be able to relieve stress by discussing specifics of their frustrations. However, intel workers had to forego those privileges.

He went on to explain Metanalysis and his partnership with Daniel.

"The Director certainly chose the right person. I know you'll do an incredible job."

"Thanks! You know your encouragement and support always mean a lot to me." Josh knew that another great aspect of having a spouse employed by NSA was that she could easily understand the need to work long hours during periods of crisis or extraordinary events.

"I wish this project had come along a few years ago," said Meihui. "There was a brilliant guy who mentored many of us in the Chinese linguist community. We worshipped him. He was half Chinese and half Japanese, and was born in Hawaii. Just before World War II started, he and his Japanese mother were visiting his father's family in China. They were trapped there when the war broke out. Because she was Japanese, they weren't harmed by the Japanese invaders. They returned home to Hawaii after the war. He was equally fluent in Japanese and Chinese, but his NSA focus was on China. Unfortunately, he passed away about five years ago."

"Wasn't that Jeff?"

"That's right. His parents named him after Thomas Jefferson."

"You introduced me to him one day when I was on assignment to the office where you and I met. He seemed like a light-hearted guy with a great sense of humor and no egotistical air about him. I never had the opportunity to have a substantive discussion with him. He'd be the perfect person to interview for a project like this."

"I forgot that I'd introduced you two. You'd have found him really fascinating. He taught us by telling us lots of stories about the tough analytic challenges he'd faced. What would you like to do for dinner this evening?"

"How about dinner at Mike's Crab House[15]? I could go for a crab dish."

"Sounds great. I'm up for one of their fish dishes. Can't wait 'til the weather warms up so we can sit outside on the deck at Mike's,

---

[15] http://www.mikescrabhouse.com

56

and enjoy the South River. Let me finish this glass of wine and the article I'm reading. You might find it interesting. It's titled, 'Everything You Might Want to Know about The Iran Nuclear Deal.' It was published yesterday in the on-line version of the *Economist*. It's a nice follow-up to the Economist article from a couple of days ago titled, "Is This a Good Deal?" Articles like these are why I worship that magazine. Of course, given all you know, you might not find anything new."

Josh laughed to himself. There was one item he'd like to know about the Iran nuclear deal that wouldn't be in the article - the identity of the Iranian spy. Like Meihui, Josh loved the British magazine because it provided him with great global insights in beautifully balanced and concise reporting style. It was journalistic art.

"Thanks! I'll take a look at the article when we get back from dinner. Let me know when you're ready to head out to Mike's."

"Will do."

When they returned home a couple hours later after a very satisfying dinner, Meihui picked up her iPad and continued to look for interesting articles in the *Economist*.

Josh decided to read the article on Iran, and then give more thought to the new projects. He first poured himself a small glass of Arak, the strong, clear, anise-flavored drink similar to Greek ouzo. This one, Golden Arak, from the town of Ramallah on the West Bank, had been introduced to him by a Palestinian-American friend.

He set his drink on a table next to an arm chair in the living room. Then, he picked up his iPad, a pad of unlined paper and a pen, and sat down. He used his iPad to read the comprehensive *Economist* article on the Iran deal. It provided the most complete and insightful picture he'd seen in open-source media.

He then began to think about how he might approach Meta - how he might most easily figure out the opposition's greatest vulnerabilities. He first considered the major components of HUMINT (Human Intelligence):

- Intelligence Acquisition Actors: The source, a possible intermediary, and the source's controller or case officer. The source could include a friendly partner government that acquired the intelligence and was sharing it with the Iranians;

- Intelligence Management, Analysis, and Distribution Personnel - The espionage organization's processing and oversight officers;

- Intelligence Recipients (Intelligence *Customers* or *Users*) - Those designated to receive the intel; and

- Unintended Intelligence Recipients - Unauthorized people who might be told about the intel by senior officials, spouses, friends, etc.

He then created a diagram of the probable relationships in the most likely scenario. That might help him and Daniel figure out the most vulnerable connections. He found that diagramming helped him sort out his thinking on complex analytic puzzles. He would change the diagrams as he gathered more data and deepened his thinking.

His diagrams complemented the spread sheets and databases he created. They also helped him think through challenging analytic problems. He found that organizing and sorting data in many different ways often helped him make discoveries he would not have made by simply thinking about an issue.

The first sketch he drew showed likely connections:

- Between the source and the Iranians,
- Among the Iranians, and
- Possibly with one or more third parties.

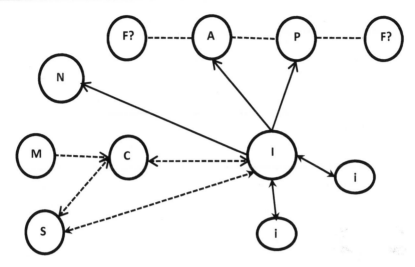

The diagrams had the four components:

1. Intelligence Acquisition Actors: S - Source, M - Middleman/Intermediary (A possibility, but less likely. Could be a third country national - a witting or unwitting partner.), C - Case officer or Controller

2. Intelligence Management, Analysis, and Distribution Personnel: I - MOIS, and entities within the MOIS, including logistical elements

3. Intelligence Recipients: A - Ayatollah Khamenei, P - President Rouhani, N - Nuclear Negotiators, including the Foreign Minister

4. Unintended Intelligence Recipients: F? - A confidant, family member, or close friend of a principal, with whom the principal might share sensitive information. (Josh knew the political reality that leaders of governments could share any information with anyone they wished. They did not need authorization.)

The second sketch he created depicted a less likely scenario - one in which the source was working with another country that was friendly to Iran or was trying to curry favor with Iran, and was passing the information to the Iranians. In the latter case, the Iranians would not likely know the identity of the original source. There were very few countries that Josh felt had both the capability and the relationship, but he couldn't rule it out. Two possibilities were Russia and Iraq.

The Russians could easily have a source. However, everything Josh had seen suggested that the Russian participation in the nuclear negotiations was genuine. In that case, they were unlikely to share any intelligence with Iran. One factor in considering any Russian role was that the sanction of keeping Iranian oil off the international market benefited the Russians, whose economy was dependent on petroleum exports. A conflicting Russian interest was that they wanted certain sanctions lifted so they could sell nuclear energy technology, advanced weapons and other military hardware to Iran.

On balance, he thought Russian involvement was unlikely. However, he wouldn't completely dismiss the possibility.

Iraq could have developed a source during the U.S. involvement in Iraq between 2003 and 2011. However, he couldn't imagine why a U.S. person might be providing the Iraqis with U.S. information about the Iranian nuclear program. It wouldn't seem that high a priority for Iraq because the Iraqi Government and the Iranians were very close. The highest Iraqi priority vis-à-vis the U.S. would be the extent to which the U.S. Government would assist in the fight against Iraq's various Sunni opponents.

While Syria and Iran were very close allies, he doubted that Bashar al-Assad's besieged government would attract a high-value American source.

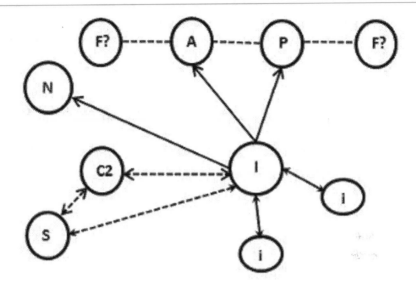

C2 = Cooperating Country

Josh then depicted a third scenario. He thought this was the least likely.[16]

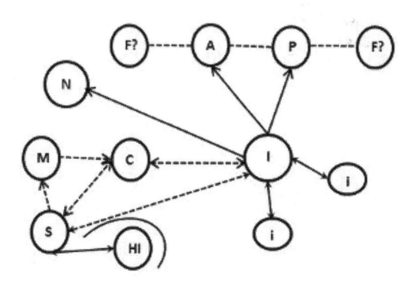

---

[16] Josh leaves it to you, the reader, to interpret **"HI"** in this diagram, or check the lexicon.

He then laid out in his own mind a set of priority actions to begin each project. He'd discuss them with Daniel in the morning and get started immediately:

A. Meta

1. Explain the possibilities to Daniel so he could begin giving more thought to actions they could take.

2. Call the FBI and CIA contacts he'd been given, and:

- Introduce himself;

- Ask how they were approaching the project,

- Make arrangements for him and Daniel to meet with them; and

- Request any comprehensive reports or any reports of MOIS activity within the U.S. during the past six months, and any earlier info they thought might be relevant.

3. Call Baeradaer Bishtaer to arrange an interview as soon as possible.

4. Call three other key analysts - one Persian and two Levantine Arabic. He would ask them to participate in Metanalysis interviews in the hope they might also provide some insight that would help with Meta.

B. Metanalysis

The more he thought about this project, the more he felt he and Daniel could complete it in six to nine months. The initial steps would be to:

1. Meet with the staff chief of each major SIGINT production organization to request the names of the best analysts to interview.

2. Meet with the British representative after confirming that Mac had secured his agreement.

3. Develop an interview list of analytic experts at NSA, other SIGINT organizations, CIA, DIA (the Defense Intelligence Agency), and other IC organizations with significant analytic responsibilities.

4. Create a set of questions to ask the experts. He'd ask Daniel to create his own list. When both had created their lists, they could discuss them and combine their ideas into a single list. He was certain the list would evolve on the basis of what they learned during the interviews.

Their daily and weekly routine would be to:

1. Start each day by reviewing the latest intel reports on Iran and looking through certain categories of Iranian intercept.

2. Conduct at least one Metanalysis interview per day.

3. Update the Admiral and Mac by email every Friday and whenever significant developments occurred.

4. Meet with the Admiral and Mac in person when developments warranted.

After Josh had given considerable thought to both projects, he sat back and finished his glass of Arak. Then he turned in for the night, with both excitement and a bit of trepidation about the challenges ahead.

Six

The Gulf Is Wide, But the Straits Are Narrow

Tuesday April 7

Josh wasn't a clock worshipper when it came to his own schedule; but on day two, he deliberately arrived a few minutes before six in order to be there when Daniel arrived. He unlocked the door, entered the office, and turned on all the computers.

At precisely six, Daniel showed up with a large cup of coffee and a bag, which appeared to be a lunch bag.

"Good morning Josh. How's it going?"

"Great so far. How about you?"

"I'm fine and can't wait to get started. I've been consumed with thinking about both projects, and can't believe I get to work on both at the same time."

"Me too. I gave them a lot of thought last night. After I make a pot of coffee, I'd really like to hear your ideas, and to share some of my thoughts."

"Sounds good. Do we have a coffee maker?"

"I brought in a coffee maker and some coffee this morning - strong French roast. Would you like some?"

"Yeah. Thanks. I love strong coffee. I'm a caféholic, and I'll be ready for more when I finish this cup."

After Josh had his coffee in hand, he said, "Let's start with Meta, since that's the most time critical."

"And the most exciting," Daniel added.

Josh began by explaining the mission, organization, history, and culture of the MOIS. He then described the three possible espionage scenarios he'd laid out for himself in diagrams the preceding evening. He used a white board to reproduce the diagrams.

Daniel clearly understood the basics of the three scenarios. He asked a number of questions to help him fully comprehend what Josh was saying. The questions were spot on, and forced Josh to clarify his own thinking. The third scenario was the most intriguing.

Next Josh provided background information about many relevant aspects of Iranian government and society, including how the Iranians operated, power dynamics within the government, decision-making processes, the pragmatists vs. ideological hard liners, the young and cool vs. conservatives, etc. Many Americans had a simplistic view of Iran, but it was a very complex society. Josh provided the information at a very high level so Daniel could understand key factors without getting bogged down with excessive detail.

Josh described key points in modern Iranian history, especially as they related to U.S. and European actions and influences, and as they related to how the current regime viewed the world.

Josh then explained a bit about Iranian ethnicity and religion. The predominant ethnic group was the Persians. However, there were many ethnic minorities, the largest of which were the Azeris. Others included Kurds, Arabs, Turkmen, Lur, Balochi, Qashqai, Galaki, Mazandarani, and Talysh. Religiously, the country was overwhelmingly Shia Muslim, with some Sunni, and a few other religious groups.

There were significant differences of opinion within Iran about the U.S. There was a strong, hardline, conservative anti-U.S. view; and there was a significant moderate view that Iran should get past its conflict with the U.S. Among the young, those born after the 1979 revolution, there were many who liked the U.S. and its culture.

Josh gave Daniel a chronology he'd prepared a year earlier for some of his junior colleagues. It started with the key driver of British interest in Iran - the discovery of oil and the creation of a British near-monopoly on that oil. He used font differences to make a visual point of how the Iranian political clergy and their followers viewed the "evil influences" of the West and secular Iranians vs. the accomplishments of the Regime and its supporters. Items in bold represented the "Satanic" doings of the West and secular Iranians, while items underlined and italicized reflected activities the regime and its supporters viewed as furthering the advancement of Shia Islam. Items in normal font were neutral. From the regime's perspective, those items might be good for Iran, but were neither regime accomplishments nor satanic evil.

Josh quickly walked Daniel through the chronology, explaining and amplifying some of the events. He emphasized that memorizing detail wasn't important. The fonts would give him a sense of the regime's world view and the change with the 1979 revolution:

1908 - **Anglo-Persian Oil Company, later Anglo-Iranian Oil Company, later BP, given exclusive oil prospecting rights in most of Iran for sixty years**

1921 - **British general selects Iranian military battalion commander, Reza Shah, to command Persian Cossack Brigade,** a division-size force and the only effective Iranian military force. Reza Shah uses the brigade to seize Tehran, preempting a Soviet plan to capture the city

1921-25 - **Reza Shah consolidates power & becomes first Shah (king) of the Pahlavi dynasty**

1925-41 - **Reza Shah modernizes & secularizes Iran, as Turkish contemporary, Mustafa Kemal Ataturk, does in Turkey: Shah clashes with clergy & requires that:**

- All but clergy wear western clothing
- Worshippers in mosques sit on chairs, not floors
- Men wear western hats with brims, preventing traditional Muslim touching the head to the floor
- Wives come to public functions without head coverings
- All cinemas, restaurants, & hotels admit women
- Women be allowed into colleges of law & medicine

He creates three pillars of support for his rule:
- Highly paid military
- Government bureaucracy with 90,000 civil servants
- Patronage controlled by his royal court

Creates industry & develops transportation infrastructure

Changes country's name from Persia to Iran (land of the Aryans)

Greatly reduces power and autonomy of tribes, and focuses on ethnic nationalism

Tries to reduce British & Soviet influence by playing them off against each other, and inviting Germans into the economy

1935 - **Shah has troops break into Meshad Shrine, killing dozens & injuring hundreds**

1941 - **Massive British - Soviet invasion forces Shah to abdicate in favor of his son, Crown Prince Mohammad Reza Pahlavi, who would rule until 1980**

1941-79 – **New Shah's rule characterized by:**
Continued modernization, secularization, and clashes with clergy
Use of SAVAK intelligence agency to suppress dissent
Corruption
Close relations with Israel
Glorification of ancient Persian Empire vice promoting Shia Islam

1953 - U.S. and UK orchestrate overthrow of democratically elected Prime Minister, Mohammad Mosaddegh, who nationalized oil industry

1963 - Shah implements American-inspired White Revolution (i.e., revolution without bloodshed):
- Expands women's rights, including suffrage
- Expropriates estates of traditional elites, and redistributes land to four million small farmers
- Institutes profit-sharing for workers in industry
- Nationalizes forests and pastures.
- Forms literacy corps

Later in 1963 - *Ayatollah Khomeini raises opposition to White Revolution* and **is arrested**, *creating widespread unrest.* **Shah uses military force to regain control.**

1964 - Shah & U.S. reach agreement that all U.S. personnel in Iran and their dependents will be immune from prosecution. (Typical U.S. Status of Forces agreement)

Later in 1964 - *Ayatollah Khomeini denounces agreement with U.S.,* **and is arrested. He is exiled to Turkey for a year, Iraq for thirteen years, and then France for a short while.**

Shah's rule also includes:
- Conflict with bazaari merchant class
- Loss of support from the working class
- Establishment of close relations with Sunni Saudi Arabia
- Occasional strains in his close alliance with U.S.

1979 – *Shah overthrown by followers of Ayatollah Khomeini*

1979 - *American hostages seized due to*:

- *Perceived* **U.S. efforts to undermine the revolution,**
- **Failed efforts to force U.S. to return Shah**
- **Long-term U.S. support of Shah**

1979 through 2015 - **Ever harsher and more crippling sanctions imposed on Iran by U.S. and many international partners due to Iran's taking U.S. hostages, terrorist activities, ballistic missile program, and nuclear weapons development program.**

1980 - <u>Failed</u> **U.S. hostage rescue operation**

1981, January 20 - Iran releases U.S. hostages the day President Reagan is sworn into office. U.S. & Iran had already negotiated the agreement, but *the Ayatollah hated President Carter so much he wouldn't release hostages until President Carter leaves office.*

1980-88 - **Iran-Iraq War**
- **Iraq starts largest conventional war ever between developing nations**
- **Massive casualties include 250,000 to 550,000 Iranian & Iraqi military killed**
- **Iraqi chemical warfare with little U.S. or other western condemnation**
- **U.S., French, Russians support Iraqis with critical weapons & intelligence**

1982 on - *Iran supports Lebanese Shia Hezbollah and Palestinian Sunni Hamas against Israel*

1983 - *During Lebanese civil war, Shia Lebanese Islamic Jihad (probably Hezbollah & probably supported by Iran) conducts devastating attacks against U.S. Embassy, U.S. Marines, and French forces in Beirut. Sixty three die in Embassy bombing in April, and 241 Marines and 58 French troops die in October bombings. This leads to U.S. and French withdrawal of troops from Lebanon.*

1984-86 - *Irangate - Reagan Administration sells arms to Iran to gain freedom for seven U.S. hostages held in Lebanon by probable Iran-associated terrorists. Thus, U.S. helps* both **Iraq** & *Iran during their war.*

2003-11 - *Iraq War*
- *Eliminates Iran's nemesis, Saddam Hussein*
- *Replaces anti-Iranian Sunni regime with pro-Iranian Shia regime*
- *Provides Iran with opportunities to attack American forces*
- *Leads to destruction of major Iranian foe - al-Qaeda in Iraq*
- **Leads to rise of Daesh (ISIS)**

2002 - Iran pursuing nuclear weapons program, with secret facilities at Natanz and Arak.

2003 - *Iran makes comprehensive proposal for negotiation on nuclear weapons, support of Palestinians, etc.* **U.S. President rejects proposal.**

2003 - Start of long, complex set of interactions between Iran, the U.S., Germany, France, the UK, Russia, China, the IAEA, the UN, and others. **Interactions include diplomacy, sanctions, threats of military action, etc.** A key player is Germany, one of Iran's most important trading partners. Germany estimates joining sanctions costs thousands of German jobs.

These actions ultimately lead to serious negotiations between Iran and P5+1, resulting in interim agreement in 2013. That leads to 2014 start of negotiations toward long-term comprehensive agreement.

After finishing the chronology, Josh spent a couple of minutes giving Daniel a high-level explanation with a print-out covering some aspects of Islam vis-à-vis Iran because of the religion's fundamental role in all aspects of Iran's government, including international relations.

Iran/Persia and Islam

History
Zoroastrianism is primary Persian religion from at least fifth century BC.
AD 610 Prophet Mohammad founds Islam in Arab Saudi Arabia.
AD 651 Arabs conquer Iran, and Iranians gradually convert to Sunni Islam.
AD 680 Islam splits into Sunni and Shia.
16th to 18th centuries – Iranians convert to Shia Islam.

Islam in the 21st Century
Sunni Islam predominates, with 87 percent of world's believers.
Iran, which is not Arab:
- Is 90 percent Shiite;
- Has 40 percent of world's Shiites;
- Has 5 percent of world's Muslims; and
- Is primarily allied with Shiite or Shiite offshoot Arab regimes/groups: Iraqi and Syrian regimes, Lebanese Hezbollah, Yemen's Houthi rebels; and on and off with Sunni Hamas.
Saudi Arabia's Sunni establishment is:
- Protector of Islam's two holiest mosques – at Mecca and Medina, and
- Major foe of Iran and its allies.

Some nations have volatile/potentially volatile Sunni-Shia mixes. One is Bahrain with pro-Saudi Sunni monarchy and majority Shia population. It is home to U.S. Navy 5th Fleet, which protects interests of U.S. and its allies in the region.

Nations with largest Muslim populations are non-Arab: Indonesia, Pakistan, India, and Bangladesh. Believers are principally Sunni.

Josh concluded the discussion about divisions within the Islamic world by pointing out that Christianity had experienced similar major cleavages in its own ranks - with Orthodox, Catholic, Protestant, Coptic, Mormon, and other denominations. Some of those divisions had led to major armed conflict.

"Wow, Professor Josh!" Daniel exclaimed, "I had no idea of the complicated nature of Iran's relationship with the West and within the Muslim world. Your chronology and explanation are extremely helpful and a lot to absorb. I now have a much better appreciation of why there's so much anger and distrust between Iran and the West. I also had no idea of the composition of the Muslim world. I thought most Muslims were Arabs. I'm going to take your great chronology and study it. Thanks!"

"Glad to do it. Your final exam on these topics will be tomorrow afternoon at three. Now I'm going to call our counterparts at the FBI and CIA, and arrange for us to meet them."

Seven

Creating the Sauce

Using the secure phone, Josh called Johnnie Dece, the FBI special agent who was the team leader of the Iran counterespionage team. Fortunately, Dece was sitting at his desk when Josh called.

"Special Agent Dece here," Johnnie answered.

"Hello, I'm Javad Shirazi from NSA. Our Director, Admiral Saunders, has asked me and my colleague, Daniel Dechado, to work with you on a special project."

"Hi! I've been expecting your call. Great to hear from you! We're looking forward to meeting you. By the way, you can call me Johnnie."

"And I go by Josh."

"We currently have four members on our team - Special Agent Shellie MacPherson and me from the Bureau's Counterintelligence Division, and two from the CIA - Farida Nasrallah, who is a counterintelligence analyst, and Gianni Portali, who is a CIA operations officer. Farida is the CIA lead.

"Our investigation is called an UNSUB, which means *Unknown Subject Investigation* because the identity of the person or persons being investigated is unknown.

"We'll be meeting here at our HQ on Thursday. We'd be happy if you and Daniel could join us."

"Let me check with Daniel, who's sitting next to me" Josh replied.

Daniel indicated he'd be available. Josh asked Johnnie to send the details of the meeting's time and venue via secure email. Johnnie agreed; and Josh provided their high-side email addresses.

Johnnie mentioned that he'd be in touch with Farida Nasrallah that afternoon. He'd let her know that Josh had called, and that he and Daniel would meet them at the Bureau on Thursday.

Josh then explained the types of studies and insights he'd appreciate from the Bureau and the CIA. Johnnie told Josh the team had already pulled together a package of that info, and would send it to him the next day via FBI courier.

After Josh hung up, he told Daniel his sense from the conversation was that Johnnie would be very easy to work with and was very organized.

After finishing his conversation, Josh immediately phoned Herman Moore - BB - at his home. Luckily, BB was home and not busy. After a bit of fun bantering back and forth in Persian, Josh explained Metanalysis, and asked BB if he'd honor Josh with an interview. As expected, BB was happy to help out. They agreed to meet on a Friday morning at ten. Josh was delighted and effusively thanked him.

Josh then phoned Marilyn to ask her help in arranging BB's visit. "Good morning, Marilyn, it's Josh. How're you doing?"

"I'm great, and you?"

"Just fine, thanks. We'd really appreciate your help with a couple of items."

"Let me know what you need, and I'll make it happen."

"Great. First, I wonder if you could make arrangements for a visitor, a retired language analyst by the name of Herman Moore."

"I'd be delighted, Josh. I remember Herman well. He's a super guy. I was once a secretary in an office where he worked. He was very kind to me and always treated me with the utmost respect - the way he treated everyone. What do you need for his visit?"

"I'd like a comfortable room where Daniel and I can interview him for a couple of hours; and I'd appreciate it if you could do the paperwork for his visit. He'll be arriving at ten on Friday."

"No problem, Josh. I'll take care of it right away. I'll get you a room here in the Director's office suite. I'll also get him VIP treatment at the Visitor Center and an escort to bring him to the interview room."

"Thanks, Marilyn. Rather than arranging the VIP escort, we'd prefer to meet him ourselves at the Visitor Center."

"I'll do it any way you want. What's the next thing you'd like my help with?"

"Well, we'd be grateful if you could set up separate forty-five-minute meetings for Daniel and me with the head of each major SIGINT production staff in the Agency, beginning tomorrow. We'd like to explain our starting approach to our project, solicit their ideas, and ask if they could provide the names and contact information of the best current and retired analysts.

"That's it for now."

"OK, I'll make it all happen. You can count on it."

"Thanks a lot Marilyn. We really appreciate your help."

"You bet, Josh. Talk to you soon."

Josh was delighted with Marilyn's attitude. She received his requests eagerly, and made him feel comfortable that she'd handle everything smoothly and quickly. He couldn't have asked for more responsive or professional support. He could see why she was working on the Director's staff.

When Josh turned away from his computer, he found Daniel waiting impatiently to talk to him. Daniel wanted to chat about the Metanalysis interview process. Josh said he'd love to get started.

Daniel first suggested that they try to have two interviews with each exceptional analyst because the first interview would likely prompt some to examine their lives and experiences more closely and carefully. That would enable them to provide additional insights in a second interview. Since problem solvers were very thoughtful people, they often continued reflecting on important questions they'd been asked.

Josh suggested a variant of that idea. They should make it clear to the interviewees that the door was always open for them to return and provide additional info. Then, one month after the interview, they could call each interviewee back and ask if they'd thought of anything further to discuss. On the basis of his own experience, Josh had observed that one type of exceptional analyst had to analyze everything, including every aspect of their own lives. The other type focused only on problem solving, and didn't think a great deal about themselves and how they'd developed in their professional lives.

Daniel thought that made sense. Then he recommended that they also interview some of the exceptional software and engineering creators to see if they had something in common with great intel analysts.

Josh loved the idea.

They then discussed how to prepare and conduct the meetings, and agreed on a number of things:

"I'd like to research artificial intelligence studies," said Daniel. "They focus on learning from expert specialists how they analyze complex problems so their thought processes can be replicated for others to use.

"Terrific idea, Daniel," said Josh. He then walked over to the white board and wrote down major topics to explore with the great ones, including:

1. Their education history, with learning experiences that may have had a significant influence.

2. Any insights as to when they first began to do analysis, and what motivated them to do that analysis.

3. The people in their lives who significantly influenced their analytic capabilities and how they did so. The types of influencers could include parents, relatives, teachers, mentors, friends, colleagues, supervisors, and even adversaries.

4. The unique special and techniques they used, including important ones they'd developed, and what prompted them to do the development.

5. Their great analytic accomplishments, and the methodologies and other factors that enabled them to succeed.

6. Any problems they'd solved when those problems had defied solution by others - and the techniques that enabled their success.

7. Any systemic impediments or barriers they'd faced, and how they'd overcome them.

8. Any improvements they might suggest in how the Agency recruited, hired, developed, supported, and rewarded analysts.

Josh and Daniel would refine this approach on the basis of their interview experiences.

Once the first round of interviews at HQ had been completed, they could travel to other major SIGINT organizations in the U.S. and abroad, and to GCHQ at Cheltenham in the UK, if the British agreed.

Josh then mentioned that in addition to BB, there were three other exceptional analysts they should interview as soon as possible because they were experts on Iran and its closest allies. They were:

- Carolyn Rainier, a Persian linguist and analyst - Her father had been an American contractor supporting the Iranian Air Force until the Shah was overthrown. She lived there from age 10 until age 19, when the Ayatollah Khomeini came into power. She had a profound understanding of Persian, and Iranian culture and society.

- Michael Harriman - a Levantine Arabic Linguist and Hezbollah - Hamas expert. He'd retired, but was working a limited number of hours in NSA's reserve program, which allowed a small number of experts to work part-time after retirement. That program was created after 9/11.

- Peter Schlauman - a Levantine Arabic linguist and expert on Syria, who was also in the NSA reserve program.

While Carolyn was an obvious choice, Michael and Peter were important because they'd analyzed partners of Iran, and might be able to provide important insights into how the Iranians did business.

Josh then asked Daniel if he was ready to share the ideas he'd mentioned the preceding day as ways to penetrate the Iranian intelligence operation. Josh was dying to learn what Daniel had in mind.

Daniel was ready. His first idea was to develop some sort of computer app, like a game, that would lure a specific person to use the app. The type of app would depend on the interests of the target person. If the intended target was an engineer, the app might be an engineering challenge tailored to the target's area of expertise. If the person was a soldier, the app could be a combat video game. Once Daniel had some details about the person's interests, he could work on developing an app. In some cases, he could probably create the app fairly quickly. In other cases, it might take a lot of research. On the surface, the app would appear to be intended for a large player group, but it would have components designed to provide a strong lure for the specific target and to identify the target if he/she used the app. One way to identify that the target using the app was to intentionally include in the app factual errors that only the target would recognize - errors that would entice the target to contact the app developers and inform them of the errors. Once the target was identified, the app would penetrate the target's computer and start the second app.

The second app would be based on a concept that Daniel had developed a couple of years earlier. He knew exactly how to write the software, and could probably create it within a week. He would have to do some research about the psychology of the target's culture and the target himself.

He'd never developed this app because it had immense potential for both good and evil. It was essentially an app that would infect a user's mind with a psychological virus. This virus would change the user's thought processes in a way that would cause him to reveal critical information in a very special situation.

Daniel said that if these concepts interested Josh, he would work on developing them. Josh thought they were great, but that they should run them by the Admiral in their Friday update. In the meantime, he encouraged Daniel to keep working on the concepts. He felt the Director was likely to approve the first app, depending on the specifics. He was not so certain about the second app. It sounded like a concept that could dramatically change the cyber world.

Wednesday April 8

Josh and Daniel spent the day meeting with the chiefs of staff of each major SIGINT production organization. They introduced themselves, explained the Metanalysis project, and requested the names of analysts they should interview. They asked not only for the names of analysts within the organization, but of great analysts they knew in other organizations.

Two of the chiefs of staff seemed very supportive of the project. The third barely concealed his view that this was just another bureaucratic waste of time.

In the afternoon, Mac Roberts phoned and advised that the British representative was very receptive to meeting with them to discuss the project.

Eight

Seeking Guides to the Dome of Damavand[17]

Thursday April 9

Knowing that traffic on the Baltimore Washington Parkway could be problematic, Daniel and Josh got an early start on the drive down to FBI HQ for their first meeting with the counterespionage team. The weather was overcast and windy, with a bit of rain. Fortunately, there were no traffic tie-ups, so they arrived at FBI HQ about fifteen minutes early. They called Johnnie's office; and he came down to meet them.

Johnnie welcomed them and took them to a conference room next to his office, where the other three team members were waiting. Johnnie introduced them first to Farida Nasrallah, the CIA counterintelligence analyst, then Gianni Portali, the CIA operations officer, and finally, Shellie MacPherson, the other FBI team member. Josh was shocked when Shellie greeted him in perfect, unaccented Persian, and continued in Persian by asking if he was related to Behrouz Shirazi (his cousin who'd been in the NSG).

"I sure am," Josh answered with a surprised reaction on his face, "He's an older cousin whom I really admire and who inspired me to

---

[17] Mount Damavand is located near the southern coast of the Caspian Sea. At 18,410 feet, it has the highest peak in Iran and the Middle East and is the tallest volcano in Asia. It has a special place in Persian mythology and folklore. (See Wikipedia.)

get into this business. How do you know Behrouz?"

"Well, when I was in the Air Force, we served together at a joint command. He was very talented and a nice guy. We used to have fun chatting with each other in Persian."

"How did you come to learn Persian? Your accent is perfect."

"I owe my fluency to my mother. She was born and raised in the Iranian Jewish community in Iran. My father, who is of American Ashkenazi Jewish heritage, was an American Foreign Service officer stationed in Iran. He was assigned to the U.S. Embassy in Tehran in 1975. He met my mother there in 1976 and married her in 1977. Luckily, he was transferred to Amman before the Shah's fall."

"After graduating from college, I joined the Air Force, went to Officer Training School, and became an intelligence officer. I served two tours in the Air Force, and then left to join the FBI.

"The Bureau provided me with counterespionage training, including surveillance. Since then I've worked against Iranian espionage efforts, and have participated in some very interesting cases."

"That's fascinating," Josh commented. "Maybe we can yak in Persian from time to time, especially when we want to pull something over on the rest of this team," he joked.

"Sounds good to me," she laughed. "Please give my best to Behrouz next time you see him."

"Will do."

Josh knew that the Iranian Jewish community had three thousand years of history in Iran. When Israel was created in 1948, there were about 150,000 Jews in Iran. Many of the poorer ones migrated to Israel. During the last year of the Shah's reign, the size of the Iranian Jewish community numbered about 100,000, of whom about ten percent were wealthy, and most of the rest were middle class. After the Khomeini revolution, many began to leave. After several decades, the number had dwindled to between 8,000 and 9,000.

Josh and Daniel would later learn that Shellie's husband, Rick, was an FBI technical expert and that they had a daughter who was a high school freshman.

As a technical expert, Daniel initially seemed the only one out of place in this group. However, as soon as he mentioned the names of a couple of FBI employees with whom he'd worked on "special projects," Josh noticed subtle changes in facial expressions and tone of voice of Johnnie and Shellie. These responses conveyed respect and increased warmth.

Daniel also mentioned the names of a couple of CIA projects he'd worked on, but neither Farida nor Gianni recognized the names of the projects or the technical experts Daniel named.

After the introductions, Johnnie pointed out the coffee and water on a side table. Josh and Daniel both poured themselves some coffee.

When they were seated, Johnnie said the four of them had decided to call their team, "Team Triad," to make it clear that it was a three-agency partnership. Josh and Daniel were really happy they'd been received so warmly.

Johnnie asked Josh and Daniel for their cell phone numbers, and he, Shellie, Farida, and Gianni provided theirs. Johnnie explained that the team needed to be able to get together quickly should some time-sensitive development occur during off-duty hours. For many jobs in the IC, it was standard practice to be on call around the clock, and even pagers were not unusual. Their world didn't work on scheduled 8-hour workdays.

Johnnie, Farida, Shellie, and Gianni told Josh and Daniel about their areas of expertise and experience. It was very clear that all four of them knew one another quite well, had often worked together, and had great mutual respect.

Johnnie was a twenty-five-year Bureau professional who'd spent his career working in counterespionage against a number of countries, principally China. He was fluent in Mandarin Chinese. He was African-American, and had grown up in the D.C. area. Josh mentioned that his wife, Meihui, was an NSA Chinese linguist.

Farida was a twenty-year CIA employee from Livonia,

Michigan. Her entire career had been in counterespionage, principally against Middle Eastern and South Asian threats. She was fluent in Levantine and Iraqi Arabic, and her ethnicity was Palestinian. Her first name suggested she was Christian, as were about five percent of Palestinians. Generally, their Christian history dated to pre-Muslim times and was Syrian Orthodox.

As a CIA operations officer - a "case officer," Gianni's expertise was in recruiting and managing foreign spies, principally in the Persian Gulf and Egypt. This gave him an offensive perspective, in contrast to the defensive perspectives of Johnnie, Farida, and Shellie. He was fluent in Egyptian and Gulf Arabic, as well as Italian and Neapolitan. As his name suggested, he was Italian-American – a native of San Francisco.

Josh was really impressed at the breadth and depth of Team Triad's FBI and CIA members.

After, those members described their backgrounds, Daniel and Josh reciprocated. When Daniel gave examples of some of his technical creations, the FBI and CIA officers were impressed, but wondered how he could possibly contribute to their effort.

Josh explained the Metanalysis cover project that he and Daniel had been assigned, and how they intended to use that project to try to develop clues by interviewing experts like Baeradaer Bishtaer and Michael Harriman.

Josh explained that he'd never worked with the Bureau before and that neither he nor Daniel had ever been involved in counterespionage cases. Josh had worked with CIA analysts on analytic challenges involving several countries. He asked the team's forbearance and help in educating him if he asked very basic questions and didn't understand very basic concepts. He said he did have a decent understanding of how intelligence organizations conducted HUMINT. Daniel seconded Josh's request.

Johnnie said they'd be glad to help, and also looked forward to Josh and Daniel educating them about NSA's capabilities. They'd all used SIGINT in the past and worked with NSA security reps, but never directly with NSA SIGINT analysts or tech experts.

Johnnie then explained that the team met at FBI HQ every Thursday morning at ten, but could come together on short notice if some development warranted. They could also meet at CIA or NSA HQ. They were very flexible.

Johnnie, Farida, Shellie, and Gianni each updated the team on their efforts of the past week. Basically, each one had combed over all the new info in their own areas of expertise. They'd looked at all intel reports from all U.S. government sources on Iran, including reports from the CIA, FBI, NSA, DIA, foreign partners, etc. While the CIA had a couple of assets within the Iranian intelligence system, none of those assets had the kind of access that could provide information on this case. The bottom line was that the team had no clue as to the identity of the Iranian source or sources.

By noon, they'd finished their discussions and agreed to meet at the same time and place the following week.

"Well," Johnnie said, "Thanks for joining our team. We look forward to working with you guys, getting to know you, and receiving your help in ending this Iranian operation. Do you have any questions before we wrap things up?"

"I don't have any questions," Daniel said. "I just hope we can make a difference."

"I have one question," Josh replied.

"Please ask," Johnnie said.

""What do you call an ointment that's used for healing a disagreement over a nuclear weapons program?"

"Oh, no!" Farida laughed, "We've got a jokester. What's the answer?"

"An atomic balm," Josh chuckled.

"Good grief!" Gianni laughed. "Get back to NSA!"

After saying their good-byes, Josh and Daniel headed back north through D.C. and up the BW Parkway to NSA.

After a quick lunch in the NSA cafeteria, they returned to their office.

Nine

Un Signe Se Présente

(A Sign Appears)

Friday April 10

Josh and Daniel arrived at the Visitor Center at about 9:45 so they'd be there if BB arrived early. He was already there.

After Josh and BB warmly greeted each other in Persian, Josh introduced Daniel. That introduction gave Daniel an immediate sense for why Josh thought BB was a very special person. He communicated a combination of warmth, respect, and intellect. Daniel liked him at once.

Josh helped BB complete the necessary procedures to get a visitor badge. Then they escorted him to the Director's suite and took him to Marilyn. BB recognized her and greeted her like a family member. After they chatted about old times for a couple of minutes, Marilyn took them to the room she'd arranged. It was very comfortable, and she'd provided water and coffee. They thanked her and she left.

Josh described the Metanalysis project in more detail than he had on the phone, and explained that he and Daniel would like to explore with BB how he'd developed his combined exceptional language and intelligence analysis skills. Josh explained a bit about Daniel's background, including the fact that he had no experience as a linguist or intelligence analyst, but had lots of experience analyzing and solving problems. Josh also mentioned that Daniel was bilingual.

Josh gave no hint of the most important aspect of the interview -

looking for information that might help with Meta.

BB said he was honored that Josh and Daniel would include him in their project.

As they asked questions, BB said he could only think of a few things in his youth that related to development of his linguistic and analytic skills. From the time he was a child, he'd been very interested in analyzing and understanding his surroundings, but he didn't know what had created that interest. His grandparents were all Irish immigrants, and the only language spoken at home was English. His parents were wonderful, but did nothing that he could remember to help him develop his language or analysis skills. His third grade teacher did a superb job of teaching her students the structure of English through diagramming sentences. In fact, he still had his third grade booklet on the subject. He subsequently applied that same technique in learning Persian.

His first exposure to a foreign language was in high school, where he took two years of French. He learned Persian in the Army. When he enlisted, he took a language aptitude test. The results were so good that the Army decided to send him to language school. They offered him a choice of Chinese, Russian, or Persian. He chose Persian because it intrigued him, and because he wasn't interested in going anywhere near the Soviet Union or China.

When he began studying Persian, he almost immediately felt some sort of emotional connection to the language, and gradually, the culture and its people. They seemed to connect with both his heart and his brain. He couldn't really explain it. Somehow, it seemed to involve the flow of the language, its sound, and later - the complex culture of Iran - its long history, its art, its poetry, and the complex relationships among its people. It was a language that seemed simple at the start, but which became much more challenging as he reached higher levels. Some languages are difficult at entry level, but seem easier after mastering the basic structure. Persian seemed quite different. There appeared to be much more deliberate ambiguity than in English.

His study of Persian and of Iran became and always remained much more than just a professional responsibility. They were a passion that he pursued both at work and at home. They really enriched his life. The constant pursuit of more knowledge added to his professional competence and led him to ever more challenging endeavors.

The conversation then moved to his operational experiences with Persian and Iran.

Until the fall of the Shah in the late 1970s and the hostage crisis, there were only a few times when there was high U.S. Government interest in SIGINT on Iran. The first and most important period was at the beginning of his career - at the time leading up to and following the overthrow of Mohammad Mosaddegh in 1953. There were other times such as during the Arab-Israeli war of 1967 and the 1973 Yom Kippur War.

The rest of the time until 1979, the U.S. Government felt it had enough American presence on the ground in Iran - with U.S. military advisers, and U.S. Embassy and CIA resources, that it did not need much in the way of SIGINT. Consequently, working on the Iranian effort at NSA was not as prestigious as working against some of the high-tension or high-conflict areas, such as Vietnam from 1965 to 1975, or the Soviet Union, or China, or North Korea.

However, that changed dramatically with the fall of the Shah and the hostage crisis. This created a surge of U.S. Government requirements for SIGINT on every aspect of Iranian Government activities. Those requirements continued to grow, as:

1. Iran's rulers:

- Created an additional security support apparatus - the Revolutionary Guard Corps - to provide a set of military forces to balance the existing conventional military forces, which the regime didn't trust because of their long training and equipment relationship with the U.S. and with other, now-hostile foreign powers.

- Undertook aggressive foreign terrorist and intelligence operations to pursue Iranian objectives such as support for Shia groups in Lebanon, Syria, and Iraq, as well as Palestinian groups intent on defeating Israel and regaining control of their homeland. The terrorist operations included the 1992 bombing of the Israeli Embassy in Buenos Aires and the 1996 bombing of the U.S. Air Force barracks in Khobar, Saudi Arabia, which killed 19 U.S. servicemen and wounded 498 people of various nationalities.

- Were probably involved with extremist elements in Lebanon who conducted the devastating 1983 attacks against U.S. and allied military and diplomatic facilities, and took U.S. hostages.

2. Saddam Hussein engaged in massive warfare with Iran.

3. The National Security Council in the Reagan White House negotiated with Iranian "moderates" and then provided arms to Iran to gain the release of American hostages in Lebanon. Basically, they traded arms for hostages.

On the one hand, these ever-increasing SIGINT requirements overwhelmed BB and his Persian linguist colleagues with more Persian-language intercept than they could begin to handle. They found themselves working long hours for days on end. On the other hand, they were energized by providing policymakers, including the President, as well as U.S. military forces, with information that greatly enhanced U.S. National Security by saving American lives and defeating many Iranian operations aimed at the U.S. and its allies. They were deeply disappointed and frustrated when they couldn't develop information to prevent attacks like the Khobar bombing in Saudi Arabia.

The new requirements led to the training of many additional Persian linguists, whom BB did his best to mentor and develop.

After discussing the evolution of NSA's Persian-language needs and BB's involvement, Josh and Daniel returned to the topic of how BB developed his analytic skills. He said there was very little light he could shed on that subject. He kept studying Iranian society and organizations at all levels, and tried to create in his own mind a three-dimensional mosaic of how it all fit together. Every time he encountered and analyzed a new problem, he looked at it from many angles to see how it fit into the mosaic. If he found something that didn't fit, and if he or someone else solved the problem, he would use the solution to refine and enhance the mosaic.

Josh and Daniel asked BB if he could lead them through some of the most difficult problems he'd solved. BB remembered all of them in great detail. He described ten that were the most challenging.

As BB spoke, both Josh and Daniel listened carefully for insights that might help them with Meta. They found s 24-karat nugget. BB didn't consider this incident particularly challenging from an analytic standpoint, but it was interesting from the standpoint of the important interplay that can occur between governmental leaders and those outside government. The Supreme Leader, the Ayatollah Khamenei, had several confidants with whom he discussed some sensitive information. His two closest confidants were another cleric and an individual who was a hero of the Iran-Iraq War. BB didn't know the name of the cleric, but the war hero was an ethnic Azeri named Mirza Behrangi. The Ayatollah was also Azeri and loved defense issues.

BB explained to Daniel that the Azeris were a Turkic-speaking group that inhabited northwestern Iran and formed Iran's largest ethnic minority. They represented between 15 and 24 percent of Iran's population. The Azeri area of Iran bordered on the country of Azerbaijan, which had been part of Iran until it was occupied by Russia.

BB only heard the Supreme Leader and Behrangi speak once, but it was a fairly long conversation. They switched back and forth between Azeri and Persian. The language switches were smooth and effortless, and seemed driven by the topic being discussed at the moment. The Supreme Leader gave his views on a broad range of domestic and foreign topics. He even joked about the then newly elected President, Mahmoud Ahmadinejad, a man that neither seemed to hold in high regard. It was very clear that the Ayatollah and Behrangi had a close personal relationship. During this conversation, the Ayatollah mentioned that Iranians would be forever grateful for Behrangi's heroism during the war.

Toward the end of the interview, BB made an observation about people who are great at some endeavor. They pursue their profession as a consuming passion, not simply as work, as a way to earn a living. They don't turn off their involvement when their work day ends. They think about it frequently, from the time they wake up until the time they go to sleep. They devote time to family or religion or sports, but when their brains have a free moment, they turn to their passion. If BB was dealing with an analytic problem as the work day ended, he wouldn't leave that problem at work. He'd think about it while he was stuck in traffic, or while washing the dinner dishes, or while brushing his teeth before bed time. In fact, he found that those times away from work were often best for discovering solutions. Silence without distraction allowed the mind to create, to innovate, to solve.

He also observed that people who were passionate about their profession would also spend their own money to constantly expand their knowledge and horizons. As he thought about it, he expanded that thought to school teachers, who would spend their own money to buy extra supplies for their pupils. They were committed to their mission to educate.

BB had met other linguists who had intellects he thought were superior to his, but they didn't have the passion for their profession. They did a good job at work, but didn't reach their full potential because, once they left the office, they gave very little thought to the language and analytic challenges they faced.

Of course, highly successful people had to have more than passion. They had to have the right mind set, the right intellect. They also had to be able to learn the subject matter relating to their language responsibilities. Understanding language is all about knowing context. A linguist or analyst who dealt with military topics had to understand concepts such as order of battle, chain of command, and strategy and tactics. A linguist who dealt with nuclear proliferation had to understand fission, fusion, enrichment, reprocessing, etc.

He had known linguists who were passionate about their language work, but could only memorize lots of language information - vocabulary, grammar, and syntax. They couldn't analyze complex language materials.

Daniel and Josh completely agreed about the importance of passion for one's profession. It was something they hadn't thought much about because it was part of their being, and they took it for granted. But when they thought about it, they realized it certainly applied to all the great individuals they knew.

When they'd finished discussing BB's own analytic experiences, he recommended the names of other exceptional analysts. They were all on Josh's list.

BB also recommended one former manager, Levy Morris, an extraordinary multitalented individual. One of his talents was to identify, at an early point in their careers, individuals who had great potential. He would mentor them and help them achieve that potential. While that was an important responsibility for managers, BB had never met anyone who fulfilled that responsibility like Levy. Perhaps Levy could help the Metanalysis project by explaining how he evaluated individuals to determine their high potential. BB said Levy was extremely adept at rapidly assembling a high-powered team of just the right individuals to respond to the type of crisis situation the Agency often had to support. Although Levy had left for the private sector some years earlier, he still performed occasional consulting work for the Agency.

Josh and Daniel thanked BB, and Josh thought that Marilyn would probably be able to get contact information for Mr. Morris.

After nearly three hours, they concluded their interesting and stimulating discussion. Josh had always admired BB, but he hadn't appreciated the full extent of his accomplishments. This man was truly exceptional.

Josh and Daniel thanked BB deeply for taking the time to meet with them. They emphasized that they'd love to meet with him again if he recalled other experiences or insights that might be relevant. BB wished them the best with their project, and said he'd be happy to return if he or they thought of anything that might be useful.

Josh and Daniel then escorted BB back to the Visitor Center, signed him out, and bade him farewell.

Josh then went to see Marilyn.

"Good afternoon, Marilyn, How's it going?" Josh asked.

"Great, Josh. How'd Mr. Moore's visit go?"

"It was terrific, thanks. He's such an incredible person. Thank you very much for arranging his visit."

"Always glad to help, Josh. Is there anything I can help you with now?"

"In fact, there is. I wonder if you know a guy named Levy Morris, and if you could find contact information for him."

When she heard his name, her face lit up. "He was one of my favorite managers. He was always so good-natured and supportive. I was really sad when he left the Agency. I can easily get his phone number. If you'd like, I can call him and see if he'd like to come and meet with you."

"That would be terrific. I'll email you a list of dates and times we're available."

"Great. I'll call him as soon as I receive the info from you."

Ten

Developing the Right Apptitude

"Very impressive guy in every respect," Daniel exclaimed, as they returned to their office. "Glad I had a chance to meet with him and hear some of the incredible things he's done. It gives me a much better understanding of what language analysis is all about."

"He's pretty incredible," Josh responded. "He's one of the best I've ever encountered. I have three important takeaways from our discussion with him. The first is that we got one major insight into what creates a great analyst, or a great person in any profession - passion. It's clear once someone mentions it, but people like us don't objectively think about our passion because it's part of who we are. We'll have to keep passion in mind when we do our other interviews.

"The second important takeaway from the interview is that we may have gotten a useful lead.

"The third is the issue of how important silence might be when an analyst is trying to solve a complex problem."

"I agree on all three counts. Can't wait to get into the office to discuss the lead and the silence issue. I think the question of passion is more straightforward."

Once inside their office, they immediately began to discuss Mirza Behrangi.

"I've never heard of Behrangi before," Josh started. "If he is a confidant of the Ayatollah, it would be great if we could find and collect his personal communications - email or cell phone. We can also hope that he has a personal computer that we can somehow access, using the techniques you mentioned. What do you think?"

"Well," said Daniel, "If we can get some info about the events that made him a hero, I'll try to develop the game app that might lure him into the fly trap to lead us to control his computer. The app would include the battle or battles where he performed the heroic deeds. I can do some Internet research on the war and its heroes."

If that app worked and if the Director approved, Daniel would then try to develop the mental virus app and remotely insert it into Behrangi's computer, if he had one. Daniel was clearly excited about the prospects for developing and applying the apps.

"There are a few things I can do as well," Josh said. "First, I can call Shellie and Farida to see if they can find any info on Behrangi in the CIA or FBI files. Second, I can check the NSA files. Third, I can do Persian-language Internet research on Behrangi. There may be Iranian Government accounts about Iran's war heroes. There may also be accounts by Iranian individuals."

"I'm anxious to work the Behrangi issue," Daniel commented, "but after we've finished what we can on him this afternoon and before we go home, I'd like to discuss the noise vs. silence issue and other things that stimulate analytic thinking."

"Sounds good. I'll let you know when I'm ready. If you're ready earlier, you can let me know."

Immediately after their exchange, Josh phoned Shellie and Farida to ask them to check the CIA and FBI databases for info on Behrangi.

Josh then searched NSA files, but the only reference he found was in the report BB had written about the conversation between the Ayatollah and Behrangi.

However, his Persian-language Internet research proved very productive. Behrangi was from the small town of Shendabad in East Azerbaijan. It was only a couple of miles from the town of Khamaneh, the birthplace of the Supreme Leader, and not far from the major city of Tabriz. Josh found a very detailed account of Behrangi's heroism in the Iranian operation to liberate the southern port city of Khorramshahr. He also found several accounts by individuals who had witnessed Behrangi's actions.

Khorramshahr was a port city located along the Shatt al-Arab waterway in Khuzestan Province in southwestern Iran, a few miles from the Persian Gulf. At the beginning of the Iran-Iraq War in September 1980, the city had a population of 220,000.

As the war began, Iraq launched a brutal operation against the city. On November 10, 1980, after fifty days of intense combat, the city fell. The devastation was so great that the Iranians called the city, "Khuninshahr" (City of Blood). It remained in Iraqi hands for nearly eighteen months.

On April 24, 1982, Iranian forces - a combination of regular Army units, the Iranian Revolutionary Guard Corps (IRGC), known as the Pasdaran, and the Basij, a paramilitary volunteer militia, launched Operation Beit al-Moqaddas (Operation Jerusalem) to retake the province of Khuzestan. This was the largest engagement of the war. The Iranian victory in that operation also marked the turning point in the war.

It took one month of fierce combat to retake Khuzestan. Each side had about 70,000 troops in the fight. The Iranian forces used massive human-wave Pasdaran and Basij assaults. During the fighting, the Iraqis sustained 15,000 killed and wounded, and 15,000 captured. Some 550 Iraqi tanks and armored vehicles were destroyed. The Iranian forces suffered some 30,000 killed and wounded.

At the time, Behrangi was a low-level soldier in the Pasdaran. Early in the operation, near the provincial capital of Ahvaz, Behrangi was in a small squad of eight troops that found itself surrounded by an Iraqi platoon of about fifty soldiers. Behrangi's squad leader was immediately killed by a sniper's bullet. Behrangi took over and used his automatic weapon to quickly kill some ten Iraqis. Inspired by his bravery, his fellow soldiers aggressively fought and overcame the Iraqis. They killed another ten, and captured sixteen. The remaining fourteen turned and fled.

As Operation Beit al-Moqaddas continued, Behrangi found himself in similar situations two more times. Each time, he demonstrated the same aggressive heroism. Given the withering fire he faced without injury, his fellow soldiers believed that Allah was watching over him. They were inspired not only by his success, but by his humility. He praised his fellow soldiers and said that their contributions were the primary reasons they were able to defeat the Iraqis, even when the Iraqis outnumbered them.

Josh summarized the story for Daniel, and said he'd work over the weekend to provide a detailed translation.

Daniel was delighted, because he'd found no mention of Behrangi in his English-language Internet searches.

Daniel said he'd use the Internet information he'd found about Operation Beit al-Moqaddas to create the game app, and would then fill in the parts about Behrangi after he received Josh's translation.

Josh printed out all the info he'd found on the Internet to take home with him. Since it was all open-source info, there was no problem taking it home. His wife was also used to him playing with Persian and other foreign-language texts and audio at home for fun, just as she enjoyed spending time on Chinese at home.

"Well, Daniel, I've done about all I can on Behrangi this afternoon," Josh said, "and I'm ready whenever you are to discuss the noise vs. silence issue and whatever related things you'd like to discuss."

"I've got a couple of minor things left, but I'll finish those after we've had our discussion."

"Are you sure?"

"Absolutely! Once this subject came up, it interested me a lot. I've never really thought about the various things that interfere with or stimulate my thinking."

"So," Josh began, "BB said that the best environment for him to analyze difficult problems was when there was silence without distractions. I wonder if that's the same for you, and if there are other situations that stimulate your creative genes."

"For some reason, I do better when there's noise, like high-energy music. I don't know why. That seems counterintuitive when I think about it.

"There are other situations as well. When someone presents me with a new problem - one that I've never encountered - it seems to generate energy in my brain, and I start turning over the challenge in my mind to look at it from as many angles as possible.

"A third stimulus is discussion of a problem with another person, especially when that person is discussing a solution that has already been developed. I start thinking about that solution and how it might be enhanced or used for some other purpose.

"A fourth catalyst is my laziness. If a particular process seems to take too much effort, I try to create ways to make it easier.

"Those are the main things I can think of, Josh. What about you?"

"I'm like BB. Silence is very important. Sometimes, a solution will jump out at me when I wake up in bed in the middle of the night or when I'm walking to the mailbox. I have trouble concentrating when I'm wrestling with a problem at work and I'm interrupted, or when a couple of people are standing near my desk and yakking with one another about a baseball or football game, or gossiping. There are exceptions however. I can get completely consumed in solving a cipher system and can tune out everything around me. And like you, I'm stimulated when I'm discussing a challenging problem with a sharp colleague."

"Very interesting. I think we should ask this question in every interview. I'll continue to think about it." Daniel commented.

"I agree."

After finishing the last few things Daniel had left, they secured the office and headed home for the weekend.

On his way home, Josh decided he'd begin to do some self-study in South Azerbaijani, the version of Azerbaijani spoken in Iran, just in case they found comms between the Ayatollah and Behrangi. All he knew about the language was its sound and that it was Turkic.

Languages from that family were really tough. He couldn't quickly pick up enough to become fluent; he just hoped it might help him a bit. He'd study at home and while he driving to and from work.

Monday April 13

When Daniel and Josh returned to the office on Monday, Josh handed Daniel a thick report with the details he'd found about Operation Beit al-Moqaddas and Behrangi's involvement.

Daniel described major components of a high-intensity war combat game he'd developed with the information he'd been able to learn about the battle. He'd even found lots of photos, which he used to help him design graphics. The game would include three major "apptributes." It would be exciting and very easy to use, and would have a few key errors that only Behrangi or a close comrade in the battle would recognize. The major error would be to greatly exaggerate Behrangi's heroism, because that was the type of error a person with Behrangi's humility would feel compelled to get corrected.

He had included an error reporting option that encouraged players to post comments about errors. The developer message would state that the developers would read all comments and do their best to correct errors in order to improve the game. The message would add that email addresses would be appreciated in case further clarification was needed.

Daniel explained that he'd built another feature into the game that might help identify Behrangi. In the segment of the game in which Behrangi's heroism was exaggerated, he'd created a tracker to determine if a given player spent a lot of time revisiting that section of the game. The tracker would highlight that player and capture his user data.

Daniel mentioned he'd need Josh's help in creating Persian-language player instructions and in making sure the game's graphics appeared authentic.

Daniel said his plan would be to make it appear that the web site hosting the game was located in a country friendly to Iran. Josh suggested Lebanon, where there was decent Internet access and where the Shia Hezbollah segment of the population worked closely with Iran.

Daniel said he'd like to get permission to bring the software into their office and run it on their stand-alone classified computer so that he could show it to Josh and so they could work on it together. Since Daniel had a very sophisticated understanding of software attacks and vulnerabilities, he knew his own software was safe.

Daniel also explained that the psychological virus app would be more challenging, not only because the concept was new, but because his knowledge of Iranian and ethnic Azeri psychology was limited to what he'd learned in some Internet research over the weekend. He hoped that between Josh's knowledge and more Internet research, he could find sufficient info to develop an effective app.

Josh decided that in view of what he and Daniel had learned and developed, it might be a good idea to meet with the Director as soon as possible in order to:

- Let him know about Behrangi;
- Present their approach to pursuing the Behrangi potential;
- Explain the extraordinary ethical implications of a mental virus app;
- Get the Director's permission and guidelines for their efforts; and
- Get the Director's permission to allow Daniel to bring his own software into the Agency to use on his stand-alone computer without restriction, and to take that software back home to work on it. That would make it much easier to develop the software as rapidly as possible, for Daniel and Josh to collaborate, and for them to demonstrate the software to the Director and Mac when appropriate.

There had always been severe restrictions on uploading outside software onto Agency high-side computers without vetting of the software, as well as restrictions on downloading software and data from those computers. However, the restrictions, procedures, and monitoring had become much tighter since the devastating losses created by Snowden's treason. The issue would not be as much of a problem with a stand-alone computer because it couldn't affect the high-side network and couldn't access data across that network.

Josh phoned Sofie and asked if they could get a couple of minutes of private time with the Director. She checked and arranged for fifteen minutes at nine thirty, which was a couple of hours away.

About a half hour before they left for their meeting with the Director, Farida called back with a bit of information about Behrangi. He'd been an enlisted soldier in the Pasdaran, and was a recognized war hero from the Iran-Iraq War. He'd served a full career in the military and was an iconic figure. His relationship with the Ayatollah was unclear. His current whereabouts and status were unknown.

Josh explained what he and Daniel had learned and what they were doing with the info. He also mentioned the planned meeting with the Dir, and said he'd call Johnnie and update him immediately after the meeting.

Josh and Daniel then left their office to meet with the Director.

When they arrived, Marilyn ushered them in. The Admiral got up from his desk, walked over to a conference table, and invited them to sit down.

They described their interview with BB, and explained what they'd learned about Behrangi. They described how they proposed to use the info to develop and deploy the war game app and the mental virus app.

Daniel explained that the objective of the war game was to find Behrangi and his personal computer, if he had one. If he didn't have one, they hoped he regularly used some other computer, such as a library or government computer.

The way the war game worked was to lead the player through a series of combat engagements in Operation Beit al-Moqaddas. The player would be acting as an Iranian combatant. There would be certain sequences in which the player would be trapped by Iraqis. The player would have the option to click on a "Unit Help" or "Hero Help" button. One of those entrapment situations replicated the first event in which Behrangi displayed his heroism. The Hero Help button would bring a Behrangi character out with weapon blazing, and performing at a superhuman level far beyond what Behrangi had done in real life. The hope was that this would prompt Behrangi to leave a player comment that would enable Daniel to locate and electronically capture his computer.

Daniel explained that the mental virus was a concept he'd developed a couple of years earlier on his own time. He knew exactly how to write the coding, but hadn't done so because of how the application could change the world. He'd waited for a situation like this so he could propose the idea in a way that would ensure it was properly considered by a key decision maker. The purpose of the app in this situation was to gain sufficient control of Behrangi's mind to elicit any information he might know about the nuclear espionage source or sources.

Both of these apps would be of no value if Behrangi had no regular Internet access or if the Ayatollah had shared nothing with him about the nuclear spy.

Daniel said he was unaware of any other mental virus app that had been developed by anyone. He reiterated his view of the **immense potential** such an app had for both good and evil. He said he would only pursue developing the app if the Director granted permission, and if the Director promised that Daniel could maintain total control over the software and it would not be shared with anyone else unless Daniel agreed. He was confident he could write the software so it would self-destruct if anyone attempted to access the coding. He could also code the app so it would self-destruct as soon as it had been activated and had transmitted the virus a single time.

The Director was delighted with what they'd learned, and he

approved development of the combat game app, but not the mental virus app. He immediately grasped the latter's wide-ranging and potentially devastating implications. So he wanted time to think about it before giving permission to develop it. In fact, he wanted to consult with the DNI to get higher level approval, perhaps even presidential approval. He realized that if someone like Daniel could develop such software, there were certainly others who could eventually develop this concept and effective software based on it.

Once the software was developed and its deployment approved, he wanted them to work through Mac to ensure that the software deployment would not interfere with any other U.S. cyber operation, nor be mistakenly taken down by another U.S. cyber operation.

Josh asked if the Director would give his assent to Daniel bringing the software into their office to upload it onto a stand-alone high-side computer, and also to take the software out of the building so he could work on it at home on a stand-alone computer. They explained their reasons for the request. The Director approved and said he'd instruct Sofie to immediately get written permission from the head of Security. The Director was very anxious to see the software as soon as it was ready.

After finishing the discussion, they returned to their office. Within fifteen minutes, Sofie phoned and said she'd have the software permission letter from the head of Security by midafternoon.

Josh then called Johnnie to update him on where things stood. Johnnie was very interested that there was some possibility of progress. Josh did not mention the mental virus app.

Josh then phoned Mike Harriman, the Levantine Arabic Linguist and Hezbollah - Hamas expert, to see if he had some time available for an interview. It turned out he was available the next afternoon, so they made a two o'clock appointment.

Josh also phoned Levantine Arabic linguist and Syria expert, Pete Schlauman, and made an interview appointment for Thursday, April 16 at two.

The interviews with BB, Harriman, and Schlauman would cover the key Iranian domestic and foreign components of the search for vulnerable connections that might not already be covered by normal collection and analysis efforts.

Shortly after two thirty, Marilyn knocked on their office door. Daniel answered, and she handed him the letter granting him permission to bring software into HQ, load it onto a stand-alone high-side computer, download it onto removable media, and take it out of HQ. Daniel thanked her for her speedy response.

He closed the door and told Josh he'd bring the first version of the software into the office in the morning.

Josh spent the rest of the afternoon typing up notes on the BB interview for use in Metanalysis.

Daniel devoted his time to studying the info from Josh about Operation Beit al-Moqaddas and Behrangi's heroism. He found exactly the kind of detail he needed to develop the game.

Tuesday April 14

The following morning, Daniel brought a fairly advanced version of the Operation Beit al-Moqaddas war game app, which he'd spent the evening and much of the night developing. He loaded it onto a stand-alone, high-side computer, and launched it. He excitedly asked Josh to watch while he navigated the game, including the point at which Daniel had grossly exaggerated Behrangi's bravery.

Josh was blown away. The game was incredible, with great graphics and exciting play scenarios. Josh was amazed that one person could develop such a great piece of software so quickly. Now he fully understood why the Director was so impressed with Daniel. The main ingredient that was lacking was the Persian-language component, including a catchy name. Josh immediately suggested the name, "Sunrise over Beit al-Moqaddas" (طلوع آفتاب در بیتالمقدس) because it would have the dual meaning of sunrise over the operation and sunrise over Jerusalem, a city that was so important for

Muslims. Daniel was happy with the name.

Josh couldn't wait to provide the Persian instructions for the game. He'd never have imagined that he'd be involved in game development. What fun and with what incredible implications!

Josh decided that the Director and Mac might like to see this version of the software, so he phoned Sofie and said, "Daniel and I were discussing some software with the Director and Mac Roberts the other day. He was very interested. We'd appreciate it if you'd let him know that we can demonstrate the software if he'd like to see it."

"OK, Josh. I'll let him know."

She called back in a couple of minutes and said, "He'd like to come at ten fifteen, if that works."

"That works. We'll be ready."

Josh phone Mac to let him know.

The Director and Mac arrived within a minute of each other. Josh exchanged the usual Persian greeting with the Director.

Once they greeted Daniel and sat down, the Director asked Josh and Daniel to repeat for Mac's benefit what they'd told him the previous day.

The reaction on Mac's face and his body language when Daniel described the mental virus app made it very clear that he had some appreciation of the implications. When Daniel finished describing that app, Mac asked if he was confident it would work. As only someone with Daniel's genius would say, he said he was certain. He also expressed his deep fear of what could be done with this type of software if the wrong people learned how to create it. He believed the methodology would be very easy to grasp and use.

When they'd finished describing the mental virus app. the Director asked Mac to give a lot of thought to its implications, and to give the Director his thoughts the next day.

Then, he asked Josh and Daniel to continue. Daniel launched the war game app, and explained it step by step. He devoted particular attention to how and why he'd exaggerated Behrangi's bravery.

They were astonished at how good it appeared. The Director was constantly amazed at the extraordinary talent and devotion that he found at NSA. He knew that brilliant individuals like Daniel could earn far more in the private sector. It was one of the reasons he constantly tried to learn and fix the things that caused such people to move to jobs outside government.

The Director joked that perhaps the Agency could set up a side business of developing and selling games.

The Director asked when they thought this app would ready to deploy. Josh explained that they had to add the Persian-language component. He also mentioned that they had two substantive interviews scheduled plus the weekly Team Triad meeting at FBI HQ. Their bottom line was that the app should be completely ready by Friday afternoon.

The Director asked how long it would take to create the mental virus app. Daniel said he could have the first version ready by the following Monday at the latest. He'd been thinking about it for a couple of years, and had already given the structure and flow a great deal of thought. He was confident he could create most of it very quickly. There were three challenging aspects of this particular one.

The first was to understand the Azeri-Iranian psychology. He said that in doing anonymous Internet research, he'd found enough English-language material to make a decent start, but was going to ask Josh to do some Persian-language research during the next few days.

The second challenge was to insert that psychology into the app linguistically. He would need Josh's help with that.

The third challenge was that there was no way to test it on a person because of the permanent impact it might have on the subject's brain. The only test would be its actual use against Behrangi.

The Director said he was scheduled to meet with the DNI late the next day to discuss a number of issues. He told Mac that he'd need Mac's views before he went to that meeting. The Director would discuss the overall approach with DNI Kraft, and would ask for her approval and guidance. The Director said he would not be surprised if the DNI felt it necessary to seek the President's guidance. The Director would advise Josh and Daniel of the results.

The Director and Mac complimented Josh and Daniel on their superb work, and then left.

After spending a couple of minutes discussing how well the meeting and demo had gone, Josh headed down to the cafeteria to grab a sandwich to bring back to the office. As usual, Daniel had brought his lunch. While Josh was gone, Daniel created a document with the English-language version of the war game's instructions and comments. He left room for the Persian translation after each English segment.

When Josh returned with his sandwich, Daniel showed him the instructions. Josh asked Daniel if he could work on the Persian at the computer, while eating lunch. Daniel said he'd appreciate that.

Within an hour, Josh had completed about a third of the Persian. However, he had to stop in order to prepare for the interview with Mike Harriman.

Eleven

RTBBDRRETK ZMZKXRHR BZM RHLOKX AD Z LZSSDQ NE KNNJHMF ZS RHLOKD OZSSDQMR[ii]

Before Mike arrived, they put away all documents relating to Meta, and Daniel shut down the game.

Mike arrived a couple of minutes after two. He was of medium height and a little on the heavy side, with dark brown hair and blue eyes. He was a bit unkempt, and hadn't shaved for a few days,

Josh greeted him in Arabic, and then introduced him to Daniel.

"Thanks a lot for coming, Mike," Josh began.

"No problem, my friend. In fact, I'm really honored that you've chosen to interview me. I just hope I can help you guys."

"How much time do you have available?" Daniel asked.

"I'll stay as long as you want. I don't have anything else scheduled. I'm always interested in substantive discussions about SIGINT - in contrast to the meaningless discussions at boring meetings in which I'm sometimes stuck."

"Great, I'd like to start by describing our project," Josh said.

When Josh finished his brief explanation, Mike said, "You know, I've never given much thought to how I developed my analytic skills. Guess I'll try to analyze my analytic skills in order to see if I can figure something out. I'm glad the Director initiated this project. Some of the previous Directors had the mistaken belief that they completely understood SIGINT analysis because they'd managed analysts or had some analytic experiences. I remember one Director describing what he thought was a new type of analysis, without realizing it had been done in parts of NSA for years. Analytic challenges have constantly evolved as the world has changed and the pace of technological change has accelerated. Many analysts have adapted, and many have not - not much different from other ventures in the public and private sectors. So it's important for guys like you to give the Director a full, unvarnished, in-depth picture of the analytic world and how it can be improved."

It was clear to Daniel early in their discussion that Mike was a sincere, straight talker who was confident and easy to talk to. "Let me tell you a bit about my background so you'll have a context for my perspective and questions." Daniel then proceeded to describe his background and why he was involved in the project.

Mike already knew Josh, and had worked with him on a couple of analytic challenges. He held Josh in very high regard.

"Well, Mike," Josh commented, "now that we've explained the project and told you a little bit about Daniel, we'd like to hear how you developed your analytic skills, including your civilian and military experiences, and your family and educational background."

"I was born and raised in Schenectady in upstate New York. My parents were both of English descent, and my family has been in the U.S. for eleven generations. We're very proud of our long history of military service to our country. In fact, we have a "Hall of Honor" in my parent's home, which our family has owned for five generations. The Hall of Honor has pictures and portraits of family military veterans. One of my ancestors was a soldier in the Revolutionary War. Another was a lieutenant during the Civil War, and fought in the 134th Infantry Regiment in the Battle of Gettysburg. My dad was a Navy officer during World War II. He served aboard the USS *Astoria* (CA-34), and participated in the Battle of Midway.

"As Josh knows, I served an enlistment in the Naval Security Group. Before I enlisted, my only experience with a foreign language was a couple of years of high school French. I enjoyed it, but never thought seriously about further foreign language study. I really liked U.S. history, world history and social studies because they seemed to make the world more interesting, and helped me understand my family's history. I loved all things military; and as early as third grade, I began to study military organization, strategy, and tactics.

"When I was in high school, I enjoyed working on cars and trying to solve their mechanical problems. In those days, cars were a lot easier to work on.

"I loved my annual deer-hunting trips with my dad, my older brother, and my uncle. My dad bought me two different rifles - a lighter one when I was in third grade, and a more powerful one when I was in high school. This taught me a bit about individual weapons, and I learned more in boot camp.

"I learned Arabic at the Defense Language Institute West Coast in Monterey. Since I did quite well on a language aptitude test, the Navy sent me to Monterey immediately after boot camp. I was really happy they sent me from Great Lakes to California because it was mid-February, and I'm not fond of winter, despite growing up in Schenectady.

"At Monterey, Arabic captured my interest in a big way. Part of that was due to one of my instructors, Boutros (Peter) Karam, a Lebanese American. He was passionate about teaching, and extremely talented. Mr. Karam recognized I had some potential and took me under his wing to mentor me.

"My Monterey course was in Modern Standard Arabic, but I spent a lot of my free time learning Levantine Arabic, the Arabic spoken by the Lebanese, Palestinians, and Syrians.

"From Monterey, I was sent to the Naval Technical Training Center at Goodfellow Air Force Base in Texas. There I learned the basics of SIGINT collection and processing.

"I was then assigned to the U.S. Naval Facility in Nicosia, Cyprus. I got there in August of 1969. My first year there was relatively calm, but at the beginning of my second year, I found myself in the midst of a flurry of activity that taught me critical lessons about the importance of SIGINT in national security.

"In a four-day period at the beginning of September, 1970, the Popular Front for the Liberation of Palestine (PFLP) attempted to hijack four international flights - one U.S., two British, and one Israeli. They succeeded with the first three, and took them to Dawson's Field, a remote airstrip in Jordan. The hijackers took 310 hostages, including some Americans. All of the hostages were released, some immediately and some in return for the release of several PFLP prisoners. The PFLP destroyed all three aircraft at Dawson's Field.

"That incident triggered a declaration of martial law by King Hussein of Jordan because of the challenge posed to his regime by the Palestinians. That started the Jordanian Civil War between the Jordanian military and the Palestinian Liberation Organization (PLO) under Yasser Arafat. That war, which the Palestinians called Black September, lasted until the Jordanians were victorious the following July.

"In those days, before the spread of microwave and satellite comms, comms not sent via land line or undersea cable were transmitted through the ether using HF (high frequency), VHF, or UHF (ultra high frequency) signals.

"HF was used for longer-range and higher-echelon comms; while VHF and UHF tended to be used for shorter-range, tactical comms.

"The three principal types of comms media used were Morse code, voice, and teleprinter; although it wouldn't be long before facsimile (FAX) began to spread.

"The quality of intercepted signals could often be very poor, resulting in "garbled" comms, because:

- Intercept sites were often far from the targeted communicants.

- Geographic features such as mountain ranges impeded the transmission of the signals. For example, the Mount Lebanon Mountain Range shielded the Beqaa Valley from Mediterranean collection activities.

- There could be interference from other signals that used the same freqs as the target comms and that were nearer to the intercept site than the target comms.

- The target communicants could be using low-power transmitters that were adequate for their needs, but not powerful enough to convey high-quality signals to the intercept site.

"Processing garbled comms could be a real challenge, making it difficult to read graphic comms, and to understand audio. Poor quality audio intercept could be very painful to the ears.

"NSG I-Branchers like me were the linguists who collected and often processed the voice signals. R-Branchers, known as "ditty-boppers," collected and processed the Morse code. We typically worked together in the same rooms.

"One of my fondest memories was using my gray Collins R-390(A) receiver to collect the HF signals assigned to me. It was well designed, dependable, and easy to operate. In fact, I bought one of those babies on eBay a couple of years ago.

"After my tour on Cyprus, I was assigned to a unit that provided, "Direct Support" aboard 6th Fleet ships in the Mediterranean.

"During those deployments, I was only tasked with collecting and recording fairly straightforward comms. This contributed to my future analytic skills because I learned the methods by which organizations and individuals communicate with one another. However, it did little for my Arabic skills because I was only tasked with collecting the comms, not analyzing them. The subject matter of these comms was very simple, and there were no expert Arabic linguists to help me significantly advance my knowledge of the language.

"As my enlistment was drawing to an end toward the completion of my second tour, I decided against reenlisting because the Navy told me my next tour would be an assignment to language school to take an intensive course in Chinese. The Navy wouldn't let me continue working with Arabic, which is what I really wanted to do.

"I also saw that, as my shipmates reached the middle enlisted rank of Second Class Petty Officer, they had to perform some supervisory duties. I had zero interest in being a supervisor.

"Even if the Navy had let me continue with Arabic, I wanted something more challenging than the typical lower-level military comms I was asked to handle.

"Since the Middle East was presenting ever-increasing threats to U.S. national security, I figured I'd have no trouble finding a job in the IC. Boy, was I wrong. When I completed my enlistment, I returned to my parents' home in upstate New York, and applied for jobs at NSA and the CIA.

"To my surprise, I was having difficulty in getting such a job because NSA was doing very little hiring in the early 1970s due to downsizing of U.S. forces and DoD support organizations as the U.S. withdrew from Vietnam.

"However, the October 1973 Arab-Israeli War changed all that, and created a need for Arabic linguists. Some of my former shipmates who were working in an office at NSA mentioned to their supervisor that I had applied to NSA, and that I was a pretty decent Arabic linguist. That supervisor asked a senior manager if he could help. That guy immediately contacted the Personnel Department. They found my application, and I was quickly processed and hired.

"Because of my familiarity with Levantine Arabic, I was assigned to an NSA organization that dealt with Levantine - Lebanese, Syrian, and Palestinian - military, police, and insurgent comms. Some of these were similar to comms I'd handled in the Navy, but others were higher-echelon, more difficult comms. Some were encrypted with manual (as opposed to machine) cipher systems or codes.

"Within a couple of months of starting at NSA, I developed a personal philosophy of how I'd learn and contribute. I followed that approach throughout my career:

"First, I'd work hard at being not only a language analyst, but also a multi-skilled SIGINT analyst;

"Second, I'd seek increasingly tougher assignments at the top end of my capabilities;

"Third, I'd look for an Arabic linguist mentor at NSA who was similar to Boutros Karam, who taught me so much at Monterey. I actually found two very talented and experienced Levantine Arabic linguists who were happy to help. One was Wayne King, an ASA veteran. The other was Samir Najjar of Lebanese Greek Orthodox ancestry (The Lebanese adherents of the Greek Orthodox Church formed the second largest Christian sect in Lebanon, after the Maronite Christians.) Both Wayne and Samir respected each other and both tried to mentor promising young linguists.

"Fourth, I'd try to get assignments that included both voice and graphic materials because I was convinced that knowledge of and experiences with either enhanced a person's skills to deal with the other;

"Fifth, I'd try to learn how to "break" (solve) manual encryption systems. I discovered that my knowledge of comms processes and language patterns specific to particular comms targets enabled me to solve manual encryption systems that professional cryppies (cryptanalysts) who weren't linguists couldn't solve.

"Sixth, I'd continue to develop my skills in Traffic Analysis (TA), the discipline of using comms contact patterns and procedures to identify and understand organizations and individuals. For example, you can identify an entire Army structure by understanding that higher-echelon entities control lower-echelon units. A division-level communications center controls its subordinate brigades. Each brigade controls its battalions, etc. With military comms, this was rather straightforward.

"Lastly, I'd never seek or accept an assignment only because it provided a better path to promotion.

"I was happy with my new job at NSA from the start because it offered me everything I wanted - interesting, high-value work in a great environment. I couldn't believe how lucky I was to find a job that was so meaningful, challenging, and fun. I occasionally encountered a manager or colleague I didn't care for, but that was relatively rare.

"Of the Levantine countries I dealt with, Lebanon was the most fascinating. As I began to deal with more complicated comms, I discovered Lebanon was much more complex than I'd initially appreciated when my primary focus was on learning Arabic and basic SIGINT skills. Lebanon would become even more difficult within a few years, as its relative peace gave way to a violent civil war and a far more difficult set of players.

"For many years, into the early 1970s, Beirut was known as the Paris of the Middle East because of its vibrant culture and night life, with a mix of Arab and French flavors. The country had only been independent for a couple of decades. Before that, it had been a French Mandate, and prior to that - part of the Ottoman Empire.

"The population comprised only a couple of million people, who identified themselves as Arabs, but also as distinctly Lebanese. Genetically and in self-identity, they had deep roots in one of the most ancient civilizations, the Semitic Phoenicians, incredible seafaring merchants, whose colonies and trading posts spread across the Mediterranean and even as far as Lisbon on the Atlantic side. The most notable of their colonies was Carthage in North Africa. The phonetic alphabet they created is the source of most modern phonetic alphabets.

"Despite the rise of Islam and the territorial conquests of its believers, a large percentage of the Lebanese remained Christian. They developed a close relationship with the European crusaders, and felt an affiliation with French culture. At one time, the majority of Lebanese were Christian, but due to large waves of mostly Christian emigration, there were more ethnic Lebanese living outside Lebanon than inside. In Brazil alone, there were probably over 5 million people of Lebanese ethnicity. There were another 1.2 million in Argentina, and large Lebanese communities in many other nations.

"The sectarian mix in Lebanon includes a variety of Muslim and Christian groups. On the ethnic Lebanese Christian side are Maronites and Melkites, both associated with the Roman Catholic

Church; the Greek Orthodox; and Protestant denominations. The Melkites are considered to be the world's oldest Christian denomination.

"On the Muslim side are Sunni and Shia.

"A third ethnic Lebanese religious group is the Druze. They represent about five percent of the population and follow a unique, monotheistic faith, which doesn't allow conversion into or out of their faith.

"Then there are important non-Lebanese ethnic groups - a large number of Palestinian refugees who either fled or were driven from Israel, Armenians, Kurds, Turks, Assyrians, and Iranians. The situation has grown even more complex during the past few years, as the brutal Syrian civil war has created a huge influx of Syrian refugees.

"As if that's not complicated enough, politico-religious movements, such as the principally Shia movement Amal against Shia Hezbollah, have created devastating intra-sectarian conflict.

"Every time I thought I'd developed a solid grasp on the current state of affairs, some major new development occurred. I continuously drove myself to learn the new players, the potential implications, and the changing directions. At the same time, I felt really badly for the ordinary people caught up in the frequent violent conflicts.

"There's been a never-ending series of painful events - the influx of Palestinian refugees in the early 1970s after the 1970-71 Jordanian-Palestinian conflict, the Lebanese Civil War of 1975-90; the taking of American hostages; the bombings of the U.S. Embassy, the Marine Barracks, and the French facility; the fighting between Amal and the Palestinians; aggressive Iranian efforts to spread the Shia religious revolution, giving rise to Hezbollah; the Israeli invasion of 1982; the Phalangist massacres of Palestinian civilians in the Sabra and Shatila refugee camps; the Syrian occupation; ad nauseam.

"All of these events put my language and analytic skills to the test. Sometimes I've made a difference, and sometimes I couldn't. I've been really upset whenever I've been unable to find SIGINT that might have prevented the loss of American lives, such as the attack against the Marine Barracks. Fortunately, I've never found a situation in which I missed or misunderstood available SIGINT. The lack of SIGINT was normally because the perpetrators didn't communicate via the ether or their comms were unknown to us. Despite public media myths about NSA sweeping up the world's comms, any serious SIGINTer knows that's an impossible feat.

"As I describe and reflect on my career experiences, I think the most important factors in developing my analytic skills have been the nonstop stream of analytic challenges, my strong drive to try to make a difference, and the availability of mentors like Wayne and Samir, who helped me understand not only the Arabic, but the cultural and religious contexts."

"You know, Mike, from what I've learned from you and others about the complexities of Lebanon," Josh explained, "I think the challenges you've faced have been much more involved than those I've dealt with."

"I'm really amazed, Mike," Daniel commented. "I always thought we techies had the greatest challenges. I'm learning how simplistic my thinking has been."

"We'd appreciate it," Josh commented, "if you could describe some of the most complex analytic problems you solved." Josh hoped one of those problems might involve some Iranian activity that would provide an insight that could help Meta.

Mike described some very sensitive analytic successes, including one that others should've figured out if they'd been more systematic in their analysis. It involved the Iranian supply of weapons to Hezbollah. In the mid-1980s, a couple of years after Hezbollah had been established, HUMINT sources reported that the Iranians were providing a steady supply of weapons and ammo to Hezbollah. However, the intel was not timely or detailed enough to enable Lebanese allies to interdict the flow. NSA collectors and analysts could find no comms related to this activity. Mike, among others, was asked to see what he could do.

He started by carefully studying known Hezbollah comms. One Hezbollah HF voice network he examined was thought to be a low-level logistics network for the distribution of food and other non-lethal supplies to Hezbollah positions within the Beqaa Valley. Mike decided to listen carefully to those comms.

In describing the voice intercept he'd heard, Mike converted Hezbollah operator discussions to American-style discussions, for Daniel's benefit.

Due to operator errors, the first thing he learned was that there appeared to be a system for encoding dates and times. The ops were using a system in which they encoded future dates by adding two days to the actual intended date and two hours to the actual intended time. For example, if an item was supposed to arrive at 1400 (2 p.m.) on Tuesday, the communicator would say that it would arrive at 1600 (4 p.m.) on Thursday.

In the first operator error that suggested this possibility, a Hezbollah op said, "The shipment of combat boots is scheduled to arrive this Thursday at 0800 (8 a.m.)." The recipient replied, "That's really early! Are you sure?" The sender answered, "Oops! I mean Saturday at 1000." The recipient responded, "Thanks. That sounds better."

Over the course of a couple of weeks, Mike heard similar errors. They always involved a difference of two days and two hours.

Similarly, when talking about the past, communicators would subtract two days and two hours. For example, when confirming that a shipment arrived on Monday at 1200, the sender was supposed to say the shipment arrived on Saturday at 1000. Similar operator errors confirmed how the system worked.

One of the vulnerabilities with any manual encryption system is operator error. Humans make mistakes. The more people who are involved in a given activity, the greater the likelihood of errors. The people who design encryption systems often fail to construct them in ways that minimize human error. Another factor contributing to vulnerabilities was inadequate operator training.

The date encoding system suggested the possibility that the names for the supplies might also be code words. For example, "combat boots" could mean "assault rifles," or even a specific type of assault rifle.

The first indication that this was the case came when two ops were discussing a food shipment. The op sending the info provided the details of a food shipment that included grapes. That seemed strange because there were plenty of grape vines in the Beqaa Valley, and this was the time of year that grapes were being harvested.

The op receiving the info quipped, "Those are the bunches of thirty that are crunchy and hard to swallow." Mike knew that thirty rounds of ammo was the magazine capacity of the two most common types of assault rifles, the AK-47 and the M16A1. The sending op replied humorlessly, "If you don't shut up, the commander might make you swallow a few of those grapes." The receiving op continued to joke, "Great! That'll test my mettle."

Over a period of a couple of weeks, Mike determined that fruit names were used to encode ammo types, including artillery ammo. Vegetable names encoded weapon types.

Through High Frequency Direction Finding (HFDF) when this net was discovered, it was determined that the control station was located at Hezbollah HQ in the Beqaa Valley, and that the outstations of the net were situated at various Hezbollah locations in the valley.

During the course of monitoring this net, Mike noticed that when the control station communicated with one particular outstation on the net, the speaker at the control station spoke Levantine Arabic with a Tehran-flavored Iranian accent, and the speaker at the outstation spoke Levantine Arabic with an Azeri accent from northwestern Iran. (Mike had an exceptional ability to identify accents, even to specific cities, and not just easy ones like Baltimore or Brooklyn.)

The two ops normally did not use names. However, on one occasion, the op at the control station slipped up and addressed the outstation op as Mirza.

When Mike checked, he discovered that this outstation had never been "DF-ed;" (i.e., no Direction Finding had been conducted against the station). He requested a DF fix, and consequently learned that the station was located in Damascus. Given the Iranian accent, he concluded that the location might be the Iranian Embassy. He also assumed both speakers were members of Hezbollah's Iranian partner and mentor, the IRGC.

Of course, the name Mirza immediately raised a red flag for Josh and Daniel. After the interview with Mike, they reviewed Behrangi's biography, and saw that it listed an unspecified "training assignment" for 1983-84. They thought there was a decent possibility that the Mirza Mike had heard was Behrangi, and that the so-called training assignment was really a cover for an assignment to work with Hezbollah. Of course, that tour did equate to a certain type of training.

Daniel said to Mike that the approach he'd used in this case was straightforward and systematic. He wondered why others had failed to properly analyze these comms.

Mike and Josh both commented that they'd had this type of analytic experience a number of times. Some analysts often look for more complicated clues and miss normal human errors. For example, in a case like this, they might quickly dismiss these comms as unimportant because the communicants were discussing fruits and vegetables, and not using an obvious and complex encryption system. They'd been fooled, just as the designers of the Hezbollah-Iranian system intended.

Mike said it was like any human endeavor involving analysis - for example medical diagnosis. Two doctors with similar training, intellect, energy, devotion to their patients, and access to the same tools and technology, could reach very different conclusions when diagnosing the same patient for the same problem. Both Mike and Josh knew family and friends who'd had such experiences with doctors.

When Daniel reflected on his own tech solutions experiences, the same was true. He counseled young tech developers to look for simple solutions first. Some who came to the Agency with the most advanced education focused on finding complex, elegant solutions that took considerable time to develop, rather than focusing on the fastest way to solve the problem. It was similar to the difference between the high-speed, revolutionary aircraft development of Lockheed's Skunk Works vs. the slow, plodding development of Lockheed's conventional aircraft.

At the end of the interview, Josh and Daniel stood at the white board in their office and listed their takeaways on how Mike developed his analytic talents:

- A drive to excel;
- Intense passion for his work;
- Examining data in a systematic way and asking himself the right questions - questions based on simple, straightforward logic about how people behave and how organizations operate;
- Identifying and seeking the support of talented mentors;
- Constantly striving to improve his skills;
- Youthful interest in history, social studies, and military affairs;
- Perhaps even his interest in auto mechanics - in having to understand how different parts of a system work together to make the whole system function;
- His push to learn all aspects of SIGINT analysis, including CA and TA; and
- His collection experience, which taught him how communications work, including operator problems and errors.

"Well, Mike, did we capture all the important points?" Josh asked.

"No." Mike said, with a smirk on his face, "You missed the biggest factor of all - luck."

"You're absolutely right," Josh laughed. "Maybe that should've been at the top of the list."

Mike, Josh, and Daniel completed their discussions just before five.

"Thanks a lot, Mike," Josh said. "What a great discussion. You've been really helpful. Thanks for your time. Please get back in touch if you think of anything else."

"It was really fun discussing my favorite subject. I'll be sure to call you guys if I think of anything else."

As soon as Mike left, Daniel and Josh discussed the interview and concluded that the reasons for Mike's success did not seem to differ from the reasons for BB's success, although Mike had the added benefits of his collection experience, and perhaps his auto mechanics experience.

They then discussed Behrangi and his "training assignment." The info didn't help with Meta, but showed that some dots were not being connected with respect to Behrangi. Josh said it was important to inform the Agency's Persian linguists and other IC analysts that they should be alert for anything relating to Behrangi. However, it should be done in a way that would not reveal the connection to Meta.

The Director subsequently indicated there was an easy mechanism for accomplishing this. He would inform the National Intelligence Manager (NIM) for Iran that Behrangi's close ties to the Ayatollah had been discovered from a sensitive NSA source and it would be useful for the NIM to issue a general requirement to all IC organizations to report on Behrangi's activities. Once NSA received that requirement, the Director would instruct the Iran office to bring to his attention any communications involving Behrangi. The Director would decide how the information should be reported. The NIM's requirement would state nothing about counterespionage or the nuclear negotiations. Consequently, if the Iranians somehow learned of the requirement, the most they might conclude was that the U.S. was aware of Behrangi's special relationship with the

Supreme Leader.

When they finished discussing the interview, Daniel said he'd download a copy of the combat game and work on it at home that evening. He'd thought of a couple of ways to make it more exciting.

Josh asked Daniel to leave a copy on the computer so he could stay for a few hours and work on the Persian instructions. He wanted to have the game available to look at as he translated the English instructions Daniel had given him. Daniel agreed.

After Daniel downloaded the software and left, Josh headed to the cafeteria and grabbed a sandwich to take back to the office. When he got back, he called Meihui and told her he'd be staying late to work on his project.

Over the course of the next few hours, Josh completed about 80 percent of the Persian instructions. Toward nine thirty, he felt he was becoming less effective, so he decided to wrap things up. He shut down his computers, locked the office, and headed home.

Twelve

In Welche Richtung?

(In Which Direction?)

Wednesday April 15

The next morning, Daniel arrived at the office with a big smile on his face and with the updated version of the combat app game. "How's the translating going, Josh?"

"I should be done by lunch. Here's a copy of what I've finished. You can incorporate it into the app if you want, and let me know if you have any questions. How's the app lookin'?"

"I'm really happy with it. Can't believe I've created this Iranian war game. If someone told me a couple of months ago that I'd be developing an Iranian combat app, I would've had a laughing fit."

With that, they both turned to their respective tasks.

About midmorning, Mac called to ask if he could stop by to let them know the opinion he planned to give the Director about the apps early that afternoon, and to see if they had any more thoughts. They told him they'd be ready and waiting.

About ten thirty, Mac knocked at the door, and they let him in.

He first asked if they had any additional thoughts about the implications of developing and deploying the apps. They told him they believed the combat game app was pretty straightforward and should be implemented. However, they were now extremely nervous about the mental virus app. On the positive side, the U.S. could use it to manipulate the minds of its enemies to steer them away from evils such as war and genocide, and to provide insights into hostile activities they were planning or conducting. On the negative side, it could be used for a wide range of hostile and evil activities from manipulating the minds of a broad segment of their countrymen to swindling and scamming masses of people. They now felt it should not be pursued.

Daniel said that the techie in him really wanted to develop this revolutionary app, but the ethical human in him understood its potentially devastating impact. He had a devil on one shoulder and an angel on the other. The angel had won this battle.

Mac agreed on both counts. He had no problem with the combat game app, but was strongly opposed to the mental virus app, feeling it posed a grave threat to the world for the very reasons they'd expressed. The app would provide the legions of malevolent actors on the Internet with the most powerful tool ever. It was the Internet equivalent of intercontinental ballistic missiles with hydrogen nuclear warheads.

If the DNI or the President approved the use of the mental virus app, the senior leadership of the Congress would have to be informed. Once that happened, it would be impossible to keep the concept secret because it had so many serious implications for the nation and the world that lawmakers would rightly feel compelled to discuss it. Once the concept's viability was revealed, the world's cyber thugs would intensively pursue its development. He also felt there'd be an understandably hostile reaction from the public.

Mac felt several things should happen with this concept. The Director should inform the DNI of its existence, and ask her to inform the President, but should recommend that NSA not develop it. The Director should instruct Daniel to develop techniques for detecting and countering such a capability in the likely event some of our enemies discovered it on their own. Mac had no doubt that if Daniel could conceive this idea, others could as well.

Mac felt Daniel and Josh should use the combat game app to try to access Behrangi's computer to see if it held any useful information, and to use the computer's microphone and camera to monitor his activities. They should also see if Behrangi's cell phone number was on the computer so that they could use SS7 (Signaling System No. 7) vulnerabilities to track him, listen to his conversations, examine his phone for useful data, and monitor his activities near the phone.

Josh and Daniel completely agreed. Mac thanked them, and said he'd get back to them with the Director's reaction.

Early in the afternoon, Mac met with the Director and explained in great detail his sentiments about both apps. He added Daniel's and Josh's views as well. The Director had come to the same conclusions. He could not in good conscience approve development of the mental virus app. He would inform the DNI and ask her to discuss it with the President. He would also recommend that no one else be informed of this concept. He said that Josh and Daniel should not share the idea with anyone else, including the other members of Team Triad.

After his meeting with the Director concluded, Mac returned to see Josh and Daniel, and said, "Well guys, I expect you know what I'm going to say."

"We're pretty sure that the Director agrees with you," Josh replied.

"You've got it. He's going to inform the DNI that you created the mental virus concept, but that we're not going to pursue it. He doesn't want you to share your idea with anyone, not even the other members of Team Triad."

"We figured that's the way it would sort out," Daniel said. "Actually, I'm relieved."

"Well guys, keep those great brains churning out ideas. See you later," Mac said, and then left.

Daniel knew he could develop the mental virus app on his own time if he wanted to. He'd created the concept on his own and had never used any government resources on it. Nonetheless, he would not write it on his own because of his conscience and his fears.

"Well, I've got to leave early," Daniel commented, "so I can get to the post office and drop off my tax return, which I just finished last night."

"I wish you luck, given the lines you'll probably find at the post office."

"I'd love to submit it electronically, but it's got some complications which require that it be submitted on paper."

"I completed my return and filed it electronically at the beginning of March. I'd have finished it earlier, but I had to wait until a couple of the mutual funds in my portfolio provided me with the 1099-Div forms. I can't understand why in this day and age of heavy computerization, the mutual fund operators can't provide the required tax data in a more timely way."

Thursday April 16

The next morning, when Daniel arrived, Josh asked how the post office adventure had gone. Daniel grunted that he had to stand in line for half an hour. Josh didn't think that was too bad, in view of the date.

Within an hour of their arrival, Marilyn phoned to say the Director wanted to see them for a couple of minutes. Josh told her they'd be right there.

When they arrived, his secretary immediately ushered them in to see him. The Director greeted them and then summarized his meeting with the DNI. "As expected, she had no problem with the combat game app, but she has instructed us not to develop the mental virus app. She had a meeting with the President scheduled shortly after our session. She said she'd inform him about both apps. She was fairly certain he would not approve development of the mental virus app.

"Assuming the President doesn't approve, we won't have to inform Congress. We only have to let them know when we're going to act on such an important development.

"Your concept has really opened our eyes to an entirely new

level of potential cyber threat, Daniel. This is just one more example of your brilliant mind."

"We appreciate your filling us in on your meeting with the DNI," Josh said. "We're not surprised. We'll work out an alternative strategy for using the combat game app, and we'll send you an email with our suggestions tomorrow."

"Sounds good. Keep those creative juices flowing."

Josh and Daniel returned to their office and prepared to set out for their weekly Team Triad meeting at FBI HQ. The drive was smooth and uneventful on this pleasant spring morning with scattered clouds and a temperature of around sixty degrees. The traffic was moderate and running smoothly.

Johnnie, Shellie, Farida, and Gianni all mentioned they had nothing new to report.

Josh described what he and Daniel had learned about Behrangi, and Daniel explained the strategy of attempting to penetrate Behrangi's computer with the combat game app.

There was a palpable sense of excitement at the possibility of progress; and Shellie's eyes immediately lit up when she heard Daniel describe the game. "I'm deep into Persian video games," she enthusiastically exclaimed. "I've got a separate computer at home that I only use for those games, and I do it with a separate Internet connection, so I don't have to worry if the computer is compromised. Would it be possible for you to bring the game here, or for me to go to NSA to check it out? I'd like to see if I can help." The rest of the group quickly chimed in that they'd love to see it too.

Josh was delighted. "Great! We'd really appreciate it if you guys would check it out and give us your ideas. I was concerned that I'd be the only person with a Persian-language background to be involved in the Persian instructions. I'd love your help, Shellie, because I don't really know Persian game vocabulary and slang. The sooner the better. We could do it tomorrow or Monday, if you're available."

"Tomorrow works for me," she replied. The others agreed as

well.

"Perhaps we could introduce you to the Director while you're there," Josh suggested.

"That would be great, Josh!" commented Johnnie.

"I'll try to arrange it."

"I apologize that our small office will be a bit crowded for a meeting," said Daniel. "We riffraff don't have a fancy room like you highfalutin guys here," he joked.

"We don't mind," Johnnie laughed. "We'll be happy to try our best to squeeze in."

"How's a ten thirty start time?" Josh asked. "Hopefully, that would be late enough to allow you to miss the worst of the morning rush hour traffic, but still have enough time to see the app, help with it, and meet the Director, if we can arrange it."

"Ten thirty's optimum," said Johnnie. "Let's do it."

With that, they ended the meeting, and Josh and Daniel headed back to NSA for their meeting with Pete Schlauman.

As soon as Josh got to his desk, he phoned Sofie and asked her to check with the Director to see if he might have a couple of minutes to meet four visitors - two from the FBI and two from CIA - who would be visiting the next day to see the software Josh and Daniel had recently shown him.

Sofie phoned him an hour later and said the Director would be happy to see the visitors, and would be available at 1:30.

Thirteen

<u>Initial</u> Observations

Pete arrived just before two. He was tall and thin, with long black hair and brown eyes. He was about Mike Harriman's age and seemed equally intense.

As Josh had done with Mike, he greeted Pete in Arabic, and then introduced Daniel. They went through the usual interview start, and then asked Pete to describe his experiences.

He was a sixth-generation German-American. His ancestors had immigrated to Baltimore from Frankfurt am Main after the failure of the revolutions of 1848-49, and the dissolution of the Frankfurt Assembly in May of 1849. In the latter half of the nineteenth century, German immigrants made up a large portion of Baltimore's white population. By 1868, one quarter of the 160,000 whites there were German immigrants. Of the remaining three quarters, two thirds had at least partial German ancestry. During the Civil War, there was a fair amount of nativist hostility toward the immigrants. The nativists tended to be pro-Southern and the Germans tended to be liberal. In an 1861 riot, the offices of the German newspaper *Wecker* were burned. Nonetheless, the German community managed to thrive.

Pete's father moved from Baltimore to Detroit to work on the assembly line in the Dodge Main Plant in Hamtramck. During World War II, the plant interrupted its automobile production, and produced military hardware such as 40mm antiaircraft weapons and Mark XIV gyro compasses.

The demographic evolution of Hamtramck, with about 22,000 people, was very interesting. It became an overwhelmingly Polish-American city, and then over time transformed into a city with the first Muslim majority in the nation, with a large percentage of Yemeni or Bengali origin.

For some reason he'd never been able to figure out, he became interested in foreign languages and cultures in high school. Perhaps it had to do with the fact that when he was young, Detroit had lots of ethnic neighborhoods. He jokingly added that perhaps it was because the foreign country of Canada was a 10-cent bus ride away across the Detroit River so he'd done lots of travel to that exotic land.

Pete attended a Catholic high school, where he studied Latin and French, and then went to Wayne State University, where he continued his language studies by majoring in Russian and minoring in German. While at Wayne, he joined an NSG reserve unit at the Brodhead Naval Armory.

Upon graduation from Wayne, he went on active duty in the Navy. Instead of utilizing his Russian or other language skills, the Navy sent him to the Defense Language Institute West Coast at Monterey to learn Arabic.

Daniel asked Pete if he was in the same Monterey class as Mike Harriman. Pete said his class started two years after Mike's, but he had several of the same instructors. One instructor Mike did not have was Pete's favorite, Fahd Sultan, who was of Syrian Sunni origin. He was a second-generation American. He'd joined the U.S Army in July, 1950, just after the start of the Korean War, and had served as an artillery officer, with time spent in combat in Korea. In 1954, he left the Army to pursue a career in teaching. He was devoted to his work, and put extra effort into helping students who showed promise. It took Mr. Sultan only a couple of class sessions to recognize Pete's talent and his laser-like focus on learning.

Since Pete had received basic SIGINT collection and transcription training during his three years in the Naval Reserve prior to active duty, he was given an operational assignment immediately upon graduation from language school.

His first assignment was to provide direct support aboard Navy ships in the Persian Gulf. In that assignment, he had some exposure to Gulf Arabic.

His next assignment was at NSA HQ, where he worked in the Levant office. His focus there was on Syria. He loved the very challenging and meaningful work they gave him. He'd developed some understanding of Syrian history, culture, and society in language school, but it was a very simple appreciation. At NSA, he learned how really complex it was. In his opinion, it was much more complex than Lebanon.

As his enlistment neared an end, he decided to apply for a civilian job at NSA rather than reenlist. His reasons were similar to Mike's. He didn't want to learn another language and he wanted to continue the high-value work he was doing. So about six months prior to the end of his enlistment, he began the application process to become an NSA employee.

Unlike Mike's situation, his conversion to NSA civilian status was very straightforward because he was physically at NSA. His supervisors tracked his application throughout the process, and made sure that the Personnel Department took all of the right actions in a timely way. The Levant office understood Pete's value and high potential, so they wanted to ensure they retained his talent.

The most important of those supervisors was Bill Bergmann, who was now Mac Roberts' Chief of Staff. He was a high-energy, no-nonsense native Baltimorean who taught Pete sophisticated analytic skills. Pete found Bill's tutelage superior to the classroom instruction he received at NSA's National Cryptologic School because Bill's training was very target specific.

As Pete's linguistic and analytic skills blossomed, his supervisors gave him ever-more-difficult assignments. He became one of a handful of Arabic experts who could be counted on to handle the toughest assignments, including deployments to support special military or CIA ops. Unlike most NSA civilian linguists, who practiced their professions from safe locations such as NSA HQ, Pete put himself at risk in places like Beirut. The one time he came very close to serious injury or death was at the time of the suicide bombing of the Marine Barracks in Beirut early on the morning of October 23, 1983. The Iranian-directed bombing killed 241 U.S. servicemen, mostly Marines. Pete had attended a meeting there the preceding day. Two friends with whom he'd gone to language school were among the dead. He would never forget this Iranian action.

He always had a good sense of his level of competence, so he only took assignments he was confident he could handle. Some individuals, motivated by career advancement, took tough assignments they couldn't handle, and ended up hurting the mission and their careers.

A major focus during his career was on the Syrian intervention and presence in Lebanon from 1976 through 2005, the year in which they were forced to withdraw following their involvement in the assassination of Lebanese ex-Premier Rafik Hariri. The principal senior players in the Syrian presence were Syrian intel officers.

Josh and Daniel asked Pete if he'd recount for them the most important analytic problems of his career, including both successes and unsolved problems. They said they'd appreciate any insights into the reasons for his successes.

He described eight specific cases, but also expressed his frustration that he'd been unable to find info that would have thwarted some of the Syrian operations, such as the assassination of Hariri, an exceptional leader who offered high promise for returning peace and prosperity to Lebanon.

Remembering the interesting info they'd picked up about Behrangi during the interview with Mike, Josh decided to ask Pete a question that might elicit similar information.

"In working with Arabic, did you ever encounter an interesting analytic problem dealing with people who were speaking Arabic, but who were not native speakers?" Josh asked.

"Yes," Pete replied, "I heard a number of such conversations, mainly by Iranians speaking Arabic. As you and I know, Josh, there are many Iranians who speak Arabic. Due to the religious and political influence of Islam, some forty percent of Persian vocabulary is of Arabic origin, and the writing system is based on Arabic script, although the two languages are structurally very different."

"Right," Josh commented. "The Pahlavi Shahs tried to diminish the use of Arabic loan words during their reigns, but after the Khomeini revolution, the use of Arabic loan words increased among the leadership."

Pete continued, "I usually encountered those conversations when they involved Iranians working with the Syrians and Hezbollah. In some situations, only one speaker was Iranian and probably used Arabic because the other speaker didn't speak Persian. In other instances, both speakers were Iranian, and they appeared to be using Arabic to conceal their Iranian nationality.

"There was one particularly interesting case. It was a phone call between a guy in Damascus and another in Tehran. It took place in the mid-1990s. The person in Damascus seemed to be there on a business trip. The guy in Tehran appeared to be a very high-level person.

"Both spoke Levantine Arabic with what I believe was an Iranian Azeri accent. The accent of the one in Damascus had a more pronounced Azeri flavor. The one in Tehran had more of a regular Persian accent. While I can't remember the call verbatim, I'll recreate a version for you now that simulates the important substance of the conversation:

"The person in Damascus initiated the call and began the conversation by saying something like, 'Greetings Excellency. It's me, M.B. How are you?' "

"The speaker in Tehran responded, 'I am fine, by the grace of Allah, and you?' "

"I am fine as well. I wanted to let you know that the mission with which you entrusted me is proceeding smoothly. I met with their big man this morning, and I gave him your regards and the letter from you. He asked me to thank you and to send you his greetings. He is very interested in your suggestions, and thinks they are viable."

"Excellent. When do you think you will conclude the work?"

"I hope to be finished by the end of next week, and then return. I will phone you in a few days to give you any new information; and I will send you a note through our channels here."

"I suggest that when you call me next time, you can address me as Sayyed and you can refer to yourself as Mubarak. You can refer to the big man as Hassan. Perhaps you can see why I chose Mubarak and Hassan."

"I am not sure, I will think about it, and ask you about it when I return."

"Good. And as for those from the large place that dislikes us, you can start their names with 'Shae.' For example, their big man would be 'Shaewika.' "

"Ah, I am beginning to understand."

"For the small place, you start with 'Shaeku.' "

"Aah. I see."

"Good, so if there is nothing else, I will look forward to your next call."

"That is all, Sayyed."

"Then God be with you."

"And with you."

"So," Pete continued, "here are my thoughts on the names used in that conversation:

"I know that Sayyed is an honorific title for males who are descendants of the Prophet Mohammed, and there are many in Iran who might be addressed that way. It sounds like this person was a very high-level official because he sent a proposal to 'the big man' in Damascus, perhaps President Hafez al-Assad. So *Sayyed* might refer to the Iranian Supreme Leader, Sayyed Ali Hosseini Khamenei.

"Then 'Hassan' might be used for Hafez al-Assad, because it contains, the first letters of his first and last names.

"When Sayyed refers to the people 'who dislike us,' he may be referring to Americans. The 'Shae' might be the first letters from 'shaeytan,' the Persian word for Satan. So Shaewika might refer to 'Devil William Clinton.'

" 'Shaeku' might refer to Israelis and be derived from the Persian words, 'Shaeytan e kuchik,' which means, 'little Satan.' "

"And the 'M' in 'Mubarak' might be the first consonant in M.B.'s first name and the 'B' might be the first consonant in his last name. I don't know whether the other letters in Mubarak might have any significance.

"I passed this information on to Al Sondheim in the Iran office, but he appeared dismissive. He said that for all he knew, it might just be a conversation between the head of some company and one of his employees. I don't know if the Iran office issued a SIGINT report on it, and kept the naming system in their files."

"I suspect you were right, Pete," Josh replied. "Sayyed may well be the Ayatollah and M.B. may be someone close to him. It's a simple enough system, and would work for very occasional use. It could easily be solved with a bit of use. Of course, explaining it on the phone is a typical amateur mistake.

"During the time I've worked on Iran, I've never seen any mention of that naming system. I also know that we rarely succeeded in collecting the Ayatollah's phone conversations. Were any NSA assets able to collect any other calls involving M.B. during that business trip?"

"Unfortunately, not. I alerted folks to be on the lookout for calls between M.B. and Tehran, but they found none. Now, I'd like to mention one thing that I know influenced my analytic skills," Pete said.

"We'd love to hear it," Josh replied.

"My Uncle Fred was my dad's younger brother and was a detective in the Detroit Police Department. When I was in third grade, I heard him discussing with my parents a case he'd just solved. It sounded very interesting, so I asked him a couple of questions. He was really happy I was interested, so he went into some detail in a way that I could understand. From then on, whenever he and his wife came to our house, we discussed the latest crimes he was either working on or had recently solved.

"There's also a very important analytic principle I learned from Uncle Fred."

"What's that?" Daniel asked.

"It's that one should never jump to conclusions about who's guilty or innocent. That happened after I heard a news story about a man who'd been tried and found guilty of murder. A year later, he was declared innocent, and released. I asked my uncle how that was possible. He told me there were two reasons. The first is that investigators sometimes jump to what seem like logical conclusions. They make their minds up about who is guilty, and then don't do enough work to investigate other possibilities. The second is that an important piece of evidence sometimes does not come to light until later. He asked me if I could think of any examples from my own life.

"When I thought about it, I remembered that a classmate and friend named Bobby had been falsely accused of stealing a teacher's money, but they later discovered someone else had done it. What happened was that the teacher made him stay after school to do additional work because he'd been clowning around in class. She left the room for a few minutes and then returned. She looked in her top desk drawer and saw that a five-dollar bill was missing. She accused Bobby and asked him to pull out the contents of his pockets and his wallet. She found a five dollar bill in his wallet and believed it was hers. She made him turn it over to her even though he said it was a gift from his grandma.

"After she told his classmates the next day, several of them came to her and said they didn't think Bobby did it because he always made a point of the importance of honesty. A week later, the parents of another boy came to tell the teacher they'd just learned that one of their sons had stolen five dollars from her. He had gone into the classroom during the lunch hour when the room was empty and had taken the money. A couple of days later, he bragged about it to his younger brother, who then told their parents.

"That lesson of keeping a very open mind has always stuck with me. Whenever I begin to analyze a situation, one of the first things I ask myself is, 'What's possible here?' "

"That's a critical point," Josh commented. "We remember the IC's major mistake in its conclusions about Saddam Hussein's nuclear weapons program, despite criticisms of some in the community who faulted some of the intelligence and analysis. It was certainly a logical assumption that he had such a program in view of his pursuit of a nuclear weapons capability dating back to the early 1970s."

"After my uncle sparked my interest in detective work, I began to read true stories of difficult crimes that had been solved. As a result of those discussions and my reading, I developed a bit of an understanding of how to analyze information. I think the types of analysis we do can be very similar to police detective work."

"That's fascinating, Pete," Daniel commented. "It certainly makes sense."

"I love it," Josh added. "It might be interesting to have a class in which famous retired detectives discuss their methodologies with our analysts and pose crime-solving problems."

"One of the factors we're looking at," Daniel commented, "is the extent to which ambient noise, like people chatting socially nearby, affects analytic focus on difficult problems. Some people like me can filter out the noise; whereas Josh prefers silence. What's your experience?"

"First," Peter started, "since much of my work involved analyzing voice comms, I was often wearing headphones or ear pieces. I did prefer quiet when I was working on graphic materials or when analyzing problems that were larger. I got the quiet I needed in a couple of ways. The first is that I got a desk in a cube in a corner of our large office. Secondly, I made a sign that said, '**Chat-Free**

Zone,' and hung it next to my desk when I really needed silence."

"Very clever!" Josh laughed. "Did it work?"

"It did. There were a couple of social animals who grumbled a bit at first. Most people knew that I could be very social and was only using the sign to help my thinking."

"I have no more questions," Josh said. "What about you, Daniel?"

"Neither do I."

"Thanks a lot for your insights and time, Pete," Josh said. "Please feel free to get back to us if you have any more thoughts."

"I'll do that. I wish you guys the best with this project. I sure hope it makes a difference."

As Pete opened the door and started to walk out, he turned to come back in and closed the door. "It occurs to me that there's one guy you might want to interview if he's not on your list."

"We'd appreciate any suggestions," said Josh. "Whom do you have in mind?"

"Do you know a guy by the name of Jean-Baptiste Espèces?" Pete asked.

"Never heard of him," Josh replied. "With a name like that, I wouldn't forget him. Sounds French."

"Actually, he's Cajun. He's a great analyst, but not a linguist. He's currently the manager of an NSA organization that specializes in using unconventional analysis to identify and track high-interest individuals like intelligence operatives, narcotraffickers, and terrorists. When he first developed and suggested his new methodologies, he was dismissed by traditional SIGINTers. However, he and his organization have been incredibly successful."

"Thanks, Pete. He sounds like just the type of analyst we'd like to interview. We'll move him to the top of our list."

After he left, Daniel said, "Looks like more unconnected dots on Behrangi."

"You're right on the mark," Josh replied. "You see how easily it can happen. It typically does not occur when comms are between identified civilian or military government officials, or between known terrorists or drug dealers. It's in unusual situations. Nowadays, when comms volume is so great and linguists are so overwhelmed, it's not surprising that dots are sometimes not connected."

"What I plan to do with the info we just got from Pete is to revise the special requirement I'd given the Director and to include a requirement that linguists be on the alert for conversations between 'Mubarak' and 'Sayyed.'

"I also plan to mention to the senior Persian linguist the system the Ayatollah suggested for referring to Americans and Israelis. I can do that by saying we learned this during a Metanalysis interview. There won't be any connection with Meta or nuclear negotiations.

"Right now I'm going to look up this guy Jean-Baptiste and call him to see if he'd be available for an interview next Thursday afternoon. I hate to wait that long, but we've got too much going on to fit him in sooner."

Josh then used the Agency high-side personnel directory to find Jean-Baptiste's high-side phone number. Josh phoned him, described Metanalysis, and asked if he'd be willing to be interviewed. Jean-Baptiste said he'd love to help, so Josh set up the interview for two the following Thursday.

Fourteen

Les Jardins où Fleurissent les Fleurs du Meilleur
(The Gardens Where the Best Flowers Bloom)

Friday April 17

Johnnie and Shellie drove up from FBI HQ to NSA together, and Gianni and Farida drove around the D.C. Beltway together from northern Virginia. Gianni and Farida arrived about 10:15, and Johnnie and Shellie at 10:25. Farida phoned Josh just before they arrived, so Josh and Daniel were waiting in the Visitor Center. Because the visitors all had IC badges, it wasn't really necessary to meet them at the Visitor Center. They could have navigated on their own to Josh and Daniel's office. However, Josh and Daniel felt that meeting them would be the hospitable thing to do.

Daniel and Josh led them up to the office, and proceeded to launch the game app. Daniel had two versions of the app on the computer - one in English and one in Persian. The English version was to make it easy for those who didn't speak Persian to understand what was going on.

Daniel took them slowly through the game, explaining each step. He devoted particular attention to how he'd grossly exaggerated Behrangi's heroism. As he proceeded through the game, he answered several questions they had. When he finished, they all commented on what an incredible job he'd done. They were absolutely blown away.

Daniel then shut down the English version; and Josh launched the Persian version. He would demonstrate it; and then Shellie could give it a go, if she wished. She said she couldn't wait.

After Josh finished a play, Shellie said she'd like to go through it once on her own without comment just to make sure she understood it. Then she'd go through it slowly to see if she could add any value.

Shellie loved the game and found it very intuitive. As she went through it slowly a second time, she had a number of ideas on how to make it more authentic. Josh wrote them down, and Daniel said that he and Josh could quickly incorporate them. They'd probably have a finished version ready for Internet launch by Monday.

Josh didn't have the kind of video game experience Shellie had, so he was really grateful for the cultural and linguistic insights she provided. Daniel was grateful as well, but didn't have the language understanding to appreciate her contributions the way Josh did.

Josh asked Shellie if she could return Monday or Tuesday to review the updated version to see if she had any further suggestions, and to see if they'd properly understood and incorporated her suggestions.

She said she'd be happy to come on Monday, and asked if 10:30 would be a good time. She'd be prepared to stay as late as necessary. Josh said that would be great. She also said it wouldn't be necessary to meet her at the Visitor Center. She'd have no problem navigating her way back to their office.

After they finished their session with the game, they went to the cafeteria for lunch. Then they returned to the office for a minute, before heading to the Director's office. Josh told Shellie that the Director knew a bit of Persian, so she could greet him in Persian if she wished.

Mac, whom Josh had informed of the meeting, was waiting outside the Director's office when they arrived. Josh introduced the visitors to Mac, and then the Director's secretary led them into his office. Josh introduced them. When he came to Shellie, she greeted him in Persian, and he smilingly responded in kind.

"Thanks for coming," the Director began. "Please have a seat." When they were seated, he said, "I'd appreciate it if you could give me a snapshot of your backgrounds."

After they'd finished describing their backgrounds, the Director commented, "I'm impressed. Looks like a great team for a tough task."

"Thank you, very much, Admiral," Johnnie replied. Adding Josh and Daniel to our team has significantly improved the odds for success. We're really awed by the combat game app."

"I'm really pleased to hear that. Let's hope it makes a difference," the Director said. "We've got to shut down this Iranian operation ASAP so we can stop the damage it's causing."

"The reason our FBI and CIA colleagues have come today," Josh explained, "is not only to see the app demonstrated, but to offer suggestions to help us refine it. Before coming to meet you, they spent several hours with us viewing and critiquing the app. Shellie is very familiar with Persian-language video games, so she's given us lots of great ideas. We'll incorporate those suggestions after they leave, and Shellie will return on Monday to review the revised version. We feel we'll be ready to deploy the game on Tuesday."

"Excellent," the Director commented. "I love the way you're all approaching this. It's a great example of the results we can produce when we all work together."

"Admiral," Josh said, "I'd like to tell you what we learned yesterday about a very interesting system the Ayatollah Khamenei created for encrypting the names of people he discusses with his confidant Behrangi, and perhaps others. We found out about it during an analysis project interview with Pete Schlauman, one of the great Arabic language analysts. He discovered it from an Arabic-language conversation he intercepted between the Ayatollah and Behrangi a number of years ago. This could be of some use in the counterespionage project." Josh then described the system in brief.

Josh added, "I've explained that system to the senior Persian language analyst in case the folks in the Iran office run across it."

"Excellent, Josh," the Director commented. "Nice to see that the analysis project could help you with the counterespionage project. I'm curious, though. How is it that the Iran office didn't know about that system? Did the guy you interviewed fail to pass it on?"

"No, sir," Josh replied. "He attempted to pass it on, but the senior language analyst with whom he discussed it at the time was dismissive, and didn't take it seriously. Fortunately, that guy retired some years ago."

"That's sad, Josh. It demonstrates how personality can block an easy path to improvement.

"Mac," the Admiral asked, "If the game is completed on Tuesday, how quickly can it be made available on the Internet?"

"Almost immediately. My Chief of Staff, Bill Bergmann, has identified an expert to work with Daniel. She doesn't know the purpose of the app, only that it has to appear to be on a foreign web site. She'll explain to Daniel how to incorporate a hidden identity feature that'll prevent U.S. cyber warriors from mistakenly disabling the game. I'll send Daniel an email with the expert's name and secure phone number."

Daniel wondered to himself if the expert might be one of the technical specialists he'd trained over the years.

"Thanks again for coming," the Director said. "And Shellie, I really appreciate your willingness to return here so soon."

"I'm really excited," she replied, "to use my gaming skills to help move us forward on this really tough and critical mission."

"We're so happy that this game app offers us some potential for progress," commented Johnnie. "It's the only glimmer of hope we have at the moment. I've informed FBI Director Pasquali, and Gianni has informed CIA Director Rolph."

"Terrific," said the Director. "Best of luck with your efforts and I look forward to helping you celebrate success."

The visitors returned to Josh and Daniel's office to pick up their things and thank them for the introduction to the Director. Then Josh and Daniel accompanied them down to the Visitor Center. As they were getting ready to leave, Shellie said to Josh and Daniel, "Please don't hesitate to call me over the weekend if you think I can help. I'd be happy to get to a secure phone in my office or return to NSA. I live in Rockville and have no plans for the weekend, other than running some errands."

"Thanks, Shellie," Josh replied. "You're great!"

"You're right on that point," she laughed. "Glad you recognize talent when you see it."

When they got back to their office, Daniel asked Josh, "Do you think it would be possible for us to get together at the office on Saturday or Sunday to work on finishing the game?"

"Sure. How about Saturday morning in case we need additional time on Sunday?"

"Great! How about starting at ten?"

"Sounds good to me."

Shortly after their discussion, Josh and Daniel received an email from Mac with the name and contact information for the expert who'd deploy the game on the Internet. Her name was Katsimba "Kat" Marcus. Daniel was delighted to see the name. She was a young African-American woman whom he'd mentored in cyber techniques in a three-year development program, starting shortly after she was hired by the Agency.

Her mother, Marian, was a retired NSA Swahili and French linguist. She'd created her daughter's name by combining the Swahili word, "Simba" (lion) with Kat (cat) as a start to motivating her daughter to be a fearless, hard charger. She introduced her daughter to both computer programming and foreign language study when she was very young. Kat enjoyed language study, but loved programming.

Daniel discovered early on that she was a creative soul who often thought of innovative approaches to problem solving. He knew she'd be perfect for the task. He called her and arranged for her to come to their office at 9:30 Tuesday morning to discuss the task.

They then started incorporating Shellie's ideas. By quarter past seven, they'd taken care of most of her suggestions. They decided to call it a night and continue the following day.

They resumed on Saturday and had completed the game by

quarter to three. They were very happy with the results, and decided it wasn't necessary to return on Sunday. Daniel said he'd play around with it at home to see if he could come up with any additional improvements.

When Josh got home about half past three, Meihui asked him how the project was going. Since he couldn't discuss Meta, he couldn't tell her about the game. He was dying to describe it because it was so amazing. All he could say was he was very upbeat about how things were going, and wouldn't have to go in on Sunday.

Un Intervallo di Sapori -

Pennsylvania Dutch & Tuscan

(A Flavors Break)

Josh then turned to more important matters. "What would you like to do for dinner?"

"I've got it taken care of," she replied. I went to The Amish Market[18] and picked up a barbequed chicken, Amish potato salad, and an apple crumb cake. We can eat whenever you'd like." The Amish Market was how most local folks referred to the Annapolis Pennsylvania Dutch Farmers Market. Josh and Meihui loved shopping at the large market, which was filled with vendors' stalls selling terrific meats, BBQ, baked goods, produce, salads, ice cream, etc. It was only open on Thursday, Friday, and Saturday.

"I'd like to eat around seven, if that's ok. I'd like to relax for a while with a glass of wine, while I do some reading in the *Economist* and *Barron's.*" These were Josh's two favorite weekly publications. Both arrived on Saturdays.

He used *Barron's Financial Weekly* to help him with investing. His father had taught him the importance of learning early about investing, and had tutored him in various investment strategies.

---

[18] (http://www.padutchfarmmarket.com)

Josh had created separate portfolios for himself and Meihui. The portfolios included the Federal Thrift Savings Plan, a mix of stock mutual funds, a couple of bond funds, and some cash. He also liked to do some short-term, on-line stock trading using *Scottrade*. He never invested more than 10 percent of their assets in stocks so that even if he made a really bad stock purchase, they could never suffer a devastating loss. His basic philosophy was to purchase only stocks with values between $5 and $55 per share and to make the purchases in 100-share increments. He never took recommendations from family, friends, or acquaintances - in order to avoid emotional complications if an investment didn't work out. It took him a couple of years to develop this approach, but once he had it worked out, he never again lost money on a stock.

They started Sunday morning with a relaxed breakfast. Meihui made xi hong shi chao ji dan - a simple and popular Chinese dish of stir-fried tomatoes, scallions, and scrambled eggs. Although the Chinese didn't eat it as a breakfast dish, Meihui and Josh both enjoyed it that way. She also served a mix of donuts that she'd bought the preceding day at the Amish market.

While they were eating, Meihui told him she planned to prepare a Tuscan dinner. His face lit up with a smile because they both loved authentic Italian cuisine of all types. He decided not to ask her what she'd be preparing, but to let it be a surprise.

They spent the day doing laundry and other weekend tasks.

As dinner time approached, Meihui asked Josh to choose a red wine. He decided on a 2010 Peppoli Chianti Classico from Marchesi Antinori. He uncorked the wine a couple of hours before dinner to give it a bit of time to open up. The Florence-based Antinori family had been producing wines since 1385. Josh had tried a number of their wines, and loved them. The head of the family, Piero Antinori, was a visionary who'd helped to revolutionize the Italian wine industry. Josh really admired Antinori and his three daughters, who shared in running the firm. Their energy, vision, warmth, kindness, ethics, and success set a wonderful example of how to make the world a more delightful place to live.

Meihui set the table with her favorite dishware – Umbrian Flowers by Dansk. The dishes Meihui was preparing were all ones they both loved and had previously made - sometimes together.

When it was time for dinner, they sat down at their dining room table in the glow of candle light from two pairs of tall white candles. The first course was already on the table. It was an appetizer of Fettunta (Tuscan for bruschetta) - grilled small bread slices with olive oil, diced tomatoes, and basil leaves. Josh poured the wine.

As they dined and sipped the luscious wine, the rich voice of Andrea Bocelli bathed their souls in waves of romantic sentiments.

Next, came Carabaccia, a wonderful Florentine onion soup that some consider the inspiration for French onion soup, when Catherine de' Medici married King Henry II of France and took Florentine cuisine to France.

That was followed by Peposo dei Fornaciari dell'Impruneta - beef stew of the tile makers of the town of Impruneta near Florence, using the recipe from the *Tuscany the Beautiful Cookbook* by Lorenza de' Medici, a descendant of the famous Florentine ruling family. Impruneta was famous for its terracotta tiles and pots. The wives of the tile makers would make the stew for their husbands to take for lunch. The tile makers would heat the stew in their tile ovens. It was easy to prepare and delicious.

The side dish she served with the stew was Carote in Stufato - a braised carrot and pancetta dish from the Tuscan town of Arezzo, using the recipe from the same cookbook.

Dessert was Strawberry Semifreddo - a type of homemade ice cream whose recipe was from the writings of Frances Mayes, author of *Under the Tuscan Sun* and *Bella Tuscany*.

Dinner was topped off with small glasses of vin santo dessert wine accompanied by cantuccini, hard almond cookies that they dipped in the vin santo to soften before eating.

The only thing that could have made the evening better would have been to experience it at a country villa overlooking the gorgeous Tuscan hills. They went to bed, showing their deep love for each other and imagining they were deep in the Tuscan hills. They could not have imagined a better life.

Vivere	**To Live**
Fiamme focose	Fiery flames
d'amore ardente	Of ardent love,
sapori squisiti	Delicious flavors,
vino vivace	Vibrant wine,
e	And
parole sensuali	Luscious lyrics
accendono insieme	Ignite together
una conflagrazione potente	A powerful inferno
di passione fortissima.	Of intense passion.
Bellissimo!	Wonderful!

Fifteen

ባንበሲቶች : ቤት : ዉስጥ : [19]
(In the Den of the Lionesses)

Monday April 20

When Josh arrived at the office, Daniel was already there and
had the game up and running. Daniel showed him a couple of
improvements he'd made at home on Sunday. They were colorful
features that added action and excitement.

Josh told Daniel he was going to try to arrange an interview for
Wednesday afternoon with Carolyn Rainier, another expert Persian
linguist. She was the last of the Iran and Levant analysts who might
provide some insights into Meta. After that, Josh would start
arranging interviews with analysts from other target areas.

Josh phoned Carolyn, described Metanalysis, and asked if she'd
be interested in being interviewed. She was available and eager. She
hoped she could contribute something of value. It turned out that
every analyst they asked was eager to be interviewed and share their
experiences. That didn't surprise Josh because there were very few
people who didn't like being recognized for excellence and being
asked to discuss the challenges they'd faced. They loved their
profession and typically had ideas on how to improve things.

After calling Carolyn, Josh did his quick daily review of intel
reports on Iran. As usual, there was no Meta-related info.

---

[19] banbesitoch bet wusTT – from Amharic, a major Ethiopian language.

Shellie arrived at about ten fifteen. When she greeted Josh in Persian, he not only replied in kind, but continued in Persian, thanking her for making the trip to NSA's rural location, something that many in the IC were reluctant to do.

She switched to English for Daniel's benefit. "I wouldn't miss the chance to come out here and work with you guys on this app. How'd it go over the weekend?"

"Very smoothly," said Daniel. "We completed most of the work on Saturday, and I added a couple of features on Sunday. What about you?"

"I came up with two more ideas for you to consider. If you'd run your new version of the game, I could see if my suggestions might work."

"Rather than us showing you the revised version," Daniel remarked, "How about if you start it yourself and play the game as if you're an on-line player."

"Sounds great. I'll give it a shot." She quickly started it up and played her way through. Then she played it two more times. "Really awesome!" she exclaimed. "It looks beautiful, and plays intuitively. The graphics are terrific and have a very Iranian feel to them. I think my suggestions would work."

"Let's hear them," Josh said.

Both Josh and Daniel liked her ideas, and Daniel quickly added them. Then, each took turns playing it four times, and tried to make it crash, but couldn't.

They interrupted their play with a quick lunch in the cafeteria.

By two thirty, they were finished and believed the game was good to go.

"Our next step," Daniel told Shellie "is scheduled for tomorrow morning. We're going to meet with a young cyber expert who's going to launch the app on the Internet. We're not going to tell her that this is a counterespionage project. I mentored her the first couple years of her career, and I'm confident she'll do a super job."

"We'll call you guys as soon as the game is launched," Josh said.

"We'd appreciate it if you'd emphasize to Johnnie, Farida, and Gianni that none of them should attempt to find or play the game on the Internet. That might alert the other side that the game is not what it seems."

Josh's cautionary remark prompted Shellie to think of a way she could help without raising suspicions. "I'm familiar with various Iranian social media sites where gamers post comments about on-line games. I could monitor those sites from my gaming computer to look for comments about the game. I won't use any techniques that would specifically point to this game. I can let you know immediately if I see anything. What do you think, Josh?"

"Beautiful, Shellie. Thanks!!!"

"Another thought I have is that you could create a couple of fake gamer IDs for Josh and he could post favorable comments about the game on Persian-language gaming web sites."

"Another great idea," Josh commented. "We'll give it a shot. I'd appreciate it if you could let me know which web sites would be best."

"I'll send you a list of URLs tomorrow."

"Thanks."

Daniel told Shellie that he'd send the team a daily update on the game's status.

Tuesday April 21

The next morning, Kat arrived as planned.

"Hi Kat," Daniel greeted her, "It's been a while. How're you doing?"

"Great, thanks to you, Dr. Dechado. How're you?"

"Terrific, thanks. You know you don't need to call me *Dr. Dechado. Daniel* works just fine. This is my colleague, Josh."

Kat knew she could never call him *Daniel.* She'd placed him on a pedestal, and he'd stay there.

"Nice to meet you, Kat," Josh said. "Daniel has told me a lot about how talented you are. I look forward to working with you."

Kat beamed at hearing about the praise from Dr. Dechado. She couldn't wait to show him how she'd progressed. "Nice to meet you, Josh."

Daniel turned to the task at hand. "I'd like to tell you a bit about what we want to do. I've written an app that's a game. Its purpose is to find a particular player and penetrate that player's computer. We want the app to look like it's on a server in Lebanon. It's important to know immediately whenever any substantive comments are posted about the game. Very short comments are probably of little value.

"We'd like to know the following things about what's happening:

- The number of unique players and the number of return players each day;

- Players' locations;

- Anyone repeatedly playing the high-interest section of the game; and

- Any effort to hack into the game or change it.

"The software includes protections that will not allow it to be changed in any way.

"Once the game is launched, we'd like you to create a couple of Persian-language game-player accounts on a couple of specific web sites so Josh can post comments about the software. When you're creating the accounts, Josh can sit next to you and handle the Persian-language part."

"No problem. I can do it all," she said. "I'll load the game onto a cloud server via a computer that's connected to the Internet, but not to any other NSA computer.

"Whenever there are comments, I'll download them onto a laptop that's not connected to any other computer, and I'll bring that laptop to your office or you can come to my office, which is about a ten-minute walk from here."

"That's going to be too cumbersome and slow, Kat," Daniel commented. "Please check with Bill Bergmann to see if he can find you a temporary office that's much closer to ours so the three of us can interact faster."

"I'll go see Mr. Bergmann immediately," she replied.

Kat called back within the hour, and said Bill had found a very small office that was just a couple of doors down from Josh and Daniel. The new office would be ready the next day. In the meantime, she'd launch the game on the Internet. She'd move the equipment to the new office as soon as it was ready.

By 1:30, she called to say the game was up and running. Josh informed Johnnie, and reiterated how important it was that no one at the Bureau or CIA attempt to find and use the game.

Then Josh wrote an email update and sent it to the Director and Mac. He reported the progress he and Daniel were making with the game app, including how they were approaching the task of spreading news about the game, and identifying the right player if he played the game. They'd immediately let the Director and Mac know if they found Behrangi.

He described how Shellie had helped them, and how supportive Kat and Bill Bergmann had been. Josh said he'd informed Johnnie Dece that the game was on the Internet. He also explained how he'd cautioned the other members of Team Triad that no one at CIA or the Bureau should attempt to find or use the game on the Internet.

The Director sent a brief reply that he was very happy, and that he would inform DNI Kraft at a meeting the next afternoon.

Fifteen

Iran Était une Fête [20]

(Iran Was a Feast)

Wednesday April 22

Carolyn arrived at two, as scheduled. She and Josh exchanged Persian greetings, and Josh introduced Daniel.

Carolyn was tall and relatively thin, with black hair and brown eyes. She appeared to be in her forties or fifties, and was very attractive and outgoing, with a warm personality. From her facial features, one might have guessed that she was of Middle Eastern heritage, but her ancestors were actually from France via Canada.

Josh started the session by asking about her background.

"My father worked for McDonnell-Douglas, which had sold the Iranian Air Force a number of F-4 Phantom fighter jets, starting with the F-4D in 1968 and subsequently the F-4E in 1969. He accepted a McDonnell-Douglas assignment in Iran, and moved our family to Tehran when I was ten years old.

"I loved Iran and immersed myself deeply in the society. I was fascinated by Tehran's Grand Bazaar, the Bazar e Bozorg, with over six miles of covered shopping lanes, each of which specialized in a different type of goods and foods like spices, carpets, gold, copper, and paper, and craftsmen like haberdashers, shoemakers, tailors, tinsmiths, and knife makers. Some areas of the bazaar had been

---

[20] This is a take-off on the French title, "Paris Est une Fête," of the French translation of Ernest Hemingway's book, "A Moveable Feast."

there for a thousand years. It was the original mega shopping center. After I left Iran, I was surprised to learn that the bazaar merchants were very conservative and were strong supporters of the revolution against the Shah because modern enterprises that he was encouraging were hurting their businesses.

"I studied Persian and spoke it at every opportunity. Since my mom and dad had hired two Iranian housekeepers, I always spoke Persian with them. I also spoke it whenever mom and I went shopping, and when we were in restaurants and shops. I loved the language, and thought it was neat that I could converse with people, and my parents couldn't understand what I was saying; and I could even be their interpreter.

"When my parents recognized my interest in Persian, they asked me if I would like my own private teacher. I loved the idea. It made me feel very special. So my parents found a very talented tutor, Farhad Esfahani, a middle-aged gentleman who was a Persian history professor at the University of Tehran. He was from a prosperous family, and did not need to work for a living. He had spent about ten years in the Iranian Foreign Service, but decided he preferred to live in Iran rather than abroad. He would come to our house twice a week, and spend an hour teaching me Persian and about Iranian culture and society. He taught me until I graduated from high school.

"One of the most important things he taught me was how to look at the world through Iranian eyes. He'd mention some event or issue, and ask me to discuss its meaning or significance in Persian. When I was finished, he'd explain to me how it would be viewed by different types of Iranians - middle class and poor, deeply religious and non-religious, male and female, etc. The more fluent I became in Persian, the more difficult a topic he would pose. At first, I felt overwhelmed because I almost never got it right; but as I came to understand Iranian mindsets, I became pretty good at making the correct interpretations, and I began to look forward to his challenges.

"About ten years after I left Iran, I learned that he had lost his teaching job at the university within a year after the revolution, and that he had passed away in poverty some five years later. I felt a great loss and sadness because he had been such a kind, caring gentleman, and had enriched my life so much. He had created a Persian part of my soul.

"After about four years of Mr. Esfahani's tutelage, one of my Iranian girlfriends at school mentioned that when I spoke Persian, I seemed to have the heart and soul of an Iranian, so she gave me the Iranian name Shirin, which means 'kind and sweet.' The name stuck, and all of my Iranian friends used it when they spoke to me. I loved it because it made me feel like I belonged.

"Those friends used to ask me questions about how Americans thought about various topics. Answering their questions helped me to develop ever deeper understandings of Iranian world views, and how they contrasted with American views. However, those world views were principally the perceptions of the secular and wealthy component of Iranian society. When I subsequently went to work at NSA, I put a lot of effort into learning the views of the Mullahcracy that governed the country. I would often discuss those views with Herman Moore, whom Josh and I call Baeradaer Bishtaer. The establishment's views were from a different Iran than the one I knew and loved. I've recently read about the changing culture of the youth in modern Iran, and I'm happy to see that they seem to be moving back in the culture-rich direction I favor.

"Like Baeradaer Bishtaer, I love the nonreligious aspects of Iranian culture, history, and society - art, architecture, poetry, people, cuisine, etc. I especially worship the intellect and accomplishments of Omar Khayyam, who lived from AD 1048 to 1131, not only for his incredible poetry, but for his remarkable works in philosophy, algebra, mathematics, astronomy, geography, and mechanics. It's a shame that very few Americans know of his genius and that he authored one of the world's most important treatises on algebra written before modern times.

"I liked him so much that I memorized over 100 of the 500 or so quatrains (4-line poems) he had written. I had the unforgettable experience of visiting his architecturally impressive mausoleum at Nishapur in northeastern Iran. It was designed and built in 1963 by extraordinary Iranian architect, Hooshang Seyhoun. I'm convinced that Khayyam's genius, with his love of wine, would have been stifled by today's small-minded religious fanatics, who wouldn't understand the gift Allah had bestowed on the earth in the form of this brilliant thinker.

"I admired Khayyam so much that I wrote one quatrain myself with a spirit I hope he'd have recognized:

> When glistening grapes from off the leafy vine
> Become the heart of love-endowing wine,
> They elevate the fullness of my soul
> To heights of rapture born of His design.[21]"

"How beautiful, Shirin," Josh commented.

"Kheili maemnun aem, Baeradaer Josh," (Thank you very much, Brother Josh.)" she replied.

"After the revolution, I came to strongly dislike the religious imperialism, the anti-U.S. activities, the restrictions on freedom of expression, the Holocaust denials, etc. I could not imagine how human beings who professed to be religious could deny the thoroughly documented, horrific Holocaust. I feel that denial in the place of compassion for immense suffering shows a complete absence of humanity."

"I feel the same as you," Josh commented, "I haven't experienced living in Iran, so I'm missing important components of your experiences. What schools did you attend in Iran?"

"The first school I attended in Tehran was Iranzamin Tehran

---

[21] Written in the style of the nineteenth century British poet, Edward Fitzgerald, who "translated" the quatrains of Khayyam. Fitzgerald's work was more paraphrasing than translation.

International School. My schoolmates were from many ethnicities and religions. After graduating from high school, I attended the University of Tehran for nearly two years, until my father moved us back to the U.S.

"About the time I was fifteen, I began to travel around Iran with Iranian girlfriends from the school. I went with them to their home towns - to Isfahan, Karaj, Tabriz, Shiraz, Qom, and Ahvaz. I loved those trips. Their families welcomed me warmly, explained their local customs, treated me to their local dishes, and took me sightseeing.

"When the security situation in Iran started to deteriorate in 1978, my father moved us back to the U.S., to Berkeley, Missouri, near St. Louis, where McDonnell-Douglas had its headquarters. He continued to work for the company until his retirement in 1991.

"In 1979, I started at UCLA, where I majored in Iranian studies. During my senior year, a friend who graduated the preceding year, told me about NSA. I applied and was hired.

"At NSA, I found that Mr. Esfahani's insight training gave me a capability most of my colleagues lacked. That often allowed me to understand when an Iranian's words meant something other than their literal meaning appeared to convey. For example, a person might appear to say he planned to carry out orders he'd been given. However, his choice of words and their phrasing showed he had no intention of doing so. Over my career, I saw a number of instances in which one of my colleagues translated the words correctly, but misunderstood the real meaning. Fortunately, I was able to identify most of those problems and correct them prior to publication of the intel.

"I was no smarter than those colleagues. I just had the good fortune of having spent considerable time in Iran. The majority of them had never been to Iran because most had learned Persian after the fall of the Shah. A few of my older colleagues had spent time in Iran, but had no experience with anyone like Mr. Esfahani.

"The one person who knew far more than I about Iran was

Baeradaer Bishtaer, whose combination of language and analytic talents were extraordinary. I never stopped learning from him, and he occasionally learned something from me. We often teamed up to handle some of the most challenging language problems.

"I did have one shortfall compared to my colleagues who'd been in the military. I had no direct experience with communications collection. Analyzing some types of communications requires an understanding of communications transmission and collection processes."

"Can you remember what it was," Josh asked, "that first created your interest in Persian?"

"I'm not sure. At the time my father moved us to Iran, I'd never been outside the U.S. and had never been exposed to a foreign language. I remember that I was captivated by this new exotic world, which was so different from my world in Missouri."

"Can you describe the most complex analytic challenges you've faced and how you solved them?" Daniel inquired.

"I put difficult analytic problems into two categories - those that have great significance for U.S. foreign or military policy and actions, and those with little significance. In some cases, the significance can't be understood until the analysis has been completed. The solution of each type can provide satisfaction, but the meaningful ones provide great psychic income, in particular, when lives are saved or when one's work affects the course of history."

Carolyn then provided examples of difficult analytic problems she'd solved in each category.

Then she said, "There was one painful and very disturbing conversation I listened to about six weeks ago. A high-level Iranian diplomat in Vienna phoned a woman in Tehran, whom I believe was his wife. In a few short sentences, he said, 'They know. I have been summoned to return immediately to meet with them. I think they will be waiting for me at the airport. If I do not see you again, remember that I love you and the children deeply.'

'Do not come,' she implored him.

'I must. They said that you and the children will pay dearly if I do not return.'

'I will pray for you, my love,' she cried.

'Good-bye, dearest,' he said, and then hung up.

"My guess about the significance of the conversation is that some powerful entity in Iran, like the MOIS, discovered something very serious about this guy - perhaps spying for a foreign government. They were using his family as leverage to get him to return to Iran. I reported that conversation. I hope it was not as dire as it sounded, but I suspect it was."

"I've never had to listen to anything quite like that," Josh commented. "I can imagine how tough it must've been."

"It was heart-wrenching," she remarked. Josh could see from her facial expressions that she was still deeply troubled by the thought of what might have happened.

"It never occurred to me," Daniel commented that linguists would have to deal with such difficult human dimensions in their work. That is not something we encounter in tech development.

"To switch topics completely, do you feel that ambient noise in the office affects your analytic work on complex problems?" Daniel asked.

"Noise around me never affects me very much. I can always filter it out. Besides, much of my time is spent working on voice intercept, so I have a headset or ear buds on, and don't really hear ambient noise."

"Well, I think we've exhausted our questions for now. Thanks for spending so much time with us," Josh commented. "I was fascinated by some of the events you dealt with and puzzles you solved before I came to NSA. I'd never heard those stories. I particularly like the one that President George H.W. Bush asked that you personally brief him. I've never known any SIGINT analyst who's been asked to brief the president."

"I was really honored. It was a great experience. Well, thanks for letting me tell you about my past and my experiences. I wish you both the best with your project."

"If you have any thoughts later, please feel free to get back in touch," Josh mentioned.

"Khoda hafez (Good-bye)," she said.

"Khoda hafez e Shomah," Josh replied.

After she left, they compared her to Baeradaer Bishtaer, Mike, and Pete. She had the same passion as the others, but there were a couple of major differences. She started her SIGINT career with a much deeper understanding of Iranian culture, society, and thought processes, and a much better grasp of the language because of extensive exposure and training at an earlier age. On the other hand, she lacked the knowledge of comms processes, cryptology, and TA that was often so critical to understanding comms. Daniel said it seemed to him that Josh possessed both types of strengths because he'd grown up in an Iranian-American culture, but also had his Navy experience that gave him the technical analytic knowledge. Josh told him that Carolyn's knowledge of Iranian culture and society ran much deeper than his because of her in-country immersion and the exceptional tutelage of Farhad Esfahani.

It seemed to both Josh and Daniel that it could be very valuable to provide linguists and analysts with substantive training in foreign thought processes - with the types of perception challenges posed to Carolyn by her tutor.

One factor that made it difficult to hire people like Carolyn was that their lives overseas posed problems to the security organization's background investigation process. There was no way security investigators could check on what she'd done when she lived in Iran. Fortunately, she lived there only through her teen years and before the revolution, so it was improbable that she'd done anything that would make her a security risk.

As for Meta, her description of the conversation involving the Iranian Foreign Ministry source who had disappeared made them feel very sorry for the man and his family. Carolyn clearly had not been told that the man was a U.S. HUMINT source.

The interview provided them with helpful insights for Metanalysis , but unfortunately, nothing she'd told them helped with Meta.

After Carolyn left, Daniel phoned Kat, and asked if she could come and share what was going on with the game. She came immediately and told them there was nothing significant yet. The game had been noticed, and there were a few players, but there was no interesting activity. Neither Daniel nor Josh was surprised. If they were very lucky, Behrangi would learn about the game within a few days. It could take much longer.

Sixteen

Les Fleuves de Notre Jeunesse Nous Guident à la Mer

(The Rivers of Our Youth Lead Us to the Sea)

Thursday April 23

Before heading to FBI HQ for their weekly meeting, Daniel called Kat to see if there were any new developments with the game. She told him that the number of people playing the game was slowly increasing, but there were no unusual usage patterns. There were a few short foreign-language comments posted.

Josh and Daniel headed down to Josh's silver Miata, and set out for their meeting. It was a gloomy morning - cloudy, windy, and chilly, with temperatures in the midfifties. Traffic on the BW Parkway was moderate and flowing smoothly until about a mile north of the Washington Beltway, when the traffic suddenly slowed to a creep. It became clear they would be at least a few minutes late, so Daniel called Johnnie to let him know.

"The FBI blockade you arranged to keep us out of town is working," Daniel joked. "I'll call back and let you know if we figure out how to get past it."

"Good luck," Johnnie replied, chuckling.

Fortunately, the traffic cleared up when they reached the beltway. There'd been an accident at the westbound ramp onto the beltway. Daniel called Johnnie to let him know they'd probably only be a few minutes late.

"Damn! I'll have to arrange a better blockade next time," Johnnie joked.

They arrived about five minutes late, and Johnnie came down to meet them. He took them up to the conference room where the other team members were waiting.

After Daniel grabbed some water and Josh got a cup of coffee, Johnnie started the meeting by asking Josh and Daniel to describe where things stood with their efforts.

Josh started by expressing how much he and Daniel appreciated Shellie's help with the game, and her idea of monitoring Iranian social media. Then he described the launch of the game, and the fact that it was getting some play, but nothing exciting yet. Josh asked Shellie if she'd seen anything interesting on Iranian social media. She'd seen a couple of positive comments and nothing negative.

Josh then described the interviews with Carolyn Rainier and the planned interview with Jean-Baptiste that afternoon. He mentioned the SIGINT report Carolyn had written about the Iranian diplomat who had probably been jailed or killed. The others had all read Carolyn's report before Josh and Daniel joined the team.

When Josh and Daniel finished, Johnnie asked the other members of the team if they'd found any new information of value, or had any new ideas about initiatives they could try. No one had anything new to offer. Gianni expressed the sentiments of the others when he said they felt frustrated that they'd been unable to come up with anything that pointed them toward the spy or spies. They'd exhausted every possibility they knew. They were keeping their fingers crossed that the innovative approach being pursued by Daniel and Josh would yield results.

After chatting a few minutes, they headed back to their respective offices.

Josh and Daniel's drive back to NSA was slowed by a traffic accident that had closed one lane of the BW Parkway just south of MD Route 197. However, they got back in plenty of time to grab a quick lunch and prepare for the interview with Jean-Baptiste.

Jean-Baptiste arrived a minute or two early. He was a bit short, and light complected, with thick, light-brown hair and brown eyes.

J. E. HARB, JR.

As he introduced himself, Jean-Baptiste asked them to call him, "J.B."

It was immediately apparent that he was like so many great analysts - a straight shooter, and not a self-promoter or political type.

As usual, Josh started by explaining Metanalysis. Since he hadn't previously met Jean-Baptiste, he told him a bit about his own background. Then Daniel did the same.

After that, Josh asked J.B. to describe his early years, including his ethnic and language background, and anything about that background that might provide insight into his analytic skills.

"Well," I'm Cajun on my father's side and German on my mother's. Our family is from an area of Louisiana called the Second Old German Coast. It's St. John the Baptist Parish along both banks of the Mississippi just above New Orleans. It was initially settled by Germans in the mid-eighteenth century. They were followed shortly after by Acadians, who were later called Cajuns, and whom the Brits had forced out of Acadia, which is now Nova Scotia Province in Canada.

"Although I speak some Cajun French, I don't have any useful foreign-language skill.

"Off the top of my head, I can't think of any childhood experiences that contributed to my becoming an analyst.

"When it came time to go to college, I decided to attend the University of Nebraska at Lincoln. People always ask me why I chose to leave Louisiana for Nebraska. I don't have a good reason. I just wanted to choose a world different from my own."

"At UNL, I majored in journalism and minored in European history. It was that combination that set me on an analytic trajectory. I owe a lot to one professor from whom I took a couple of courses, including one on investigative reporting. She taught us how to gather, organize, and analyze information. She also stressed the importance of keeping an open mind and not jumping to conclusions, an action which can bias outcomes.

"During the second semester of my senior year, in 1983, I asked her if she had any suggestions about where I should look for a job. I expected she'd mention some newspapers or magazines. Instead, she suggested I consider employment at an intelligence agency like the CIA or NSA. She told me she thought I might make a good intelligence analyst. She suggested that I read 'The Code-Breakers' by David Kahn and 'The Puzzle Palace' by James Bamford. She also suggested a couple of books about the CIA. I read everything she suggested, and was intrigued, so I applied to both agencies.

"Each offered me a job with the same starting salary, so I flipped a coin, and ended up choosing NSA. I think it worked out great for me. I started in the reporting intern program. When most outsiders hear the word 'intern,' they think of traditional, non-paid positions, in contrast to NSA intern programs which are essentially three-year paid educational and experiential development programs in specific professional fields such as engineering or language.

"In the intern program, I had the typical four six-month assignments and a final one-year assignment. Each assignment was in a different analytic office - the Soviet Air Force, the Chinese Army, counterproliferation, counternarcotics, and counterterrorism. During those assignments, I took a number of classes, principally in analysis and reporting, at the National Cryptologic School.

"The Soviet and Chinese efforts didn't interest me at all. Given the large nature of those targets, the analytic efforts against them were large and hierarchical. They didn't offer the types of challenges, creativity, and freedom I wanted. However, I enjoyed the other three efforts which focused on tracking and analyzing international equipment, software and services transactions, and on people, often involving phony front organizations designed to camouflage true intent.

"As I was finishing my final year in the intern program, I found the organization where I am now. It's responsible for identifying and tracking the movements of high-interest, foreign individuals such as intel officers. Traditional SIGINT has involved collecting and analyzing the comms of target governmental organizations such as intel services, military forces, diplomatic services, and security services, as well as terrorist and narcotics trafficking organizations.

"Our work is very different. We focus primarily on international internet transactions and comms related to commercial activities involving travel, purchases, finance, etc.

"When we started our effort, the NSA organizations that focused on traditional target comms thought our focus was a waste of time. Many remain unconvinced, despite our many successes. Others have told me that the skeptical response is a typical reaction to new endeavors. One of my acquaintances is a senior counterproliferation analyst who was in on the startup of that effort in the mid-1970s, when the U.S. became concerned about 'The Dirty Dozen' countries that were most likely to develop nuclear weapons. One event that prompted U.S. concern was India's test of a nuclear explosive device 'for peaceful purposes' in May 1974. NSA created a counterproliferation analytic office in response to new requirements from U.S. policymakers.

"Despite the high-priority requirements for SIGINT on nuclear proliferation, the new endeavor often met resistance from traditionalists when it came to sharing limited collection capabilities. Fortunately, the counterproliferation office persisted and collaborated with Department of Energy (DOE) experts to develop very successful capabilities.

"We met similar resistance, but didn't enjoy the high-priority intel requirements they had. Nonetheless, we persisted and figured out innovative ways to use hardware and software to overcome some of the unique challenges we faced. We don't give up easily because we know the value of our work."

"What sort of challenges?" Josh asked.

"Before I answer your question, I'd like to make one thing really clear. When I talk about overcoming resistance and figuring out innovative ways to work, I always say 'we,' not 'I' because it's a team effort. We constantly look for innovators, regardless of pay grade or age or gender or whatever. If one of us is chatting with an

Army private who seems dissatisfied with a current job and who seems like a sharp go-getter, we try to get him or her to join us.

"In a very micro way, it's like following some of the collaborative ideas of Linus Torvalds, the software engineer who created the Linux kernel. He accepted ideas from more and more people on how to grow Linux until it became a huge, nonstop innovation machine. And I use the word 'collaborative' in the way Linus uses it - not collaboration in a kissy-huggy way, but in a challenging and sometimes combative way, to produce great results. We also focus on solving individual problems, not on elegant mega solutions. We gradually developed a unique set of analytic tools and processes. It has often been difficult, but it has worked. So I just want to emphasize, it's a 'we' effort, not an 'I' effort.

"Now to your question about the challenges we faced. For starters, the volumes of comms involving travel plans and reservations is extraordinarily large and continues to grow with globalization and the increase in wealth and the economies of countries like China that enable many more people to travel. We can't begin to collect and process all the available information to find only the few bits of information of high value to us. The volumes were bad enough before the Internet. Since the mid-1990s, the volumes have been growing exponentially.

"Secondly, there are many, many variables. Spelling of personal names is one. For example, the name Muhammad, which is spelled one way in Arabic, can be transliterated into many different spellings in the Latin alphabet. Josh certainly knows that, but let me write some for you, Daniel." J.B. wrote: Muhammad, Muhammed, Mohamed, Mohammad, Mohammed, Mahamed, and Mahomet.

"There are also many different ways that dates and times are written and different calendar systems.

"These variables really complicate our search efforts.

"We've learned over time that every group of people has its own bureaucracy that handles its most mundane activities, such as travel and lodging. Each group has its unique processes, practices, regulations, likes, dislikes, special benefits, prohibitions, etc. It doesn't matter whether the organization involves terrorists, or intel officers, or military personnel, or drug traffickers, or scientists. We analyze each organization in many ways. For example, we talk to IC partner organizations, look at social media, read intel reports, prepare questions for interrogations of prisoners and defectors, etc. When we can't find info about a particular group, we develop hypotheses based on how similar organizations in the same or other countries work. We include considerations such as culture, ethnicity, and religion."

As Josh listened to J.B.'s explanation of his organization's methodology, he reflected on how perfectly that aligned with his own concept of *Group Discovery and Affiliation Analysis.*

"One factor that complicates our work is that we can't target the comms of U.S.-owned companies like hotel chains or airlines. Those companies are responsible for a large percentage of the world's travel and lodging activities.

"The work we do occasionally results in the discovery of a U.S. person spying for a foreign power. The way that happens is that when we report to CIA the travel of a foreign intel officer, the CIA may surveil that officer at his destination. The officer may have traveled to meet with an American spy at a location outside the U.S. If the CIA officer spots the foreign officer meeting with an American, then an investigation of that American is initiated.

"Our work can also provide the CIA with recruiting opportunities. For example, in once case in the early 1990s, we learned that a physicist from the Libyan clandestine nuclear weapons program was traveling to an international conference in Europe. The CIA was able to recruit him there and develop him as a source.

"In another case, a CIA officer was using one of our tips to surveil a Russian intel operative who traveled to a Caribbean nation. The CIA guy discovered the Russian meeting with an employee of the German intelligence service, the BND, with which the U.S. has partnered a great deal since the 1950s. The CIA tipped off the BND, which then investigated and found that the employee was spying for the Russians. The Germans arrested him and put him on trial.

"Those are just a couple of examples. There are many, many others."

At that point, Josh commented, "I've worked a lot on Iran. I'm curious as to whether or not you've tracked MOIS officers."

"Yes. We've identified and tracked a number of them over the years. In one case, we provided information that foiled a terrorist attack they were planning in South America. In another case, we helped the French identify an Iranian source in one of their security agencies."

"How were you able to identify the French spy?" Josh asked.

"Well, the French suspected the employee might be spying for someone, but they didn't know for whom or how. Their suspicions were based on changes some of his colleagues had noticed in his behavior at work. The suspect was scheduled to take an Aegean cruise that would start in Athens and take him to the Greek Isles, Kusadasi-Ephesus, and Istanbul." The French gave his itinerary to the CIA and asked if the CIA could help. They turned to us, and we looked for the travel of intel officers that might correlate to that itinerary. We found an Iranian who'd made a hotel reservation in Kusadasi at the same time the Frenchman's cruise ship was scheduled to stop there. CIA provided that info to the French. They had a small team surveil the guy, and saw him meet with the Iranian at a cafe there. The French couldn't do anything there because they were on Turkish soil. However, when the guy returned to France, they confronted him with photos of the meeting, and he admitted that he'd been spying for the Iranians for some five years.

"Actually, there was another CIA request in February. They asked if we could look through our data to see if we had any info about a possible MOIS officer traveling to Ribeauvillé in Alsace. We found a hotel reservation and a car rental. We couldn't say the guy was definitely MOIS, but he used some of the MOIS travel practices.

"We've also met with the CIA to discuss how they could

examine their own vulnerabilities to avoid exploitation of their travel practices. Since they'd had years of experience arranging travel for their officers, they were skeptical that we could provide any useful advice. When we described our methodology, they looked at their own practices and realized how very vulnerable they were.

"One interesting aspect of our effort is that it requires very little in the way of foreign-language skills.

"One problem we do have is occasional turf disputes with NSA geographic organizations because they feel that anything involving their target country should be handled by them. Our view is that our work, which involves analysis of transactions of international commercial organizations, often requires very different techniques and skills. I understand their view, but we know from years of experience that our processes work better for this type of endeavor, and their processes work best for handling governmental comms.

"We do our best to resolve the disputes by suggesting that we work as teams and not as disconnected rivals. That usually works, but personalities sometimes make it difficult to resolve our differences. It's not that one side is bad and the other is good. Each side is dedicated to getting the job done and serving the American people. They just have different views of the most effective way to do that.

"There's one thing that I feel helps me advance our analytic efforts. I try to closely track how technological changes create behavioral changes in foreign societies, creating new vulnerabilities among our targets. Whenever possible, I purchase new personal electronic equipment or software that has communications implications. By not only reading about new technology, but by using it myself, I try to understand its potential. I've encouraged that same mind set among those who work for me. In fact, we have monthly brown-bag lunch sessions in the office to brainstorm about the significance of new hardware, apps, etc.

"I think I've pretty much covered my analytic career. Is there anything else you'd like me to describe?"

"Yes," Josh said. "Have you found that ambient noise interferes with your analytic efforts? For example, when people are yakking socially nearby."

"Not really," J.B. responded. "I feel like I've got a noise filter that I can activate in my brain whenever I need it. Noise doesn't seem to impact my analytic efforts one way or another."

"Can you think of any specific conditions that stimulate your analytic thinking?" Josh asked.

"The one thing that always energizes the analytic gears in my brain is a new challenge. I'm driven to look for answers. I believe they're out there and just need to be intellectually discovered."

"Thanks, J.B.. That's very helpful. That's all I have at the moment," Josh commented. "What about you, Daniel?"

"I can't think of anything either. I have to say that I'm really impressed."

"Like Daniel, I found our discussion fascinating," Josh added. "I was completely unaware of your efforts. Aah! There is another question that I almost forgot. It relates to your youth."

"Please ask," J.B. responded.

"Well, this is something I started thinking about after reflecting on the first interviews we did. I wonder if either or both of two factors might have helped your problem-solving abilities.

"The first is that people who live in heavily urbanized areas have access to lots of goods and services. For example, it's easy to head to the nearest Home Depot or Lowe's or Wal-Mart to buy inexpensive replacement parts. Those resources are far less accessible in rural areas, and even less so when you were growing up. Today, people in rural areas can use the Internet to order hard-to-get parts or tools. That also wasn't available when you were growing up.

"Secondly, families who have limited financial resources often save money by trying to do their own maintenance and repair. That involves analyzing diverse problems and developing solutions.

"When I was growing up," Josh continued, "we lived in an urban area and my dad had a good-paying job. He also was very busy at work, so he was quick to pay others to provide needed goods and services, and those items were readily available where we lived.

"So I wonder first about the extent to which your family had to solve its own maintenance problems, and the extent to which your parents involved you and your siblings."

"Interesting! I've never given that much thought. First of all, we lived in a very rural area. Secondly, while my father earned enough money to provide us with the basic necessities, he didn't have much money to spare. Consequently, he tried to solve as many problems as he could on his own, whether they were mechanical or electrical, and whether they involved our house, or our car, or our equipment. Whenever he worked on a problem, he pulled in my older brother and me. He initially used to explain the problems and show us how to fix them. As my brother and I learned, dad started asking us to diagnose the problems ourselves, and figure out solutions. In some cases, he would show us how to jury rig solutions in unconventional ways that would allow him to avoid buying replacement parts. In those days, automobiles and equipment were far simpler, so it was much easier to diagnose and solve problems.

"I'd never given any thought to that, but you may have hit on something. I've always been grateful to dad, because what he taught me has helped me solve problems around my own house. I never connected that learning to my analytic work. I wish dad was still around so I could thank him even more."

"Thanks! I think we'll need to ask Baeradaer Bishtaer, Pete, and Mike if their situations were in any way similar to yours," Josh said. "We're going to have to thank Pete Schlauman for recommending that we talk to you."

"Well, Pete's a great guy. He and I have solved some interesting problems by teaming up," J.B. answered. "I really enjoyed talking about my favorite subject. I probably won't have too many more opportunities because I'm planning to retire in a couple of months."

"I think that'll be a big loss to the Intel Community. Hopefully, we'll have a chance to meet with you again. Are you planning to go back to Louisiana?"

"No, my wife and I are thinking of moving to someplace on the coast of New England. Please give me a call any time before then. I'd be happy to come back and chat with you some more."

Daniel and Josh wished him well.

When he left, Josh commented, "What a great guy. We have to keep him very much in mind. If the right opportunity presents itself in our efforts to uncover this Iranian spy, we'll have to ask the Director and Johnnie if we can invite J.B. to join Team Triad."

"My sentiments exactly," Daniel agreed.

"As soon as we finish discussing the interview, I'll give Johnnie a call and suggest that he and the others keep J.B.'s talents in mind," Josh added. "What new conclusions have you reached from this interview?"

"I'll take a stab at four thoughts. I'm fairly confident about the first two because they also relate to my work. However, I'm not that confident about the other two because I don't have your depth of experience," Daniel commented.

"Go ahead. I'm willing to bet we're on the same wave length."

"Well, the first that I feel most comfortable about relates to the team approach to some analytic solutions. The second involves sometimes trying to solve small individual problems rather than attempting to create elegant mega solutions.

"The team-solution approach is different than the individual expert approach that BB and Mike and Pete and Carolyn and you represent. To me, the type of approach that works best depends on the problem. Neither is the only solution. I've found many instances in which two or more minds come up with better and faster solutions than one individual, especially when the players have very different backgrounds or training or mind-sets.

"I've also found that addressing small individual problems can lead to faster solutions, and then combining some small solutions can create a large set of solutions that complement one another. That's what happened with Linux. Torvalds didn't start to create a mega system. It just developed that way as thousands of people all over the world contributed individual solutions to small problems.

"The first observation that I feel less comfortable about is my impression that J.B.'s unique analytic skills have something to do with his education in investigative journalism, but perhaps the Cryptologic School has similar training," Daniel said.

"I suspect you're right about the journalism training. We'll have to see if the Cryptologic School offers that kind of training. If not, it might be interesting to incorporate some form of it into the school's curriculum. Let's explore that further and perhaps include a suggestion about that in our final report. What's your second conclusion?"

"I'm wondering if there are two factors that left him more open to non-traditional SIGINT. The first is that he wasn't in the military and didn't receive strong military training in the basics of SIGINT. The second involves the mix of intern tours. The two that he had in traditional SIGINT turned him off because they were too limiting; while the three tours in non-traditional SIGINT gave him a lot of freedom and taught him skills that would help with tracking analysis."

"Again, I agree completely," Josh responded. "You clearly see to the heart of things. Perhaps an important suggestion we can make is that all new analysts be exposed to both traditional and non-traditional analytic endeavors.

"There's one thing I wish we could explore in some substantive way; and that's the extent to which ethnic background might contribute beyond obvious factors like learning one's ethnic language. Look at the ethnic mosaic of the people we've interviewed, plus you, and Kat, and me. Lots of talent, but with very diverse ethnic backgrounds. I'd appreciate it if you would think about how we could analyze that issue."

"I'll give it some thought," Daniel replied, "but I'm not optimistic that I'll be able to suggest anything. Although in my case, it's simply a matter of native genius. Ha! Ha!"

"Then that native genius should be able to find a solution," Josh joked.

When they finished discussing the interview, Josh phoned Johnnie and described J.B.'s skills and how they might contribute at some point.

While Josh was talking to Johnnie, Daniel called Kat in the hopes of hearing about some interesting developments. There was nothing exciting. The number of players using the app was steadily increasing, but there were no major comments and there was no unusual use. Daniel was disappointed, but not surprised. He thanked her, and said he'd call the next day before they sent the Director an email update. Daniel informed Josh when he got off the phone with Johnnie.

Josh then said he'd like to begin moving on to interviews with outstanding analysts in other Agency organizations. He thought it would be a good idea to do three interviews per week, on three different afternoons - Monday, Wednesday, and Thursday. If there were Meta developments that required action, they could reduce the number of interviews. Daniel agreed.

Josh estimated there were probably about 20 additional analysts and language analysts for them to interview at NSA HQ. After that, they could interview exceptional problem solvers from other NSA professions such as CA and engineering. Then they could consider analysts at other locations away from NSA HQ, at military organizations, at Cyber Command, at other U.S. intelligence agencies and at GCHQ.

Daniel suggested that perhaps they could try to interview some experts who were visiting NSA on other business. That would save time and money. Josh thought that was a great idea and said he'd contact the organizations of interest and discuss making the necessary arrangements.

Josh then started calling and arranging appointments with some of the analysts on their list of people to be interviewed. He set up interviews for the following two weeks.

Seventeen

Morris Code

Friday April 24

Marilyn Carter arranged a nine thirty meeting for Josh and Daniel to interview Levy Morris. Since she admired him so much, she convinced Josh to let her meet Morris at the Visitor Center and escort him to their office. They arrived on time. As Morris walked in the door, Daniel and Josh noted his demeanor and body language - he was very relaxed, and had a warm, engaging smile. They noticed that Marilyn looked at him with open admiration. He was a good-looking guy, probably in his early sixties.

Josh began the conversation - "Thanks for coming Mr. Morris."

Morris interrupted - "Please call me Lev." He then turned to Marilyn and thanked her for accompanying him.

"It was my pleasure. It's always nice to see you."

"The feeling's mutual. You're always so supportive and helpful." Marilyn smiled, then turned and left.

Josh and Daniel introduced themselves and invited Lev to sit down.

Lev told them that Marilyn had briefly described their project, and had aroused his curiosity. He loved innovative efforts to improve NSA's capabilities, and felt it was very important to complement NSA's excellent traditional classroom training with out-of-the-box, innovative development efforts for two reasons. First, the rate of technological change and advancement was far faster than It had been in the past. Second, high-interest, innovative training and development could help motivate tech experts to continue to work for the government, and not leave for much higher pay and benefits in the private sector.

Josh and Daniel proceeded to give Lev a detailed description of the project. Then they went through their usual approach of describing their own backgrounds.

As Daniel began to talk about his background, Lev interrupted. "I don't know if you remember this, Daniel, but you and I had some interaction on Project Panache in the late 1980s, early in your career. You created Merlin, a powerful software solution to a complex SIGINT challenge. The software had very broad application and was based on your unique adaptation of an open-source, private-sector development. Since that time, I've followed your career very closely."

Daniel was a bit embarrassed because he didn't remember Lev.

"You must be thinking of a different Daniel Dechado," Josh joked. "This one usually depends on me for creative solutions."

"Thanks for the compliment," Daniel reacted, ignoring Josh's remark. "I was really happy with how that application turned out." Daniel then talked about his background prior to being hired by the Agency.

When Daniel finished, Josh asked Lev if he could describe his background, as well as his career at the Agency.

"I was the grandson of Jewish immigrants from Odessa in the former Russian Empire and what is now the Ukraine," he began. "They fled after the October 1905 anti-Semitic pogrom in which a number of Jews were massacred.

"I was born and raised in the Jewish community in Manhattan's Lower East Side. Both my grandfathers worked in garment factories, and my dad owned and operated a children's clothing store. I worked in his store from the time I was in second grade until I graduated from NYU. From my grandfathers and my father, I learned every aspect of clothing and operating a small business. My mother was an intellectual who loved English literature and philosophy, as well as foreign affairs and culture. She inspired in me a devotion to life-long learning. My parents and grandparents were not religious. However, they drilled into me the importance of treating all others as equals, no matter their race, religion, ethnicity, or gender. That value included never telling jokes that implied stupidity of other groups. I once made the mistake of telling a Polish joke and was severely chastised. They explained that belittling other groups is divisive. It's a tactic that demagogues use to move majorities in the direction of 'solving' problems with minorities. What some view as 'politically correct,' I view as unifying.

"I loved the culture of the Lower East Side - the delis, like Katz's; the bakeries, like Kossar's Bialys; the pickle stores, like Guss' Pickles, etc.

"At NYU, I majored in government and politics, and minored in Middle Eastern Studies. In my senior year, I heard about and attended an NSA recruiting presentation at NYU. Even though the recruiters said very little about what NSA did, I was intrigued by what little they did say; so I applied and was accepted.

"At NSA, I became deeply involved in the collection and analysis of Soviet comms. Over time, I became experienced in almost every aspect of those comms, some of which were extremely challenging.

"About a third of the way into my career, I became a supervisor. As I advanced into middle and upper management, my responsibilities grew to encompass ever larger collection activities."

"We hear that you're very skilled at identifying and developing talent in others," Josh commented. "Can you explain how you do that?"

"To me, those two responsibilities are among the most important a manager has - both for the success of the manager's own operation, and for his entire agency or company. Even though I've primarily been involved in managing collection operations, I believe that what I'm about to say applies to any endeavor in which creativity and problem-solving are important.

"When I interview applicants for jobs that are challenging, or even when I just meet young people, I ask them questions which help me understand how they think. I might ask a simple question like, 'How do you open a drawer?' Most would reply, 'You pull it, of course.' However, some sharper individuals immediately analyze my question and guess my motive for asking. I look for an answer like, 'It depends on what a user needs. If a person needs both hands to hold items going into a drawer, you could have a foot pedal opener, or for handicapped people, you might have a spring-loaded drawer that opens by pressing a button.' In today's high-tech world, I like an answer suggesting a voice-activated opening and closing mechanism. I don't really care about the specific solution. I just want to get a sense of their creative genes.

"Another example of a question I ask is, 'What would you do if one of two toilets you have won't stop running?' I look for the person who says, 'I'd try to figure out what's wrong and fix it,' not the one who says, 'I'd call a plumber.' "

"When talking to more experienced people, I try to distinguish between 'experts' who have only memorized standard problems and solutions, and those who love to solve new problems.

"I ask all of them to describe the most difficult challenges they've solved, not just at work, but in any aspect of their lives. I try to look beyond appearance and personality, 'though that can sometimes be difficult. Often, the sharpest technical people have little or no interest in appearance.

"Once I identify and select those I feel are right for my organization, I try to give them experiences and training that will develop their talents as quickly as possible. I choose responsibilities which I think are at the upper edge of their capabilities, but not beyond. It can be a disaster to give an individual an assignment that is beyond his or her capabilities. It can crush the person and create major problems for the mission.

"I pair inexperienced people with talented professionals who'll tutor them as they work together. Additionally, I try to distinguish between several types of talented people - those who are egocentric and those who work easily with others. Some extraordinary people are good at teamwork and some are terrible. I try to develop both, but in different ways. Both types can make major contributions in different types of situations, so it's best to match the type of individual to the type of challenge.

"When the best ones move on to other jobs, I try to keep in touch and mentor them. I let them know they can come to me for advice any time they face really tough challenges.

"With regard to exceptional people, I recommend that you read the bios of some of our greatest cryptologic pioneers like William and Elizebeth Friedman, and Lambros Callimahos. All three were incredibly talented, fascinating individuals. Both William and Lambros were immigrants brought to the U.S. by their parents. You might get some clues from their bios about what made them so great.

"William Friedman was born in the former Russian Empire in what is now Moldova. His family emigrated to the U.S. to escape anti-Semitism. He originally worked in genetics at Riverbank Laboratories, a private-sector organization, but became interested in cryptanalysis because Elizebeth, a co-worker and love interest who later became his wife, was working in that field. He joined the U.S. Government during World War I, and brought mathematics and scientific methodology to cryptology.

"Elizebeth was a superb cryptanalyst who was the nation's first female in that profession. She solved well in excess of 12,000 messages herself. She may have been a better cryptanalyst than William.

The Friedmans were so important to U.S. cryptology that the Ops 1 building at NSA is dedicated to them.

"Callimahos was not only brilliant and multitalented, but was quite a character. He was born of Greek parents in Egypt in 1910 and his parents brought him to the U.S. in 1914. He studied law at Rutgers, got a music degree from Julliard, and toured as a flutist. He joined the Army in 1941, and taught cryptology and Italian. Then he studied Japanese. After that, he was assigned to the China-Burma-India Theater in World War II. Following the war, he worked as an assistant to William Friedman. He created an advanced course in CA and taught it for many years, training the most advanced cryptanalysts at NSA. He created a society for his graduates, and named that group the Dundee Society, after an empty jam jar on his desk. He created that name in order to give the society a name that was totally unrelated to the organization's purpose.

"Another important factor to consider is management style. The old Industrial Revolution model of managers who are dictatorial and micro-managers does not always work for today's great talent, the best of whom have many job options. The wrong type of manager can drive away top talent and create poor morale and productivity among those who remain. Of course, there are brilliant old-style managers like Steve Jobs, so we can't dismiss them. You may want to explore that issue."

Josh and Daniel thanked Lev for his insights. He said it was his pleasure and he'd be happy to return for further discussion. Josh called Marilyn, who came and escorted Lev back to the Visitor Center.

After Lev departed, Josh and Daniel what they'd learned from him and how to incorporate it into their recommendations to the Director.

"Terrific guy!" Josh remarked. "Too bad he's no longer at the Agency. What jumps out at you from that interview, Daniel?" Josh asked.

"Two things. First, I think it would be useful to include in the hiring process techniques that help to identify those who not only have superior technical skills and academic knowledge, but those who are-out-of-the-box thinkers. Second, we should recommend a special, high-powered mentoring program for the most talented young innovators. My ideas apply not only to analysts, but to techies as well. What do you think?"

"I completely agree. I can't add anything to that."

"Of course you can't! I'm always at the leading edge of progress," Daniel joked. "Hopefully, you'll learn something from my observing my brilliant thought processes."

"I'll do my best," Josh laughed.

Josh decided it might be useful to do an in-person update with the Director and Mac, because there were a number of topics to cover. He called Sofie and asked to meet with the Director. She told him he'd be available at five, so Josh called Mac to let him know.

Just before five, Daniel checked with Kat to see if there were any major game developments. There were none.

Josh informed the Director and Mac of the game status, the main takeaways from the interviews with Carolyn, J.B., and Lev, and the interview schedule they'd developed for Metanalysis.

Both Josh and Daniel commented on how impressed they were with the analytic specialty of J.B. and his colleagues. The Director and Mac were aware of the endeavor, but hadn't had detailed discussions about it. The Director told Josh to let Sofie know he wanted a briefing on the topic from J.B.

After the update session, Daniel called Kat and asked her about her plans to monitor the game status over the weekend. She said she'd come at midafternoon on Saturday and Sunday, and would let them know if she found anything.

Eighteen

A One-Room Ephishiency[22]

Sunday April 26

At about three in the afternoon, Daniel was at home developing a hardware-software cyber defense tool when the phone rang. "Hi, Dr. Dechado, it's Kat. I hope I'm not calling at a bad time."

"No problem, Kat, I'm just in the middle of developing the greatest cyber defense tool ever."

"I'm sorry. Should I call back at another time or should I call Josh?"

"Just joking, Kat. What's going on?"

"Well, there's an interesting development you might like to see."

"Great. I'll call Josh to see if he's available. Then, I'll come in. See you shortly."

Daniel phoned Josh, and greeted him with "Saelam Agha," the Persian greeting he'd heard Josh use with others.

"Hey Daniel, you're getting into the Persian thing. Good show! What's going on?"

"Kat just called to say there's something we might like to see right away. Are you available?"

"Your timing is great. I just finished installing a new faucet in our kitchen sink. I'll head into work as soon as I take a couple of minutes to clean up."

"Great. See you soon, and khoda hafez."

---

[22] From "phishing."

"Khoda hafez e shomah," Josh answered with a chuckle. Josh was grateful he'd finished the faucet installation, which had been a pain because of the tight working area beneath the sink.

Josh couldn't easily explain to Meihui why he suddenly had to go into work. She was used to such call-ins, but not for something like an analytic project that was not time-sensitive. He could only tell her that Daniel had learned something of high interest to the Director, and that they'd have to discuss it with him in the morning. He didn't expect to be gone more than a couple of hours, but would call her if he had to stay longer.

Both Daniel and Josh arrived at Kat's office within half an hour. Their trips were fast because Sunday afternoon traffic was very light along their usual routes to work.

Daniel arrived first. "Hey, Kat. What's going on?" he asked.

"Well, there've been two very interesting developments," she answered, as Josh entered.

"Hi, Josh," Daniel greeted Josh. "Kat tells me she's got a couple of interesting things to tell us about."

"Hi, Kat. I'm all ears. What's going on?"

"First, one individual has played the game many times over the course of three hours. That same player posted a very lengthy comment after playing the game. The comment is in a foreign language with a writing system like Persian or Arabic. I've got the player's comment up on the screen."

"It's Persian," Josh said "From a quick scan, I can see that the player's a guy - a former soldier. He says the game's very interesting and he enjoyed playing it. He appreciates that the game developers tried to capture the essence of a military action called Operation Beit al-Moqaddas. He feels it's important to let the developers know that they've exaggerated the heroism of a soldier named Mirza Behrangi. The player says it's Allah who inspired Behrangi, and it was Behrangi's comrades who did the bulk of the fighting. The player says he was present at the battle, and he then proceeds to describe how the action took place. He says he'd be happy to provide any additional details."

"Great show, Kat," Daniel said with a big smile. "That's our guy!"

"I've identified the player's computer and gained unlimited access to it. I've also found his contacts file." She brought up a screen which showed the player's hard drive and contacts file.

"That's fantastic! Can you make a copy of the contacts file?" Josh asked.

"I thought you might want it, so I've already done it. Here it is," she said as she displayed it for Josh to see.

He searched through the file and found four phone numbers of high interest - a cell phone number and a land line number for "Sayyed," and the same for the computer user.

"Can you access the user's email account?" Daniel asked.

"I've already done that too, and I've copied all his emails into a file on this computer," she said.

"Could you please open the email file?" Josh asked.

"Sure. Here it is."

"Thanks, Kat," Josh said as he began to read through the emails. After reading a few, he said, "This is our guy. You've done an incredible job, Kat! Now I see why Daniel thinks you're so talented."

Josh described to Daniel the game changes that Behrangi had suggested, and asked Daniel how long it would take to make those changes. He said he could easily make them in the morning.

Next, Josh responded to the player's comments by thanking him and stating that the developer would be happy to make the suggested changes.

After that, Kat informed Daniel and Josh that the player's computer mike and video camera were activated. They'd be able to hear anything he said within range of the mike, and to see anything in view of the camera. In other words, they could do a one-way Skype.

She'd also made copies of all of the player's file folders for Josh and Daniel to browse.

They again complimented her on the superb and thorough job she'd done. She was especially pleased by her mentor's compliments, and beamed with pride. Daniel was delighted to see that another of his protégés had done so well, and it was very rewarding to see the results of his efforts to develop young talent.

Daniel told Josh they could now use the SS7 vulnerabilities of the Supreme Leader and Behrangi to monitor their activities. He suggested they inform the Director before exploiting the cell phones.

Josh agreed and said he'd request an appointment with the Director first thing in the morning.

Josh told Kat he'd like to browse the user's file folders for a bit before heading home. She brought up the directory with the folders and turned the computer over to Josh. As he looked through the folder names, one jumped out at him. It was, "Shaediha-Shaejoro," which seemed to fit the name encoding system the Supreme Leader had set up with Behrangi years earlier. If the Ayatollah's name encoding system had been used to name the folder, it would refer to two Americans.

Josh knew that no professional intel service like the MOIS would use such a system. They'd use cover names that bore no relationship to the real name of the source. However, the Supreme Leader and Behrangi were not intel professionals. Like many amateurs, the Supreme Leader had concocted a system that was fairly susceptible to analysis, given sufficient context.

Normally, an intel service would not share the real identities of its sources with others except the most senior government official or officials, like a president or a prime minister. In this case, the MOIS probably shared the identity with the Supreme Leader, and he may have shared it when meeting in person with Behrangi.

Josh opened the folder and found two subfolders - one labeled Shaediha, and the other named Shaejoro. Each contained only one small document that was a mix of letters that made no sense - probably a cryptogram. Each cryptogram document file had the same name as the subfolder it was in.

The Shaediha document was:

TCTTAHREFEAEUSLSSALIOWNASS
WVDTNSSIEUSKLIOSOYEHHEOTL
IFDXLAECWOTSHOXDRTBNSLHITX
FDBUEIWTDNAISULEENIEEEHREE
UIYLRDS

The Shaejoro document was:

ICSRTYSFEEVORFTRUNHULHTHD
STEXYRACSFIENLWNHUIGSEELP
IOANTRDXYZDOMONIELEWILSYW
EIYPXSTORAWXYZAYHSUEEESIS

He asked Kat to print a copy of each document for him.

Daniel and Josh then thanked and complimented Kat again. They said there was no reason for her to stay longer. They'd call her in the morning as soon as they found out if and when they could meet with the Director. They'd check with her then to see if there were any new developments.

They left her and went to their office, where they chatted for a couple of minutes about meeting with the Director.

Josh wanted to take a shot at solving the two cryptograms before heading home, so he called Meihui to let her know he'd be staying a couple of hours longer.

First he took a close look at the Shaediha cryptogram. The frequency of various letters suggested it might be a columnar transposition encryption system rather than a substitution system. A transposition system is one in which the original letters are not enciphered. Instead they are transposed in a systematic way. For example, the original letters of a message are written into rows of a matrix. The letters are then taken out of that matrix in columns. The columns are extracted from the matrix in a scrambled order.

In the following example, the message, "Security is my most

important duty" is written into a matrix in rows.

	1	2	3	4	5
1	S	E	C	U	R
2	I	T	Y	I	S
2	M	Y	M	O	S
4	T	I	M	P	O
5	R	T	A	N	T
6	D	U	T	Y	X

The columns are then extracted in groups of 5 in the order 5, 3, 1, 4, 2:

RSSOT XCYMM ATSIM TRDUI OPNYE TYITU.

Josh counted the number of letters and saw that the total came to 110. He then noticed the three Xs, and figured out a couple of interesting things about them mathematically. That allowed him to easily figure out their function. He solved the cryptogram within a couple of minutes.[iii] Josh shared the very interesting results with Daniel.

Josh then examined the Shaejoro cryptogram. He concluded it was also encrypted using columnar transposition. The total number of letters came to 100, which suggested a 10 x 10 matrix. This one was also easy to solve, despite the fact that the unencrypted text was written into the matrix in a very different way.[iv] Josh shared this equally interesting text with Daniel.

It seemed clear to Josh that Behrangi was keeping notes for himself, but trying to use three layers of protection to prevent others from understanding the substance. First he encrypted the names of the subjects - Shaediha and Shaejoro - using the naming system devised by the Ayatollah. Second, he wrote very cryptic notes to himself. Third, he encrypted those notes. Without the insights Pete Schlauman had given them in his interview, they'd have had no clue as to the significance of the cover names.

While Josh always enjoyed the mental exercise of solving

cryptograms, there was far greater psychic income when the resultant plaintext provided high-value information.

By now, it was nearly half past eight. Josh and Daniel were delighted with the significant progress they'd made. They decided to call it a night, so they locked up and headed home.

When Josh arrived home, he told Meihui that he and Daniel had a very interesting discussion, and that they hoped to meet with the Director in the morning. It was now very clear to her that Josh was involved in some sort of effort that was time-sensitive, or that there was some unusual aspect to the Metanalysis project that she didn't appreciate.

Monday April 27

When Josh and Daniel were both at the office, Josh phoned Sofie and said it was very important that he and Daniel see the Director as soon as possible, and that Mac participate if he was available. She called back in about ten minutes and said the Director and Mac would be available at nine fifteen. Josh thanked her.

Before meeting with the Director, Josh phoned Kat to see if there was anything new. There wasn't.

Josh informed the Director and Mac that the game had produced results. On the basis of the two cryptograms and their file names, it was possible that the Iranians had two American sources. The first probably had the initials, "D.H." It appeared the Iranians had something they were holding over the source's head. There was nothing to tie this possible source to the nuclear leaks. The creation date of the file was October 1, 2014, indicating the source had begun to work for the Iranians prior to that date.

The second possible source probably had the initials, "J.R." and might be a DOE employee. His motivation appeared to be money. There was also nothing to tie this possible source to the nuclear leaks. The creation date of the file about this source was April 14, 2014.

Josh said he planned to spend the day reading through Behrangi's folders and email to see if he could find more information of value.

Josh asked the Director for permission to exploit the phones of Behrangi and the Supreme Leader. The Director assented and instructed that all material from the Supreme Leader's phone, including phone calls, texts, and contacts should only be processed by Josh until the spy had been identified and stopped. The Director did not want to risk losing this potentially valuable source. If the workload became too great, the Director would revisit this approach. He added that any SIGINT published from this source had to be sent "eyes only" to the President, the DNI, the Secretaries of State, Defense, and Energy, and the CIA and FBI Directors. It could also be discussed with Team Triad members. The Director wanted to review such reports before they were distributed.

Mac said he'd make the necessary arrangements.

Josh and Daniel praised the great work that Kat had done. Daniel was very proud of her accomplishment.

The Director and Mac complimented Daniel and Josh on their success, and the admiral said he'd call the DNI immediately to let her know. He asked Josh and Daniel to inform him right away if they learned anything more related to the nuclear spy.

Josh and Daniel returned to their office, where Josh phoned Johnnie to give him the promising news. He told Johnnie that he'd personally call Shellie to tell her and thank her for her contribution. Johnnie said he'd work with Shellie, Gianni, and Farida to look for individuals with the initials D.H. and J.R. who had access to high-level briefings on intel relating to Iranian nuclear activities and the negotiations with Iran. Johnnie asked Josh to phone immediately if he found any new info about D.H. or J.R.

The two left their office to go work with Kat. "Hey Kat!" Daniel began, "Josh and I just had a great meeting with the Director and Mac Roberts. We told them what a great job you've done." Her face really lit up. It wasn't often that someone at her grade level was praised to the Director and Mac. "Of course," joked Daniel, "I explained that your success was mostly due to mentoring and inspiration from me."

"Well," she said, "A lot of that's true. You've made a big difference in teaching me how to approach difficult problems."

"Could you please download all of Behrangi's emails, contacts, and folders onto a DVD so I can take them and upload them onto the stand-alone, high-side computer in my office?" Josh asked.

"Sure thing," she replied. She quickly downloaded Behrangi's data and gave it to Josh.

"I'd also be grateful," Josh said to Kat and Daniel "if you guys could get a copy of the Ayatollah's contact list, and make a copy for me."

"You bet," Daniel replied.

When Josh left, Daniel worked with Kat to begin exploiting the cell phones of Behrangi and the Supreme Leader. It turned out that Behrangi's cell phone was not a smart phone, so they could only use their access to track his movements and listen to his phone calls.

On the other hand, the Ayatollah's phone was a smart phone with lots of data, primarily contacts. There were also some apps. Since they were in Persian, Daniel couldn't figure out what they were. He made a copy of the Ayatollah's contacts, and apps, downloaded them onto a DVD, and took them to Josh.

When Daniel arrived at the office, Josh had already uploaded Behrangi's data and had begun to read through it. Josh stopped what he was doing and uploaded the Supreme Leader's contact list. He began looking through it and found a contact of very high interest - the head of the MOIS. Josh asked Daniel if he'd ask Kat to work with Mac to make sure he received a copy of any phone calls between the Supreme Leader and the head of the MOIS. When Josh examined the apps, he found they were all religious.

Josh then resumed reading through Behrangi's computer data.

Daniel returned to Kat's office and passed on Josh's phone call request.

After Daniel finished with Kat, he returned to his office and began to update the game on the basis of Behrangi's input. He finished the update by early afternoon, and then took the revised version to Kat to update the on-line version. She did that immediately.

By the end of the day, Josh had scrutinized all Behrangi's files, emails, and contacts. He was disappointed to find nothing else relating to the possible nuclear spies. He did find a couple of interesting-sounding contacts, but nothing exciting.

By the end of the afternoon, Mac had worked out a process to rapidly transfer to Josh and Daniel the audio of phone calls between the Supreme Leader and Behrangi or the head of the MOIS, the audio picked up by the mike on Behrangi's computer, and new emails to or from Behrangi.

Within a week, a couple of things would become clear. The Ayatollah rarely used his cell phone to discuss substantive issues with anyone. Behrangi called the Ayatollah once or twice per week to chat. They usually did not discuss sensitive government issues, but they did gossip about key individuals, both Iranian and foreign.

When Josh listened to the two men talking, he saw that they easily fit in with his *Group Discovery and Affiliation Analysis* concept. It was clear that each belonged to a different group. Even if a listener knew neither man, the listener could make certain observations about them on the basis of how they articulated their views. It was obvious that the Ayatollah was a senior religious figure who held some sort of power and who looked at the big picture. Behrangi, on the other hand, was a straight-talking military guy who respected authority, and who was in a different and lower class than the other speaker. What they had in common was respect for each other, common ethnicity, and devotion to religion and country.

Tuesday April 28

Josh phoned Johnnie to see if they'd found any individuals with the initials D.H. or J.R. who had the right kind of access.

"Well, we've got a wealth of possibilities who have the initials D.H. and who've attended high-level briefings on the Iran negotiations. The seven individuals are:
- A State Department staffer supporting the negotiations
- A midlevel CIA manager
- A DIA analyst
- A National Security Council staffer
- A senator on the SSCI
- A congressman on the House Armed Services Committee
- A Congressional staffer on the HPSCI (House Permanent Select Committee on Intelligence)

"All of them are possibilities, but none of them stand out. The congressman and senator have both come out in strong opposition to the nuclear deal with Iran, but that's no surprise because there's fairly wide opposition to the deal on the Hill.

"Fortunately, there are only three candidates with the initials J.R. - a DOE staffer supporting the negotiations, a senior Defense Department official, and a congressman on the HPSCI.

"I hope to have more info to discuss at our weekly meeting on Thursday."

"I've got nothing new," Josh said. My best hope would be to get a phone call in which the Supreme Leader or MOIS director would reveal some new clue. I'll call you if we get anything new before Thursday."

"OK, Josh," take care.

In the afternoon, Josh and Daniel met with the Director and Mac. Josh, Daniel, and Mac updated the Director on the actions they'd taken and processes they'd put in place to exploit any new material quickly and properly.

Nineteen

Le Renard Rusé Qui Se Deguise en Poulet Dodu

(The Wily Fox Who Disguises Himself as a Plump Chicken)

Thursday April 30

At the Team Triad meeting, Johnnie reported further details regarding the individuals with the initials "D.H." and "J.R."

The Bureau had researched their past business, education, and travel connections with the Middle East and South Asia.

There appeared to be nothing out of the ordinary with the D.H. individuals. If more information surfaced, something that appeared ordinary might be bear closer examination. For example, what appeared to be ordinary vacation travel might suggest other possibilities.

Since there were only three people with the initials "J.R.," it was easier to find something that might cause one to stand out from the others. That was the case with the DOE staffer, Jonathan Rothstein. He was a member of a team working round-the-clock to provide support to the Secretary of Energy during times when the secretary was preparing for or participating in nuclear negotiations with the Iranians

However, the reasons he stood out had nothing to do with Iran. They had to do with his finances and a connection with Israel. While many Jewish-Americans had strong emotional connections with Israel, with rare exceptions like Jonathan Pollard, they were loyal Americans and had nothing to do with espionage on Israel's behalf.

Rothstein was in his midthirties, divorced, and had no children.

He lived in Alexandria, Virginia, just across the Potomac River from the southern part of Washington, D.C. A cursory examination of his finances suggested he was spending a lot more than he was earning, yet he had no debt. National Security Letters[23] were being used to obtain further details on his finances from banks, credit card companies, etc., and to examine his phone records.

In the second half of September 2013, he had spent two weeks in southern Spain, visiting Cordoba, Seville, the Costa del Sol, and Granada. In January 2014, he had traveled to Caracas, Venezuela for a couple of days. In the second half of September 2014, he had spent two weeks in France's Côte d'Azur and Provence at Nice, Antibes, St. Remy, and Aix. On all three trips, he was unaccompanied, rented a car and drove himself.

He had spent the summer after university graduation working on an Israeli kibbutz. He had since returned to Israel twice - in 2009 and 2012. His email address included the Hebrew word, "Herut." which means, "freedom."

Finally, they learned from his Facebook page that he was planning a 9-day trip to the Amalfi Coast beginning Saturday, May 16. He would be spending several nights in Amalfi and several in Sorrento.

It was unusual that he would take significant time off work, given his involvement in supporting the Secretary of Energy at the nuclear negotiations, which were at a critical stage.

Johnnie said the Bureau would search Rothstein's home and office, including his computers. Both efforts would pose problems. Searching the office would be a challenge because Rothstein's team was working round-the-clock so frequently. The Bureau would have

---

[23] A National Security Letter (NSL) is an administrative order that the FBI is authorized to issue, without judicial approval, to financial institutions, telephone companies, Internet service providers, etc. in situations involving national security. The NSL requires the recipient to provide transactional information regarding financial transactions, phone calls, and email exchanges. However, it does not cover the content of phone calls or emails.

to work with the DOE security office to find a time when the Secretary was not at the negotiations and the team was not working round-the-clock.

Searching Rothstein's residence in Alexandria would be a bit difficult because it was a row house. The neighbors on either side were retired couples who always seemed to be present, and would likely inform Rothstein of anything suspicious. The best time to search might be while Rothstein was in Italy. It would be best to conduct the search toward the beginning of the trip in case they discovered any info about a planned meeting with a foreign contact. The search team would install surveillance equipment in Rothstein's residence.

Agents could enter the residence under the pretext of being utilities repairmen dealing with some sort of emergency. Even that would be touchy because the neighbors might send Rothstein an email about workmen entering his residence.

Johnnie asked Shellie to work with DOE to identify a time when the Bureau could search Rothstein's office. Johnnie would work on arranging a search of his residence while he was in Italy.

The itinerary for Rothstein's trip was:

May 16 Depart U.S.

May 17 Arrive Naples, rent a car, and drive to Amalfi

May 17-19 Overnight at Amalfi, with visits to Ravello & Positano

May 20-22 Overnight at Sorrento, with visits to Pompeii & Capri

May 23 Return to U.S.

There were no specific flight or lodging details.

Josh asked if there was any indication Rothstein would be traveling with someone else. Johnnie said there wasn't.

Gianni suggested that perhaps he and Shellie could form a 2-person team to go to Italy and surveil Rothstein on his trip to see if he met with a possible foreign agent. Gianni felt that Shellie, with her Iranian background, might recognize an Iranian. With Gianni's experience as a case officer covertly meeting with spies, he might detect contact between Rothstein and a case officer. Gianni was very familiar with the area. Both sides of his family were from nearby Naples, and he'd spent three of his grade school and middle school summer vacations there with his maternal grandparents. During those vacations, he'd learned to speak the Neapolitan language, which is very different from standard Italian, and is spoken by millions of people in southern Italy.

In addition to the summers with his grandparents, he'd taken vacations to the area and other parts of Italy with his wife, son, and daughter, when he and his family were stationed in Egypt and Bahrain.

Shellie said she'd be happy to participate. However, in all her years at the Bureau, she'd never seen a surveillance operation performed by only two people. Teams were needed so given team members would only follow the suspect for a short distance and then hand the tracking over to another. That reduced the possibility of detection by the suspect. She understood the reasons for a small team - the sensitivity of this case and conducting the surveillance in another country. Doing this surveillance with just the two of them would be very challenging.

Gianni explained that the only reason this was doable was that the towns Rothstein would be visiting were small and the street layouts conducive to easily finding and observing a target. It would never work in a major urban area like Rome or Naples.

Farida said she'd once visited the area, and decided it was the one place in Italy where she wouldn't consider driving - because the main road along the coast was so narrow. She joked that the road's shoulder was a mile below the road.

Gianni laughed and said it was no big deal. In fact, it was fun. Perhaps he had Italian driving genes in his DNA.

Daniel added that if they were interested, he could go along to identify and hack into wireless network connections to look for possible intel officers. They said they'd love to have him.

The whole team liked Gianni's suggestion, and Johnnie said he'd present the idea to Director Pasquali.

Josh then added a suggestion of his own. He described in detail what he and Daniel had learned about the people-tracking analysis of J.B. and his colleagues. Josh suggested that J.B. might be able to provide unique support if he became a member of Team Triad. He could perhaps identify one or more foreign intel operatives traveling to the same places at the same time as J.R., and he could search for other relevant movements.

The others liked that idea as well, and Johnnie said he'd add that to his recommendations to Director Pasquali. He'd let them all know the results by the end of the day.

After completing their lengthy discussions, the group returned to their offices.

As soon as Josh and Daniel got back to NSA, Josh called Sofie and asked if he and Daniel could meet with the Director that afternoon. Sofie said she'd let him know shortly. Sofie, who'd never been briefed on Meta, could not imagine why Josh and Daniel had to meet with the Director so often and on short notice when they were supposedly working on a long-term project that wasn't time-sensitive. And, the Director always responded positively to their requests. Something else had to be going on. She wished she could ask.

She called Josh back to let him know they could come at three.

Josh then phoned Mac to let him know. Mac wasn't available to take his call, so Josh informed Mac's secretary about the meeting. If Mac couldn't come, Josh would phone him afterwards with the details.

When Josh and Daniel met with the Director, Mac wasn't there. They apologized for interrupting him so frequently when he was so busy. The Admiral responded that they were doing exactly what he wanted. He'd let them know if he wanted any changes in their criteria for meeting with him on short notice.

Josh updated him on what the Bureau had learned about D.H. and J.R.; on Gianni's surveillance recommendation, including Daniel accompanying them; and on Josh's suggestion that J.B. become a member of Team Triad.

The Director thanked them and said that if the FBI Director approved, Josh and Daniel could brief J.B. on the project and invite him to join. J.B. would continue to work out of his own office and could not tell anyone else about the project. His job would be to use his tracking techniques to look for movements of intel officers. He wouldn't be allowed to track either J.R. or D.H. because they were U.S. persons and beyond NSA's scope of authority without a court order. Daniel could accompany the surveillance team, and target the wireless use of foreigners, but not of J.R.

Josh and Daniel thanked him and left. Josh phoned Mac and updated him.

Just after four, Johnnie called Josh to inform him that Director Pasquali had discussed the surveillance initiative with CIA Director Rolph, and they'd approved it. The CIA Director would call the CIA Chief of Station in Rome to let him know and advise him not to share the information with anyone. The director also approved the recommendation that J.B. join the team.

Josh immediately phoned J.B. and asked if he could come to meet with him and Daniel ASAP to discuss a special request.

J.B. arrived within minutes, eager to find out what was going on. He couldn't imagine how their work on the Metanalysis project would require an urgent meeting.

Josh explained that he and Daniel were working for the Director on an extremely sensitive project, in addition to Metanalysis. They could only discuss the project with a handful of people, whom they named. They'd recommended to the FBI Director and to Admiral Saunders that J.B. join them. They asked if he'd be willing to take on the task.

J.B. said he couldn't imagine what it would be, but if it required approval from the heads of the NSA and FBI, it had to be of high value and very interesting. He'd love to be involved.

Josh then explained that he and Daniel were actually working on two very different projects, the Metanalysis project, which he knew about, and an effort to identify one or more Americans spying for the Iranians. When they'd interviewed him a week earlier, they'd been very impressed, and thought he might be able to contribute to the counterespionage effort, which they called *Meta*. They'd learned something that very morning that led them to believe he could be of immediate assistance.

They described all that had occurred to date on Meta, ending with Rothstein's upcoming trip to the Amalfi Coast and the planned surveillance by Gianni, Shellie, and Daniel.

They explained the possibility of Rothstein meeting with a foreign intel operative - an Iranian, or an Israeli, or perhaps both. They hoped J.B. could uncover the travel of one or more intel officers to the Amalfi Coast at the time of Rothstein's trip. They asked J.B. to let them know immediately, including during weekends, if he learned anything of interest. Time would be of the essence.

J.B. said it was the type of challenge he lived for. While he'd previously done work involving Iranian travel, he'd never done anything involving the Israelis. Nonetheless, he explained there were often little indicators of intel operatives' travel - in contrast to tourist travel and travel of regular government employees.

He then repeated to Josh and Daniel what he'd just heard from them about every aspect of the project to be sure he understood all of its objectives, nuances, and limitations. He wanted to confirm he'd missed nothing.

When he described what he thought they'd said, they told him he was spot on. It occurred to Josh that this might be another indicator of the technique of a skilled analyst - make sure you really understand all the details.

Josh then gave J.B. the dates of Rothstein's travels and stops at specific locations. They didn't know his lodging plans or the sequence of his day trips at each stop.

As they were finishing the discussion, J.B. offered to help in another way. "If the team members planning the surveillance in Italy haven't made their travel arrangements, I can give them tips that'll help avoid detection by foreign intel services. Most of them devote significant resources to uncovering activities of other intel organizations."

"Great idea!!" Josh replied. "We always think offense, but I suspect we don't pay sufficient attention to defense. I'll call the head of our team as soon as you leave. What about you, Daniel?"

"I'd appreciate any travel tips. I have no experience with this sort of travel."

"OK," said J.B. "If we're finished, I'll head back to my office and get started. I'll put additional collection in place, and start analyzing the data we already have."

"Thanks J.B. Talk to you soon," Josh concluded.

It was now about five. Josh phoned Johnnie and informed him of J.B.'s offer regarding defensive travel arrangement tips. Johnnie liked the idea. He'd let Gianni and Shellie know.

Gianni called within fifteen minutes to ask if he and Shellie could meet with J.B. at NSA the next morning to discuss travel arrangements, because there wasn't a great deal of time before the trip.

Josh checked with J.B. who said he'd be available and happy to help. Josh gave him a time of ten thirty, and then phoned Gianni to inform him.

Friday May 1

Gianni and Shellie showed up on time for the travel conversation with Daniel and J.B.

Gianni thought it would be useful to spend a couple of minutes discussing the on-the-ground portion of the operation in Italy, including the nature of Amalfi and Sorrento, where Rothstein would stay, and Ravello, Positano, Capri, and Pompeii, which Rothstein's postings said he'd visit on day trips. Gianni and Shellie would do most of the physical surveillance. He thought the most productive times for Daniel to try wireless network penetration would be in the morning or evening, when the subjects were at their lodgings. If Daniel wanted, he could help at times when wireless monitoring would be least useful. Daniel agreed.

The towns involved were very popular tourist destinations, particularly from mid-spring through mid-fall. So it would be very easy to blend in.

Amalfi, where they would start, was a beautiful small town at sea level and on a hillside. It was once a powerful Maritime Republic. Positano and Ravello were close by. Each was famous and each had a very different charm. Ravello was only four miles from Amalfi, but it was 1,200 feet above sea level and was reached via a very serpentine road. It offered breathtakingly spectacular views of the coast and had provided inspiration to musicians like Richard Wagner and artists like Salvador Dali. It was here, in 1880 at age 67, that Wagner, who was staying at Villa Rufolo, was inspired to write the second act of his opera, Parsifal.

Positano was another picturesque small town, located about twelve miles west of Amalfi. It started at sea level and filled the hillsides. Gianni said it would be easier for him to handle the Ravello portion of the surveillance because it was not served as frequently by bus, so he could drive. In fact, rather than stay at Amalfi, he'd stay at Ravello, but drive to Amalfi and Positano to help there.

Both he and Shellie could handle Positano. For her, there was good bus and ferry service between Amalfi and Positano. It took the bus about an hour to travel the twelve miles from Amalfi to Positano because it was a local bus that made a number of stops, and because of the heavy traffic and the nature of the road. The ferry trip took about half an hour.

Shellie said that if Rothstein went to Ravello the first day, she could do a practice trip to Positano that day and familiarize herself with the transportation and the town. She could take the ferry in one direction and the bus in the other.

Daniel suggested that he help with the Positano surveillance because there'd be very little wireless surveillance for him to do during the middle of the day. If Rothstein went to Ravello the first day, Daniel could make the practice trip that day, and help with surveillance the next. He'd take the bus both ways. Gianni and Shellie agreed.

Sorrento was a picturesque town; the Isle of Capri was a short ferry ride away; and the archaeological site of Pompeii was an easy train ride. The layout of all three would facilitate surveillance. Sorrento would require coordination by all of them. Gianni could do Pompeii himself.

After Gianni finished, J.B. began the discussion about travel. He first asked when they planned to depart. Gianni said they'd leave on May 15, the day prior to Rothstein's departure, so Daniel and Shellie would have time to familiarize themselves with the area before Rothstein arrived. They'd return on May 24, the day after Rothstein's return, to give them time to adapt to any changes in Rothstein's return plans.

J.B. asked what types of foreign travel they'd performed for clandestine and other U.S. government business, and what sorts of travel they'd done in Italy.

As a CIA operations professional, Gianni had a great deal of experience operating abroad, including foreign travel for clandestine purposes. As a CIA case officer, he'd managed and held clandestine meetings with foreign sources whom he'd recruited to spy for the U.S. He had lots of training on and experience with making such contacts. He'd traveled to Italy for pleasure, but never on government business.

Shellie had never traveled to Italy. She'd been abroad on typical military assignments while she was in the Air Force. She'd also traveled abroad for pleasure, but never on FBI business.

Daniel had traveled abroad a number of times on NSA business, including one trip to Italy. He used an official U.S. Government employee passport and did classified, but not clandestine work with U.S. military personnel on a U.S. military base. He hadn't traveled abroad for pleasure, but did have a U.S. tourist passport.

None of the group ever had any contact with Italian Government officials.

J.B. commented that because Daniel had gone to Italy on an official U.S. passport, he could be identified in an Italian database as a U.S. Government employee, He reminded Daniel to use his tourist passport for this trip.

He asked whether Gianni and Shellie planned to travel as a couple or to operate separately. He also wondered whether or not Daniel planned to travel with them.

Gianni and Shellie said they planned to travel and operate separately, but in a coordinated way. It would be a bit difficult because they didn't know Rothstein's specific plans and lodging arrangements. They hoped he'd post them.

J.B. asked very detailed questions about the way they planned to make flight, lodging, rental car, and shuttle reservations, and the flight routes they planned to take. Gianni thought he already knew the best way to make those arrangements through a CIA travel specialist. However, J.B. pointed out four vulnerabilities that Gianni was unaware of.

Shellie and Daniel planned to make flight arrangements very similar to those of Gianni. J.B. pointed out that would be a major mistake.

He described the best way to make each type of arrangement. He added that the best possible approach would be for the three of them to meet together with a single CIA expert from the office that made clandestine travel arrangements to have that person make the arrangements, and to have the person incorporate J.B.'s suggestions.

They all agreed and suggested J.B. join them at that session to make sure nothing was missed. He agreed. They decided to schedule their session for the following Tuesday afternoon, by which time they hoped to have some idea of Rothstein's lodging arrangements. If not, they'd have to make educated guesses. When Gianni returned to CIA HQ, he would arrange to have a travel support specialist meet with them, and he'd call to let them know when.

J.B. then asked what type of smart phone use they planned. Gianni said he planned to provide both Daniel and Shellie with an unused smart phone of the type they preferred - an iPhone or a Droid. The CIA station in Rome acquired and activated phones, and provided prepaid talk, data, and text service from Italian carriers. The phones were not directly acquired by the station or identified with the embassy in any way. They should not turn the phones on or start using them until they arrived in Italy. That way, there'd be no geographic connection to the U.S., especially to the Langley or Ft. Meade areas.

Daniel said if Gianni gave him all three phones, he'd have an expert at NSA analyze them to ensure they were clean of any harmful software, hardware, or firmware. Daniel said he'd like a Droid, while Shellie said she'd prefer an iPhone. Gianni said he'd provide the phones the next time they met.

J.B. and Gianni then both explained how Shellie and Daniel should study the local food and attractions so they'd appear to be knowledgeable tourists and avoid making mistakes that might create complications. Gianni explained how to behave like pleasant tourists. He offered to arrange to have a CIA expert brief them. They accepted.

When they finished, they expressed their gratitude to J.B. Gianni wondered if J.B. would be willing to brief some of his colleagues once this counterespionage operation was completed.

J.B. said he'd love to. He'd already done some presentations to small groups at CIA, and those presentations had been well received.

J.B. left and returned to his office.

Gianni told Shellie and Daniel that if they were interested, he could meet them at CIA HQ the following week and brief them on important aspects of the Italian language, and Amalfi Coast food and culture. Italian was probably one of the easiest languages for an

American to pronounce correctly. It had no difficult sounds. He could also teach them Amalfi Coast practicalities like how to use ATM machines, and take buses and ferries. It was all very easy.

Shellie and Daniel accepted, and settled on meeting at CIA HQ the coming Wednesday, May 6 at ten.

After Shellie and Gianni left, Josh sent the Director and Mac an email reporting their briefing of J.B., his start on Meta, and his briefing to Gianni, Shellie, and Daniel on making secure travel arrangements.

Twenty

Poison Pills within the Wazir's Wells

When, at length, the Partners Eight
Had reached a crucial caravanserai (کاروانسرا)
Along the road to Solhestan (صلحستان)[24],
Who would know that feigning friends
Had planted poison pills
Deep within the Wazir's wells?

Saturday May 2

At about six, Josh, who was still sleeping, got a phone call from Kat. "Sorry to bother you so early in the morning, Josh. I've got something you might want to see."

"No problem, Kat. I should be there in about an hour."

Josh told Meihui he needed to go to work. He got dressed, had a bowl of Wheat Chex, and headed to the office. It was now very clear to Meihui that Josh must be involved in some project other than the Metanalysis project, or that the project had some time-sensitive aspect that Josh hadn't included in his description of the project. She wished she could ask him about it, but she knew he'd let her know if he could.

At work, Josh found a relatively long phone conversation between the Supreme Leader and Behrangi. They discussed a number of interesting topics. They attempted to disguise the more

---

[24] The Province of Peace

sensitive substance, but revealed a great deal, as is often the case when speakers start out trying to talk around a subject. They get caught up in the content and flow of their discussion, and let down their guards. Fortunately, most of their conversation was in Persian.

Probably with respect to the nuclear deal, the Supreme Leader said, "On the one hand, I am constantly working on ways to keep Mojaezae and Harou from giving away too much to the other side. It is difficult because they are so driven that they are too friendly and cooperative. Mojaezae gets along too well with Shaejoka.

"On the other hand, what we are learning from Shaediha makes me think this is all a façade and the other side may not really want a deal. They may be pushing us too hard in the belief that we will stop with them. Mojaezae assures me that is not true. He says he understands Shaejoka very well, and believes he sincerely wants agreement.

"There are also your friends who are trying to block this. I think some of them do this because they earn lots of money from the current status. I try to balance both sides."

"With regard to my friends," Behrangi replied defending them, "Many are concerned that we are giving away something very important that we must have for our country. Those friends are not concerned about money."

"Yes, I understand." The Ayatollah answered, "That is true with most, but I have very reliable information about others."

Josh assumed that Mojaezae was Iranian Foreign Minister, Mohammad Javad Zarif, that Harou was Iranian President Hassan Rouhani, and that Shaejoka referred to the U.S. Secretary of State. He believed that Behrangi's "friends" were the IRGC players.

"And," the Supreme Leader continued, "there is Shaejoka's number one, Shaebahuo. They say many of his people believe he's a secret Muslim. You remember that when I first heard this, I told the special group to study his religion and tell me what kind of Muslim he is so we can use that to our benefit. The special group created a team of experts to study that for six months. They found nothing except that his father was a Muslim, became a Christian as a child, and later became an atheist. The father left before the son was three years old. I told the special group there must be more, but they told me there was nothing. I ordered them to look again. They came back to me in another month, and said they could find absolutely nothing credible.

"If this man is a Muslim, it seems to be so secret that he himself does not know it, nor his wife, nor his daughters – the way they dress, and talk, and are so independent. And he strongly opposes us, and on the apostate side, he kills so many Daesh and Taliban with his drones. If he is Sunni, why does he kill so many Sunni. If he is Shia, why does he not help Shia."

"You are so right, Sayyed, and they say that proof of his Muslim belief is that he will not use the term *Muslim radicals* or *Muslim extremists* to describe Daesh. They do not understand that the Daesh wish to be called Muslim extremists and radicals. They wish to be called an Islamic State – ISIL or ISIS. That validates their so-called caliphate. That is their goal. They hate to be called *Daesh*."

"Yes, yes," said the Ayatollah. "This must be the only area in which I agree with Shaebahuo. To destroy a group's ideology, you must destroy their prestige, their essence. Shaebahuo's Muslim allies know this and always use Daesh, just as we do."

"Of course, I am happy to see that Shaebahuo's opponents hate him so much and are so blind. That makes it easier for us to accomplish our goals."

Josh was surprised to hear the Supreme Leader's view that the U.S. might not really want a deal. He wondered if at least one spy was not only providing the Iranians with intel, but might be adding false information. There were only a couple of reasons a spy might provide false information to his handlers.

The first was that he could be a double agent for another power, and had been tasked with providing false information. Josh doubted that the subject was a U.S. double agent, because if he was, there would be no counterespionage effort. However, he could be an agent for another country that was trying to mislead the Iranians for its own objectives. That was the third scenario Josh had initially diagrammed when he was considering possibilities. It was the scenario he had judged least likely. If another country was involved in trying to undermine the negotiations, one had to put Israel at or near the top of the list.

The second was that the source wanted to mislead the Iranians for his own reasons.

The third was that he had misunderstood U.S. policy. That was unlikely.

By midmorning, Josh had finished processing the conversation and had prepared a report. It would be interesting to see the reaction of the Director, the Secretary of State and others. He called the Watch Director of NSA's twenty-four-hour operations center and informed him that he had something of high interest to show the Director.

The Watch Director asked what the topic was. Josh replied that the Director would know. Josh said he'd be waiting in his office to hear where and when the Director would like to be briefed. The Watch Director called back and informed Josh the Director would be at Josh's office within half an hour.

The Admiral, whose residence was nearby on another part of Fort Meade, arrived within twenty minutes, and Josh showed him the report. When the Admiral read it, he was very concerned about the portion that suggested the U.S. might not really want an agreement. He asked Josh if there was any possibility this meant something else. Josh assured the Director that he was confident the translation was accurate. The Director said he could think of only two possibilities. The first was that the spy was deliberately providing false information for some reason. The second was that the Iranians were misinterpreting some information the spy had provided.

In any case, this report would likely help the Secretary of State strategize how to convince the Iranians of U.S. sincerity.

While they were talking, Josh received a phone call from J.B., who said he was hoping Josh might be at work. He had some info that might be of interest. Josh invited him up, and told the Director J.B. would be coming.

When J.B. knocked on the door, the Director opened it. Josh and the Director chuckled at the expression on J.B.'s face when he saw the Director. Josh introduced J.B. to the Director, who expressed his pleasure at meeting him, and told J.B. he'd heard great things about him from Josh. He was looking forward to being briefed on J.B.'s work.

J.B. said he'd found possibly relevant information about travel reservations to Sorrento and the Amalfi Coast by three individuals – one Iranian and two Israeli.

He was fairly confident the Iranian was an MOIS officer. He had not previously been identified as such, but his travel patterns fit those of the MOIS, and his travel arrangements indicated he would be traveling under cover in Italy. He was stationed at the Iranian UN Mission in New York. He had rented an apartment in Zurich, Switzerland from May 18th to May 25, using HouseTrip, a European company similar to Airbnb. His Iranian name was Farhad Ahmadi. An individual with the same initials, but with the French-language name, Fernand Amédée, who claimed Swiss citizenship, would be in Sorrento when Rothstein was there. Amédée was scheduled to fly from Zurich to Naples Capodichino Airport via Rome. He had reserved a rental car for pickup at Naples, and lodging reservations for the nights of 20-23 May at the Hotel Antiche Mura near the Piazza Tasso in the heart of Sorrento. The connection between Ahmadi and Amédée was the email address that Ahmadi had provided as contact information for his Zurich reservation and that Amédée had given for his Antiche Mura reservation. His Swiss pseudonym was similar to his real name.

With respect to the Israelis, there were two possibilities. One individual was more likely than the other to be an intel operative. The more likely one was Shmuel Feld, who was traveling round-trip from Vienna, Austria. He would depart Vienna the day before

Rothstein departed the U.S., and fly to Naples via Rome. He'd reserved a rental car at Naples. He would stay at Amalfi the nights of 16-19 May. Then he would leave for an undetermined location. He would fly back to Vienna from Naples the day after Rothstein returned to the U.S. J.B. had looked up the official Israeli list of its embassy personnel in Vienna. Feld was listed as the First Secretary. That was a cover assignment position often held by intel officers operating out of diplomatic missions.

The second Israeli was Aharon Mandelbaum, who was traveling round trip from Tel Aviv to Naples via Greece and Rome. He would be arriving at Naples two days before Rothstein's arrival and returning to Tel Aviv two days before Rothstein's return to the U.S. It was not clear where this individual would be going or staying. He appeared to be an Israeli Government official.

The Director asked J.B. for his interpretation of the travel data of the Iranian and the most likely Mossad officer.

J.B. said his answer would be a best guess based on patterns he'd seen in several other double-agent cases. If the Mossad officer was really involved, he'd meet first with Rothstein to prep him for the meeting with the Iranian. That preparation might include providing Rothstein with information to feed the Iranian. J.B. would also have expected the Mossad officer to meet with Rothstein to get feedback after the Iranian had departed. However, since both the Iranian and Rothstein would be departing on May 24, J.B. felt that Rothstein would not meet with the Mossad officer after meeting with the Iranian. Perhaps Rothstein would meet with the Israeli back in the U.S. to let him know how the meeting with the Iranian had gone. However, that was all only conjecture based on previous experience. It was first important to make definite connections between Rothstein and any foreign intel officer.

The Director agreed that if this was a double-agent situation, the scenario suggested by J.B. was the most likely. The Director was really pleased with what J.B. had been able to learn in less than two days, and with his analysis. He thanked him for his great work and said he thought this would really help the surveillance effort.

The Director hand-carried Josh's report to the Watch Director and gave him very detailed instructions to send it via special channels to a very limited number of recipients, including the Secretary of State. The Director decided to spend a couple of hours in his office to phone the DNI and update her, and to wait and see if he would get a reaction from any of the recipients.

Within an hour, he received a phone call from the Secretary of State to discuss the substance of the report. This sort of direct call was very unusual. The Secretary said he wanted to be absolutely sure the translation was accurate. The Director explained Josh's background and competence level, and said he had pressed Josh on the very same question. The Secretary thanked the Director and said this information had revealed the need to figure out how he might better assure the Iranians of U.S. sincerity and intentions.

Following that discussion, the Director phoned the DNI to apprise her of the Secretary of State's phone call and of the Secretary's assessment of the value of the intelligence in adjusting his negotiating strategy.

Twenty-one

Il Viaggio dei Tartufai[25]

(The Trip of the Truffle Hunters)

Monday May 4

Josh phoned Johnnie first thing Monday and told him about the Saturday conversation between the Ayatollah and Behrangi, and about what J.B. had discovered about the travels of Ahmadi and the Israelis. Johnnie would ask Farida and Shellie to research CIA and FBI files to see if they could find anything about Ahmadi and the two Israelis. Shellie would check with the Bureau's New York office for information about Ahmadi and for recent photos of him.

Johnnie mentioned that he had some interesting info. On the preceding day, Rothstein had posted his Amalfi Coast lodging plans on his Facebook page. Shellie had just sent the lodging details to everyone on the high side, and Gianni was in the midst of using those details to work out a lodging proposal for himself, Shellie, and Daniel. He wondered if Josh, Daniel, and J.B. could come to FBI HQ that afternoon for a Team Triad session to discuss the details.

Josh checked with Daniel, who was sitting next to him; and Daniel agreed. They'd have to cancel an interview they'd set up for

---

[25] Italian truffles, fungi related to mushrooms, are a precious commodity. The best are white truffles, found in the Piedmont in the northwest. Delicious black ones are found in the forests of Umbria, Tuscany, Emilia-Romagna, Campania, and elsewhere. Finding them requires specially-trained dogs or pigs. So this title refers to the difficult search for a precious commodity - a spying fungus.

the afternoon, but that wasn't a problem. Josh would check with J.B. to see if he was available. They set a meeting time of one.

Josh called J.B., who was more than happy to go. Josh then checked and found Shellie's email with Rothstein's lodging plans. In Amalfi, he'd be staying at the Marina Riviera, whose room rates ranged from over $300 to over $1,000 per night. In Sorrento, he'd be staying at Maison Tofani, where the room rates ranged from over $200 to over $300 per night. Both had great reviews and ratings.

Since Gianni was very familiar with Amalfi and Sorrento, he quickly laid out his lodging suggestions:

A. Amalfi

1. Daniel - Marina Riviera on the eastern side of this small town.

If there was a Mossad officer, he would probably not stay at the Marina Riviera where Rothstein was staying, but would likely stay at a nearby hotel like the Luna Convento which was located on one side, or the Residence Hotel, which was nearby in the other direction. If Daniel was in the middle, he might have a higher probability of success with his wireless network efforts. The distances from those hotels would be too far for normal computer wireless reception, but Gianni assumed Daniel's gear would be far more sensitive.

2. Shellie - Residence Hotel, very close to the Marina Riviera on the west side, and very close to the Piazza Flavio Gioia, where intercity buses, including the one to Positano, stopped. It was also very close to the ferry pier.

3. Gianni - Hotel Giordano in Ravello, a very short walk from the Piazza Duomo, the Cathedral Piazza. The town's main parking lot was very close to the piazza, and the intercity bus stop was only a couple of blocks away. Most people coming to town would certainly come to the piazza to visit the cathedral, or walk through the piazza to get to a couple of major sights like Villa Rufolo and Villa Cimbrone. During the day, Gianni could hang out at an outdoor table at the Duomo Caffè located on the piazza, and keep an eye out for Rothstein.

B. Sorrento

1. Daniel - Hotel Antiche Mura where the Iranian operative was staying. There, Daniel could hope the Iranian would use the hotel's Wi-Fi, and that Daniel would be able to identify him and monitor his on-line activities. If the Iranian used Persian, as was likely, Daniel would simply collect the Iranian's emails and details of his Internet activity, then forward it to Josh for analysis.

2. Shellie - Hotel il Faro, very close to the Marina Piccola (Small Harbor) of Sorrento, where the ferries departed to and arrived from Capri. It would be very easy for Shellie to hang out near the ferry ticket sale area looking for Rothstein. There were so many people passing through the area that she wouldn't stand out. When she saw Rothstein, she could buy a ticket for the next ferry to Capri, then text Gianni and Daniel to let them know.

3. Gianni - Hotel Nice, a budget hotel on the Corso Italia - about a block from the train station, at the corner of Corso Italia and Via Ernesto de Curtis. Rothstein's posting said he planned to take the train to Pompeii. Anyone walking to the train station from the direction of the Iranian's hotel or Rothstein's hotel would pass by the Hotel Nice.

When Gianni finished his proposal, he emailed it to Johnnie and asked him to print copies for the meeting.

Josh, Daniel, and J.B. drove to the Bureau in Daniel's 2013 silver Prius. The weather was nice, with a temperature in the midseventies, and a partly cloudy sky. The traffic was very smooth. Josh was thankful their trips to the Bureau were always outside rush hour and generally without incident. He was also happy they rarely had to travel around the Washington Beltway to CIA HQ. He felt sorry for colleagues who lived on the east side of NSA in areas like Pasadena, and took a two- or three-year assignment at CIA. They would have to add a round-trip beltway commute each day, tacking on an extra hour of commute time each way when the traffic was running smoothly. It could add an extra 80,000 miles of driving over the course of a three-year assignment. If they wanted to avoid that, they had to move to a new residence for three years, and then move back when they finished their assignment. Such an assignment involved a certain amount of sacrifice because the extra mileage equaled five extra vehicle years and the extra driving time added up to at least 1,500 hours.

When the meeting at the Bureau started, Johnnie asked Josh to summarize the conversation between the Ayatollah and Behrangi. What most interested and surprised all of them was that either or both of the spies were providing not only factual intel, but probably false info suggesting the U.S. really didn't want a nuclear deal. It pointed in the direction of Israel trying to poison the negotiations through the use of a double agent. It was very difficult to accept that premise.

Gianni asked Josh how confident he was that the Iranians had deliberately been given false information, and that it was the Israelis who had done so. Josh said there was nothing in the Ayatollah's words that confirmed that the info about U.S. intentions was false info that had been deliberately planted, and not simply a misunderstanding. Nor was there any proof that it was the Israelis who had planted any information at all. These just seemed to be the most likely conclusions based on the possibilities.

As all of them except Daniel, whose focus was on technology, understood from years of analyzing intel, the info available for analysis was often incomplete and ambiguous. Those who criticized the IC for "intelligence failures" never considered the ambiguities and misunderstandings that occurred in their own lives, when even spouses who had been together for decades misunderstood each other because of the natural ambiguities of language, or due to accidentally leaving out key information when speaking with each other.

Johnnie asked J.B. to describe what he'd learned from his tracking analysis. J.B.'s description of a probable Mossad officer traveling to Amalfi and another area in that part of Italy, and of an MOIS officer traveling to Sorrento seemed to support the double-agent hypothesis.

After J.B. finished, Shellie said she'd asked the FBI office in New York what was known about Ahmadi. She learned that he supposedly held a low-level clerical position at the Iranian UN Mission. No photos were available, but the New York office would obtain photos as soon as possible. Neither she nor Farida had uncovered any other information about Ahmadi or the two Israelis. Farida added that she had sent requests to the CIA stations in Vienna and Tel Aviv to see if they had any info about the Israelis. She expected she would have answers by the following morning.

Shellie gave Gianni and Daniel each a set of four current photos of Rothstein taken from different angles. She had found the photos on his Facebook page. He looked to be of medium height, with a solid build. He was clean shaven, had black hair and brown eyes, and a very distinctive, good-looking face, with a warm, contagious smile. He also had a nice tan. He was always very fashionably dressed, even when he was in casual clothing. She noted that many of the photos on his Facebook page showed him in the company of beautiful young women.

Next, Johnnie gave everyone copies of the proposed lodging arrangements prepared by Gianni, who proceeded to describe the arrangements. He explained that the limited number of local transportation options and the logical street routes in all the towns should make it relatively easy to find Rothstein much of the time, and hopefully allow them to detect meetings he might have with foreign intel officers.

In discussing Daniel's lodging at the Marina Riviera Hotel in Amalfi, Gianni commented that he loved the Marina Riviera and wished he could stay there himself. It had been owned and operated for decades by the Gargano family, which did a superb job of serving the hotel's guests.

Gianni asked Daniel how easy it would be for him to do wireless network penetration.

Daniel said he could not predict the probability of success. He'd had plenty of success against other targets, but had never done anything involving the Iranians or Israelis. He could only give it his best.

Gianni said his biggest concern at the moment was whether the hotels he suggested still had vacancies. There were some available when he checked a couple of hours earlier, but they could disappear quickly. Amalfi and Sorrento were extremely popular tourist destinations, and May was one of the best months because of the pleasant weather. Sorrento was larger, and offered more lodging options suitable for their operation.

As Gianni promised the previous Friday, he'd made arrangements for himself, Shellie, Daniel, and J.B. to meet the next afternoon with a CIA clandestine travel specialist in his office at one thirty.

Next, Gianni gave Daniel the three smart phones to take to NSA for testing. Daniel said he'd have it done by their meeting on Thursday. It would be done in a facility which would block the signals from leaving. That would prevent the signals from connecting to any tower and tying them to a U.S. location.

Gianni also gave Daniel and Shellie the phone numbers for each phone, and then asked if anyone had any questions.

Shellie and Daniel both had questions about the mechanics of working in the Amalfi and Sorrento areas, but they'd hold the questions until Gianni briefed them on Wednesday.

Johnnie reported he'd made arrangements for Washington-area surveillance of Rothstein to begin the following day. He mentioned that the Bureau had obtained additional information on Rothstein's financial activities. In November 2014, he'd paid $55,000 in cash to purchase a 2015 Porsche Boxster. His only debt was a mortgage whose payments were $2,100 per month. He had three credit cards, but only used them for on-line purchases or automated payments for recurring expenses, like monthly cable bills. He seemed to use cash to pay for items like restaurant meals and groceries.

When they finished their substantive discussions, Gianni

explained the proper pronunciation of Capri was different than the typical American pronunciation. The accent was on the first syllable, not the last, and the "a" was like the "a" in "father," not the "a" in "was." With that tidbit, they concluded the meeting.

When Josh and Daniel were back at NSA, Daniel called a friend in the Information Assurance organization, and asked him if he could expeditiously check out three phones for an impending operation. The friend said he'd have it done by Wednesday afternoon.

Tuesday May 5

As planned, Daniel and J.B. met with Shellie, Gianni, and a CIA clandestine travel specialist. Fortunately, the specialist was able to make the lodging arrangements Gianni had proposed. He was also able to make flight reservations. In both cases, he used a couple of J.B.'s suggestions to minimize tying the three travelers together in any way, or suggesting that they were government employees. They had the cheapest possible tickets, left at different times, and flew via different routes. Daniel would depart from BWI Airport. Shellie and Gianni would fly from Dulles, but on different airlines.

When all the reservations were set, they thanked the travel specialist and went to Gianni's office. Although they'd planned to meet the following day for Gianni's travel briefings, he was prepared to brief them now so they wouldn't have to make the trip the next day. J.B. said he could also do what he'd promised. Fortunately, everyone was available for the early briefings.

Gianni started by suggesting they watch YouTube and other on-line videos of each location they'd be visiting - Amalfi, Positano, Sorrento, and Capri.

Next he gave both Shellie and Daniel a set of tourist pamphlets and maps covering the Sorrentine Peninsula and the Amalfi Coast; the city of Sorrento; the towns of Amalfi and Positano; and the Isle of Capri. They wouldn't need maps of Ravello and Pompeii because he'd be the only one going there. He said that maps and pamphlets like these, which were produced in the areas to be visited, were great because they often provided details that guide books or apps wouldn't have.

They asked where he'd gotten maps like these on such short notice. He told them he collected multiple copies when he was traveling for business or pleasure because he never knew when they'd come in handy for his own work or for friends and colleagues. He described how his wife chided him for stuffing the file cabinets in their house full of these items. He was an unrepentant tourist pamphlet hoarder.

Gianni gave both of them a list of Android and iPhone apps for travel, transportation, and sightseeing on the Amalfi Coast, Sorrento, and Capri. The transportation apps were great, with bus and ferry schedules. If they wanted to use the apps, they should download them onto their phones after arriving in Italy, so the phones would not be connected to the Washington area.

As mentioned the preceding Friday, a traveler could choose a coastal ferry or a bus to go between Amalfi and Positano. Tourists often took the ferry in one direction to enjoy fantastic views of the coasts from the sea. They would take the bus in the opposite direction to take in some of the most breathtaking views he'd seen anywhere. The bus ride could be a bit scary because of the very narrow winding coastal road, the SS163. The road was so narrow in some places that buses going in opposite directions would have to slow to a crawl, pull their mirrors in, and creep past each other, making sure they did not come into contact. The bus drivers there possessed amazing driving skills.

Conveniently, the Amalfi departure points for the bus and ferry were just a few feet from each other by the Piazza Flavio Gioia. The ferry ticket kiosks were on the edge of the piazza and the bus tickets could be purchased in the little Bar il Giardino delle Palme (Garden of the Palm Trees) on the piazza. Hopefully, Shellie would be able to detect Rothstein in the piazza and figure out whether he was going to take a ferry or bus to Positano. If she was really lucky, a foreign contact would be with him.

He said that Shellie and Daniel would have few language problems because English was widely spoken throughout the area due to the high level of foreign tourism. However, it would be useful to learn a little bit about standard Italian, which is based on Tuscan Italian, and which became the national language after Italian reunification in the mid-nineteenth century. Standard Italian was the language used in the media, business, education, etc., and between Italians from different parts of Italy. It would be very helpful for Shellie and Daniel to learn a few polite phrases, to be able to pronounce menu items properly, etc.

This was one of the easiest languages for an American to pronounce. It had no phonemes (sounds) that were difficult for Americans. Italian phonemes were even closer to Spanish, which Daniel spoke. Unlike English, each letter was always pronounced the same or nearly the same. For example, *a* was always like the *a* in father. In written English, the letter *a* could be pronounced at least five different ways, as in *father*, *hat*, *hate*, *a*, or *fall*. Double consonants in Italian were always pronounced twice as in *penne* - pen-ne. (If one only pronounced *n* once in *penne*, that changed the word to *pene* - the part of the male anatomy beginning with the same three letters in English.) The "sch" as in *bruschetta* was pronounced like the *sch* in *school* not the *sh* in *shoot*. He gave them a simple, one-page explanation of Italian pronunciation. Once they understood the simple rules, they could easily pronounce any word they saw in print, unlike English in which you had to memorize words - like pronouncing the vowels in *foot* vs. *boot*, or *have* vs. *gave*, or *was* vs. *has*.

He then described a few things about greetings, politeness, civility, ordering food, etc. He explained how to use ATM machines, which even had English menu options. He mentioned that crime was not really a problem, except for pickpockets in Naples.

He taught them an interesting alternative technique for using

TripAdvisor reviews to select restaurants or lodging. Most people looked at reviews in their own language. However, there were a couple of ways to use reviews in the local language, even when the visitor didn't know the local language. Local language revealed what host country natives thought about the place in the review. They had a much more informed perspective about authenticity, service, and quality. TripAdvisor pages about a given restaurant, lodging, attraction, etc., indicated how many reviews there were in each language.

A foreign traveler could sort the reviews by language and then simply look at the number of ratings locals had given in each category from top through bottom. With languages that had some words similar to English, the traveler could look for highly complimentary words like *fantastico*, *perfetto*, or *eccelente*. The technique for examining reviews by language was simple. The review menu had language boxes one could check. The default box for American users was English. It was simple enough to click on another language, and later to click English again.

One example he gave was reviews of the Marina Grande, an Amalfi restaurant he liked. Of 249 Italian-language reviews, 227 were either excellent or very good. Only two were terrible. That showed most Italians loved the place.

While Daniel and J.B. were with Gianni and Shellie at CIA HQ, Josh met with the Director and Mac to update them on the operational plans and preparations.

When Josh finished, the Director said, "Tell me, Josh, how're you finding the cooperation on your interagency team? It seems pretty smooth. There've been a few instances in which I've had to interject myself to ensure complete cooperation between NSA and its counterparts, and even between different organizations within NSA. The most well-meaning, dedicated individuals can be blinded by their wish to be protective of their organization, its mission, and its capabilities. I've seen that in both the public and private sectors throughout my career. It's a natural human tendency."

"It couldn't be better. It started on a positive note when the FBI and CIA members named our group *Team Triad* to make it clear it was a three-agency partnership. There's been no hint of parochialism, even when J.B. suggested improvements to the CIA travel arrangements. I think there are important reasons for the absence of friction."

"I'd love to hear those reasons, Josh."

"Well sir, first, our mission is of the highest importance and is time sensitive. Second, our effort is clearly visible to each agency Director. There are no intermediate level managers in the way and no turf issues. Third, the CIA and the FBI had no leads, so we offered them a possibility. I think there was some initial skepticism about what Daniel might bring, but they now appreciate his unique talents. Fourth, the FBI and CIA team members know one another quite well and respect one another. Fifth, the personalities of all the team members mesh well together."

"Makes perfect sense, Josh. I'm delighted to hear that."

Wednesday May 6

J.B. called Josh and informed him that he'd obtained further travel information on the second of the two Israelis, whom he'd thought might be a Mossad officer. The additional information strongly suggested that this individual was a tourist and nothing more. He had no further info on the first Israeli or on Ahmadi. He reiterated that he was most confident Ahmadi was an intel operative and less confident about the first Israeli. Even if he was an intel guy, he could simply be going on vacation.

Josh thanked J.B. and asked if he'd be able to attend the weekly Team Triad session at the Bureau the following day. J.B. said he'd go in case anyone had any questions or requests.

Thursday May 7

The weather was really nice when Josh, Daniel, and J.B. headed down to the Bureau. Temperatures were in the low seventies, the sun was shining, and there was no wind. Dogwood trees were in full bloom in the wooded areas along the parkway.

When the meeting started, Johnnie informed the team that the previous evening a team of two agents had searched Rothstein's desk at the DOE; and two forensics experts searched his desktop computer there. Their exhaustive search produced absolutely nothing suggesting Rothstein was involved in espionage.

Johnnie then gave both Daniel and Gianni two photos of Ahmadi. (He'd given Shellie pics earlier in the day.) Ahmadi would be very easy to pick out.

Next, Daniel reported that the NSA examination and testing of the smart phones for the operation indicated they were all clean in every respect. Gianni thanked Daniel, and said Shellie could take hers, he'd take his, and Daniel could hold onto his, so Daniel gave Shellie and Gianni their phones.

While they were discussing phones, Gianni suggested how they should communicate with one another in Italy. He suggested they limit their communication to reporting sightings and movements of Rothstein, any companions he might have, and possible intel contacts, and to emergencies.

He then proposed cover names they could use for various individuals. They could refer to Rothstein as "Rob." They could use Italian pseudonyms for probable foreign intel contacts. Ahmadi would be "Enzo," which had four letters like "Iran." An Israeli would be "Silvio," with six letters like "Israel." If there was a second Iranian, they could refer to him as Enzo's brother or sister. They could use a similar approach for a second Israeli.

There was no reference to a traveling companion on Rothstein's Facebook postings. A companion would make it awkward to meet with an intel contact. However, just to be prepared, they could refer to a male traveling companion as "Bud," and a female as "Gina."

As for themselves, he suggested they use Italian names:

- "Dani" for Daniel. It was the Italian diminutive of "Daniele."

- "Stella" for Shellie because there was no Italian equivalent for Shellie,

- "Nino," for Gianni. "Gianni" and "Nino" were both diminutives of his full first name, "Giovanni."

Gianni began a discussion of how they could construct their text messages. For instance, if Daniel thought Rothstein might be heading up to Gianni's location at Ravello, he could text, "Rob might be coming to see you this a.m." If Shellie was following Rothstein to Positano, she could text, "Might meet Rob at our favorite place." They proceeded to discuss various scenarios and how they might describe them in an innocent-sounding way.

After they'd completed the phone discussions, Johnnie asked J.B. if he had any new people-tracking info. J.B. repeated what he'd told Josh the preceding day.

Johnnie reported that Rothstein was continuing to post his anticipation of his upcoming trip. However, he'd posted no new info that might help the team.

Shellie said she'd checked out all flights departing Dulles or Reagan National on May 16 and reasonably connecting to flights arriving in Naples on May 17. She felt the very earliest Rothstein could reach the Marina Riviera after arriving at Naples, passing through customs and immigration, getting his rental car and driving to Amalfi was about 12:30; and that was a stretch. So the team would have plenty of time to get ready.

Gianni said that on the 17th, he would drive down from Ravello and help in the first part of the surveillance to confirm Rothstein's arrival and to see if he met anyone. There was no point in staying in Ravello on that date because it was unlikely Rothstein would consider going there on the day of his arrival.

Gianni laid out a detailed street map of Amalfi. He explained that, because of the location of the Marina Riviera's entrance, there

were challenges to confirming Rothstein's arrival. He would
probably be driving from the east on the SS163, named the Via
Pantaleone Comite. There were two locations from which his arrival
would be most visible.

The first was a short section of the Via Pantaleone Comite, about
450 feet long, which extended from a few feet on the west side of the
entrance to a small and picturesque tower called the Torre Saracena
(Saracen Tower) 400-500 feet beyond the entrance. It was very easy
to see the entrance from outside the tower, which housed a restaurant
that belonged to the Luna Convento Hotel just across the road. The
tower was one of a series of coastal fortifications built hundreds of
years ago to protect against pirates and Saracen invaders. The area
next to the tower was a good place to take photos west toward
Amalfi and of the coast east of Amalfi. Since there was no sidewalk
along this section of the road, it was very important to pay attention
to the traffic.

Marina Riviera from the Ferry Pier

From the west, where Shellie's hotel was located, it would be

very difficult to see anyone arriving at the street entrance of the
Marina Riviera. The best place to do it from that direction would be
at the edge of the Piazza Flavio Gioia closest to the water, or on one
of the two piers off the piazza. A person would have to use compact
binoculars or a camera-binocular combination.

Another approach would be for Daniel to spend some time using
the desktop computer available for guests at the Marina Riviera. It
was located very close to the check-in desk. Its location wasn't
optimum because the user had to face away from the desk. Daniel
would also not be able to see the vehicle because the registration
desk was one floor above ground level.

Gianni suggested a way they might work together to watch for
Rothstein's arrival. Starting at about quarter past noon, the three of
them could take forty-five-minute turns walking past the hotel to the
tower, sightseeing and taking photographs. When Shellie was not
doing that, she could go to the Piazza Flavio Gioia or the closer pier
and look from there with binoculars or a special camera. When
Daniel was not out on the street, he could spend some time at the
desktop computer near the registration desk.

If Rothstein arrived early enough and was not wiped out from the
trip, he would probably unpack, wander around town for a bit, have
dinner, and then go to bed. Gianni suggested they try to surveil him
if he walked around town. Shellie could look out the window of her
hotel room and watch for Rothstein to walk from the Marina Riviera
to the Piazza Flavio Gioia. If she saw him coming, she could text,
"Rob wd like to go downtown." Gianni could wait at the Piazza
Flavio Gioia, and watch Rothstein's movements through the piazza.
Daniel could wait in the nearby Piazza del Duomo.

Gianni again raised the remote possibility of Rothstein traveling
with a companion. That would make surveillance a bit easier
because Rothstein would probably not include his companion in a
meeting with the foreign intel officer. The most likely time of any
intel contact would be between the end of the day's sightseeing and
the start of dinner. Rothstein might tell his companion that he wanted

to go out to buy some necessity. Another possible time would be between the end of breakfast and the start of the day's sightseeing activities. So it would be important to be particularly vigilant during those times.

Gianni then brought up the Ravello visit. Since that town was very small, he'd be staying there, and Rothstein would probably start out at the Piazza Duomo, the cathedral square. He didn't think it was necessary for Shellie and Daniel to take the bus up to Ravello.

In the case of Positano, it would be easy for Shellie to determine if Rothstein was going to go there by bus or by ferry. That's because the bus and ferry departure points were very close to each other. Once she saw which form of transport Rothstein chose, she could buy the appropriate ticket for herself. She could then text Gianni and Daniel. Gianni could drive there from Ravello and Daniel could take the means of transportation not used by Shellie and Rothstein. If Shellie took the ferry, Daniel could take the bus, and vice versa.

Gianni then turned to the Sorrento phase of the operation. He folded up the Amalfi street map, and then opened up a street map of Sorrento. He showed Shellie and Daniel the key points:

- Maison Tofani, Rothstein's hotel,

- The Antiche Mura Hotel, where the probable MOIS officer and Daniel would be staying,

- The Hotel il Faro, Shellie's hotel,

- The Hotel Nice, where he would be staying,

- The pier where the ferries to and from Capri docked,

- The train station, from which Rothstein would probably go to Pompeii, and

- The Piazza Tasso, the main piazza in the heart of Sorrento.

Even though Shellie's hotel and the ferry pier appeared close to all the other locations horizontally, those two were at sea level and the other locations were much higher - probably about 190 feet above sea level. The two areas were connected by the steep and winding Via Luigi de Maio. There was bus and cab service between the two areas. He showed her a photo of Sorrento which clearly revealed the height difference between the sea level areas and the plateau on which the main part of the city was located.

Sorrento – Elevations

He explained that two parts of the surveillance would be easy to start with - following Rothstein to Capri and Pompeii. Watching him in those locations could be easy or moderately difficult, depending on what he did. It would be very easy for Shellie to hang out near the ferry ticket kiosks each morning, and wait for Rothstein to come and purchase a ticket to Capri. Once he reached the island, it would depend on what he did. Pompeii would be similar. Rothstein would have to walk past Gianni's hotel to the train station. Gianni could follow him and buy a train ticket to Pompeii.

Watching Rothstein in Sorrento could be slightly challenging. It would be easy for Gianni or Shellie to sit at an outdoor table at one of the eateries on the Piazza Tasso, old Sorrento's main piazza, and find Rothstein if he walked from Maison Tofani east along the pedestrian-only Via San Cesareo in the direction of the piazza. It would be more difficult if he were to walk in the opposite direction on Via San Cesareo. Just west of Maison Tofani was a very narrow walkway, Via degli Archi, onto which Rothstein could turn right or left. There was no eatery with an outdoor table where one could watch for him. The Via San Cesareo was a very busy street with many little shops and lots of tourists wandering around. In fact, it was one of the busiest tourist shopping areas in town. Gianni suggested how they might position themselves. Shellie could be on the Piazza Tasso side of Maison Tofani. From that position, she could look for the Iranian to come from Antiche Mura and for Rothstein to come from Maison Tofani. Gianni could wander around the shops on Via San Cesareo and hopefully locate Rothstein if he walked west from Maison Tofani.

Gianni raised one potential complication in this operation. If one of the Italian security services knew the Iranian and/or the Israeli intel officer and surveilled either or both, they could stumble onto the U.S. team. So it was extremely important to keep that possibility in mind.

Shellie raised the subject of photographic documentation of Rothstein's espionage-related contacts or actions. She and Gianni knew the techniques and had the equipment to take the photos unobtrusively. They gave Daniel a few tips on how to do this with both a camera and a smart phone. Johnnie said he'd provide Daniel a special camera suitable for this purpose. Daniel couldn't wait - another device to feed his tech addiction.

Gianni raised the topic of communication between Johnnie, Farida, and Josh in the Washington area and the team members in Italy. There was a good chance that they'd have to exchange important info, for example, if Rothstein's itinerary changed, or if the team in Italy discovered something that would be helpful to the Washington team or that required urgent action.

Daniel said he could make the necessary comms arrangements. First, the laptop he would bring was one of the hack-proof laptops he'd created. It would be impossible for anyone but him to use it or alter it in any way. He'd set up an encrypted cloud capability that would have no association with the U.S. or the U.S. Government. Josh and Daniel's connection to that cloud account would be protected with powerful encryption. Both he and Josh could upload encrypted files into the account; and only they would have the capability to decrypt and read those files. The encryption algorithm and the passwords would be powerful enough that they would be unbreakable. Within the account, there would be two major folders - one for items from Italy to Washington, and one for items from Washington to Italy. Whenever they performed encryption or decryption, they'd do it in stand-alone mode, disconnected from the Internet.

When Daniel finished, Gianni asked if anyone had any additional thoughts or questions. No one did. They felt all the bases had been covered.

When they'd finished their substantive discussions, Daniel suggested that they have their next weekly meeting the following Wednesday, May 14, rather than Thursday, when they would be focused on final preparations for their Friday departure. They all agreed.

Wednesday May 13

The final meeting at the Bureau prior to their departure was straightforward and uneventful. There'd been no new phone conversations between Behrangi and the Supreme Leader; there was no other new intel; and Rothstein's plans seemed unchanged.

Johnnie reported several items of interest from the surveillance of Rothstein:

First, on the preceding Friday and Saturday evenings, he'd gone out to eat with the same woman, and had then gone to her apartment in Arlington. Her name was Julia Martin. She worked in a prestigious law firm in Washington. Martin was married and her husband was a U.S. Army lieutenant stationed in Afghanistan. That is probably why Rothstein never mentioned her on his Facebook page. There was one odd aspect of Rothstein connecting with a woman in that law firm. One of the firm's partners had very effectively represented three clients accused of espionage in three separate cases. They'd all gotten off with very light sentences. It raised the question of whether Rothstein had met the woman while seeking advice at the law firm, or whether he'd met her in some other way. The surveillance team had taken a couple of pictures of Martin and provided them to Johnnie. He showed them to the rest of the team.

Second, the surveillance team noticed that when Rothstein worked normal hours, he took the Metrorail Yellow Line subway from Alexandria to the L'Enfant Plaza Metro Station, not far from DOE HQ on Independence Ave. He always got on the same subway car in each direction and always took the subway at the same time, even when he reached the platform in time to take an earlier train. The team hadn't seen him interact with any of the other passengers in a suspicious manner.

After Johnnie finished discussing the surveillance results, the team members reviewed all their plans and procedures for the coming two weeks.

Twenty-two

Una Terra Sensuale

(A Sensual Land)

Friday May 15 – Departure Day

Shellie, Gianni, and Daniel headed to Dulles and Baltimore airports for their flights to Naples. Shellie and Gianni took separate flights from Dulles to Naples via Paris. Daniel departed from Baltimore and flew to Naples via Newark and Munich. The weather on departure was decent, with cloudy skies and moderate winds.

Saturday May 16

The weather on arrival in Naples was cloudy, with light winds and a pleasant temperature of about seventy degrees Fahrenheit.

Daniel arrived the earliest - at about eleven. Shellie arrived at about noon, and Gianni in midafternoon. Daniel and Shellie both used the same transportation company - Amalfi Car Service - to travel from Naples Airport to Amalfi. Gianni had rented a car to drive to Ravello. It was a tiny, blue Fiat 500 with manual transmission - like most European vehicles.

For Shellie and Daniel, the first three quarters of the drive was simple enough, but when they saw the nature of the road on the last 13 miles of the drive, they both were very grateful to have professional drivers. The drive from Naples Airport to Amalfi was about 50 miles, and took an hour and forty minutes. Both drivers took the same route past Mount Vesuvius and then around the northern, eastern, and southern sides of the Lattari Mountains:

- The three-lane A56 Autostrada (expressway) for a couple of miles. Traffic was relatively light.

- The mostly three-lane A3/E45 Autostrada southeast for about 35 miles to Vietri sul Mare, just west of Salerno. Traffic was light and much of the scenery was uninteresting, with businesses and some residential buildings. There were often berms which blocked the view. However, nothing could block the view of Mt. Vesuvius off to the left. Farther along the expressway, they saw the beautiful, forest-covered Lattari Mountain Range ahead and to their right. The expressway skirted the north side of this range and then went down the east side. Near the southeast side, they exited at Vietri sul Mare, which as its name implied, was located at the edge of the sea - the Tyrrhenian Sea.

- At Vietri sul Mare, they picked up the SS163 regional highway, which they followed west for about 13 miles along the Amalfi Coast of the Tyrrhenian Sea to the town of Amalfi. The views were absolutely spectacular as this narrow winding road clung to the hillsides and passed through several small towns. Although they were both very tired from the long trip, the breathtaking views kept them wide awake. Even though the distance between Vietri sul Mar and Amalfi was short, this portion of the trip took nearly an hour because of the nature of the road.

On the other hand, even though Gianni was very tired from the long trip, he was energized to be driving in Italy again, especially when he was driving along the Amalfi Coast. He followed the same route as the drivers who took Daniel and Shellie except for the last leg, when he turned north onto regional road SS373 to drive the last couple miles uphill to Ravello.

Another route he could have taken was to exit the A3/E45 due north of Ravello and take the provincial roads - the SP2b and the SP1 up over the top of the Lattari Mountains. However, that was a very winding route, much more so than the SS163, and it didn't afford the SS163's beautiful sea views.

Daniel checked into the Marina Riviera[26] at about 1:45. It was as amazing as its TripAdvisor reviews and the photos on the hotel's web site indicated. Daniel's room was situated in a way that he had a breathtaking mix of views. His room overlooked the sea, which was only a few yards away across the road. From his balcony, he could see the port of Amalfi, the coast toward the west, and some of the mountains overlooking the town. The room itself was spacious and comfortable. He only wished he was on vacation, and that his wife was with him. He knew she'd love it. He decided he'd have to bring her here on vacation.

Amalfi from Daniel's Room at the Marina Riviera

Once Daniel had unpacked, he set up his laptop to check out the hotel's wireless network signal. He was disappointed to see how weak it was. That was not a problem for his extremely sensitive gear. However, it would be a problem for the ordinary hotel guest. He suspected most people would have to sit in the lobby to get a reliable

---

26 http://www.marinariviera.it

connection.

Shellie loved her room at the Hotel Residence[27], which was built in the eighteenth century as an aristocratic palace. The room was nicely appointed and comfortable, and it had a sea view. Gianni had specifically requested a sea view room for her because the street that ran below the rooms was the Corso delle Repubbliche Marinare[28]. The corso was *the* street leading from the Marina Riviera Hotel to the Piazza Flavio Gioia, where the ferry and bus tickets were sold, where the buses arrived and departed, and from which the ferry pier extended. She'd be able to look out onto the street and its sidewalk to see Rothstein approaching. She'd have an even better view of the corso from the hotel's breakfast dining terrace.

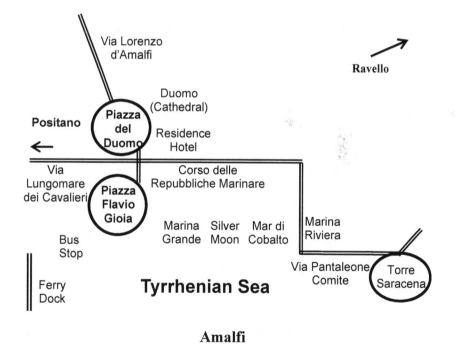

Amalfi

---

[27] http://www.residencehotel-amalfi.it
[28] Avenue of the Maritime Republics. Named after the five Italian Maritime Republics - Amalfi, Ancona, Genoa, Pisa, and Venice- which existed for varying periods of time starting in the tenth century AD. Some of them were fairly powerful in the context of their times.

After unpacking and freshening up, she walked out onto the small balcony of her room and spent a bit of time looking in all directions. She could see the Piazza Flavio Gioia, the intercity buses waiting there, and the ferry docks. As she looked toward the Marina Riviera, she saw Daniel walking from there toward the piazza. She quickly looked around her room to see if she could find something to "accidentally" drop from the balcony in front of him as he passed below. She found a tourist pamphlet and dropped it. It floated down and he noticed it. He looked up, saw Shellie, and smiled. He kept walking.

A few minutes later, she walked out onto the corso and to the piazza. There she found the ferry ticket kiosks and examined the times and schedules posted there. She then found the Bar il Giardino delle Palme where the bus tickets were sold.

Next Shellie wanted to check out the buses, which were operated by a company called SITA. The bus route was Amalfi - Positano - Sorrento. Before coming to Italy, she'd printed out the SITA bus schedules in both directions between Amalfi and Sorrento. There were twenty-six trips per day in each direction. She walked to the area where the buses were arriving and departing. There was no covered bus station. There were ten large buses parked there.

After checking out the buses, she walked out onto the boat pier, where a ferry had just arrived and was disgorging its passengers. There was a very large cruise ship anchored just off shore, and there were several large sailboats out on the water. She turned around and looked at the town, with buildings sprinkled across the hillsides amidst woods, terraced groves or orchards, and bare rock. She would later learn that the planted areas were lemon groves, olive groves, and vineyards.

Next she decided to walk through the center of town. She walked the short distance of about a block up the narrow Via Duca Mansone I, with her hotel on the right, to the Piazza del Duomo, with the impressive Cathedral of Sant'Andrea (Saint Andrew), named after the apostle Saint Andrew. The cathedral, with its colorful façade of marble and stone with interlocking arches and a beautiful mosaic at the top depicting the "Triumph of Christ" and the Twelve Apostles, towered over the square. It had a broad set of sixty-two stairs leading up to the entrance, with the first bronze doors in Italy. They were made in Constantinople. The Cathedral had been built at the end of the thirteenth century to house the relics of St. Andrew, which crusaders in the Fourth Crusade stole from Constantinople and brought to Amalfi. The beautiful façade, however, was built in the late nineteenth century, after the original collapsed in 1860. There'd been churches on this site since the end of the sixth century.

Cathedral from the Piazza del Duomo

A centerpiece of the piazza was the beautiful Fontana del Popolo (People's Fountain). The piazza was filled with tourists who were obviously enjoying themselves.

She continued out the north side of the piazza onto the narrow main street, whose name kept changing - from the Via Lorenzo d'Amalfi to the Via Pietro Capuano to the Via Cardinale Marino del Giudice. The street was lined with shops selling souvenirs, jewelry, ceramics, clothing, produce, lemon soap, etc. Narrow walkways rose up off the left and right sides of the main street. She thought people living there must certainly get their exercise just running daily errands around town.

The street kept going uphill and the interesting looking shops were running out. So, she turned around and walked back downhill to the Corso delle Repubbliche Marinare. She turned left and followed the corso to the Via Pantaleone Comite to the Marina Riviera, and strolled beyond it to the Torre Saracena[29].

She now felt she had a decent appreciation for the parts of Amalfi that were important to her role in the operation. She'd already checked these areas out through on-line videos and map street views. However, there was no substitute for walking them in person.

After exploring the town, she decided she should have supper and get some sleep. Like Daniel and Gianni, she wanted to push herself to stay awake until at least eleven to try to adapt her body to the time difference as soon as possible.

This would be the only night available before Rothstein arrived and work got serious, so she decided to have a nice, leisurely dinner. She chose the Marina Grande restaurant[30], which was located at the water's edge along the corso close to her hotel. She chose the restaurant on the basis of the example Gianni had given about how to look at Italian-language TripAdvisor reviews.

She started with an antipasto[31] of seared scallops, sweet pepper,

---

[29] http://www.torresaracena.net/
[30] http://ristorantemarinagrande.com/
[31] "Appetizer" - literally, "before the meal."

pancetta bacon, and fried mozzarella bread. Next she had a pasta dish - scialatielli with seafood. Scialatielli is a local Amalfi pasta that is short and chewy. It is made with semolina dough, parsley, and grated Grana Padano cheese, and can include milk and eggs. Next she had a dish of San Daniele prosciutto (ham) and Buffalo Mozzarella (Mozzarella di Bufala). The San Daniele, produced in the northern Italian region of Friuli-Venezia Giulia, was the one palate-pleaser in which she diverted from locally produced food. It is probably Italy's best prosciutto. She'd enjoyed it in the U.S., but wanted to do so in Italy. Mozzarella is a southern Italian cheese. For dessert, she had a pear and chocolate semifreddo, a type of soft Italian ice cream.

She accompanied her meal with a couple glasses of a local red wine - the A. Sammarco Costa d'Amalfi Ravello Giardino di Klingsor made with 50 percent Piedirosso and 50 percent Aglianico grapes.

The meal was superb, and she hoped it signaled the beginning of a successful operation.

She didn't realize that while she was dining at the Marina Grande, Daniel was having dinner a few doors down at the Ristorante Pizzeria Silver Moon[32], which he'd chosen on the basis of its TripAdvisor reviews. The restaurant's outdoor dining area had a very nice view of the port, and also of the Marina Grande. In fact, if Daniel had looked hard enough, he would have seen Shellie, who was having her dinner at the same time.

A waiter quickly came to his table. "Good evening, and welcome to the Silver Moon. Here is our menu. Is there something I can bring you to drink while you read the menu?"

"I would like some water, please."

"Would you like bottled water?"

"Yes, please"

"With gas, or still?"

---

[32] http://www.silvermoon.it/?l=2

"Still, please, and could you recommend a pizza for me to eat? I have never been here before and would like to try a pizza with a local flavor."

"There is a very nice pizza I recommend. Do you like food with a lemon taste?"

"Yes, I do."

"This pizza has lemon, zucchini, and anchovies. How does that sound?"

"It sounds like an unusual mix of flavors, but I will try it."

"I think you will enjoy it. Is there anything else I can bring?"

"No. That's it for now. By the way, what is your name?"

"It's Oleg."

"That doesn't sound Italian."

"It is Russian. I came from Russia, but I have lived here for a while, and I consider it my home."

Oleg soon brought the pizza.

When Daniel had finished about half the pizza, Oleg returned. "How do you like the pizza?"

"It's delicious. I'm really surprised. I've never heard of pizza with zucchini and lemon."

"One reason I recommend this pizza is that lemons are a very important fruit grown in this area, not just the town of Amalfi, but the whole Amalfi Coast and Sorrentine Peninsula. The local lemon is called the Sfusato Amalfitano. Let me get one from the kitchen to show you."

The lemon Oleg brought was very large and had a large point that looked like a nipple. "You can see how large it is. These lemons are very tart and have very few seeds. They are grown along the cliffs near Amalfi, and they are used in many of our foods and drinks. One famous local drink is a liqueur called limoncello. However, only the zest of the lemon is used to make this liqueur, not the juice. We also make a wonderful lemon cake."

"Thank you, Oleg," Daniel said. "While I am in Amalfi, I will have to try other food with lemon."

When Daniel had finished his pizza, Oleg returned. "It looks like you really enjoyed your pizza."

"It was wonderful, Oleg. Thanks again."

"Can I bring you anything else?"

"I was originally only going to have pizza, but I would like to try the lemon cake you mentioned."

"I will bring it."

Oleg returned with the cake and also with a small glass of liquid. "Here is your cake, and I have also brought you a little gift of limoncello liqueur."

Although Daniel didn't care for wine or alcohol in general, he enjoyed this liqueur and decided he would later buy some to take home. He'd soon discover that many local restaurants served complimentary after-dinner limoncello to their guests. Daniel quickly began to look forward to it.

After dinner, Shellie and Daniel each returned to their respective hotels. Between the time change and the travel, Shellie was feeling very tired and immediately went to bed. Daniel, however, spent nearly two hours checking out wireless users to see if he could find any evidence of a foreign intel operative. The way he approached the task was to determine the available wireless network signals and then attempt to look at the users of each. If the wireless network signal was unencrypted, he would simply check out the users. If they weren't Americans and were a high-interest target, like an intel officer, he'd analyze their activities. If the signal was encrypted, he'd use an app to break the password. This was often easy because of some of the incredibly simple passwords. To his frustration, he found nothing of interest, so he finally gave up and went to bed.

Gianni knew Ravello well. After checking into the Hotel Giordano[33] and unpacking, he spent a bit of time walking around town to see if anything had changed since his last visit four years earlier. As is often the case with the streets and shops of Europe,

---

[33] http://www.giordanohotel.it/en/history

little had changed. Satisfied that he was comfortable with the layout of the town, he returned to his hotel.

Just after sunset, at the respectable dinner hour of eight thirty, he walked over to the restaurant Principe Compagna[34] at the Hotel Villa Fraulo. He skipped ordering an appetizer because he knew the rest of the meal would be more than filling. For a first course, he had paccheri pasta with cream of asparagus and diced shrimp and scallops. Paccheri is a local, very wide, short, hollow tubular pasta that was supposedly created to smuggle garlic from Italy into Austria. Italian garlic was more flavorful than Austrian garlic, so the Austrian Government had banned the import of Italian garlic in order to protect Austrian farmers. In response, the Italians created the paccheri noodles, each of which could hide several cloves of garlic.

His next course was lamb chops crusted with pistachios and sun dried tomatoes with an aromatic herb sauce, accompanied by a vegetable strudel. For dessert, he had lemon cake with wild berries. With his meal, he ordered a couple of glasses of Marisa Cuomo Costa d'Amalfi Furore wine made with half Piedirosso and half Aglianico grapes. Furore was a wine-producing area up in the hills about half way between Amalfi and Positano. The meal was superb. He relaxed after dinner with a glass of limoncello. Then, feeling the effects of his long day, he paid for the meal, returned to his hotel, and went to bed.

---

[34] http://www.principecompagna.com/en/

Twenty-three

Arrivano il Volpe e la Sua Preda Squisita

(The Fox and His Delicious/Exquisite Prey Arrive)

Sunday May 17

When Shellie awoke, she walked to the window and looked out at the Tyrrhenian Sea. It was a gorgeous, clear, sunny morning, and the sea was calm. After getting dressed and putting on her makeup, she walked to the breakfast room. She decided to sit inside rather than on the outdoor terrace, because temperatures were in the midsixties. She had a couple of pastries, fruit, juice, and coffee while she thought about the day ahead. She hoped that Rothstein's travel had not been cancelled, or his lodging or itinerary changed.

After breakfast, she again strolled around the most relevant parts of town - the Piazza Flavio Gioia, the intercity bus boarding area, the ferry ticket kiosks, the pier, the corso, and the Via Pantaleone Comite to the Saracen Tower. Then she returned to the hotel to prepare to start the surveillance. On her way back, she passed Daniel, who was just leaving the Marina Riviera and heading to the Saracen Tower. When he smiled a stranger-to-stranger greeting at her, she smiled back.

Daniel had roused himself reluctantly when his alarm went off at six thirty. It was half past midnight at home. After getting out of bed, he opened the door to the balcony and enjoyed the incredible view of the sea.

Before getting dressed, he powered up his laptop and checked the wireless network to see if he could find anything of interest.

There was nothing, so he shut down the computer.

After getting dressed, he walked down to the breakfast buffet area. The selection looked mouthwatering, and he could not resist. He had scrambled eggs, sausage, mozzarella di bufala, prosciutto, cannoli, and coffee. Unlike Shellie, he decided to sit outside on the balcony to enjoy his breakfast. Since he preferred cooler temperatures, he thought the outside temperature was perfect.

After breakfast, he returned to his room and tried the wireless network again for about an hour. Still nothing. He decided to walk around town - a walk Shellie had already nearly completed. He noticed her coming toward him as he first headed to the Saracen Tower. He smiled a greeting at her as though she was a stranger, and she returned the greeting.

Gianni had no problem getting up when his alarm went off. He was fully charged and ready to go. He had a quick breakfast, then got in his car and made the short drive down to Amalfi. He wanted to get there early enough to find (paid) public parking before it filled up. He found parking on the west side of town at a lot by the Piazzale dei Protontini and Via Lungomare dei Cavalieri. Then he walked to Piazza Flavio Gioia, where he confirmed that everything was as he remembered it from his last trip. He walked along the Corso delle Repubbliche Marinare. There, almost at the entrance to Shellie's hotel, he encountered Daniel heading toward the Piazza Flavio Gioia. They did the stranger-to-stranger smile. Gianni continued all the way to the Saracen Tower, then headed back.

When he reached the point where the Via Pantaleone Comite met the corso, he stopped at an outdoor table of the Bar Gran Caffè[35]. The table was sheltered from the sun by a large umbrella. Boxes of beautiful flowers separated the table area from the rest of the sidewalk. He ordered a pastry and a coffee, and did some people watching. It was too bad the tables were located just out of view of the Marina Riviera's entrance.

---

[35] http://www.bargrancaffeamalfi.it/default.asp

Just after noon, he paid and left to begin the first shift of the surveillance on the Via Pantaleone between the Marina Riviera and the Saracen Tower. He would be first, then Shellie, then Daniel.

Gianni's turn was pleasant, but uneventful. At one, he left, and Shellie started. Nothing happened during her time. Daniel was about twenty minutes into his turn, and at the Saracen Tower when he saw Rothstein drive by. It was about 2:05. Rothstein was in no ordinary rental car. It was a bright red Ferrari 458 Spider with the top down. The car had to retail for well over $200k. And it turned out that Rothstein was not alone. Seated next to him was Julia Martin, the woman he'd been seen with the preceding weekend. In person, she was even more beautiful than in the photos Johnnie had shown the team a couple days earlier. She was a strikingly beautiful blonde who appeared to be about ten years younger than Rothstein.

Daniel texted the arrival of "Rob and Gina" to Shellie and Gianni, and then began walking back toward the Marina Riviera's entrance. As he was doing so, Rothstein quickly raised the vehicle's top back into position. A member of the hotel staff came down and greeted the couple. He said something to them, and took their luggage up one floor to the registration desk. While the couple was waiting for the hotel employee to return, Daniel managed to get a good photo of them standing next to the vehicle.

When the hotel staff member returned, he asked Rothstein if he would like him to take the vehicle to a private parking garage. Rothstein agreed, gave the staffer the Ferrari's key, and then, holding hands with Martin, headed up to the registration desk.

Daniel entered the hotel a few minutes later, hoping to hear something as he walked past the registration desk. The only thing he heard was Rothstein calling Martin something that sounded like "Gillie" or "Jilly." It didn't sound like "Julia." Perhaps it was a nickname.

Daniel headed to his room and stayed there for a while. He was happy that Rothstein had arrived. The expensive car seemed to validate the Bureau's analysis that Rothstein was living beyond his means. It was puzzling that Rothstein had brought Martin because it was unlikely that he would include her in a meeting with a foreign intel officer, unless she was somehow complicit. While possible, it seemed unlikely.

If Martin wasn't involved, Rothstein would have to leave her alone at some point - more than once if he was going to meet with an Israeli at one time and an Iranian at another. Daniel typed and encrypted a note to Josh that Rothstein had arrived in a bright red Ferrari Spider convertible, and that he was accompanied by Martin. Daniel then uploaded the file and the photo of Rothstein and Martin into the encrypted cloud account he shared with Josh.

Daniel needed to let Gianni and Shellie know about the vehicle because it would be very easy to spot when the couple was driving. He knew that Gianni would be waiting in the Piazza Flavio Gioia to watch Rothstein in case he decided to walk around town after unpacking. Daniel left the hotel and walked to the piazza. As he walked past Shellie's hotel and came to the piazza, he saw Gianni sitting at an umbrella-shaded table of the Savoia Pasticceria[36], which was located just across the narrow Via Duca Mansone I from Shellie's hotel. It offered a perfect view of anyone walking up the Corse delle Repubbliche Marinare to the piazza. The Via Duca Mansone I also led to the Piazza del Duomo, and was one of the most logical ways to reach that piazza.

Daniel walked over to the Savoia and took a seat at the table next to Gianni's. He ordered an iced coffee and one of the Savoia's incredible pastries. When the waiter walked inside to get the order, Daniel said only loud enough for Gianni to hear, "Rob's driving a bright red Ferrari, and he's with Julia Martin." "Thanks," Gianni replied.

At about the time Gianni and Daniel were at the Savoia, a team from the Bureau was beginning a search of Rothstein's residence in Alexandria. It was about nine in the morning in Washington. A day

---

[36] http://savoiapasticceria.it/

prior to the search, the Bureau had informed the Alexandria police department that it would be conducting the search under the cover of fixing a utilities problem. When the Alexandria police contact checked the address, he noted that one next-door neighbor was a retired Alexandria policeman. The contact asked if the Bureau wanted the department to ask the neighbor not to inform Rothstein. The Bureau did.

A team of four agents conducted the search. Two were computer forensics experts, one of whom was Shellie's husband, Rick. They hit the jackpot. They found a group of folders containing some seventy-five classified documents from the DOE and other U.S. Government agencies. The documents were filed in date order. The computer experts found soft copies of each document on the hard drive of Rothstein's desktop. The classifications of the documents ranged from a high of **TOP SECRET** to a low of **UNCLASSIFIED//FOR OFFICIAL USE ONLY**. In the hard drive folder that contained those documents, they also found a simple database that was entitled DocOr, and that contained only three fields, and a number of records equivalent to the number of documents in the folder. Two fields had dates and the third field had a digraph. The digraphs were Bl, Bg, Cn, Ec, Fo, Lt, Mi, Nt, Ti, Wj, Wp. The headers for the date columns were: SD and DD, and the digraph column had the header S. The only field the agents could figure out was the second one, which seemed to be the date of origin of each document. The date in the first field was always one or two days prior to the date in the second field.

SD	DD	S
11/1/2014	11/2/2014	Ec
11/15/2014	11/16/2014	Ec
11/21/2014	11/22/2014	Nt
11/24/2014	11/25/2014	Wp

Sample Records from the DocOr Database

The agents were unable to find any evidence that Rothstein had provided these documents to the Iranians or that he was in any way dealing with the Iranians or anyone else. Nor did they find any evidence of equipment that Rothstein might be using to communicate with the Iranians.

The agents discovered a handwritten ledger with a list of monthly sums of $9,500. Each sum was followed by a date. The first date in the ledger was March 25, 2014. The total came to $138,000. They wondered if these dollar amounts represented Iranian payments. They could only speculate.

Finally, in one of the desk drawers, they found a thumb drive that contained an app that appeared to be for encryption and decryption, and a file with a series of numbers that appeared to be something like encryption keys.

The agent heading the team at Rothstein's residence called Johnnie and told him what they'd found. Johnnie was delighted. He inquired about the earliest date in the ledger - because he remembered that Josh had mentioned the date Behrangi's J.R. cryptogram had been created was April 14, 2014. He also asked about the date of the most recent document. Interestingly, it was dated May 7 - two days after the Bureau had initiated its surveillance. That meant he might have passed the document to someone while he was under surveillance.

Johnnie asked the team chief to have someone bring him the thumb drive the next morning so he could pass it to NSA for analysis.

In Amalfi, about an hour and a half after Rothstein had checked in at the Marina Riviera, Shellie was looking out of her hotel room, and saw him and Martin coming from their hotel. She sent the agreed-upon text, "Rob and Gina wd like to go downtown."

Rothstein and Martin spent about an hour wandering around the piazza and then walking out onto the piers to see all of the beautiful views. They then came over to the pasticceria, and each had some gelato and iced coffee at an outdoor table. Unfortunately, Gianni had already finished at the Savoia. He was nearby in the piazza and could see that the couple was completely engaged in enjoying each other's company. He snapped a photo of them.

When the couple finished, they walked to the Piazza del Duomo, looked in all the shop windows, and walked up the broad staircase to the entrance to the cathedral. From the cathedral balcony, they took photos of the piazza below. They didn't realize that the photos included a CIA officer surveilling them. After they finished snapping photos, they paid the admission to the cathedral and went inside.

When they were back down in the piazza after touring the cathedral, Martin pointed out that just to the left of the staircase was an almost hidden restaurant called the Taverna degli Apostoli (Tavern of the Apostles), probably named after the Twelve Apostles depicted on the church façade. She walked up to the taverna and took a look. She liked what she saw, and suggested to Rothstein that they consider eating there one night. He agreed.

Then they walked up the Via Lorenzo d'Amalfi to the Via Pietro Capuano to the Via Marino del Giudice, walking into shops along the way. In il Ninfeo[37], a ceramics shop with ceramics from all over Italy, she purchased a ceramic plate from Vietri sul Mare, an Amalfi Coast town famous for its ceramics.

At around seven thirty, they headed back to the Marina Riviera. At about the same time, Gianni returned to his car and left for Ravello. He wanted to complete the drive before sunset.

Daniel decided to have dinner at the Eolo Restaurant[38], which was operated by the daughter of the owners of the Marina Riviera. He wanted to have a light meal close to the hotel and return to his room to focus on wireless network searches. Some of the tables at the Eolo had a beautiful view of Amalfi. The food was supposed to be excellent and the wine list superb. Of course, the wine list meant little to Daniel, who didn't care for wine. He decided he would only

---

[37] http://www.amalficoastceramics.com/OurCeramicsShop.asp?l=2
[38] http://www.eoloamalfi.it/

have a dish of pasta and then return to his room. He chose scialatielli pasta and ham.

Rothstein and Martin also decided to have dinner at the Eolo. They arrived just as Daniel's waiter was bringing him his pasta. They were seated at one of the window tables - a table that was only one table away from his. Since he was so close, he decided to order a main dish and dessert in order to prolong his stay and see if he could hear anything interesting. The entire time he was eating, the couple just engaged in lighthearted banter about the beauty of Amalfi, the smoothness of their trip to Italy, and their anticipation of upcoming adventures. The only insight he gained from listening was that they had a very close relationship.

After Daniel returned to his room, he spent nearly four hours searching and monitoring wireless networks, but again found nothing suggesting the activities or identity of an intel officer. For her dinner, Shellie decided to try Trattoria da Gemma39, an antique trattoria which had been established in 1872 and which was located at Via Fra Gerardo Sasso, up a sidewalk of stairs. It had a sheltered outdoor dining terrace above the Via Lorenzo d'Amalfi. She had a caprese appetizer that was a trio of small dishes in three different styles - a traditional caprese salad, a mousse, and a deep-fried tomato mozzarella cake. Then she had paccheri pasta stuffed with burrata cheese and covered with conch sauce. For dessert, she had tiramisù.

---

[39] http://www.trattoriadagemma.com/en/

Twenty-four

Una Sinfonia Incredibile di Giardini, di Colline, del Cielo e del Mare

(An Incredible Symphony of Gardens, Hillsides, the Sky and the Sea)

Monday May 18

It was a sunny morning with a temperature of about seventy.

Like the previous morning, Daniel got up about half past six. He decided he'd first shower, shave, and get dressed. Next, he'd work on wireless exploitation in his room 'til eight. Then he'd take his laptop to the breakfast area, have a leisurely breakfast, and do wireless while waiting for Rothstein and Martin to come to breakfast. He figured he'd look like a computer-addicted geek.

When they finished breakfast, he'd wait 'til they left the breakfast room. Then he'd drop the laptop off in his room, and stroll on the road in front of the hotel, walking to the Saracen Tower and back. He'd let Gianni and Shellie know when the couple left the hotel.

Rothstein and his companion walked into the breakfast room at eight fifteen. They sat outside at a table overlooking the sea, and spent half an hour enjoying breakfast and chatting. Then they left.

Daniel left a few minutes later, dropped off his laptop, and walked down onto the Via Pantaleone Comite for his surveillance stroll. About ten minutes later, a hotel staff member left the hotel entrance, and soon returned with the red Ferrari. Rothstein and Martin came out of the hotel and got into the car. Rothstein lowered the top; and they drove up the Via Pantaleone Comite toward Daniel and the Saracen Tower. As they passed, he captured a good photo of the pair in the Ferrari. He assumed they were headed toward Ravello, so he sent Gianni the agreed-on text, "Rob & Gina might be coming to see you." To Shellie, he texted, "Rob & Gina prob gonna see our Nino." After that, Daniel returned to his room, transferred the photo he'd just taken, encrypted it, and uploaded it to the shared cloud account.

In accordance with the plan if Rothstein went to Ravello on the first day, Shellie set out for Positano. She decided to go there by bus and return by ferry. She took the bus at nine thirty. Daniel followed on the next bus – an hour later. They separately spent a couple of hours familiarizing themselves with the tourist shopping and dining streets of Positano, and had lunch there at different restaurants along the waterfront.

When Gianni received Daniel's text that Rothstein and Martin were en route to Ravello, he headed over to the Piazza Duomo. About twenty minutes later, Rothstein and Martin came strolling hand in hand from the nearby parking area into the piazza. First they walked into a couple of the ceramics shops, which carried the beautiful (and expensive) ceramics for which Ravello was famous. There were a number of other such shops around town.

Then they walked into the twelfth century Duomo, the cathedral, with its simple white façade. Like the cathedral in Amalfi, it had a pair of the few remaining bronze doors in Italy. Their fifty-four beautiful relief panels depicted biblical scenes, saints, and warriors. They were designed by Barisano da Trani in Italy and cast in Constantinople in 1179.

One superb feature in the interior was the Pulpit of the Gospels. The mosaic-covered pulpit rested on six spiral columns each resting on the back of a lion statue.

After leaving the cathedral, they visited the Villa Rufolo[40], a

---

[40] http://www.villarufolo.it/home.html

magical place that was built in the thirteenth century by the wealthy Rufolo family. Over time, many changes were made, and the villa eventually fell into decline. It was purchased in the mid-nineteenth century by a Scottish botanist, who brought it back to life. It had many interesting Arab-Norman[41] architectural features, beautiful gardens, and incredible views of the Amalfi Coast. Each year from late June through early September, it hosted a variety of musical concerts.

Gianni took a couple of good photos of the pair while they were strolling in the flower-filled garden, and he was looking down from a terrace above. Any observer would think he was photographing the garden. As he took in the spectacular views of the coast from this position and others in Ravello, he was sorry Shellie and Daniel wouldn't have the opportunity to share the experience.

The Amalfi Coast toward the East from Villa Rufolo

---

[41] There is significant Arab and Norman architectural influence in southern Italy due to various Arab and Norman conquests and rule of Sicily and the southern mainland starting in the ninth century AD.

After leaving the villa, Rothstein and Martin had lunch at the Sigilgaida Restaurant[42] of the Hotel Rufolo. With its windowed walls, the restaurant offered spectacular views of the coast, similar to the views from Villa Rufolo.

At about the time they were having lunch, Josh examined the shared cloud account, and found Daniel's note about Rothstein and Martin's arrival and the Ferrari rental. He also found the photo of Rothstein and Martin in the Ferrari. He called Johnnie, informed him, and said he'd send him a copy of the photo via secure FAX.

Then Johnnie described what the FBI team had found at Rothstein's residence, including the thumb drive. Josh asked if Johnnie could have someone from the Bureau courier the thumb drive to him as soon as possible so he could arrange for cryptanalytic experts to examine and analyze it. Johnnie said he'd make the arrangements right after he got off the phone.

On the one hand, Josh was thrilled with what had been discovered at Rothstein's residence. On the other, he wished the team had found some connection to the Iranians. Josh thanked Johnnie, and immediately phoned Sofie to ask for a couple of minutes on the phone with the Director. She said he was in a meeting, but would let him know as soon as the session ended. The Director called about a half hour later. Josh informed him of the discovery of the documents and the thumb drive, and of the nature of Rothstein's arrival in Italy. The Director thanked Josh and complimented him on how the work by Josh, Daniel, and J.B. had led to this point. Josh thanked the Director, and commented that the key to their progress was the teamwork of the entire team.

After Josh got off the phone with the Director, he called J.B. to let him know.

Following their lunch in Ravello, Rothstein and Martin went to visit the gardens of another villa - Villa Cimbrone[43]. The first villa

---

[42] http://www.hotelrufolo.com/th portfolio/sigilgaida-restaurant-2/?cats=18
[43] http://www.villacimbrone.com/en/home.php

had been built on this site in the eleventh century, but had fallen into decay. An English lord bought the property in the early twentieth century and had a large villa and beautiful gardens built there. It was now a 5-star hotel. Visitors who weren't staying at the hotel could pay to visit the gardens, which offered even more smashing views of the coast than Villa Rufolo. Among the many famous guests who'd stayed at Villa Cimbrone were Winston Churchill, Greta Garbo, D.H. Lawrence, and T.S. Eliot. The villa was a considerable walk from the Piazza Duomo.

When Rothstein and Martin finished enjoying the gardens, they returned to the Piazza Duomo and started walking around town, stopping in more ceramics shops, where they made several purchases.

At a little after six, Gianni saw them pass through the Piazza Duomo and head toward the parking lot. He assumed they were returning to Amalfi. He tipped off Shellie and Daniel by text. Although Gianni had watched the couple a number of times during their visit to Ravello, he'd never observed them making contact with anyone other than waiters and sales people. He hadn't really expected any contact when he saw Rothstein arrive in Ravello with Martin.

By that time, Shellie and Daniel had been back in Amalfi for about two hours. Daniel had taken the 3:10 p.m. bus from Positano to Amalfi so he'd be back in plenty of time to prepare for Rothstein's return. Shellie had returned on the three thirty ferry.

When Daniel received the text, he walked down to the Via Pantaleone Comite to watch the couple arrive. They reached the hotel about twenty minutes later, with the top down on the Ferrari. They went through the same drill as on their arrival the preceding day.

Daniel returned to his room and texted Shellie. She texted back that she was going to have a snack at a coffee bar. He figured she meant at an outdoor tables at the Bar Gran Caffè. She did. He decided to spend some time searching the Wi-Fi. He again found nothing, so he headed to the Bar Gran Caffè to replace Shellie. When she saw him, she left and returned to her hotel room.

Daniel and Shellie both guessed separately that since the couple had eaten at the Eolo Restaurant the previous evening, they'd try a different restaurant this evening. A waterfront restaurant was one good possibility, and the Taverna degli Apostoli was another. Of course, Amalfi offered many other good options.

Daniel ordered an iced coffee and sat facing in the direction of the Marina Riviera. As he was sipping his coffee, he heard a male voice behind him exclaim, "Daniel, dude, how're you doing?" Daniel turned and saw Ed Yelnovic, a senior NSA Human Resources expert, whom Daniel knew from an earlier assignment. Everyone called him, "E.J." He was a SHRM[44]-certified innovator who stayed on top of HR change in the public and private sectors, and figured out how to adapt them to NSA's special requirements. Daniel had known such a chance encounter was possible, so he was prepared.

"Hey, E.J.! What a surprise! I'm doing great. Amalfi's so incredible. How're you?"

"I'm great. I love it here. Is your wife here with you?"

"No. She went to see her good friend in Tampa. She doesn't like to travel abroad, so I decided to come here myself. Always wanted to do it. Sure glad I did. What about you?"

"I'm here with my wife, Lani, and our 19-year-old son. We wanted to introduce him to his ethnic heritage on my wife's side."

"Where are you staying?"

"We're at the Luna Convento[45]," E.J. replied, pointing to the area just beyond the Marina Riviera. "What about you?"

"I'm at the Marina Riviera, very close to you. Where've you been so far?"

"We started at Naples, where Lani's maternal grandmother came from. We spent three days there and then came here. We're going to

---

[44] Society for Human Resources Management
[45] http://www.lunahotel.it/

spend two more nights here. Then we're going to spend a couple days in Sorrento and make day trips to Pompeii and Capri. After that, we'll travel east to the Adriatic side of Italy - to Puglia, where Lani's paternal grandfather was born and raised. We're going to make a day trip to Positano tomorrow. What about you?"

"I got here a couple days ago, and I'll also be staying here for two more nights. I might go to Positano tomorrow too. I'll decide in the morning. Then I'm going to spend a couple days in Sorrento, like you. After that, I return home."

"You ought to spend more time in Italy. It's so great."

"I'd like to, but I want to be back home for my wife when she returns."

"Maybe you could make a few extra bucks spying while you're here." E.J. joked.

"Hey, thanks for the tip. I'll have to try that next time. Maybe you could use your HR talents to help me find one of those jobs," Daniel joked back.

"If I could find a job like that, I'd have to get out of HR and get into operations. Well, take care, Daniel. Gotta get back to the family. Maybe we'll see you again in the next few days."

"You too. Hope you guys have a great time. See ya."

E.J. then left and headed toward his hotel.

As E.J. walked back toward the Luna Convento, he thought to himself, "Gee, what if Daniel is on some kind of mission here?" Then he thought, "No, that's not possible. I can't imagine any type of mission he'd do on the Amalfi Coast. Not the sorta thing NSA does. I could understand if he was at some U.S. military base helping support a mission in the Middle East or North Africa, but nothing in Amalfi. Oh, well."

As soon as E.J. left, Daniel texted Shellie and Gianni, "Just saw friend from work who's here with family." He wanted to let them know in case they saw him talking to E.J., or E.J. and family, at some point.

About twenty minutes after E.J. left, Daniel saw Rothstein and

Martin approaching. He texted Shellie that Rob and Gina would probably go out to dinner. She texted back that she hoped to join them.

Looking out from her room, she saw them coming. When they'd almost reached her hotel, they turned into the Stella Maris di Esposito[46] restaurant, right next to the Marina Grande where she'd eaten dinner the first night. Fifteen minutes after their arrival, she went to the Stella Maris and was seated four tables away. She could also see the beautifully lit section of Amalfi to the right of the restaurant toward the harbor. She decided to have a long leisurely dinner to observe them as long as possible.

She ordered a glass of Sammarco Bianco wine, a caprese salad and a small bowl of Cerignola olives. Next she had a plate of Scialatielli pasta with mussels and clams. She followed that with parmesan-crusted cod. For dessert, she had lemon cake with limoncello. She ended her meal with a cup of espresso.

Rothstein and Martin also had a multicourse meal. Throughout, they engaged in lively conversation, and appeared to greatly enjoy each other's company. Even though they started their meal before her, she finished before them. She returned to her hotel room, from which she hoped to observe whether they returned directly to their hotel room or walked about town. When they emerged from the Stella Maris, she saw them head back toward their hotel. They walked very slowly holding hands, and stopping occasionally to face out toward the water.

Shellie decided she wasn't quite ready to go to bed, so she strolled out to the end of one of the piers and looked in toward the town. As she stood on the pier, she reflected that this was the strangest surveillance she'd ever done. Normally, she was a small part of a large operation conducted in a challenging urban environment with little time to eat anything more than fast food. This was in a captivating, exotic location with mind-boggling sights and

---

[46] http://www.stella-maris.it/index_en.html

incredible food. Nonetheless, she couldn't really relax and enjoy the experiences because of the uncertainty of success and the need to stay focused and constantly on the alert. It would all be for naught if they couldn't find some connection between Rothstein and a foreign intel officer. She was keeping her fingers crossed that their efforts would yield results, and that they weren't on a wild goose chase.

Johnnie phoned Josh late in the afternoon, and said the Washington team that had surveilled Rothstein confirmed that the woman in the photo was indeed Julia Martin. Johnnie also mentioned that a Ferrari Spider like Rothstein's rental vehicle retailed for about $280k in the U.S., so it must have been extremely expensive to rent. Johnnie mentioned that someone from the Bureau would be bringing Rothstein's thumb drive to Josh the next morning.

Josh used the cloud account to confirm to Daniel that Rothstein's companion was definitely Martin.

Twenty-five

Posa! Posa![47]

(Put down! Put down!)

Tuesday May 19

It was another beautifully calm and clear morning with a temperature of about seventy.

Shellie awoke around six and began to get ready for a probable trip to Positano. She had a quick breakfast in the breakfast room, and returned to her room to watch for the target couple.

Daniel woke up about the same time. He took his laptop and went to the breakfast area as soon as it opened. Rothstein and Martin showed up at eight. They had a quick breakfast and left.

Daniel texted Shellie and Gianni when they finished. When Shellie saw the time, she guessed they might be giving themselves time to catch the first ferry to Positano at nine twenty. The next one would be at ten thirty. She got her things ready, and when she saw them coming at about ten to nine, she headed down to the lobby. When they passed the hotel, they headed straight for the ferry ticket kiosks. She headed there as well. She purchased a ticket just after they did. Then she walked out onto the pier, and texted Gianni and Daniel that she'd be going for a boat ride.

As soon as Daniel received her text, he went to the Bar il Giardino delle Palme on the Piazza Flavio Gioia, bought a bus ticket,

---

[47] The phrase from which Positano reportedly derived its name. Explained in this chapter.

and got on the bus scheduled to depart at nine thirty.

Gianni had already driven through Amalfi en route to Positano when he received Shellie's text. He knew he could be in place near the ferry arrival point when the ferry reached Positano at about 9:55 a.m.

The ferry passengers embarked about 9:45, and the ferry departed as scheduled. There was no wind, so the sea was very calm. Like many of the passengers, Rothstein and Martin, and Shellie all sat on the open upper deck. The views along the mountainous coast were breathtakingly beautiful. Just as she'd seen above Amalfi, Shellie saw terraced groves, bare rock, and woods. In several places, there were deep gorges cutting into the coast. One of those gorges was the Fjord of Furore. It included the town of Furore, which started at sea level and extended up to about 1,800 feet above sea level. They also passed the town of Praiano.

Approaching Positano by Ferry

Coming to Positano by sea offered a great view of the town, which started at sea level and climbed very high up the hillsides. The residences and businesses clinging to the hillsides were mostly subdued in color, with many whites, and yellows, but there were also some reds. At the center at sea level, was a beach. It was grayish in color. At the center above the beach and in the heart of town was the Church of Santa Maria Assunta, with its striking dome of green, yellow, and blue majolica tiles. The church was named after the town's patron saint, the Virgin Mary of the Assumption.

The ferry arrived on time and the passengers debarked. As Shellie was getting off, about 15 passengers behind Rothstein and Martin, she spotted Gianni standing alongside a wall not far from the ferry arrival point.

Rothstein and Martin started wandering around the streets and pedestrian walkways of the town, checking out the shops and restaurants and taking photos. It was easy enough for Gianni and Shellie to wander around in the same way and observe them.

About fifteen minutes after the ferry reached Positano, Daniel arrived at the bus stop on the main coastal road high above the beach. Right next to the bus stop was a street that went down into the heart of town - the Via Cristoforo Colombo (Christopher Columbus St.). On his right were shops and lodging, and on his left for a short distance was a nice view of the sea and the beach. Lower down were shops and eateries on both sides of the street.

After a while, he came to the Via dei Mulini[48] on his left. He turned and followed this pedestrian walkway down toward the beach. At places along the way, there were blooming wisteria vines on an overhead pergola. They created a colorful, live ceiling. At various times as he walked around the tourist areas of town, he saw Rothstein and Martin, Gianni, and Shellie. At about 12:45, he ran into E.J. Yelnovic, his wife Lani, and their son Chris in the area by the beach outside the Ristorante la Pergola. E.J. introduced Daniel to

---

[48] Street of the Mills

Lani and Chris, and they all chatted for a couple of minutes.

At about one, Daniel saw Rothstein and Martin enter La Pergola[49], apparently for lunch. That gave Daniel the idea of suggesting that E.J. and family have lunch with him in La Pergola. They liked the idea. They could see it had a great view of the beach and the glistening sea with bobbing boats. It had three open sides and an overhead pergola canopy of leafy vines. It also offered a nice view of a beautiful hillside portion of Positano. They entered La Pergola and were seated about four tables away from Rothstein and Martin.

Daniel's only worry was that E.J. would start talking about the Agency - not about classified information, but about people they knew, assignments, etc. He needn't have worried. E.J. and Lani were entirely focused on their trip. Their son was having the time of his life, and his parents were delighted.

At one point, E.J. asked their waiter to take a picture of the four of them. Daniel saw that Rothstein and Martin would end up in the picture, so he asked the waiter to take the same photo for him.

Daniel asked the waiter if he could recommend a local pasta and a local seafood dish. For the first dish, the waiter recommended Gnocchi alla Sorrentina - Sorrento-style potato dumplings with tomato sauce, mozzarella, and basil. The suggested seafood dish was Pezzogna all'Acqua Pazza - Sea Bream in Crazy Water - an Amalfi Coast specialty. It was a very simple dish in which a whole sea bream was poached in water, salt, a local heart-shaped cherry tomato called Pomodorini al Piennolo, celery, carrots, garlic, Italian parsley, and extra virgin olive oil. Daniel took the recommendations. Chris had Spaghetti alla Carbonara, and E.J. and Lani shared a Pizza Capricciosa - pizza with tomato sauce, mozzarella, ham, mushrooms, artichokes, and olives. All of the dishes were delicious. After lunch, they wished one another well and continued their separate wandering around town.

---

[49] http://www.bucapositano.it/ristorante-en.html

Gianni had lunch at Ristorante Le Tre Sorelle (The Three Sisters Restaurant) just to the right of La Pergola, and facing the water. He could see Rothstein from his table. Shellie found a nearby snack bar where she bought a light take-out lunch.

After a long leisurely lunch, Rothstein and Martin walked up to the Church of Santa Maria Assunta and went inside. The most important feature in the interior was a large, Byzantine icon of the Black Madonna above the main altar. The town got its name from this icon. Saracen pirates trying to take the Madonna from town were faced with a large storm that wouldn't let them leave. The Madonna supposedly said, "Posa, posa!" (Put (me) down! Put (me) down!), so the pirates put the icon down, and were then able to leave town.

After leaving the church, Rothstein and Martin walked slowly up Via dei Mulini and then up Via Cristoforo Colombo toward the bus stop, whose location they'd learned from a shop owner. They were carrying several bags with purchases they'd made.

Shellie felt she shouldn't ride back to Amalfi with Rothstein and Martin on the bus because she'd been with them on the ferry. She didn't want to raise their suspicions by spending too much time near them. She texted Daniel and Gianni that she felt like a boat ride. Daniel picked up the hint and texted that he liked bus trips better. Gianni texted that he'd drive to their favorite town. He planned to get to Piazza Flavio Gioia in Amalfi before the bus arrived.

Rothstein and Martin just missed the 5:10 p.m. bus, so they'd have to wait forty minutes for the next one. In the meantime, Gianni walked to where he'd parked his car - the paid parking lot by Piazza dei Mulini at the intersection of Via dei Mulini and Via Cristoforo Colombo. He paid the parking fee and drove to Amalfi, arriving just before six - with plenty of time to park his car and await the arrival of the bus. After parking, he walked over to the Savoia pasticceria and ordered an iced coffee and a pastry. He was served by the same waiter who'd served him two days earlier. The waiter remembered him, and greeted him warmly. He decided he'd wait in the area until about seven thirty, and then head back to Ravello.

The bus from Positano arrived about six forty. When Daniel saw that Rothstein and Martin appeared to be heading back to the Marina Riviera, he decided not to follow them, but to kill a little time in the Piazza del Duomo. He saw Gianni as he walked past the Savoia and turned up the narrow Via Duca Mansone I toward the Duomo. After a few minutes looking in shops, he headed back to the Marina Riviera, to spend some time on his Wi-Fi hunt.

Unfortunately for Shellie, she just missed the ferry at five, so she'd have to wait until the day's last ferry at six thirty. Of course there were worse fates in life than having to hang around Positano for an extra hour and a half. She purchased a ferry ticket, browsed in a few shops, and enjoyed people watching until about six fifteen. She then moved to the ferry landing, and boarded when it arrived.

The ferry reached Amalfi just before seven, and Shellie debarked and headed toward her hotel. She also noticed Gianni at the Savoia, and he saw her walk past. She freshened up in her room and then began to watch for Rothstein.

At about half past seven, Gianni left for Ravello as planned.

At eight thirty, Shellie saw Rothstein and Martin coming from the Marina Riviera. They passed below her window and turned right onto Via Duca Mansone I. She hoped they were heading to the Taverna degli Apostoli for dinner. She texted Daniel and Gianni, "Planning to join friends for dinner." She waited fifteen minutes, then headed to the taverna.

She entered and saw Rothstein and Martin seated at a table underneath what appeared to be an abstract modern painting or poster of Marilyn Monroe's face.

She was seated on the other side of the room. She ordered an appetizer of tomato bruschetta and a main dish of Spaghetti al Pesto di Limone - Spaghetti with Lemon Pesto. The pesto was made with lemon zest, olive oil, walnuts, almonds, mint, parsley and cheese. The spaghetti in this dish was "alla Chitarra" - guitar-style spaghetti, which is made with durum wheat semolina, egg, and salt. The spaghetti gets its name from being cut into shape on a frame of wire strings that are like guitar strings. The spaghetti strands are square rather than round.

Along with her spaghetti, Shellie had a side dish of fried eggplant with cherry tomatoes and basil. For dessert, she had Babà al Limoncello - limoncello cake, followed by a small glass of limoncello and coffee. She also had a glass of local white wine with her pasta and side dish.

Her observation of Rothstein and Martin throughout their meal was that they were completely relaxed and thoroughly engaged in light-hearted conversation. To this point, she'd seen no indication that this trip was anything other than a vacation.

After dinner, Rothstein and Martin wandered around town for an hour or so, and then returned to their hotel.

While Rothstein, Martin, and Shellie were having dinner, Daniel walked around town with his laptop , checking out different wireless network signals. Near Shellie's hotel, he found an interesting user who sent an English-language email to someone in Israel and signed it S.F. The sender said, "Having a great time. Heading to C. tomorrow. Regards to guys at the office." Daniel thought this could be Shmuel Feld. He wondered if "C" might be Capri. He knew he was just speculating. If this was Feld and he was a Mossad officer, there was no indication of any contact with Rothstein. Daniel decided to pass this info to Josh. He also texted it to Shellie and Gianni. "Think Silvio's here. Might head to isle tmw."

Back at NSA HQ, Josh received Rothstein's thumb drive from the Bureau in the morning. He immediately called Mac to ask for help in having experts examine the drive. Mac asked Josh to bring him the drive, and he'd have the right folks analyze its contents on an urgent basis. Josh immediately took the drive to Mac.

Mac contacted Garland Von Greif, the NSA's chief cryptanalyst, and asked for an immediate analysis of the thumb drive because it was of the highest national interest. Von Greif, who was a brilliant cryptanalyst himself and a protégé of Lambros Callimahos, told Mac he'd put a couple of his best guys on it right away.

Twenty-six

Sull'Incantesimo delle Syrene

(Under the Spell of the Sirens)

Wednesday May 20

The morning started out clear, with a temperature of sixty-five degrees and no wind.

Daniel and Shellie each enjoyed a leisurely breakfast, but Gianni decided to eat quickly, check out of his hotel, and drive down to Amalfi. He hoped he'd be lucky enough to find a parking space in the Piazza Flavio Gioia. When Rothstein left to drive to Sorrento, Gianni would follow. He knew Rothstein would have to drive through the piazza on route SS163 which would follow the coast, turn north, connect to the SS145 and lead to Sorrento.

At about ten thirty, Gianni and Shellie received a text from Daniel that read, "Just said good-bye to Rob & wished him a good trip." A few minutes later, Gianni saw Rothstein's red Ferrari, with its top down, pass through the piazza headed west. Gianni got into his car, waited a few minutes, and then followed on the SS163.

Rothstein took the SS163 west along the coast through Conca dei Marini, Praiano, and Positano, stopping several times along the way so they could enjoy the views of the coast, and take photos. Each time Gianni saw Rothstein pull over, he'd pull over a kilometer or so ahead, and wait for Rothstein to pass. Then he'd continue. About eight kilometers west of Positano, he followed the SS163 as it turned north and wound through the hills. They passed some grape vines

271

and olive trees. As they dropped down lower toward Sorrento, they passed lemon groves with trees surrounded and covered by netting to protect them from frost and hail.

When they reached the lowlands along the coast, the Plane of Sorrento, they turned left onto the Corso Italia, the main street that went through the heart of Sorrento, a city of about 61,000 inhabitants. The corso was very busy, and was lined with shops, restaurants, and lodging.

Maison Tofani[50], the Sorrento hotel where Rothstein would be staying, did not have its own parking, so Rothstein took his car to the Central Parking garage on the Corso Italia, about half a mile east of Piazza Tasso. The garage offered free valet service to and from hotels. The valet service only took Rothstein and Martin to the Piazza Tasso, very close to the hotel, because the hotel entrance was on a pedestrian street, the Via San Cesareo. Gianni parked in the same garage, which was only a couple of blocks from the Hotel Nice[51] where he'd be staying. Gianni, and Rothstein and Martin arrived at their respective hotels at about the same time - around twelve thirty.

Daniel checked out of the Marina Riviera at eleven, and an Amalfi Car Service van picked him up at quarter past. The same vehicle picked Shellie up at her hotel a few minutes later. The company, which did not realize they knew each other, had checked with each beforehand to see if they'd be willing to ride to Sorrento with another passenger. Both agreed.

When Shellie got into the vehicle, she introduced herself to Daniel, as if they'd never met. The driver explained that the trip was a distance of 32 kilometers (about twenty miles) and would take about an hour and ten minutes, with no stops and normal traffic. He offered to point out interesting sites along the way, and to stop at a couple of places that had beautiful views so that they could take

---

[50] http://www.maisontofani.com/
[51] http://www.hotelnicesorrento.com/

photos if they wished or just enjoy the views. They thanked him and said they'd be grateful if he'd do both.

The whole way to Sorrento, they chatted as if they were friendly strangers. The portion of the drive along the Amalfi Coast was, of course, spectacular. Both Shellie and Daniel had already done the Amalfi-Positano portion of the trip by bus. However, the unobstructed view from the van was far superior.

The driver stopped at two places along the coast for them to enjoy the views and take photos. The first was near the point of Conca dei Marini, where they had a beautiful view facing back east toward Amalfi. The second was just west of Praiano, at the Church of San Gennaro, with its colorful dome. From there, they had a great view of the coast west toward Positano and beyond.

On the SS163 Looking West Toward Positano and Beyond

The driver then continued, following the same route to Sorrento that Rothstein and Gianni had taken.

On reaching Sorrento, the driver first took Daniel to his hotel, the

Antiche Mura[52] (Ancient Walls), near Piazza Tasso, the main square. The hotel was so named because it sat along the fifteenth century walls of the town, with a portion of the walls preserved inside the hotel. Daniel thanked the driver, paid him, and added a nice tip. He wished Shellie well on her trip, and said he looked forward to meeting her again some day. She reacted in kind.

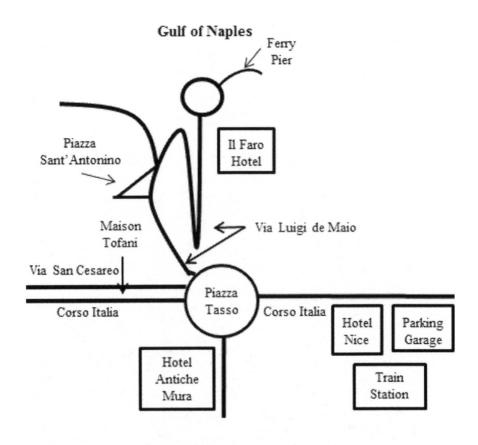

The Heart of Sorrento

The driver then drove her down the steep Via Luigi de Maio to

---

[52] http://hotelantichemura.com/

her hotel, the il Faro[53] (The Lighthouse), located very close to the ferry landing. Like Daniel, she thanked the driver effusively, paid him, and added a generous tip. It was about one thirty when she checked into the il Faro. Her room had a view out toward the waterfront, including a clear view of the ferry ticket kiosks. However, she decided that in the morning, she would hang out around the kiosk area to watch for Rothstein and Martin. From that location, she could purchase a ferry ticket quickly when she saw them purchase theirs.

After settling into his room, Daniel started his laptop and put a short encrypted message into the shared cloud account. It read, "Arrived at second loc. No contact yet."

As he was doing that, he and Shellie received a text from Gianni that read, "Having lunch in PT with Rob & Gina." Both assumed PT was the Piazza Tasso. Gianni had headed to the piazza right after checking into his hotel. He had correctly hoped that Rothstein and Martin would be lured to have lunch at either the Bar Ercolano[54] or the Fauno[55] Bar, both of which had lots of shaded outdoor tables facing the piazza. They chose the Bar Ercolano, which was right next to where the valet from the parking garage had dropped them off. While Rothstein and Martin were having lunch, Gianni was having his lunch at an outdoor table at the nearby Bar Syrenuse[56], from which he could watch them.

Shellie read Gianni's text just after checking into her room. She freshened up, then left the hotel and caught a bus up to the Piazza

---

[53] http://www.hotelilfaro.com/
[54] Italian name of the ancient Roman city of Herculaneum, just north of Pompeii. Like Pompeii, it was buried by the eruption of Mt. Vesuvius in 79 AD.
[55] "Fauno" in Italian, "faun" in English. A mythical creature that was half human and half goat. From the waist up, it was human, but with goat horns on the head. From the waist down, it was a goat. http://faunobar.it/en/index.php
[56] "Sirens," named after the Sirens of Greek mythology who are said to have inhabited an eponymous set of islands near Sorrento.
http://www.barsyrenusesorrento.it/en/index.php

Tasso. She started strolling around the piazza, and soon saw Gianni at the Bar Syrenuse. She went to the Syrenuse and got a table there. She showed no hint of recognizing Gianni. He paid for his lunch and left. Instead of walking directly toward Rothstein and Martin, he circled away from them and walked all the way around the piazza past the front of the Fauno Bar and onto the Corso Italia headed west. He walked to the Via degli Archi and then turned north to the Via San Cesareo. There, he started wandering into the shops and keeping an eye out for Rothstein and Martin.

After reading Gianni's text, Daniel logged into the hotel's wireless network system and started checking out users. In short order, he found one who was using Persian script. He was able to differentiate Persian script from Arabic by using a few techniques Josh had taught him. The Persian script was based on Arabic script, but had four additional letters.

Daniel was excited to find several emails the user had sent in the past few hours. One was sent just minutes earlier. He copied them, encrypted them, and put them in the shared cloud account. He asked Josh for a quick translation. The timing of the request could not have been better. It was about 2:15 p.m. in Italy and 8:15 a.m. at NSA.

Josh quickly read the emails, and found one that sounded very interesting. The other two appeared to be social emails of no value. The one of interest read:

"Friend just arrived, but not alone. Will see him in early evening."

Josh immediately uploaded that short translation into the account folder and added a note that the other two emails were of no interest. Josh was excited and crossed his fingers that the team would see a contact in the evening. If so, Josh might hear something during his workday.

Daniel knew he had to let Gianni and Shellie know right away. Prior to the trip, they'd agreed on different texts Daniel could send them if he learned of a scheduled contact Rothstein might have. If the contact would be in the evening, it would read, "Boys night out."

If there was any info about time or location or the intel operative, that would be added. Daniel texted, 'Boys night out with Rob & Enzo." When Gianni and Shellie received the text, they both assumed the meeting was likely to take place before dinner, perhaps between five thirty and eight. That was more likely than after dinner, but it was just a guess. They figured Rothstein and Martin would wander around and browse in the shops for a couple of hours, then return to Maison Tofani. Rothstein would give some excuse for going out on his own, and then meet with the Iranian.

After lunch, Rothstein and Martin began to walk around and look in the shops. They strolled on the east to west streets - the Corso Italia, the Via San Cesareo/Via Fuori, the Via Accademia, and cross streets like the Via Torquato Tasso and the Vico Primo Fuoro. There was a large mix of shops selling clothing, jewelry, ceramics, "home-made" footwear, leather goods, toys, luggage, inlaid wood, etc. There was a lemon-themed shop selling towels, candies, soaps, limoncello, etc. There was Bartolucci - which sold hand-made wooden toys, and had a spectacular full-sized, hand-made wooden motorcycle out front. Some of the shops were Italian and some foreign. The eateries included not only-interesting looking Italian restaurants, but the "Scottish Tilted Kilt" pub, an Irish pub, and a British pub.

During their walk, Martin added to her Italian ceramics and also purchased lemon soaps and towels. At about half past five, they returned to Maison Tofani.

At six thirty, Daniel saw the Persian-language user disconnect from Antiche Mura's wireless network. He speculated that the user could be preparing to head out for his meeting. Daniel texted, "Night out cd be soon." Then he immediately walked out the front of the hotel and to the other side of some deep ruins, the Vallone dei Mulini. He faced the hotel as if to take a picture of the hotel itself. About a quarter to seven, when he saw a person who looked like Farhad Ahmadi, he snapped a photo. Then he texted, "Think Enzo's coming now." Daniel returned to his hotel room, encrypted the photo of the probable Iranian, and uploaded it to the shared cloud account. Josh downloaded the photo and passed it to Johnnie.

Several minutes later, Shellie saw a man who closely resembled Ahmadi coming to the Piazza Tasso from the Antiche Mura. When he reached the Fauno Bar, he turned right and circled carefully all the way around the piazza to the Bar Ercolano. Then he walked onto the Via Luigi de Maio. Shellie texted, "Past me."

A few minutes later, Gianni saw Rothstein come out of Maison Tofani, turn left (west) onto Via San Cesareo, and then right onto the very narrow Via degli Archi. Instead of following Rothstein directly onto Via degli Archi, Gianni went one block further west to the parallel Largo Padre Reginaldo Giuliani. Gianni knew that Via degli Archi only went one block north to Via Santa Maria delle Grazie, so Rothstein would have to turn left or right there. He turned right, and Gianni could see him. Gianni gave him a couple of minutes, and then followed. After one block, Via Santa Maria came to the small, triangular-shaped Piazza Sant'Antonino, which was named after the eleventh century basilica by that name on one side of the piazza. There were a couple of park benches in the piazza. Gianni saw Rothstein sit down at a bench on the side of the piazza facing the basilica. He sat next to a man who looked like Farhad Ahmadi. Bingo!

Gianni did not stop to look. Instead, he walked past and crossed the Via Luigi de Maio to Ristorante Pizzeria L'Abate[57] (the Abbot Restaurant and Pizzeria), which was located next to the entrance to the basilica. The restaurant had lots of outdoor tables, and had just opened for dinner. Gianni asked for an outdoor table near the street, and was seated facing the piazza. A few minutes later, he saw Shellie walking down Via Luigi de Maio toward him. When she saw Gianni and then Rothstein in the piazza, she knew Gianni had everything under control, and she continued down the street, following it all the way downhill to her hotel. She was excited that they seemed to have

---

[57] http://www.labatesorrento.it/en/

caught Rothstein in the act.

Gianni was delighted because he was perfectly situated to observe Rothstein and his case officer. He was even able to take occasional covert photos. After the pair chatted for a few minutes, the probable case officer pulled out a manila envelope, and handed it to Rothstein. Rothstein looked into the envelope then put his hand inside. It looked like he could be counting money. Gianni captured that in a photo. After Rothstein pulled his hand out and closed the envelope, he said something to the case officer in an animated way. Gianni wished he was close enough to hear the conversation. Rothstein then handed a small envelope to Ahmadi, who thanked Rothstein. Gianni snapped a photo of that exchange.

The two continued to talk for another ten minutes or so. Then the case officer left and walked back up Via Luigi de Maio toward Piazza Tasso. When he was out of sight, Rothstein looked back inside the envelope and smiled. He closed the envelope, got up, and left, heading back the way he had come. Gianni knew there was no point in following. The meeting was done. He texted Shellie and Daniel - "night out done. DPT22" The abbreviation meant, "Daniel, Piazza Tasso 2200 hours (10 p.m.)." That indicated Gianni would meet Daniel to give him a micro SD card with pics to upload for Josh. Gianni continued with his dinner. He ordered the Pezzogna all'Acqua Pazza (Sea Bream in Crazy Water), which Daniel had eaten at La Pergola in Positano. He accompanied that with a bottle of Feudi di San Gregorio Rubrato, made with 100 percent Aglianico grapes. He had something to celebrate.

Back at Antiche Mura, Daniel saw the Iranian log back into the hotel's wireless network, and send a short Persian-language email.

Daniel copied the email, disconnected from the wireless network, and encrypted the email. He also wrote and encrypted a note - "Nino at mtg. Pics later." He reconnected to the wireless network and uploaded the encrypted files to the cloud account. He couldn't wait to learn the contents of the email. The time at Ft. Meade was about 2:15 p.m.

Josh translated the email, which read, "Met friend and received gift. Gave him bonus. He said it was not enough. I said we need better. He said we give more or there's nothing. I said if nothing, we tell. He said if we tell, no one trusts. Should I give more? Will meet him same time tomorrow." Josh loaded the encrypted translation to the cloud account.

He then phoned Johnnie, and informed him that Rothstein had met with his case officer, and that the meeting had been observed by Gianni. Photos and details would be coming soon. Josh explained the contents of the case officer's email, which described the meeting. The Iranian reported that Rothstein threatened to stop working for them if they didn't give him more money. The case officer warned Rothstein that if he stopped providing info, they'd reveal his activity. Rothstein said that if they did that, others wouldn't trust them. The case officer wanted to know if he should give Rothstein more money, and stated that he was scheduled to meet with him again the next evening.

Johnnie was excited. He said he'd confirmed that the individual in the photo Daniel had sent was Farhad Ahmadi. Hopefully, with the photos of the meeting, and other evidence they might obtain, they could arrange to arrest Rothstein when he was passing through Customs on reentering the U.S.

If Ahmadi had given him more than $10,000 in cash, he would probably have that money on him. Any person entering the U.S. with $10,000 or more in cash or other financial instruments had to submit to Customs on arrival a declaration of the amount of those funds. The declaration could be made on a paper FinCen 105 report form or on a receipt from data the traveler entered into an Automated Passport Control kiosk. Johnnie doubted that Rothstein would make the necessary declaration.

Josh phoned Sofie and asked to meet with the Director. She said he was away for a meeting with the DNI, but she expected to be talking with him by phone in about an hour. Josh said it was very important that he talk to the Director in private at that time if at all possible. She said she'd inform him and he could call Josh if he had the time.

Josh phoned Mac and updated him. At that very time, Daniel was looking into one of the windows of A. Gargiulo & Jannuzzi[58], a large, upscale store that carried beautiful inlaid woodwork, ceramics, linens, furniture, etc. It was located at the edge of Piazza Tasso next to the Bar Fauno, and had been in business since 1852. Gianni started looking into another of the many windows of the store. They moved toward each other. When they were at the same window, Gianni inconspicuously passed Daniel a micro SD card with photos of Rothstein and Ahmadi. Daniel returned to the Antiche Mura, encrypted the photos and uploaded them for Josh.

The Director called just after four fifteen, and Josh provided him with the latest developments. The Director was very happy, and said he'd immediately inform the DNI.

After getting off the phone with the Director, Josh checked the cloud account and found four sharp photos of Rothstein meeting with Ahmadi. He left Daniel an encrypted note that read, "First pic did trick."

Daniel ended the evening with a text to Shellie and Gianni, "Mtg again same time tmw. GOOD night."

---

[58] http://www.gargiulo-jannuzzi.it

Twenty-seven

Un Gioiello del Mare

(A Jewel of the Sea)

Thursday May 21

The day began with no wind and scattered clouds. Temperatures were in the low sixties and would remain that way all day.

Shellie, Gianni, and Daniel all got up around six and quickly prepared for the day, unsure of where Rothstein would go. If he and Martin decided on Capri, they could take a ferry as early as 7:15. The trains to Pompeii departed as early as 6:25.

Before leaving the Antiche Mura, Daniel logged into the hotel's wireless network. He found the Iranian logged in and discovered he'd received an email in Persian. Daniel went through the usual process to get it to Josh. He knew Josh wouldn't see it for at least six hours because it was just after midnight at Ft. Meade. When Daniel observed that the Iranian had disconnected from the wireless network, he also disconnected. Then he prepared for the day.

When he was ready, Daniel left the Antiche Mura and headed to the Bar Syrenuse at Piazza Tasso to see if he could determine which way Rothstein and Martin were going. At about ten to eight, he saw them come to the piazza and catch a cab. It headed down the Via Luigi de Maio toward the ferries at Marina Piccola. Daniel texted, "boat today."

Shellie saw them arrive at a ticket kiosk a couple minutes later. The first available tickets were for a high-speed ferry at eight thirty.

Those ferries took twenty minutes to get to Capri, and the regular ferries took half an hour. Shellie bought a ticket as well. Another ferry ride with Rothstein and Martin. She texted the time to Gianni and Daniel.

Gianni replied, "Will go a bit later." Daniel added, "Me too." They both headed down to the ferry dock. They'd end up on the high-speed ferry at quarter to nine.

Shellie boarded the ferry about forty passengers behind Rothstein and Martin. Since the ferry carried several hundred passengers, it was easy to blend in.

As the ferry departed, Shellie looked at Sorrento. The view from the Bay of Naples was spectacular - with the small harbor, the sheer cliffs, the city on the plateau, and the hills above. To the north, she could see Mt. Vesuvius under scattered clouds. She was looking forward to seeing the island in person after watching so many on-line videos and reading so many interesting articles. She learned from her research that the Roman Emperor Tiberius had ruled the empire from his Villa Jovis on the island for the last ten years of his reign - from AD 27 to 37. She wondered what the people of Capri had seen when Mt. Vesuvius erupted with massive force across the bay in AD 79 and buried Pompeii and Herculaneum. She read that Capri was famous for caprese salad, which means, "Capri-style salad," and which originated on the island in the 1950s. Its colors of white mozzarella, red tomatoes, and green basil represented the colors of the Italian flag. In Italy, it was typically served as an antipasto. She also learned that the island was the inspiration for Capri pants, which had been created in 1948 by renowned fashion designer Sonja de Lennart, who designed a "Capri Collection," and whose family loved Capri. The pants became popular when they were worn by actress Mary Tyler Moore playing Laura Petrie on the Dick Van Dyke show in the 1960s. Amusingly, they were considered risqué.

The sea was very calm, so the ride was exceptionally smooth. Rothstein and Martin were taking in the views and chatting away.

The ferry soon pulled into Capri's Marina Grande (Large Harbor), which was filled with small and medium-size boats; and its waterfront was lined with buildings that were three to five stories high and in a variety of colors - red, yellow, orange, blue, white, etc. There were restaurants and shops on the street level. Residences and other buildings dotted the hillsides; and the town of Capri sat high up on a hill overlooking the port, with mountains towering above.

When Rothstein and Martin got off the ferry, they immediately headed for a dock where there were Blue Grotto and round-the-island tour boats. They immediately bought tickets for a round-trip to the Blue Grotto cave, one of the most famous sights on the island. The water inside was lit by natural azure blue light, creating a beautiful glow. It could only be entered from the sea via a low entrance that was only about six feet wide and three feet high. Visitors took a motor boat to a floating ticket office near the cave entrance; purchased a ticket to enter the cave; then transferred to a small row boat to be rowed into the cave. Passengers had to lay flat in the boats during entry. The boats only stayed inside for a couple of minutes.

Shellie knew there would be no value in following them on the grotto tour. It would be impractical for Rothstein to have substantive contact with anyone of interest during that tour. She decided to await their return at a covered outdoor table at a cafe along the waterfront. She selected Caffè Augusto at Via 20 Cristoforo Colombo, not far from the ferry dock. She also texted Gianni and Daniel, "Rob & Gina on Grotto tour. Coffee stop for me."

While Daniel and Gianni were on their ferry ride to Capri, Daniel sat in the center section of the passenger compartment and Gianni on the port side. As Daniel looked around, he noticed Ahmadi seated alone near a window forward on the starboard side. Daniel immediately texted Gianni and Shellie, "Enzo's along for the ride." Gianni began looking around, and finally saw Ahmadi.

Gianni, Shellie, and Daniel all gave some thought to why Ahmadi might be going to Capri. They could think of a variety of reasons, particularly if Rothstein had mentioned the outing at their meeting the previous evening. Ahmadi might want to:

- See if Rothstein contacted anyone else;
- Get a look at Rothstein's traveling companion, and perhaps get a sense for the relationship between the couple;
- Determine if Rothstein had told the truth about his outing;
- Travel to Capri for his own pleasure; or
- Some combination of the above.

In any case, they were glad they'd detected him. They'd now have to be more cautious in their surveillance.

When the ferry docked, Daniel and Gianni maneuvered themselves to get off at a distance behind Ahmadi. They noticed that he continuously monitored his surroundings. He quickly headed to one of the many eateries with covered outdoor tables. Fortuitously, he chose Caffè Augusto where Shellie was having her coffee and pastry. He seated himself just two tables from her.

"Saelam agha, khosh amaedid be kapri. Hal e shomah che tor?" (Hello sir. Welcome to Capri. How are you?), the waiter greeted Ahmadi in Persian.

The Iranian reacted with surprise and a smile at the same time. "Besiar khub aem, mersi, vae shomah?" (I'm fine, thanks, and you?)

"Besiar khub aem, mersi," the waiter replied.

"Where did you learn Persian?" the Iranian continued in Persian.

"Just here. We have visitors from many countries. But now I have spoken almost all my Persian."

"I compliment you," the Iranian switched to American-accented English. "Your pronunciation is very good."

"Kheili maemnun aem," (Thank you very much) the waiter replied in Persian. "I hope you enjoy Capri."

"I always do. It is so beautiful. By the way, how did you know I was Iranian?"

"It is the way you dress and walk. I see many customers from all over the world, so I can usually identify their country. Now, how may I help you?"

"I would like a cappuccino and a cornetto" (a crescent-shaped Italian breakfast pastry similar to a French croissant).

"I shall bring them right away."

Shellie texted Daniel and Gianni that Enzo had joined her, and that he was familiar with the area. They chuckled to themselves. If only Ahmadi knew who was seated near him.

Ahmadi appeared to be in his early-to-mid forties. He was about six feet tall, and trim. He had a full head of black hair, but no mustache or beard. He had a distinguished thin face with a long nose that had a slight bump. His attire was nicer-than-tourist casual, with a plain, long-sleeve, pressed, light beige shirt with collar, tan slacks, and sharp, light-brown leather shoes. He was wearing a smart watch on his wrist. His demeanor and interaction with the waiter were polite and self-assured, with a manly demeanor. He constantly scanned the people walking by and those in the cafe. His appearance certainly didn't fit what one would expect of a low-level clerical employee, even at a diplomatic facility like the Iranian UN Mission; nor would one expect such a person to be able to afford an Amalfi Coast vacation.

Shellie noticed that he looked at her a couple of times, seeming more to evaluate her as a woman than to think of her as someone who might be surveilling him. She used her phone to get a photo of him, as she pointed the phone toward the waterfront snapping photos in different directions.

Shellie beckoned to the waiter and ordered another pastry so she could stay longer and watch Ahmadi.

Gianni felt Shellie and Daniel had the waterfront covered, so he decided to go up to the town of Capri which was about 450 feet above sea level, almost directly above Marina Grande. The town was a natural next stop for Rothstein and Martin after visiting the Blue Grotto and the Marina Grande. There were other options, like taking a boat tour around the island or visiting the town of Anacapri. Both towns offered stunning views. The town of Capri was where all the action was - with more shops and eateries. The town of Anacapri was quieter, less crowded, and more quaint. Consequently, tourists who were visiting the island for a single day tended to choose Capri over Anacapri.

There were several ways to get from Marina Grande up to the town of Capri - by funicular, bus, or cab, or even by walking, but that was time-consuming and tiring. The funicular ride to the top was the fastest - about four minutes - if the waiting line wasn't too long. Gianni bought a funicular ticket at the ticket window, and then got in the short line. He knew how to position himself in a funicular car so he could face the sea and catch the most beautiful views.

When he got to the top, he walked out of the exit and took a few steps over to a railing, where he took in the incredible views of the sea, of Monte Cappello rising to about 1,600 feet on his left, and of Marina Grande far below. Another example of why he loved southwestern Italy so much.

He walked around the corner into the Piazza Umberto I, which was known as "la Piazzetta" (The little piazza), and which locals called a "chiazz." It was now about half past nine. He found a seat at an outdoor table of the Al Piccolo Bar. He knew it would be expensive because of its location, but it offered a great view of people coming to the town of Capri by funicular or bus. It was a few feet from the funicular station, and it was about a block from the intercity bus stop on the Via Roma.

In one corner of the piazzetta was its famous clock tower (Torre dell'Orologio). Around the piazzetta were four eateries, which at times filled the little piazza with their outdoor tables, where the rich and famous often mingled with tourists. There was also the town hall, a tourist information office, an upscale shop called La Parisienne (The Parisian Woman), and a bank. Overlooking the piazza was the Chiesa di Santo Stefano (the Church of St. Stephen).

While Shellie was at the Caffè Augusto and Gianni was in the piazzetta, Daniel wandered around the Marina Grande waterfront, familiarizing himself with the shops, the eateries, the funicular station, the bus stop, and the ticket offices. Ferries continued to arrive from Naples, Sorrento, and Positano, disgorging more and more tourists, most of whom were probably day-trippers.

Just after ten, Shellie saw Rothstein and Martin return from their Blue Grotto tour, and walk off the pier and onto Via Cristoforo Colombo. They started walking along the waterfront and into shops. When they walked past the Caffè Augusto, she saw that Ahmadi had detected them and followed them with his eyes. They did not see him. She texted Daniel and Gianni that Gina and Rob were back.

Shellie decided she'd stayed at Caffè Augusto long enough. She paid her bill, and then started walking around Marina Grande, visiting the shops. She kept an eye out for Ahmadi, as well as Rothstein and Martin. Ahmadi remained at the cafe.

Daniel decided to take the bus up to the piazzetta. He texted to Gianni and Shellie "Taking bus up."

After about forty-five minutes of shopping at Marina Grande, Rothstein bought funicular tickets, and he and Martin headed up to the piazzetta. Shellie texted Gianni and Daniel, "Rob & Gina on fast route up."

She then saw Ahmadi leave the cafe. Instead of going to one of the transportation modes to get to the piazzetta, he walked over to a ferry ticket kiosk and bought a ticket. He then headed to an embarkation point and boarded a ferry. Perhaps he felt it would be difficult to avoid running into Rothstein and Martin in the town of Capri because of the layout of the streets. She texted Daniel and Gianni, "Enzo back on boat. I'm coming up."

When Daniel learned that Ahmadi was returning to Sorrento, he decided it would be best to return to see if Ahmadi logged into the wireless network. Daniel did not want to miss any of Ahmadi's comms. He texted Shellie and Gianni, "Gonna be a boat person." He went to the funicular station, bought a ticket, and returned to Marina Grande. There he bought a ferry ticket. While Shellie was waiting in line to get on the funicular, she saw Daniel exit, and silently wished him a smooth trip back.

Daniel departed Marina Grande about twenty minutes after

Ahmadi. When he reached Marina Piccola at Sorrento, he caught a cab directly back to Antiche Mura in the hope of arriving and logging into the hotel's wireless network before Ahmadi arrived. He was successful. However, that was of little value. Ahmadi logged into the wireless network and then his email account. He found nothing new and logged out of both.

Daniel logged into his shared cloud account. He found the translation of the email that had been sent to Ahmadi. It read, "Give another 10. Tell him he must do better or will reduce gifts."

On Capri, Gianni saw Rothstein and Martin walk into the piazzetta. They looked around for a couple minutes, and then continued through. Gianni felt it would be too difficult to follow them around the narrow streets of Capri without being noticed. They knew Rothstein wouldn't be meeting Ahmadi on Capri since he'd already returned to Sorrento. Gianni doubted that Rothstein would meet another contact with Martin present, especially given how he'd met Ahmadi alone the previous evening. Gianni texted Shellie, "Will have lunch & go back."

She replied, "Ok. enough here. Did u like last night's dinner?" She wanted to convey to Gianni the message that she could have dinner at L'Abate restaurant and surveil the upcoming meeting between Rothstein and Ahmadi - to reduce the possibility of detection.

He understood her message and answered, "Yeah. U shud try it."

She sent, "Thanks. Will go tonite."

Shellie wished she could have continued the surveillance on Capri. After studying the shopping there, she thought Martin would be lured in by the upscale shopping on Via Vittorio Emanuele and Via Carnerelle with high-end shops like Versace, Bulgari, Dolce & Gabana, Ferragamo, Gucci, Louis Vuitton, and interesting local shops. These shops were certainly a reflection of the wealth that flowed through Capri.

Gianni decided to have lunch at Ristorante da Giorgio[59] located a few steps from the piazzetta on Via Roma. It had incredible views and good food. He walked down the stairs into the restaurant, and luckily got a table at an open window overlooking the Bay of Naples, and with a clear view of Mt. Vesuvius in the distance. He had a Caprese salad followed by a dish of Ravioli alla Caprese (Capri-style ravioli). He also had a small bottle of Taurasi wine, a Campania wine made from Aglianico grapes.

Shellie felt she couldn't leave Capri without having a meal there. Thanks to TripAdvisor, she discovered the Pulalli Wine Bar up some stairs next to the Clock Tower on the piazzetta. The owner, Fabrizio, seated her at a table overlooking the piazzetta. Like Gianni, she had the Caprese salad and Ravioli alla Caprese.

After their meals, Gianni and Shellie took separate ferries back to Sorrento. Shellie jokingly thought she should recommend to the Bureau that all agents be given overseas surveillance sabbaticals in places like this. She'd volunteer to be first.

After arriving in Sorrento and stopping in her hotel room, Shellie decided to hang out at the area between her hotel and the pier to look for Rothstein and Martin's return. There were so many tourists and others around the area that it was easy to blend in.

She saw them arrive at about five thirty, grab a cab and head up Via Luigi de Maio, presumably to Piazza Tasso and then on to Maison Tofani. She texted the info to Gianni and Daniel.

Since she'd sat so close to Ahmadi earlier in the day at Caffè Augusto, and since she wouldn't be far from him at L'Abate restaurant, Shellie altered her appearance by changing clothes, redoing her hair, and donning glasses. In view of the chilly temperatures, she put on a light jacket that was different from the one she'd worn to Capri. She hoped it was enough.

At about six forty, she caught a cab up to Piazza Sant'Antonino and L'Abate Restaurant. She arrived about ten minutes before the

---

[59] http://www.ristorantedagiorgio.com/en/index

restaurant opened, so she stood by the entrance waiting. Ahmadi showed up about five to seven, and sat at the same park bench where he'd met Rothstein the previous meeting.

The restaurant opened and Shellie asked for an outdoor table. She pointed to one with a good view of the meeting place. Rothstein showed up about five minutes late. After greeting each other, Rothstein sat next to Ahmadi, and they engaged in an animated conversation. After a couple of minutes, Ahmadi pulled out a manila envelope and gave it to Rothstein, who opened the envelope, looked inside and smiled. He talked to Ahmadi for a few minutes longer. Ahmadi seemed to be speaking forcefully about something, and Rothstein kept nodding in agreement. Then they concluded the discussion. Ahmadi got up and left. Rothstein departed a few minutes later. The meeting lasted no more than eight minutes. Shellie managed to snap a couple of photos, including one of Rothstein looking into the envelope. Fortunately, the waiter left her alone long enough for her to get the photos.

She sent Gianni and Daniel a text identical to the one Gianni had sent the preceding evening, "night out done. DPT22" She would be meeting Daniel in Piazza Tasso at ten to give him the micro SD card with the pics. Gianni was walking around the Piazza Tasso to see if Ahmadi would pass through and return to the Antiche Mura after the meeting with Rothstein. A couple of minutes after Shellie's text, he saw Ahmadi crossing through the piazza en route back to the Antiche Mura. He texted, "Enzo's going to Dani's."

After Shellie had sent her text, she ordered dinner, starting with an appetizer of Prosciutto di Parma and Mozzarella cheese, followed by a plate of Gnocchi alla Sorrentina. The Sorrento-style gnocchi were potato dumplings with mozzarella, southern Italian tomato sauce, and basil leaves topped with parmesan cheese - a delicious and very filling dish. She chose a lemon sponge cake from L'Abate's big dessert trolley and followed that with limoncello and a double espresso. She then returned to her hotel and waited until it was time to meet Daniel at Piazza Tasso.

After receiving Shellie's text about the conclusion of Rothstein's meeting with Ahmadi, and Gianni's text about Ahmadi's return, Daniel logged onto Antiche Mura's wireless network and waited for Ahmadi to log on. He did not disappoint. About fifteen minutes later, he sent a very short Persian-language email. Daniel copied it, signed off the wireless network, encrypted it and added a note "Stella at mtg tonight. Pics later." He then logged back on, and uploaded the email and note to the shared account. Since it was about 1:30 p.m. at Ft. Meade, he hoped he would get a quick translation from Josh. He did. The translation read, "Met friend. Gave. He agreed. Don't trust. Return as planned." Josh added, "Great stuff."

Josh immediately informed the Director, Mac, and Johnnie.

Johnnie told Josh that he now had Rothstein and Martin's return itinerary. They would depart Naples just after noon local on May 23, change planes at Paris Charles de Gaulle, depart Paris at 5 p.m. local, and arrive at Dulles at 7:25 p.m.

The Bureau would have a team of agents in the Dulles arrivals area to observe Rothstein from the time he reached his arrival gate until he reached the final Customs and Border Protection (CBP) Officer. Once Rothstein completed the Automated Passport Control kiosk process and presented his receipt to a CBP Officer; or when he submitted a customs declaration, he would be taken aside, questioned, and searched. Hopefully, he'd have undeclared cash in excess of $10,000 on his person. Even if they didn't find the cash, he'd be placed under arrest because of all the evidence they had. Martin would be detained, questioned, and searched. However, since there was no evidence or even any hint that she was complicit, Johnnie expected that nothing further would be discovered, and that she'd be released.

After receiving Josh's translation and compliment, Daniel walked to the Fauno Bar in Piazza Tasso for dinner. The piazza was now closed to traffic for the evening. It was alive with people out for La Passeggiata - the traditional Italian evening stroll. The sun would not set for another hour, but when it did, the piazza would be brightly lit.

Not surprisingly, the Fauno Bar was crowded. Luckily, Daniel was seated quickly. He ordered a dish of Cannelloni alla Sorrentina, a pasta dish with a sauce that normally included beef or veal, Fior di latte[60] cheese and ricotta cheese, tomatoes, white wine, basil, olive oil, and grated Parmesan. Before the pasta arrived, the waiter brought him nibbles of local olives, nuts, and crisps. The olives in particular were terrific. When the pasta came, it was delicious. He followed the pasta with a strawberry dessert, a limoncello, and coffee. He thought the restaurant had delicious food and friendly, professional service, despite being in such a mega tourist location.

Since Gianni could not really contribute to the surveillance after seeing Ahmadi return to the Antiche Mura, he decided to treat himself out of his own pocket to a very special dinner at L'Antica Trattoria, a restaurant that he loved and that was one of his favorites in southwestern Italy. It was located on the Via Padre Reginaldo Giuliani, two blocks west of the Piazza Sant'Antonino. He was greeted at the entrance by the owner, Signor Aldo Doria, whose family had owned the restaurant since 1930. Signor Doria seated him at a table on the garden terrace. Gianni ordered the four-course set menu known as the Menu Sinfonia (Symphony Menu). The dishes were truly a culinary symphony:

- Zucchini flowers fried in a delicate batter with fuscella ricotta (a cows-milk ricotta produced in Campania), cubes of prosciutto, and sweet Tropea onions (from Calabria) in a sweet and sour sauce. (Fiore di Zucchine con Ricotta di Fuscella e Brunoise di Prosciutto in Pastella Delicata, Salsa all' Agrodolce e Petalli di Cipolle di Tropea)

- "Mediterranean Concerto" fresh, triangular egg-pasta with delicate Sorrento cheese, zucchini, zucchini flowers, basil pesto, and marjoram. (Triangoli "Concerto Mediterraneo" di Pasta Fresca

---

[60] "Milk's Flower" - a type of mozzarella cheese made from cow's milk as opposed to "Mozzarella di Bufala" (Buffalo Mozzarella), which is made from Mediterranean water buffalo milk.

all'Uovo ai Formaggi Delicati di Sorrento con Maggiorana, Zucchine, Fiore di Zucchine, e Pesto di Basilico)

- Pork medallions with mustard, and herbs, with Savoy cabbage and green onions, fresh Annurca apples (a type of small apple from Campania) in a cream sauce, dried dates, and cranberry sauce. (Medaglione di Filetto di Maiale alla Senape, alle Erbe, con Verza al Cipolotto, Fresco Cremoso di Mele Annurche, Datteri Secchi, e Salsa al Mirtillo)

- Sorrento Lemon Delight (Delizia di Sorrento al Limone) - sponge cake covered with Chantilly lemon sauce.

To accompany his meal, he had a 2013 red wine called Dedicato a Marianna (Dedicated to Marianne) Sciascinoso, made with Sciascinoso and Aglianico grapes. It was produced in the Irpinia area of Campania, just east of Mt. Vesuvius.

During the meal, a very talented mandolin player wandered around the restaurant enthusiastically serenading the diners. The meal was superb. Gianni felt a bit guilty about enjoying this symphonic culinary interlude, but he couldn't resist.

At 9:50 p.m., Daniel left his table at the Fauno Bar and walked to the opposite side of the piazza near the Bar Syrenuse. He saw Shellie, and walked toward her. As he passed close to her, she surreptitiously handed him the micro-SD card. He returned to the Antiche Mura, inserted the micro SD card into his laptop, and took a quick look at the photos Shellie had taken. They were nice and clear. He encrypted them, logged onto the wireless network, and uploaded them. At that time, he also found a note from Josh that Rothstein would be departing Naples just after noon on Saturday. Daniel texted Shellie and Daniel, "Friends leave after noon Sat."

When Josh downloaded and decrypted the file Daniel had sent, he was delighted by Shellie's photos. He immediately passed them to Johnnie, who was very happy. He was also relieved that there was no indication of Israeli involvement. That would have created many complications.

Twenty-eight

Scavi e Misteri

(Excavations and Mysteries)

Friday May 22

The day started out clear, with no wind, and with a temperature of around sixty. Temperatures would rise into the high sixties in the afternoon.

On the basis of Ahmadi's email the previous evening, Gianni, Shellie, and Daniel all doubted there'd be another contact with Ahmadi prior to Rothstein's departure from Italy, but they couldn't ignore that possibility or the possibility that he might meet with an Israeli. So Daniel went to the Bar Ercolano on Piazza Tasso at about quarter past six, shortly after it opened. He knew Rothstein and Martin would almost surely pass by if they headed to the train station to catch the train to Pompeii. He ordered a cappuccino and a cornetto pastry. He would end up having a couple of each before they walked by at about seven thirty. When he saw them pass not far from his table, they were headed east across the piazza to the Corso Italia. He texted Gianni and Shellie, "Rob & Gina want choo choo."

Gianni knew there was very little shade within the vast Pompeii historical site, so he dressed appropriately, including a wide-brimmed hat and a light jacket. As soon as he received Daniel's text, he left the lobby of the Hotel Nice, turned right onto Via Ernesto de Curtis, and walked one block to the train station of the

Circumvesuviana (around Vesuvius) rail line. Sorrento was the last station on the Circumvesuviana. He went to the "Train & Bus Ticket Point" on the ground floor, and purchased a one-way ticket to the Pompei Scavi-Villa Misteri[61] Station, the one that served the Pompeii historical site. He immediately walked up the stairs to the platform. He wanted to be up on the platform when Rothstein and Martin arrived, so it would not look like he was following them.

The couple arrived a few minutes later, and walked to a different section of the platform. When the train arrived, the couple and Gianni got on different cars, both of which were fairly crowded. The train departed at 7:55 a.m. The views along en route were not particularly interesting. The track ran through industrial areas, tunnels, and apartment clusters. There were a couple of scenic views and some lemon groves and scattered orange trees. The train arrived at Pompei Scavi-Villa Misteri, the 13th station after Sorrento, at 8:25 - a half-hour trip.

Gianni let Rothstein and Martin walk outside the station first. When he exited, he walked around as if he was trying to figure out what to do, even though he knew what was outside the station. For example, there was an individual trying to pitch a private tour, and there was an office selling group and private tours.

Gianni watched Rothstein make a call on his cell phone. Within a couple of minutes, a man walked up, and introduced himself. There were two possibilities. Most likely, he was a private tour guide whom Rothstein had booked in advance. It was also possible he was an intel contact. He could be both a professional guide and a conduit for passing materials. The cover would be perfect.

From the man's behavior and personal interaction, Gianni was almost certain he was only a professional guide. He handed each a

---

[61] Means, "Pompeii Excavations - Villa of the Mysteries." The ancient town of Pompeii and the Villa of the Mysteries together form a UNESCO World Heritage site. The villa is about a quarter mile from the town. It is large and remarkably well-preserved, with beautiful frescoes. The Italian spelling of Pompeii is "Pompei."

couple of documents - probably site maps and guide booklets. Gianni took photos of the document handover. The photos could be closely scrutinized later for any indication of an abnormal transaction.

If the tour was a bona fide tour, as Gianni believed, it would probably last two to three hours. A good, two-hour private tour could cost €150 or more, depending on the season; while nice, small-group tours were very reasonably priced.

Gianni had been to Pompeii several times, and knew the logical tour sequences used by guides. One of those sequences was on the self-guided audio tour visitors could rent. He saw the guide take Rothstein and Martin to the Porta Marina (Sea Gate) entrance, which was the closest to the train station. The gate was at the coast in Roman times, but after the eruption of Mt. Vesuvius in AD 79, the coast ended up half a mile away.

The couple bought their own park entrance tickets, and then the three entered the site.

Gianni also went to Porta Marina and purchased an entrance ticket with cash because they didnt accept credit cards. He requested and was given a free map and guide booklet. He rented an audio guide, which he didn't need, but pretending to use it would allow him to seem absorbed while he was actually observing his targets. He had to leave a credit card as security until he returned the audio player.

Gianni entered the historical site and began to follow Rothstein and Martin at a distance. Because of the large numbers of tourists, it was easy to blend in. He would take photos throughout the trip.

Pompeii had been a prosperous Roman town with approximately 11,000 inhabitants, a third of whom were slaves. Pompeii and the nearby smaller town of Herculaneum were destroyed by the eruption of Vesuvius. Pompeii was buried under sixty feet of ash, not lava. Most of the population had evacuated before the catastrophe, but 2,000 stayed and perished. A major earthquake seventeen years earlier caused severe damage to both towns.

Pompeii and Herculaneum were rediscovered in the eighteenth century, and excavations were begun. About a third of Pompeii remained unexcavated.

The town had a complete running water system that worked without pumps. Water pressure was maintained by a series of towers throughout the town and by a system of double sets of lead pipes. The dwellings of the rich had running water and toilets. There were public baths and fountains.

Mules were the only transport animals permitted in town because horses were not good at walking on the uneven stone streets.

Unfortunately, during World War II, Allied bombers sometimes mistakenly bombed Pompeii, causing serious damage.

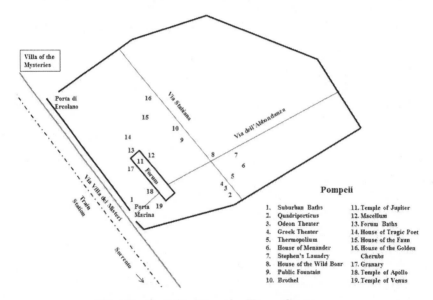

The Rothstein-Martin Tour Sequence

The guide took Rothstein and Martin to a number of places in town, but not all:

- The Suburban Baths - public baths at the Porta Marina entrance to Pompeii. Visitors arriving by sea could clean up there while enjoying the interesting and erotic mosaics.

- The Quadriporticus of the Theaters - a square, open area

surrounded by covered walkways with columns. The gladiators' barracks and training facility was relocated here when the earthquake of AD 62 damaged their original barracks.

- The Odeon, a small Roman theater, used primarily for musical performances. It held 1,000 - 1,500 spectators, and probably had a wooden roof.

- The large Greek Theater, used primarily for drama. It held 5,000 spectators and could be covered by a temporary canopy.

- A thermopolium – an ancient food vendor's stall where fast-foods like soup, bread, meat, chicken, beer and wine were sold. The bitter-tasting wine could be mellowed with honey or water.

- The huge first-century-BC House of Menander, with at least 50 rooms. It had a well-preserved fresco of the ancient Greek dramatist, Menander, and many other frescoes, including some about the Trojan War. It had a concubine meeting room and a glass case with three skeletons found in the house during excavation.

- Stephen's laundry (Fullonica di Stephanus), a commercial laundry that used urine to clean clothes. When Vespasian became emperor, he decided to raise money by taxing urine. (Gianni figured a lot of people were pissed about that tax.)

- Up Via dell'Abbondanza[62], which was lined with shops, to the intersection with Via Stabiana, where there was a large public water fountain, with water still flowing, and visitors filling their water containers. In Roman times, the general public relied on these fountains for their water, and used them as reference points for giving directions. Rothstein et al., who were about 100 ft. ahead of Gianni, turned right onto Via Stabiana. As Gianni approached the fountain, he saw a small private tour group of ten moving toward the fountain from the opposite direction. As Gianni scanned the group, he noticed Ahmadi, who had done nothing to conceal his appearance. He glanced toward the Rothstein trio several times but made no effort to follow them. Perhaps he was validating

---

[62] Street of Abundance

Rothstein's itinerary or looking for other Rothstein contacts. Gianni texted, "Enzo enjoying visit here."

- The major brothel in Pompeii - the Lupanare, which means, "Place of the She Wolves." It had very graphic frescoes to which patrons could point to indicate desired services. The bed inside was a stone bed. (Ouch!!)

- The House of the Wild Boar, with a large black and white mosaic floor depicting a wild boar being attacked by a dog.

- The Forum, and the Temple of Jupiter.

- The Macellum, the food market on the east side of the Forum.

- The Forum Baths (Terme) on the north side of the Forum - one of three sets of public baths in Pompeii. The complex included a cold bath (frigidarium), warm bath (tepidarium), and hot bath (calidarium).

- The House of the Tragic Poet, with its famous large black and white mosaic floor depicting a growling dog, with the words, "Cave Canem" (Beware of Dog).

- The 27,000 square ft. House of the Faun, the largest home in Pompeii, named after the bronze statue of a mythical faun.

- The House of the Golden Cherubs, an elegant, midsized home with rooms opening onto a peristyle with garden, named after gold-laminated cherubs that had decorated one room.

- The Granary on the west side of the Forum. Gianni again spotted Ahmadi with the small group. This time, Rothstein noticed him and appeared surprised. Ahmadi remained with his group and Gianni wouldn't see him again.

- The Temple of Apollo on the lower west side of the Forum.

- The Temple of Venus, the patron goddess of Pompeii.

They ended up back near the Porta Marina, where the guide chatted with Rothstein and Martin, and pointed toward the northwest corner of the park. Gianni assumed the guide was describing the fascinating Villa of the Mysteries outside that area of the park. They could get there fastest via the Herculaneum Gate (Porta Ercolano). Rothstein and Martin appeared to nod in agreement.

The large, well-preserved Roman villa was just outside the walls of Pompeii. It suffered only minor damage when buried under ash from Vesuvius. It was named after a series of beautiful frescoes in one room. They illustrate the initiation of a woman into some Greco-Roman cult, and are probably the best of the small number of surviving ancient Roman paintings.

The guide also pointed to the book and souvenir shop close by at the Porta Marina. Rothstein handed the man an envelope, presumably with a cash payment. The man looked in the envelope, and then thanked the couple. Rothstein and Martin in turn thanked him effusively, and shook hands. The guide then departed.

The couple spent about fifteen minutes in the book and souvenir shop, and came out with a couple of purchases in hand. Rothstein scanned the area around the shop, perhaps looking for Ahmadi. Then, he and Martin started walking toward the Herculaneum Gate. There was no one else walking in that direction, so they would easily have noticed Gianni if he followed them. He thought about it and decided there was no point. It was improbable they'd meet Ahmadi or anyone else there. There was only one way they could come back toward the train station. That was outside the walls of Pompeii along the Via Villa dei Misteri. He returned his audio guide, retrieved his credit card, and exited through the Porta Marina.

It was now 11:50 a.m. Gianni calculated that the couple would be gone about sixty to seventy-five minutes - about ten to fifteen minutes to walk each way to and from the villa, and thirty to forty-five minutes to tour the villa. He figured that after they arrived back near the train station, they'd look for a restaurant or a food stand to have lunch.

He decided to pass the time by having lunch himself. He chose Chalet Hortus[63] Porta Marina just outside the Porta Marina. Even though the restaurant looked like it might be a typical tourist trap

---

[63] Latin word for, "garden." Source of the English word, "horticulture." http://www.pompei-hortus.it/en/

near the park's entrances, he knew better. He and his family had enjoyed a good lunch there in the covered outdoor dining area which was filled with a plethora of plants of all types, creating a very pleasant atmosphere.

He had a simple lunch - a Minerva Sandwich (salami, mozzarella, tomato, and lettuce on focaccia bread), a glass of Lacryma Christi red wine, and a small bottle of mineral water. The wine was especially appropriate for Pompeii. White, red, and rosé Lacryma Christi wines were produced with grapes grown on the slopes of Vesuvius. The red was produced with Piedirosso and Sciascinoso grapes. The name means, "Tears of Christ."

Gianni finished his lunch within an hour and started browsing the souvenir stalls outside the Porta Marina. Just after he started, he saw Rothstein and Martin approaching. They entered the restaurant he'd just left. He knew there weren't enough snack bars and souvenir stands by the Porta Marina for him to browse the whole time they were having lunch, so he walked the short distance down to the Piazza Porta Marina Inferiore[64], where there were additional stands and shops. Forty-five minutes later, he returned to kill time near the Porta Marina and train station.

About 2:25 p.m., they emerged from the restaurant and headed toward the train station. He knew from the train schedule that the next train to Sorrento was at 2:47 p.m. He figured they'd catch that train. He'd take the next train, but would let Shellie and Daniel know they were coming. He texted, "Rob & Gina returning in 20 min. I'm gonna shop here a bit." Daniel replied with a copy to Shellie, "Thanks. Gonna chill on PT[65] C u soon." Throughout their time in Pompeii, Gianni hadn't seen Rothstein do anything suspicious.

Gianni went to the train station at 2: 55 p.m., and purchased a ticket. When he walked onto the platform, he didn't see Rothstein

---

[64] Means, "lower," not, "inferior," because it is a bit downhill from Porta Marina.
[65] Piazza Tasso

and Martin, so he assumed they'd departed. He caught the next train at 3:17 p.m., arrived at Sorrento at 3:47 p.m., and returned to his hotel. He was surprised he hadn't received a text from Daniel about Rothstein and Martin passing through Piazza Tasso. He immediately texted Daniel and Shellie, asking, "Have you seen Rob & Gina?"

"See them coming now," Daniel replied. Apparently they'd stopped somewhere between the train station and Piazza Tasso. Gianni hoped he hadn't missed Rothstein making some contact.

Shellie texted, "Will ask if they want to do last-minute shopping." She expected they might walk around town a bit on their final full day in Sorrento. About four thirty, she took a bus from her hotel up to Piazza Tasso. She walked to the Via San Cesareo and spent time checking out the same shops she'd visited there before.

About five, Rothstein and Martin came out of Maison Tofani and headed toward Piazza Tasso. Shellie followed them at a distance. They went to a ticket stand next to the Bar Syrenuse, and purchased tickets for the Sorrento City Train, a wheeled sightseeing "train," with a small locomotive that was probably on a truck chassis, and a passenger car with about six rows of seats, each of which could accommodate four passengers. The train took its passengers on a thirty-five-minute tour of some of the most interesting parts of town. Passengers were given headsets and could listen to commentary in any of seven languages. No sooner had Rothstein purchased tickets, than Shellie saw Ahmadi walk up to the ticket kiosk and buy a ticket. She watched to see how Rothstein and Martin would react. She saw a surprised and questioning look on Rothstein's face, but no reaction on Martin's part. She continued chatting with Rothstein as if nothing unusual was happening, which strongly suggested that Martin didn't know Ahmadi. This was the third time in two days that Ahmadi had been near Rothstein and Martin without talking to them.

When the train arrived, Rothstein and Martin got into the third row. Ahmadi sat immediately behind them. When Shellie saw there were still a couple of spaces available on the train, she quickly purchased a ticket and boarded the train in the last row. Rothstein and Martin plugged in their headsets, but Ahmadi didn't. The train departed about five fifteen. Shellie watched Ahmadi during the entire trip. He rarely glanced at the scenery, even when there were a couple of very nice views of the coast and the Bay of Naples. He was focused on the interaction between the couple. Martin seemed oblivious to Ahmadi's presence, chatting away and pointing to sites she found interesting. Rothstein seemed a bit reserved. During the ride, Shellie texted, "Enzo, Rob, Gina, & Stella sightseeing. DPT22." She felt Johnnie should know that Martin apparently didn't know Ahmadi, so she wanted to meet Daniel in Piazza Tasso at ten and give him the info to forward.

When the train returned to its starting point, Ahmadi strolled over to the Fauno Bar and was seated outside, facing the piazza. Rothstein led Martin down the Via Luigi de Maio. Shellie followed at a distance until they reached Piazza Sant'Antonino, where Rothstein had twice met Ahmadi. They then turned left onto Via San Francesco. Shellie followed, and didn't know that Rothstein was taking Martin to the Villa Comunale, a public garden park full of beautiful palm trees and other plants. It was high above the Bay of Naples and offered a beautiful view of the coast, the beaches below, and Mt. Vesuvius in the distance. It also had an elevator which the public could use to go down to the beaches. The city train had stopped at the edge of the Villa Comunale during the ride around Sorrento. After enjoying the views, taking photos, and chatting, they walked a short distance along the Via Veneto to Piazza della Vittoria[66], where they walked to the decorative concrete railing near the edge and took in more great views of the coast and the Gulf of Naples. While following the couple, Shellie texted, "enjoying walk with Gina & Rob."

From Piazza della Vittoria, Rothstein and Martin headed back up the Via Veneto and Via San Francesco to Piazza Sant'Antonino. Ironically, Rothstein led Martin to Ristorante Pizzeria L'Abate, from

---

[66] Piazza of the Victory, a memorial to victory in World War I.

which Shellie had had observed him the preceding evening and Gianni the evening before that. Like Shellie and Gianni, they chose an outdoor table. Shellie mused that perhaps she should write a TripAdvisor review that the restaurant was a popular gathering spot for spies and counterspies.

Shellie decided to sit and watch them for a few minutes from the Piazza Sant'Antonino. She sat at the very bench where Rothstein and Ahmadi had sat the previous two evenings at about the same time. After watching them, reflecting on Rothstein's previous meetings, and considering the time left in the evening, she was fairly confident Rothstein would not meet with a case officer that evening.

She left and decided to have dinner at Ristorante Pizzeria Sant'Antonino[67], a block east of L'Abate. It was a rooftop garden restaurant with lemon-tree trellises above. She had a local meal, with a main dish of seafood scialatielli pasta (Scialatielli ai Frutti di Mare), and a dessert of Sorrento Delizia al Limone - sponge cake covered with Chantilly lemon sauce. Her drinks were mineral water and a half bottle of Fidelis Aglianico del Taburno - a red wine made with ninety percent Aglianico and ten percent Sangiovese and Merlot grapes. While she dined, there were a couple of musicians serenading the diners. The meal was very pleasant.

After dinner, she walked through the Piazza Sant'Antonino on her way to Piazza Tasso to meet Daniel. She glanced at L'Abate and saw that Rothstein and Martin were still there.

Gianni's dinner choice was O'Murzill, a tiny mom and pop place on Via dell'Accademia. It was an intimate eatery with only six tables. The name meant, "The Morsel" in Neapolitan. He'd read incredible Italian- and English-language reviews about O'Murzill, as well as a few really bad reviews. He had an appetizer of caprese salad, followed by paccheri pasta with amberjack (Paccheri con la Ricciola). Next was grilled swordfish (Spada alla Griglia). Swordfish was very popular in Italy. For dessert, he had Lemon Cake (Torta di

---

[67] http://www.ristorantesantonino.com/english/

Limone). The wine he chose was a half-bottle of Per'e Palummo, from the comune of Bacoli, west of Naples. The Per'e Palummo grapes were another name for Piedirosso. He really enjoyed the meal.

For dinner, Daniel returned to Bar Fauno, which he loved. He couldn't get enough of enjoying good food while people watching at the edge of Piazza Tasso. He again thought about his wife, and wished she could be with him. He was sure he'd bring her here. He was served by the same waiter as the previous evening. The waiter remembered Daniel and asked in English if he was enjoying Sorrento. Daniel said he loved it. The scenery was beautiful and the people so warm and welcoming. The waiter appeared to sincerely appreciate the complimentary words. Daniel ordered the Gnocchi alla Sorrentina and Sorrento-style filet of sole in citrus sauce (Sogliola agli Agrumi di Sorrento). He only had mineral water to drink. For dessert, he had a plate of mini-pastries, accompanied by the usual complimentary limoncello. Throughout the meal, he kept his eye out for Ahmadi and the others, but saw no one he knew.

By 9:50 p.m., he'd finished and paid for his meal. He walked across the piazza to a store called Italica Ars, which had been in business since 1856. Among other things, it specialized in selling an incredible variety of chess sets. He stared in the window looking at some of the artful items for sale. Shellie soon sidled up alongside. She quietly said, "When Gina and Rob bought tickets to ride on the city train today, Enzo came up and bought a ticket, and then sat right behind them. Rob noticed him, was surprised, and seemed restrained the entire time Enzo was there. Gina clearly didn't know him. She's probably not involved. Please pass this on for Johnnie."

"Got it," he replied. "I'm gonna come here at 6:30 a.m. to watch for their departure. No idea when they'll leave."

"I'll come at 7:30."

"Great. Let's let Gianni know."

"Right."

Daniel walked back toward Antiche Mura, and Shellie caught a cab to her hotel.

In his room, Daniel typed Shellie's message onto his laptop, and encrypted it. He added a note of his own that Ahmadi had sent and received no emails that day, and had spent no time browsing. He then signed onto the hotel's wireless network and left both notes in the shared account. After that, he texted, "PT breakfast at 6:30." Shellie immediately responded, "Enjoy, will eat at 7:30." Gianni got the message, and responded, "Sleeping in. Not going 'til 8:30."

Josh saw Daniel's note and Shellie's message almost immediately. Just as he prepared to phone Johnnie, he received a call from Mac, who said Garland Von Greif of the cryptanalytic organization had just called with the results of the analysis of the thumb drive found at Rothstein's residence. The encryption/decryption app on the drive was very powerful and had the unique signature of an Iranian creation. In fact, they'd encountered this specific app in an MOIS device that had been obtained in a special operation. While the encryption/decryption keys on the drive appeared to be randomly generated, they were pseudo-random, and the cryptanalysts studying the drive had figured out the key-generation algorithm.

Josh was delighted and wished he could have personally thanked Von Greif.

He phoned Johnnie to let him know about the note from Daniel, Shellie's message, and the thumb drive analysis results. He said he figured that sometime between midnight and 4 a.m. Washington time (6 a.m. and 10 a.m. in Italy), Daniel would send a note about Rothstein and Martin's departure. When that happened, Josh would send Johnnie a high-side email.

Jonnie asked Josh to alert him by phone instead because he wasn't sure where he'd be in the middle of the night. He gave Josh a special Bureau number to call. Josh agreed.

Josh indicated that J.B. would check throughout the weekend for any new info on Ahmadi's travel to Zurich and then to the U.S.

Josh also said he'd ask Kat to alert him immediately to any

comms between the Supreme Leader and Behrangi.

Josh said that when he got off the phone, he'd update the Director, and recommend that the Director instruct the Iran office to monitor certain types of Iranian comms around the clock for unusual activity by Iranian intel or diplomatic entities focused on the U.S.

Johnnie thanked Josh and told him the details of the Bureau's plans to arrest and question Rothstein on arrival, as Johnnie had previously explained. Johnnie said he thought it likely that when news of Rothstein's arrest hit the press, Ahmadi would learn about it quickly through MOIS channels and would cancel his return to the U.S. If he did come back, the State Department would declare him persona non grata, and give him twenty-four hours to leave the U.S. Ahmadi could not be arrested because he had diplomatic immunity.

Josh wished Johnnie and his Bureau colleagues the best in their operation to arrest and question Rothstein. He concluded by saying that after updating the Director, he'd go home and catch a few hours' sleep. Then he'd return to the office to await Daniel's note.

When Johnnie and Josh completed their conversation just past five, Josh phoned Sofie to ask if he could see the Director as soon as possible. Sofie called back and said Josh would have to come immediately. The Director was about to head home. He had a full slate of activities scheduled throughout this Memorial Day weekend.

After the Director and Josh exchanged their usual Persian greetings, the Director said, "Well Josh, I hope our country's going to get a special gift for Memorial Day. It would be a nice way to honor those who've made the ultimate sacrifice."

"We hope so, Admiral. We're keeping our fingers crossed. The Bureau now seems to have all the evidence it needs to arrest Rothstein and charge him with espionage. I'd like to update you on where things stand, including our arrangements, and to make a recommendation to you. Then I'd like to get your guidance."

"Go ahead Josh."

Josh proceeded to brief the Director and recommend putting the Iran office on twenty-four-hour alert.

The Director thanked Josh and said, "Since you alerted Mac and me earlier in the week about the plans to question and arrest Rothstein tomorrow evening, I've asked Mac to stand in for me on this issue all weekend in view of the many military commitments I have. I've asked him to inform me immediately about key events like the actual arrest. However, I'd like Mac to take any necessary executive actions in managing NSA's role in this phase of the operation. I know he'll be here a couple more hours this evening. I'd like you to contact him, and update him. I approve your recommendation about the Iran office. You can let Mac know, and ask him to issue the necessary instructions. Best of luck Josh. Thanks for the great work you guys in Team Triad have been doing. It's very impressive."

"Thank you, sir. Have a great weekend. I'll call Mac as soon as I get back to my office."

Josh immediately phoned Mac, who asked Josh to come to his office. Josh agreed, but said he wanted to first call Kat to try to catch her before she left for the weekend.

He phoned Kat just in time. She was just getting ready to walk out of her office. She said she'd be delighted to support Josh throughout the weekend. She had no special plans.

Josh then hurried down to Mac's office. After briefing Mac, he returned to his office, made a last-minute check of the shared cloud account, and headed home. Fortunately, the route home was one that didn't involve main roads affected by heavy, intercity holiday traffic.

When he got home, he profusely apologized to Meihui, telling her that he'd probably be tied up at work most of the weekend, but would try to do the traditional Memorial Day commemoration activity that they did together every year.

She told him not to worry. She understood. She didn't add that she was dying of curiosity to know what he was involved in. She was sure it was very interesting. It had to be extraordinary, otherwise, he could have told her something when they were at work.

Twenty-nine

I Tartufi non Hanno Nessun Sapore

(The Truffles Have No Taste)

Saturday May 23

Daniel got up at six and checked the hotel's wireless network. There was no sign of Ahmadi. He got dressed and headed to the Bar Ercolano, where he sat at an outdoor table. The waiter recognized him and greeted him. He ordered a cappuccino and a cornetto. At half past seven, Shellie arrived at the Bar Ercolano. Daniel paid the waiter, thanked him, and returned to the Antiche Mura. As he walked through the lobby, he saw Ahmadi checking out. When he got to his room, he texted, "Sayonara to Enzo." Daniel typed and encrypted a short note to Josh about Ahmadi's departure. He then uploaded it to the shared cloud account.

At half past eight, Gianni arrived at the Bar Ercolano and Shellie left. She decided to walk down Via Luigi de Maio to her hotel.

At about nine, Gianni saw Rothstein and Martin come to the piazza with their luggage. They were met by a valet from the parking garage, who loaded their luggage into his vehicle and drove them toward the garage. Gianni texted, "Rob & Gina leaving." Daniel immediately reported the departure to Josh.

Josh, who was continuously monitoring the shared account, saw Daniel's note immediately. He downloaded and decrypted it, then called the special Bureau phone number Johnnie had provided. It was now about three thirty in the morning Washington time. Since Rothstein and Martin had left Sorrento, it was unlikely Josh would hear any more from Daniel other than reporting the team's departure from Sorrento the next day. The only reason that might change would be if Rothstein and Martin's flight from Naples was canceled and they returned to Sorrento.

Since Gianni, Shellie, and Daniel had a Saturday to kill separately, they each did something of interest to themselves. Daniel had been fascinated by what he'd read about Pompeii, so he took the train to visit the ancient ruins. He was beginning to feel very comfortable traveling on his own using all types of public transportation.

Shellie hadn't really been able to explore Capri when she was doing surveillance there, so she took a ferry back to the island. The one experience that would leave an indelible memory was of the stunning views from the Belvedere di Tragara, a viewpoint which was a one-mile walk from the Piazza Umberto I - the Piazzetta. The beautiful sights included the sea, the hillsides of Capri, and most impressive of all - the Faraglioni, three majestic towering rock formations rising up from the sea. She vowed to return with her husband and daughter.

Gianni spent his Saturday wandering around Sorrento. If his family in the Naples area knew he was in southwestern Italy and hadn't come to visit them, they'd have been really upset. He hoped they'd never find out, because it would be very hard to explain.

Rothstein and Martin's flight arrived at Dulles at 7:20 p.m., five minutes early. By 7:50, they were standing at Automated Passport Control kiosks next to each other. They each went through the process, with Rothstein finishing a couple of minutes faster. Then they walked together to a CBP Officer and gave him the receipts printed out by the kiosks.

When the CBP Officer looked at Rothstein's receipt, he asked, "Have you thoroughly answered the customs declaration questions?"

Rothstein said he had.

"Do you have $10,000 or more in cash or other financial instruments with you?" the officer continued.

That question raised a red flag in Rothstein's mind. He wondered if the customs officials had some reason to suspect he had undeclared cash. He thought it might be safer to answer that he did, because if they searched him and found the money he was carrying, he'd be in a lot more trouble and might face serious legal problems. He'd already prepared answers. "Yes I do. About $40,000."

"Why didn't you include that on your declaration?"

"I thought that question only applied to cash being brought into the country for the first time. I took the money with me when I went on my trip."

"The declaration requirements cover any cash, not just cash obtained outside the country."

"I didn't know that. I'll change my declaration."

"You can change your declaration. However, I have some further questions regarding the undeclared funds."

"I'd be happy to try to answer your questions."

"What is the source of the $40,000 you have with you?"

"It's from savings I've kept at my house. Those savings are a combination of money I inherited from my grandmother and money I've saved over the years."

"Were you traveling for business or pleasure?"

"Pleasure."

"It's very unusual for a vacation traveler to be carrying so much cash. Was there some particular reason?"

"Yes. I traveled to Italy and was considering buying a vacation condo there. I wanted to have some cash to make a down payment if I found the right place."

"Did you check out any real estate while you were there?"

"Yes. My friend here and I visited a real estate office in Sorrento, Italy. We talked with a realtor about the types of properties that were available and the prices."

"Do you have any proof?"

"Yes. In my wallet, I've got the business card of the realtor in Sorrento. I also have in my luggage a pamphlet from the realtor. She was with me," Rothstein said, pointing to Martin.

"That's true." Martin replied. "We spent about half an hour with the realtor yesterday afternoon when we returned from Pompeii to Sorrento."

"Well, I think we're going to have to discuss your trip a bit more. Let me call my supervisor."

"Ok," they replied.

A minute later, another uniformed CBP Officer walked up to them and introduced himself. "My name is William Rasmussen. Please follow me." He led them to a row of rooms in another part of the building. He asked Martin to enter the first room. He said someone would come to the room very shortly. Martin entered and seated herself at a table with four chairs. She was a bit nervous, but thought that everything that Rothstein said was on the up and up. She'd never seen him being deceitful.

Rasmussen then took Rothstein to another room located at the other end of the row of rooms. He opened the door and asked Rothstein to enter. On entering, he saw three men seated at a table, also with four chairs. One of them was Johnnie, who asked Rothstein to take a seat.

"Mr. Rothstein, we are from the FBI, and would like to ask you a few questions about your trip. This is Special Agent Tanaka; that is Special Agent Mellese; and I am Agent Dece. Here are our official IDs."

Rothstein immediately understood that the issue was about much more than the cash he had failed to declare. "I'll do my best to answer your questions."

"Can you tell us why you met with an Iranian intelligence operative in Italy?" Johnnie asked.

"How do you know I met with an Iranian?"

"We have some photos," Johnnie said, showing Rothstein two photos, one each from the two meetings in Sorrento.

"I'm not prepared to discuss that subject without consulting my attorney."

"How long you have been providing classified information to the Iranians?" Agent Tanaka asked.

"I've never provided classified information to the Iranians, or to any other foreigners or unauthorized Americans."

"Then how do you explain the classified documents we found in your home?" Agent Tanaka asked. He unlocked and opened a briefcase and pulled out a document they'd printed from Rothstein's computer. This one was unclassified but had the **FOR OFFICIAL USE ONLY** caveat. "Here's one of them. We've taken the classified ones to a secure facility and are holding them as evidence of your treason."

"None of those documents contain classified information, nor would you have any proof that I gave those documents to anyone."

"How can you say that none of those documents are classified when they all have classification markings - including headers, footers, and paragraph markings?"

"First, I obtained all the information in those documents from open-source print and broadcast media, or I made it up."

"Can you prove that?" Johnnie asked.

"Very easily. I presume you saw both the printed versions of the documents and the soft copies on my computer."

"We did," Johnnie affirmed.

"In the same computer folder with the documents, you should've found one database that contained three fields and one record for each document," Rothstein explained.

"We found the database," Agent Mellese commented. "Can you explain it?"

"Sure. The first field, SD, is the date of the open-source material I used to create the document. The second field, DD, is the date I created the document. The third field uses digraphs to indicate the source of the information in each document. The sources are: *Bloomberg Business Week, The Boston Globe, CNN, the Economist, The Los Angeles Times, The New York Times, Time Magazine, The Wall Street Journal, The Washington Post*, and my imagination. If you check, you'll find the open source for every single document, except the ones I created out of thin air."

"What about the classification markings?" Agent Tanaka asked.

"I put them all on myself so that the documents would appear authentic. If you look at the font sizes and types, you'll find they're very different from those used in official DOE and other U.S. government documents. Not a single one of those documents is legitimate. That's all I'm going to say without consulting my lawyer. "Since I haven't lied to you or anyone else about my activities, and since I haven't disclosed a single secret to any unauthorized party, I doubt you can charge me with espionage or lying to the FBI. It would seem silly to charge me with scamming the Iranians, if you can even prove I gave them to Iran. If you drop the charges, perhaps I could help you out.

"Also, I want to assure you that the woman I was traveling with was not involved in any way with the meetings that your source photographed. I'd like to phone my lawyer now."

"I'm very skeptical of your explanation," Johnnie replied. "In order to determine whether or not your story holds water, we'll analyze the documents you say you created and the source database you created. We do know for sure that you met with an Iranian intelligence officer twice, and that he probably gave you two manila envelopes full of cash. We have other evidence that you were working with the Iranians. It also appears that you tried to bring a large sum of cash into the U.S. without declaring it. Consequently, we're now placing you under arrest, and we're ordering you to give us the $40,000 in cash you brought into the country without declaring it - money we believe you got from the Iranian you met."

Rothstein pulled out an envelope with the cash and handed it over to Johnnie, but Johnnie handed it back and asked Rothstein to pull the cash out and count it in front of them so they could agree how much cash was there. Then Johnnie had Rothstein reinsert the cash and Johnnie took the envelope. Johnnie didn't touch the cash because Bureau experts would examine it for fingerprints.

Johnnie told Rothstein where he'd be incarcerated so he could inform his lawyer.

Within a few minutes of watching Rothstein walk in the door, Johnnie's emotions had gone from elation to deep frustration - from what he thought was a slam-dunk serious espionage case against an important Iranian spy to realizing that the target of the investigation was a clever, bit player and con man. The major Iranian spy was still at large and presumably still damaging U.S. national security. Perhaps Rothstein could be useful in providing insights into Iranian methods and techniques, and perhaps Team Triad could rattle the real spy by crafting the right type of press releases about uncovering Rothstein.

"We'll leave you for a minute to let you phone your lawyer," Johnnie commented, before pointing to a phone at one end of the table. "Do you have his phone number with you?"

"I do." Rothstein had done a lot of research prior to and during his interaction with the Iranians. He figured he had created a methodology that would keep him from being discovered. He knew that if he was very careful in how he carried out his operation, he might only face a few minor charges if his activities were ever uncovered. However, in the event he was found out, he would need the right type of legal representation. In researching recent espionage trials, he learned about a lawyer named Sean F. Chandler III, who was a partner in a prestigious Washington, D.C. law firm and who had successfully defended three clients accused of espionage in three different cases. Chandler's success equated to his clients spending relatively little time in jail, not to their being found innocent. Rothstein met with Chandler and liked him. At their meeting, Chandler explained how he worked and described the provisions and conditions of his representation, should the need ever arise. Rothstein agreed, and they signed a contract. He kept Chandler's business card in his wallet in case he needed to contact him right away.

Chandler thought it was really strange that an individual charged with nothing should come to him and have such a discussion. Normally, individuals sought representation after they were accused of a crime, not before. He wondered if Rothstein was conducting or planning to conduct espionage.

What Chandler didn't know was that when Rothstein came to meet with him, Rothstein immediately hit it off with Chandler's secretary, Julia Martin. Soon after meeting, they began dating, despite the fact that she was married. Chandler would be very upset when he learned of the relationship, which was against the partnership's policy prohibiting romantic relationships with clients.

While Rothstein was being questioned, Martin was being interviewed by two other special agents, Donna Lawrence and Emma Jennings. They asked her about her relationship with Rothstein. Martin explained she'd met Rothstein in February when he came for an appointment with a lawyer at a law firm where she worked. They'd been dating for a couple of months. She'd accepted his invitation to join him on a trip to Italy at his expense.

The agents said they were aware that her husband was in the Army and on assignment in Afghanistan. They could see that she was embarrassed that they knew. They explained that Rothstein was being charged with espionage, and that he had met with a foreign intelligence officer during their trip. They could see that she was genuinely surprised. She said she was with him the entire time except for a total of less than an hour on each of two evenings in Sorrento - Wednesday, May 20 and Thursday, May 21. Each of those times, Rothstein told her he was going out for a short walk alone, and he was gone less than half an hour. The only time they met with anyone together was a half hour they had spent with a realtor in Sorrento to discuss Rothstein's interest in buying property in the area.

They advised Martin that other agents had searched her luggage and texted that they'd found nothing suspicious. The agents asked her if she'd let them examine the contents of her purse and carry-on bag. She agreed and allowed them to look through everything. They found nothing relevant to Rothstein's espionage activities. They informed Martin that she was free to leave. However, she might be called in for further questioning. They told her where to find her luggage.

As Martin left, she began fretting about her image - about what people would think about her hanging out with a spy and cheating on her husband while he was in Afghanistan. When she'd first given in to Rothstein's advances, she thought she could have a little fun, while keeping it secret from those who knew her. She gave no thought to how she'd explain the relationship to her husband. She'd decided that she didn't like being married to someone who was likely to have other assignments away from her. She needed more attention and felt that HER life was more important.

After Martin left and Rothstein had been taken away, Johnnie met with the other four agents to discuss the two interrogations. When they finished, he asked Special Agents Tanaka and Lawrence to put together a detailed report. Then he phoned Director Pasquali and informed him of the disappointing outcome. He also wanted to discuss the sort of press release the Director would want the Bureau to issue in light of how things had turned out. The Director wanted the first release to be something very simple until they'd had a few hours to consider something more substantive that might have an impact on the Iranians and their other spy, the unidentified subject with the initials, "D.H." Director Pasquali said he would immediately phone his senior counterparts - the DNI, the Directors of the CIA and NSA, and also the Secretary of Energy, because it was one of his employees. Johnnie mentioned that the Secretary of Energy was probably aware that something like this might happen because DOE security personnel had been involved in the search operation at Rothstein's office. Presumably, they'd informed the Secretary.

Johnnie prepared a short and simple press release which stated that a DOE employee had been arrested for conducting espionage on behalf of a foreign government. He then passed the press release to the appropriate office in the Bureau.

Next, he phoned Josh and Farida to let them know. Both were surprised and very disappointed. Johnnie said there was no point in trying to contact the members of the team in Italy, who'd be leaving the country in a few hours. There was nothing they could do, and there was nothing to be accomplished by informing them. Josh said he'd watch for any reaction by the Ayatollah and Behrangi. He would also take action to have someone inform the Iran office at NSA that an American had been arrested on charges of spying for the Iranians.

Josh immediately phoned Mac to pass on the results and ask Mac to inform the watch office at NSA so they could alert NSA's Iran office to look for relevant Iranian governmental comms, such as MOIS efforts to contact Ahmadi, who was scheduled to return to the U.S. from Zurich in two days. The Iran office was still unaware that Josh was involved in Meta, so he wouldn't contact them directly about such issues.

Josh then headed home to catch a few hours' sleep.

Thirty

Sed Libera Nos a Malo[68]

(But Deliver Us from Evil)

Sunday May 24

It was a cloudy day, with no rain, almost no wind, and temperatures in the midsixties.

Gianni, Shellie, and Daniel each had a flight that departed Naples between early and midafternoon. They'd all checked out of their hotels by nine thirty and were en route to Naples Capodichino Airport - Gianni in his rental car, and Shellie and Daniel in separate Amalfi Car Service vehicles. Since it was Sunday morning, the traffic was relatively light and the trips were quick.

As the car carrying Shellie approached the front of the terminal building, the roadway divided into three separate curving roadways that were only a couple of feet apart from one another. The two closest to the terminal, which was on the right, were limited access roadways. Her car was on one that had two lanes, and ran next to a short-term parking lot on the left. The driver stopped in one of the spaces dedicated to picking passengers up or dropping them off. The space was just before a pedestrian walkway from the short-term parking lot to the terminal entrance. The driver opened her door, and then took her luggage out of the trunk. She paid and thanked him.

With her surveillance experience, Shellie was constantly alert to

---

[68] From the Latin version of the Lord's Prayer

her surroundings. As she looked to her left, she saw a young man walking out of the short-term lot toward the terminal entrance. He was pulling a wheeled duffle bag, and was wearing a completely zipped-up jacket that appeared too heavy for the midday temperatures. There was a slight bulge at the waist. He was wearing a glove on his left hand, but not on his right. There might've been an innocent explanation for wearing a single glove, or perhaps he was using it to conceal the trigger for an explosive device. The duffle bag was long enough to contain an assault rifle. The young man had a very intense, focused look on his face. He was looking around, but didn't pay attention to Shellie. He stopped for a second, leaned over, and unzipped the duffle bag. She could see the stock of an assault rifle, as he was fumbling around with something inside the bag near where the magazine would be. She was now certain he was a suicide attacker.

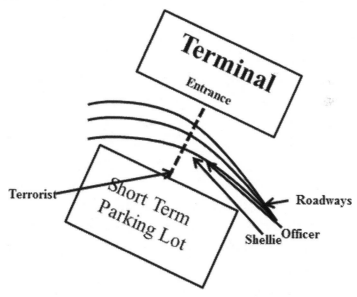

The Encounter

Shellie knew she had only seconds to figure out what to do. With her law enforcement ethos, she gave no thought to herself. The question was how to stop him and protect others. It wasn't simply a question of grabbing him and bringing him under control. With her FBI training, that would've been simple to do. However, he could easily detonate the explosive device with the concealed trigger as she was taking him down. She had only two options. Neither was fail-safe.

The first involved a special weapon that she'd long ago built into the handle of her carry-on suitcase for use in a life-threatening situation. It was an extendable metal rod with a very sharp tip coated with an instant-acting, deadly poison. To an x-ray machine, it would look like part of the suitcase handle structure. She could quickly push a special release, pull it out of the handle, walk up behind the target, and stick it into the back of his neck. This would probably cause a pain so intense that he wouldn't be able to detonate the explosive before collapsing and dying. The operative word was, "probably." Since she was traveling as a tourist, she wasn't carrying a firearm.

The second option involved engaging an Italian security officer whom she saw standing a few feet from her and who was armed with an assault rifle. She'd observed many law enforcement officers and security personnel during her career. This one appeared very professional and capable. She'd have to communicate to him the urgency of taking decisive action. Since they were at an international airport where many travelers spoke English, she hoped the officer understood it.

She walked the few feet to the officer. Turning her back to the attacker, she faced the officer and asked if he spoke English. He said he did and asked if he could help her. She turned slightly and pointed to the attacker in a way the attacker would not see. She said clearly and slowly, "I fear that young man is a suicide attacker. I can see a rifle in his duffle bag and I think he might be wearing a suicide vest under his jacket."

The officer made a quick assessment. He could see the rifle stock, which was still partially visible. There was absolutely no innocent reason to take an assault rifle into the terminal. The overly heavy jacket bulging at the waist, the glove, and the young man's countenance all pointed in the direction of an attack. The officer knew that if he killed the man and was wrong, he would have taken an innocent life. If he failed to act, and the man was an attacker, many innocent lives could be lost and many people could be injured. He knew he had no choice. He didn't shout or say anything to alert the attacker, who'd begun to zip the duffle bag closed. The officer simply raised his weapon and fired a volley of shots into the attacker, who fell to the ground, dead. The officer immediately pulled out a small tactical radio and called for assistance. Then he ran up to the downed attacker.

In the meantime, Shellie blended into the dozens of travelers who had quickly scattered away. When she traveled, she always dressed in a very low key manner. She'd been wearing sunglasses, a hat, and a sweater. She removed all three, and hoped that the officer had paid more attention to the attacker than to her, and wouldn't remember her. The last thing she wanted was come to the attention of the Italian Government while on this sensitive mission.

Within seconds, six more security officers converged on the scene. They looked around to determine if there might be other attackers in the area. Two of them kept people away from the dead attacker. Soon, sirens wailed as a vehicle brought explosives specialists to the scene. They were able to disarm the explosive device worn by the attacker. They also found the assault rifle and a number of magazines in the duffle bag.

As soon as the shots rang out, the four entrance doors to the terminal were secured. The officers then began to walk around and question bystanders as to what they had seen. Most of them had observed nothing until the shots rang out and the attacker died. Shellie acted like the rest, and said she'd seen nothing. Fortunately, the officer she'd alerted was involved in explaining the situation to another officer - probably his superior. Within forty-five minutes, the entrance doors were reopened and passengers were again allowed to enter the terminal.

Shellie entered, shaken by what had just happened. She could easily have failed to stop the attacker, and many might have lost their lives. She might also have perished, without ever seeing her daughter and husband again. She passed through security with no problem and caught her flight on time. She couldn't wait to get home to hug her daughter and husband. She was also eager to learn what happened to Rothstein.

While Shellie, Gianni, and Daniel were en route back to the U.S., Rothstein's lawyer, Sean Chandler, met with Rothstein in jail. As soon as they sat down together, Chandler informed Rothstein that Martin had phoned him when she arrived home the previous evening to tell him about the arrest and her trip with Rothstein. He advised her not to discuss the case with anyone without first clearing it with him. Chandler said it was the first he'd been aware of the relationship between Martin and Rothstein. He was upset and disappointed that one of his employees would have a relationship with a client, against company policy.

Rothstein apologized for the relationship with Martin, and then described what the Bureau knew about him. He said the bottom line was that he'd never shared classified information with the Iranians or any other unauthorized party, foreign or domestic. Moreover, he'd never lied to the FBI or anyone else. He had failed to report unauthorized contact with foreign intelligence and the receipt of large sums of cash. He had also falsified government documents. However, he figured the U.S. Government wouldn't prosecute him for that because the only reason he did it was to con the Iranians.

Chandler said the U.S. Government was very upset with Rothstein because he had put people's lives at risk and had cost the U.S. Government a great deal of money to investigate his case. Chandler thought he could negotiate a deal with the FBI that would let Rothstein off with no jail time, except the time waiting for an agreement to be approved by the Bureau and Justice Department (DOJ) lawyers. However, the agreement would require a number of concessions from Rothstein, and would have a major impact on his life. The agreement that Chandler would offer the government would mean that Rothstein would:

- Lose his job and security clearance;

- Have to turn over to the government all the funds he had received from the Iranians or the assets he had purchased with those funds;

- Never again be able to work for the federal government or a federal government contractor;

- Fully cooperate with the FBI and tell them everything he knew about the Iranians' methods, equipment, personnel, etc.;

- Never accept any money to tell his story in interviews, books, movies, etc.; and

- Give up his passport and agree not to travel outside the U.S. without the Bureau's permission.

If Rothstein reneged on the deal in any way, he would face jail time.

Rothstein was crushed that he'd made such a major miscalculation and that his life would be ruined. He realized that Chandler was one of the best in the business, and that his only viable option was probably to go along with the deal. After a bit of additional discussion for clarification and a little hesitation, he decided to accept such a deal.

Chandler said he'd call the FBI on Tuesday to discuss a deal. Monday was out because it was Memorial Day. So Rothstein would have to spend at least a couple of days in jail. In the meantime, he should not discuss the case with anyone without first clearing the discussion with Chandler or having Chandler present.

When Daniel arrived at BWI Airport late that evening, he picked up his luggage and headed home. Even though it was late, he was so curious that he couldn't resist calling Josh to see if he could get some sense of the outcome with Rothstein.

Josh warmly welcomed Daniel back and asked about his trip home. Daniel said it was very smooth. (He was unaware of Shellie's encounter with the terrorist because he was already at his departure gate when it happened.) Daniel then asked about "Rob."

Josh had a strange response. "He's not free, but he might soon be. Very strange developments. If you meet me at work in the morning, I can fill you in. I'm planning to be there about eight for a short time to look for incoming. I know that doesn't give you much time to sleep after a long trip."

"Doesn't matter, Josh. I'll be there. See you in the a.m."

"Right."

Gianni's conversation with Farida was similar.

Shellie's conversation with Johnnie was very different. "I've got to see you right away," she said. "Can we meet at the office ASAP?"

"Sure," he answered. "Are you OK?"

"Thank God," she replied.

"Ok. See you shortly." Johnnie noticed a hint of stress in Shellie's voice. This was very unlike her. He'd been with her in some extremely difficult situations, and her demeanor had always been very calm. He couldn't imagine what might be going on.

Shellie then phoned her husband, and informed him that she'd be stopping by the office to meet with Johnnie on the way home. "I think you're in for a surprise," he commented. "Johnnie will get one too," she said.

When Shellie arrived at the office, Johnnie was waiting.

"Hi, Shellie. I'm worried about you," he said. "From your call, it sounds like there's been some kind of problem."

"I'm lucky to be alive. I've just been through my nearest brush with death. I'm still shaken by the whole experience."

"What happened?"

"Just after I arrived at Naples airport and was getting ready to enter the terminal, I noticed a young man whom I was sure was a terrorist who was within seconds of pulling off an attack with an automatic weapon and an explosive device. I alerted an airport security officer who immediately killed the guy. It was a miracle that no one except the attacker was killed or injured. Thank God for the skill of the security officer. I'm so thankful to be alive. I've thought about this the whole way home."

Johnnie was flooded with emotions as he listened to her, and understood how close she'd come to tragedy. He thought about her bravery and quick thinking, and about the people who were safe because of her - the typical selflessness of a law enforcement officer.

"What a frightening experience! It sounds like a lot of people owe their lives to you. They're fortunate you were there and reacted the way you did."

"I think any special agent would've done the same. The timing was really fortunate. If I had arrived a couple of minutes earlier or later, everything might have turned out differently, and I might not be here. It's also fortunate that the security officer spoke English and understood what I was saying. No one could have responded faster or better than he."

"Did the Italians question you?"

"No. Their entire focus was on looking for any accomplices the guy might've had and for taking care of the explosive device."

"That's fortunate. They could've kept you in Italy for a couple of days to question you to see if you could add any info."

"I think you're right. There's very little I could have told them."

"Because of the implications of this incident, I'd better let the Director know as soon as we're done discussing it. I'd also like you to come into work tomorrow to write up a detailed incident report."

"OK, but before you call him, I'd like to know what happened to Rothstein. Did you guys nail that creep?"

"Well, Shellie, you're not gonna believe this, but the guy was not giving the Iranians any classified information."

"What? I don't believe it. He met with Ahmadi in Sorrento, and it looked like Ahmadi gave him some kind of payment. The Iranians wouldn't do that for nothing. Did the search of his residence turn up anything?"

"We found lots of stuff there and it all had classification markings. He claims he got all the info from open source or made it up. He's got a log of the source for every single document - sources like *The Washington Post* and *The Economist*."

"What about the classification markings?"

"He says he put those markings on the documents himself and that he used different fonts than the government fonts in order to show that he'd done it."

"I'm stunned. You mean he's nothing more than a con man?"

"You've got it. When they brought the SOB into the room at Dulles where three of us were waiting, I was confident we had an airtight case against him. I could never have imagined how it would play out."

"So our whole operation in Italy was a waste of time?"

"Not really. If you guys hadn't gone there, the terrorist at Naples might have succeeded; and a lot of people might have suffered. We also uncovered Ahmadi as an MOIS operative, and he'll be kicked out of the country."

"I see what you're saying, but trying to take it in is a bit difficult. Between the Rothstein outcome and the terrorist incident, my world's been turned upside down in the last 24 hours."

"I'll bet. The Rothstein thing was tough enough for me, but you guys put so much effort and energy into the Italy operation. Then add the terrorist incident. The only thing I can say is you should keep thinking about the lives you've saved.

"Tomorrow morning, I'm going to call the other members of our team," he continued, "and ask everyone to meet here on Tuesday morning to discuss the Italy operation, the current status of trying to find out who might be spying for Iran, and the way ahead. Now, I think I'd better call the Director to let him know what's happened."

"Needless to say," Shellie said, "I'll be at the meeting on Tuesday."

Johnnie called Director Pasquali and explained what had happened. The director asked to speak to Shellie. He asked her how she was feeling, and then praised her for her heroism. He said he wanted to meet with her and Johnnie on Tuesday morning to further discuss the incident, as well as the Rothstein case.

Monday May 25

Memorial Day I

Josh met Daniel at the office at eight. Daniel said he was really puzzled by Josh's suggestion in their phone call that Rothstein might go free. When Josh explained the situation, Daniel couldn't believe what he was hearing. He'd flown all the way home confident that Rothstein would be convicted and sent to prison for a long time. Josh said that he, Johnnie, Farida, and J.B. all felt the same way. Johnnie told Josh he'd never seen anything like this in his entire career.

Josh wasn't sure what would happen next. He'd come into the office to see if there was any indication that the Iranians were aware of the arrest. There was nothing yet.

While they were talking, Johnnie called. He first explained what had happened to Shellie. Josh was stunned. He told Johnnie that Daniel was standing next to him, and had made no mention of the incident. When Josh asked Daniel if he was aware of an attempted terrorist attack at Naples Airport at the time he was departing, Daniel replied that he wasn't. Daniel understood from hearing Josh's side of the conversation with Johnnie that something had happened, but he couldn't tell what. Josh said he'd fill him in as soon as he got off the phone.

Johnnie then asked if Josh had seen any reflection that the Iranians were aware of Rothstein's arrest. Josh had seen nothing.

Johnnie said he'd like to have a Team Triad meeting at the Bureau at ten the next morning to discuss the operation and the way ahead. Josh and Daniel said they'd come, and that Josh would contact J.B.

When Josh got off the phone with Johnnie, he explained to Daniel what happened to Shellie at Naples. Daniel's jaw literally dropped. He experienced strong emotions similar to what Johnnie and Josh had felt, but there was the added feeling about how close he'd come to death or serious injury.

When they finished discussing Shellie's heroic actions, Daniel said he planned to stick around the office and write up an account of his actions in the surveillance operation. When he was finished, he'd email a copy to the others.

Josh said he'd be leaving, and that he and Meihui had Memorial Day plans to honor the fallen.

Thirty-one

Our Deepest Gratitude

Memorial Day II

To Josh, Memorial Day was much more than a holiday. It was a day to commemorate the sacrifice of those who had given their all to enable him to have the wonderful life and freedoms he enjoyed. He had his own special way of dedicating this day to honoring the valiant fallen men and women of the U.S. military. Each Memorial Day, he went to Section 60 of Arlington National Cemetery, where many of those who'd died in Iraq and Afghanistan were buried. There, he would place a beautiful bouquet of fresh flowers on the grave of Fred Simmons, an Army sergeant and Special Forces Operator who'd been a classmate in Pashto language class and who'd become a good friend.

When Josh and Meihui arrived at the cemetery, there were strong winds with gusts up to 25 mph, and the sky was mostly cloudy. Temperatures were in the mideighties. There were many visitors - family and friends - honoring the loved ones they had lost.

They walked to Fred's grave and placed the bouquet there in one of the flower cones provided by the cemetery. Josh spent a while remembering and reflecting on all the good times he'd spent with Fred, a talented SIGINTer, who loved the Army and who was dedicated to his country. He was a great guy, with a terrific sense of humor. He was always there for his friends. Tragically, he'd been

331

killed while participating in a SOF[69] mission in Afghanistan in 2008. He left behind a wonderful wife and two young children. Josh kept in touch with Fred's family and sent the children Christmas presents every year. Josh would never forget Fred, and considered his Arlington visits a way to honor his friend and keep his memory alive.

Since Josh's marriage to Meihui, she'd always accompanied him to Arlington Cemetery, even though she had never known Fred. She knew how much it meant to Josh.

---

[69] Special Operations Forces

Thirty-two

Le Renard Avare Se Fait Cuisiner[70]

(The Avaricious Fox Is Grilled)

Tuesday May 26

The first thing Josh did at work was to see if there were any comms between Behrangi and the Ayatollah. There was nothing. He phoned Sofie and asked to see the Director before nine. She called back and said the Director wasn't available. Josh told her he'd pass the info to the Director via Mac.

Josh phoned Mac and told him about the Naples Airport incident and the upcoming meeting at the Bureau. He emphasized that Shellie's involvement was being closely held.

Then Daniel, Josh and J.B. headed down to the Bureau. The skies were overcast, and it was very windy. The temperature was in the high seventies.

Johnnie began the meeting by recognizing Shellie for what she'd done. She thanked him, but said it was the sort of response she felt any of her fellow agents would have had.

Johnnie then complimented the Italy team on their superb work. Gianni commented that the mechanics of the operation had worked smoothly, but the outcome was hard to accept. Rothstein's greed had cost the U.S. Government a lot of money, as well as wasted time and

---

[70] A double entendre. Similar to the dual meanings of the English verb, "To grill," the French verb, "cuisiner," can mean, "to cook food" or to "grill (a suspect)."

energy. They all agreed, but Johnnie added that a lot of lives had been saved at Naples because Shellie was there.

Johnnie mentioned that he and Shellie had met with their Director at nine to discuss the operation and the foiled terror attack.

Johnnie then said that he, his boss, and two DOJ lawyers were scheduled to meet with Rothstein's lawyer, Sean Chandler, at one. On the basis of previous experience with Chandler, his boss expected the lawyer would make a detailed proposal to the Bureau. That proposal would likely include provisions that Rothstein cooperate fully with the Bureau and turn over all his ill-gotten gains. Johnnie hoped Chandler's proposal was one that could be approved quickly in order to get Rothstein's cooperation in a way that might reveal the other spy, "D.H." Johnnie asked the team members to stick around to learn the outcome of that meeting, so they could make future plans.

Johnnie informed them that the FBI team that surveilled Rothstein locally would have two team members team on the morning and afternoon subway car Rothstein normally took to and from work. They'd try to determine if some individual on both the morning and afternoon train might be Rothstein's contact, and might be trying to get in touch with him. If they saw an individual in the afternoon that they'd seen in the morning, they'd follow the person. They suspected that once Rothstein was discovered to be missing, the possible contact would not be on that subway car again. The local surveillance team also arranged with the Metrorail authorities to take a video of the passengers in the car, to use that video to see if they could spot a possible suspect. They didn't know if the subway car was the venue for Rothstein's contact with the Iranians, but they couldn't pass up the opportunity to see if it might be.

Gianni asked if Ahmadi had returned to the U.S. Johnnie said he'd arrived at JFK the previous evening, as scheduled.

Johnnie then asked the Italy surveillance team members to recount the main points of the surveillance of Rothstein in date order. He asked Gianni to lead the discussion, since he was most familiar with foreign operations and with Italy.

The Italy team proceeded to cover the key events and observations.

When they finished, Johnnie again complimented them on a well-executed operation. He asked them to compile a detailed report on their operation, as well as a profile of Ahmadi - the way he dressed, his demeanor, his interaction with Rothstein and with the waiter on Capri, his English-language fluency and accent, his computer use, etc. Although he would soon be declared persona non grata, and expelled from the U.S., the CIA, DIA, or some other U.S. Government entity might encounter him somewhere abroad.

The group, except Johnnie, then broke for lunch. Johnnie went to his desk to prepare for the meeting with Rothstein's lawyer.

As expected, the lawyer presented a very well-thought-out proposal. The Bureau said it could accept the proposal if three provisions were added. First, Rothstein wouldn't be released until the FBI had completed an exhaustive interrogation and was satisfied that Rothstein had candidly and truthfully revealed everything. Second, Rothstein could not talk to the press without Bureau approval. They didn't explain that they didn't want Rothstein to reveal any information that might jeopardize their search for "D.H." Third, Rothstein had to agree to testify against any American who'd acted as a contact between him and the Iranians.

The lawyer felt the additional provisions were reasonable. He said he would have to get his client to assent. He could probably do that by phone if the Bureau could arrange for him to present the idea to Rothstein by phone as they were meeting. Johnnie placed a call to the jail and asked that Rothstein be brought to a phone. When Rothstein came on the phone, Johnnie handed his phone to the lawyer. Chandler presented the additional conditions to Rothstein, and recommended that he accept them. Rothstein agreed.

The DOJ lawyers said they'd return to their office and consider the proposal. They expected to have an answer by late afternoon. Chandler gave them his card and told them which number to use to reach him.

Johnnie then met with the other Team Triad members and told them he hoped the DOJ would approve the agreement by late afternoon. If that happened, agents would begin questioning Rothstein the next morning. He hoped the questioning would reveal some aspect of Iranian methodology that would help them discover D.H.'s identity. Another hope was that the Ayatollah and Behrangi would have a conversation when the MOIS discovered Rothstein was missing or under arrest.

Beyond that, he didn't think there was much that could be done unless they found some other clue. The others agreed, and returned to their offices. They were all unhappy that Rothstein was likely to get off so easy. He deserved more.

By late afternoon, the DOJ agreed to Chandler's proposal, with the addition of the provisos from the Bureau. They informed Chandler, who said he'd typed up a revised agreement with the additional provisos. He'd take it to Rothstein immediately for his signature. Chandler would then FAX it to the DOJ and the Bureau.

Johnnie arranged for the interrogation of Rothstein to begin at nine thirty the next morning, provided there was a copy of the agreement signed by both Rothstein and the DOJ. Johnnie would participate in some of the interrogation sessions, but Shellie would not. Rothstein might recognize her from the Italy trip, and then reveal that information in a way that might get back to the Italian Government. The Italians would be very upset to learn that such an operation had been conducted on their soil without their permission.

Wednesday May 27

When Josh arrived at the office at six, he found that a call from Behrangi's cell phone to the Ayatollah had been collected an hour earlier. It was very short. After exchanging greetings, Behrangi said, "I wonder if Shaejoro is discovered. There was some news of an arrest." The Ayatollah replied, "I believe this is possible. I am told that we cannot contact him. If such is true, we must hope they do not discover the big one." Josh called to tell Johnnie, and then informed the Director.

About an hour later, Johnnie got a call from the head of the local Rothstein surveillance team that had checked the Yellow Line subways the previous day. They'd identified one suspicious person. The Special Agent who had Rothstein's smart phone said that two texts had been sent to the phone. Each only had a time of day. One was the time Rothstein might take the subway to work. The other was the time he might arrive back from work. One of the people who boarded the subway at Rothstein's home station, the King Street - Old Town Station, only traveled to the next station north, Braddock Road, and exited. That evening, the same person got on the subway at Braddock Road and exited at King Street - Old Town. One of the agents followed the man to his car and got the plate number.

At first glance, the individual could've been an ordinary commuter, but their research strongly suggested this subject was Rothstein's Iranian contact. First they checked out the license plate and identified the vehicle's owner, Bart Wilson. Then they checked out the phone number of the individual who had sent the texts to Rothstein's phone, and found out the number was Wilson's.

When they looked into his background, they discovered some very interesting info. He had been a U.S. Navy officer. In his last assignment, when he was a lieutenant, he was assigned to a logistics position at the U.S. Naval Base in Manama, Bahrain. He'd been caught accepting bribes from local companies so they'd be chosen to provide supplies to the Navy. He was court-martialed, served one year in prison, and was dishonorably discharged. The team leader said they'd taken a photo of Wilson and would get it to Johnnie. Johnnie thanked the team leader for their great work.

Since the Bureau now had a legally binding agreement signed by Rothstein and the DOJ, a small team of Agents began to question him about his cooperation with the Iranians. Johnnie was present at the morning session, which started at half past nine.

Rothstein said he conceived the idea of selling phony intelligence to the Iranians in December of 2013, when he was assigned to work on the Iranian nuclear issue at DOE. In January 2014 he flew to Caracas, Venezuela and approached the Iranian Embassy there. He chose Caracas because the Venezuelan Government was very hostile to the U.S., and would not likely inform the U.S. of an American visiting the Iranian Embassy. He was introduced to Mirza Rashidi, a member of the embassy staff, with whom he discussed his proposal for a couple of days. He assumed that Rashidi was an Iranian intelligence officer. He spoke very clear and articulate English, with a British accent.

Rothstein told Rashidi that he worked on the DOE nuclear negotiations support team, and had access to nuclear negotiations-related policy papers of the DOE, the State Department, and the Defense Department. He was participating in writing some of those documents. He also had access to a fair amount of intelligence.

He showed his ID card and a pay statement as proof of employment, and showed an administrative document that revealed his Top Secret clearance. He told Rashidi that, in exchange for $9,500 per month, he would provide sensitive information on U.S. positions and actions relating to the Iranian nuclear program.

Rashidi asked Rothstein the name of the city where he lived and how he commuted to work. Rashidi said he needed the information to determine how to make contact arrangements between Rothstein and the Iranian government. Rothstein explained he lived in Alexandria, Virginia and commuted to DOE HQ in Washington, D.C. via the Yellow Line subway of the DC Metrorail system. He named the subway stations he used in Alexandria and Washington.

The discussion on the first day lasted about two hours. Rashidi said he'd submit Rothstein's proposal to his superiors and would let Rothstein know the answer the next day. They agreed to meet at ten in the morning.

At the start of the meeting on the second day, Rashidi informed Rothstein that his superiors in Tehran had accepted Rothstein's proposal. They would pay him the requested monthly sum for two months. If the information he provided was satisfactory and useful, they would continue the relationship.

Rashidi then said he would instruct Rothstein on how to pass information to the Iranians. He would transfer encrypted files from his cell phone to a contact who would be near him at the King Street - Old Town metro station. Whenever Rothstein had information to pass, he should send a text msg that contained only a time of day - the time Rothstein would arrive at the subway station. The contact would be at the station at the same time. Rashidi would give Rothstein a smart phone whose Bluetooth had already been paired with another smart phone that would be sent to the U.S. and given to the contact. The phones had an app that automatically searched a specific file folder on each phone for messages to transfer.

The Bluetooth had a maximum range of about 30 feet, so Rothstein would have to be relatively close to the contact, who would be standing near the end of the overhead protective canopy at the north end of the platform. The first time the contact would be on the platform, he would be wearing a Washington Redskins jacket and baseball cap. He was white and had a beard, mustache, and black hair.

Rashidi then asked Rothstein whether he preferred an iPhone or an Android device. He preferred the latter, so Rashidi pulled out a new Galaxy S4. He showed Rothstein a Bluetooth device name that was the name of the device the contact would have. He also showed him the file folder where Rothstein should put new messages.

Rashidi had paired two iPhones and two Galaxy S4's to be ready for whichever Rothstein wanted. After Rothstein made his choice, Rashidi would use a diplomatic pouch, which would be free from inspection, to send the paired partner phone to the Iranian UN Mission in New York. An MOIS officer there would get the phone to Rothstein's contact.

Rothstein asked what he should do if he had information to pass on a weekend. Rashidi told him he should text a time to the contact and then go to the subway station. After passing the message to the contact, he should take the subway somewhere so it would appear he was making a normal subway trip.

Rothstein asked how he should encrypt the files. Rashidi gave Rothstein a thumb drive that had an encryption/decryption app, and a file of encryption/decryption keys. Rothstein should use them in the order they were listed in the file. Rashidi then used his own desktop computer to demonstrate how to use the app. It was very easy. One of the interrogators commented to Rothstein that the team that searched his residence found the Iranian thumb drive in his desk.

Rashidi said that if Rothstein had any requests to make or needed anything, he should encrypt the request and pass it in the same way that he passed information.

Rothstein asked how he'd receive his monthly payments. Rashidi told him that, on the morning of the second Saturday of each month, a delivery man would bring to Rothstein's residence a package containing his cash payment. The delivery man would be the contact with whom he would be exchanging information via the paired smart phone. Rothstein would sign for the package. If he could not be home that morning, he should text another weekend date and time.

Rothstein asked what he should do in the event of an emergency. Rashidi gave him a U.S. cell phone number, but cautioned that the number should only be used in an extreme emergency.

When Rashidi and Rothstein finished their discussions, Rashidi said he had recorded all their discussions on video. Rothstein said he'd anticipated that.

After Rothstein finished describing his meetings with Rashidi in Caracas, Johnnie asked if Rothstein had met with any other Iranians. Rothstein answered that in addition to meeting with Farhad Ahmadi in Sorrento, he'd met with one other Iranian, an individual named Rahim Ghorbani, - twice in Antibes, France in the second half of September 2014. In August of that year, the Iranians used an encrypted message passed via his Alexandria contact to ask Rothstein to meet one of them outside the U.S. Rothstein responded that he would be traveling to southern France in late September, and sent his itinerary. If they wanted to meet him during that trip, they should pay his travel expenses. They agreed to $5,000, and chose Antibes as a meeting location. The purpose of the meeting was to question him about how the U.S. nuclear negotiations were supported; namely, who were the people supporting the negotiations and what were the processes they used.

One of the interrogators asked Rothstein if he had provided Ghorbani with the requested information. He said he had. The interrogator commented that the Iranians probably wanted that information to help them further penetrate the U.S. nuclear negotiations support structure, and to identify people to recruit. The information provided by Rothstein could have put some of the support personnel, including his DOE colleagues, at risk.

The session then broke for lunch. At that time, a member of the surveillance team gave Johnnie the photo of Bart Wilson. When the interrogation resumed, Johnnie showed Rothstein the photo and asked if Rothstein recognized the man. He replied that he did - it was his contact. Johnnie asked if Rothstein had any information - documents, audio, or video - to prove that this man was his contact. Rothstein did not.

Johnnie left the session and initiated action to obtain a warrant to arrest Wilson and search his home.

Johnnie returned to the session, and asked Rothstein the total amount the Iranians had given him. Rothstein said he'd received $178,000, including the monthly payments, $5,000 for the trip to France in September 2014, and $40,000 during the trip to Italy. Of that money, the FBI seized the $40,000 he received in Italy and he had spent over $50,000 on his Porsche Boxster. One of the investigators said they found nearly $60,000 when they searched his house. Rothstein said that was all the remaining money, because he'd spent the rest.

By the end of the day, the team had exhausted all the lines of questioning they had for Rothstein. If they thought of no further questions overnight, they would release him the next morning.

Thursday May 28

The interrogation team had no further questions for Rothstein. One member of the team drafted a detailed report for the others to review. Johnnie sent an email with the relevant details of the interrogation to his Team Triad partners.

By midmorning, the Bureau had received warrants to arrest Wilson and search his residence. They immediately executed the warrants. Wilson was home and seemed to be expecting them. When they searched his home, they found nothing implicating him in working for the Iranians. They couldn't find a Galaxy S4, on which they hoped they'd find pairing for Rothstein's phone, and the encryption/decryption app. They seized his computer and gave it to the computer forensics team in the hope of finding and retrieving deleted files of interest.

When they arrested Wilson, he was very hostile. He said he'd done nothing wrong and wouldn't answer any questions without a lawyer present. They told him that Rothstein had informed them that Wilson was his contact. They said they had proof from his phone company and on Rothstein's phone that he'd exchanged text messages with Rothstein. They also told Wilson that if he would cooperate fully, they might be able to release him without filing any charges. They then allowed Wilson to contact his lawyer.

In the meantime, Johnnie recommended to Director Pasquali that the State Department be asked to declare Ahmadi persona non grata for involvement in espionage activities inside the U.S. The Director approved and the request was sent to State, which approved the request. The next morning, State informed the Iranian UN Mission that Ahmadi had been declared persona non grata for espionage activities, and had twenty-four hours to leave the U.S. The Iranians vehemently denied the accusation, but said Ahmadi would depart as ordered. They had no choice but to comply.

Thirty-three

فیل در اتاق

(The Elephant in the Room – Fil Dar Ataq)

Friday May 29

Early in the afternoon, Josh and Daniel were alerted to a cell phone call from Behrangi to the Supreme Leader's landline. The time of the call was about eleven thirty in the evening Tehran time. Josh rushed to listen to the call, which turned out to be very interesting.

"Good evening Sayyed. It is I, Mubarak. I am sorry to call you so late, but I wonder if you have heard the news."

"Good evening Mubarak. It is no problem. I know that you would only call me if it was important."

"Have you heard that they have now taken Shaediha for his deeds?" Behrangi asked.

"Do not worry. It is a different one, not our Shaediha," the Supreme Leader answered.

"You mean they have another whose name is Shaediha and who is in the same organization and who has perpetrated the same evil?"

"Yes. Perhaps there are more. They have many such evil ones in their land. Even among the religious men. However, the one they have taken is old and did this many years ago. Do not worry. Inshallah, the other one will not be discovered."

"Thank you Sayyed. I'm sorry that I bothered you."

"Do not be concerned. With you, it is never a problem. Good night."

"And good night to you."

Josh immediately called Sofie and requested a meeting with the Director ASAP. While he was holding for an answer, he told Daniel what he'd learned.

Sofie got back on the phone and told Josh he'd lucked out. The Director was available.

Josh and Daniel rushed to the Director's office, and Sofie escorted them in.

"What's going on, Josh?" the Director asked.

"Sir, we think we've just discovered the probable identity of the main Iranian spy, D.H."

"Who is it?"

"We strongly believe it's Florida Congressman Daniel Haston, who's on the House Armed Services Committee."

"Why do you think it's him?"

"Behrangi just phoned the Ayatollah. He apparently heard the news about the indictment of former House Speaker Dennis Hastert, and confused the names because they are so similar. He asked the Ayatollah if he'd heard that D.H. had just been arrested. The Ayatollah told him not to worry because it wasn't the same person. The Supreme Leader also confirmed that the two men were in the same organization, which could be either house of Congress. It sounded like the Iranians were blackmailing Haston for the same type of activity Hastert had perpetrated."

"Good grief! In this job, I never know what strange thing I'm going to be hit with. Please immediately prepare and bring me a verbatim translation of that conversation, and then I'll phone the DNI, and inform her. Don't distribute any other copies until I talk to her and get her guidance as to who should receive the translation."

"I'll go prepare the translation, and bring it to you."

Josh rushed back to the office and translated the conversation. Fortunately the audio quality was great. Josh relistened to the call five times to make sure he'd made no mistakes. He then printed the translation and rushed it to the Director, who had cancelled his next appointment and was waiting. The Director read the report carefully, and then described to Josh what he understood the translation to mean. The Director knew from experience that language could be ambiguous, and it was not hard to misread a translation, even one that was perfect.

Josh told the Director his understanding of the translation was spot on.

The Director asked Josh to stand by while he phoned the DNI.

She instructed the Director to provide the transcript only to her, and to the Directors of the FBI and the CIA. She would ask FBI Director Pasquali to inform the Speaker of the House. The DNI said she would inform the President.

Josh asked the Director if he required anything else at the moment. The Director said he did not, but that he wanted Josh to stay at work until about seven in case the DNI or the other two directors had any questions.

Josh said he'd be glad to, and that he'd let the Director know immediately if anything further developed. In the meantime, he'd phone Johnnie.

When Josh returned to his office, he called Johnnie and gave him the details, including the fact that Admiral Saunders would be informing FBI Director Pasquali.

"My compliments to you and Daniel on your success. It looks like you guys may have finally identified the culprit. However, it's really important to keep in mind that this is just a start. The information you've developed certainly points to the congressman. However, since he hasn't been clearly named, it's possible there's some mistake or misunderstanding. The congressman is innocent until proven guilty. It's critical to thoroughly investigate to determine if there's evidence."

"Thanks, Johnnie. The Rothstein situation is my first experience involving an American breaking U.S. law, so I'm still learning the legal dimensions of a case like this."

"Shellie, Gianni, Farida, and I have had a number of such

experiences, so we're very familiar with the complexities," Johnnie explained. "However, we've never dealt with a situation involving a member of Congress. That makes me really nervous.

"I'll immediately check with Director Pasquali to make sure he's informed and to request permission to initiate close surveillance of the congressman. Then I'll inform the other members of our team. It's very important that we meet as soon as possible to develop a plan to try to ascertain if it really is the congressman, and to figure out who else might be involved. I suggest we meet on Monday morning at 10:30 at our HQ. The weekend will give me time to research the issue, talk to the Director and some of my colleagues, and think about strategy and tactics.

"You probably remember that in late April, we looked into the backgrounds of the congressman and the six other individuals who had the initials D.H. and who had access to high-level intel on the Iranian nuclear negotiations. We looked at possibly relevant info from FBI and police records, and publicly available information, for example foreign travel, as well as criminal records or financial problems, but we found nothing suspicious.

"Over the weekend, I'll reexamine the data on the congressman in greater detail. I know that neither you guys at NSA nor the folks at CIA have any intelligence information about the congressman because that's prohibited. However, the congressional liaison offices at each of our agencies would have routine records on the briefings they've given the congressman, and his intelligence information requests."

"Thanks, Johnnie," Josh replied. "Daniel, J.B., and I will see you and the rest of the team on Monday."

As a result of the conversation with Johnnie, Josh realized that someone should check with the NSA congressional liaison office to find out what interactions the congressman had with NSA. Josh knew he could not make such a request himself without arousing suspicions. His only approach would be through the Director. He phoned Sofie and asked to see the Director again before the end of the day.

She called back and said he could come in half an hour. Josh continued to be amazed that he could get access to the Director on such short notice, given the Admiral's heavy workload as head of two major organizations. Moreover, the Director was always laser focused during their discussions.

In the meantime, Josh phoned Mac and updated him.

Josh returned to the Director's office and asked him if it would be possible to make the request of the NSA congressional liaison office. The Director said he'd already asked, and expected to have the answer within the hour. He'd phone Josh when he had it and had a minute to discuss it.

Josh informed the Director of the upcoming meeting with Team Triad at FBI HQ, and said him he'd informed Mac.

At five, Sofie phoned and said the Director wanted Josh and Daniel to come to his office immediately. They did.

The report from the Agency's congressional liaison office was very interesting. Over time, the congressman had been briefed on a number of topics, some at his specific request and some as an attendee at briefings to the House Armed Services Committee. The topics he'd requested most frequently had to do with Iran, especially its nuclear program, and Israel-related topics, such as Hamas, the Palestinian Authority, Syria, and Hezbollah. Despite being a member of the Armed Services Committee, the congressman had rarely requested information about Iraq, Afghanistan, or Pakistan, or for that matter, Russia, China, or North Korea. That was quite surprising given his responsibilities on the committee.

While the congressman's information interests did not provide any evidence of espionage, they were certainly focused in a way that could support espionage activity involving Iran and Israel.

Josh thanked the Director, and then returned to his office to call Johnnie to relay that info.

When Josh reached Johnnie, Johnnie said he'd received Director Pasquali's permission to initiate close surveillance of the congressman. It would begin the next morning, Saturday, May 30 in the congressman's home district. The congressman had been there since late on May 21, after Congress had adjourned for the Memorial Day holiday recess. He would probably return to Washington on the morning of Monday, June 1, when the House was scheduled to begin a legislative session.

Josh passed on what he'd learned about the topics on which the congressman had requested NSA briefings.

Un Intervallo di Sapori - Persian

Saturday May 30

Josh decided he'd prepare an Intervallo di Sapori Persian dinner, using family recipes he'd learned from his mother. The night would have accents from Shiraz, His ancestors' home town. He expected he wouldn't be called in to work during the evening because of the time difference between Washington and Iran.

As always for their special dinners, the dining room was lit by two pairs of white candles on the table.

They began with Khashk-e Bademjan dip with lavash bread. The ingredients of the dip were eggplant, yogurt, walnuts, onion, dried mint, garlic, salt, pepper, cayenne, and vegetable oil. The lavash bread, also known as Armenian bread, was an unleavened, soft, flat bread used throughout Iran, Azerbaijan, Armenia, and Turkey.

Then Josh brought Khoresh-e-Fesenjan - a chicken stew with pomegranate syrup, walnuts, onion, and butternut squash. He served the Fesenjan with chelo rice - an elegantly fluffy, Persian-style, white rice.

The stew and rice were accompanied by Mast-o Khiar yogurt-cucumber salad made with yogurt, English cucumber, shallots, garlic, salt, and pepper. This salad was also used as a sauce or dip and was similar to Greek and Middle Eastern sauces and salads such as Tzatziki and Khyar bi Laban, with slight changes such as the use of dill or garlic.

For dessert, Josh made Shir Berenj, Persian rice pudding, which he served with topping choices of pomegranate molasses, honey, and chocolate syrup.

The wine he served was a nice 2011 Signature Series Shiraz from the Iran-style Darioush Winery[71] in the Napa Valley. The owner of the winery, Darioush Khaledi, had grown up in Shiraz. The wines were on the expensive side for Josh and Meihui, but he'd occasionally serve one for a special dinner.

While they dined, they were serenaded by the beautiful Persian songs of Leila Forouhar, whom they both loved. They pretended they were in an imaginary Iran which would be a fun place to visit if it ever came to life.

After they finished, Josh surprised Meihui by reading love poetry in Persian from the famous 14th Century lyric Persian poet whose pen name was Hafez and who was a native of Shiraz. He was considered the greatest Persian poet, and was the most popular poet in Iran. His poetry praised love and wine.

Meihui knew only a few words of Persian, but she delighted in the mellifluous way Josh read the poetry and lovingly looked at her as he read. He ended the poetry session by reading an English quatrain (four-line poem) he had written in the style of Hafez.

Our Love
Our love in Eram's[72] garden glows
As soft Shiraz inside us flows.
A tide of love from Leila's lyrics
And sensuous sauce from Hafez grows.

---

[71] The winery is interesting not only for its wine, but for beautiful, ancient-Persepolis-style Persian Empire architecture, built with materials from near Persepolis - https://www.darioush.com/

The thirteenth century enclosed Eram Garden (Garden of Heaven) with beautiful Qavam House and pool is located in Shiraz. It is decorated with tiles that have the poetry of Hafez.

Thirty-four

From the Higher Slopes of Damavand, the Summit Looms Ahead

Monday June 1

At about 9:30, Josh, Daniel, and J.B. went to Daniel's Prius, and left for the Team Triad meeting. It was mostly cloudy, with a temperature of eighty degrees and wind gusting to over twenty miles per hour. The traffic on the BW Parkway flowed smoothly, and they arrived early.

At about the same time, Congressman Haston's flight from his home district was landing in Washington. The House of Representatives would be back in session at noon.

Johnnie started the meeting by informing the team that he was scheduled to meet with Director Pasquali at three thirty to update him. After that, the Director would meet with the Speaker of the House to brief him on suspicions about the congressman.

Johnnie asked Josh and Daniel to recount for the team all the latest info. Josh's update included what he'd learned about the congressman's interactions with NSA.

Josh reminded the team of the May 2 phone conversation between the Supreme Leader and Behrangi, in which it sounded like the spy or spies might be including false information with the intel that he or they were providing. Although the team had suspected Israeli involvement in Rothstein's case, that turned out to be wrong.

Johnnie explained what had been learned about Congressman Haston. All of the team knew by now that he represented a district in a major Florida metropolitan area.

Johnnie fleshed out the picture. He was in his midfifties, a native of Florida, and a successful retired businessman who'd developed a large insurance agency that had an excellent reputation. He was first elected to Congress in 2010, and was a member of the Tea Party Caucus. He was a widower with two grown children. He had no criminal record and his finances appeared to be on very solid ground. There wasn't the slightest hint of the Hastert-like pedophilia. Unlike Hastert, he'd never held any job or volunteer position involving children.

Not surprisingly, given his party and caucus affiliation, he was opposed to just about every initiative of the current administration, so it was no surprise that he was strongly opposed to the Iran nuclear negotiations.

Shellie said she'd checked with the Bureau's congressional liaison staff, and found that he'd once requested and been given a briefing on Iranian espionage in the U.S. The briefing covered known cases of Iranian espionage since the 1979 revolution, including the 2011 plot to assassinate the Saudi Ambassador to the U.S., and to bomb the Saudi and Israeli embassies in Washington. The FBI did not brief the congressman on the details of its methods, just the results.

Gianni had checked with CIA's congressional liaison office, and discovered that the congressman had requested and been given briefings similar to those NSA had provided him; and similarly, he hadn't requested other briefings one might expect would interest a member of the Armed Services Committee.

Shellie said the congressman's normal schedule was like that of most congressmen from outside the D.C. area. If the House had a full week of legislative days, it would be a four-day week that would start at about noon on Monday or Tuesday and end early to midafternoon on Thursday or Friday. There were many weeks when the House was not in session or there were shorter weeks - due to holidays, elections, etc.

In a normal legislative week, Congressman Haston would take a direct flight from his home district to Washington's Reagan National Airport. From there, he would take a subway to the Capitol South Metro Station and walk to his office in the Longworth House Office Building. When Congress adjourned on Thursday or Friday, he would immediately take the subway back to the airport and fly home to his district. There, he would spend a great deal of time in meetings with his constituents, either individually, or in events like town hall gatherings.

Every Saturday afternoon, precisely at three, he would go grocery shopping at his local Publix supermarket. He was devoutly religious, and attended church services every Sunday with his two adult children and their spouses. Then they would have dinner together. He had a very busy schedule.

He had an apartment in D.C., and still owned the family home where he and his wife had raised their children.

He'd made one foreign trip on his own within the past two years - a one-week unaccompanied trip to Italy in August of 2014. He flew into Florence, where he spent three nights. Then he took a train to Rome, where he spent three nights, before returning home to Florida. He'd also made several trips abroad as a member of congressional delegations. One of those trips had been to Israel.

Shellie suggested to J.B. that he look for info on any Iranian, Israeli, or other intel officers traveling to or staying in Florence and/or Rome on the dates in question. She felt a bit silly asking about Rome because, with so many embassies there, lots of foreign intel officers traveled to Rome or passed through.

J.B. said he'd check as soon he got back to his office.

Farida also reacted to the Italian travel info. "There's a very remote possibility I'd like to pursue with regard to that trip. I doubt it'll yield anything, but I'd like to give it a try. If you can give me the dates when the congressman was in Florence and Rome, I'll do some checking, and let you all know if I discover anything."

Johnnie said the congressman had arrived in Florence on Sunday,

August 17, 2014, and departed for Rome on Wednesday, August 20. He had returned to the U.S. on Saturday, August 23.

Johnnie said he was checking with the FBI liaison officer, known as the Legal Attaché, at the U.S. Embassy in Rome to see if the congressman had contacted the Embassy for any sort of assistance during his visit to Italy.

When Farida returned to CIA HQ, she phoned Kathrina "Kathy" Georgiadis, a friend in another office at HQ, and asked if she could come to chat with her for a couple of minutes. Kathy invited her up.

The previous October, Kathy had returned from a three-year assignment to the CIA Station at the U.S. Embassy in Rome. Farida knew Kathy because she was Kathy's replacement in an assignment to the U.S. Embassy in Tel Aviv. Farida remembered a conversation in the fall of 2014 in which Kathy mentioned a short vacation trip she'd taken to Florence a couple of months before returning to the U.S. Kathy had mentioned something about seeing a Mossad officer when she was in Florence. She had a photographic memory, and never forgot the face of anyone she met.

After exchanging greetings, Farida said, "I'd like to follow up on something you mentioned when we were chatting last fall, when I first saw you after your return from Italy. This might help me on a project I'm working on, but unfortunately, I can't share any details."

"I understand. You work for the CIA and would have to kill me if you told me. What would you like to know?"

"You mentioned that a few months before you came home, you went up to Florence on holiday for a couple of days."

"That's correct. I love Florence - Firenze. I've been there a number of times."

"Would your trip have been in August by any chance?"

"Yes, it was. I arrived on the evening of Friday, August 15 and departed on Tuesday, August 19."

"I believe you said you saw a Mossad officer while you were there."

"That's correct. On Monday evening, I was having dinner by

myself at one of my go-to eateries in Florence - the Trattoria Ponte Vecchio[73] along the Arno River. It's a stone's throw from the famous Ponte Vecchio Bridge. When I arrived at eight forty-five, this Mossad guy was there dining with another guy. There was only one other pair of diners in the restaurant because it was early for dinner by Italian custom."

"Was he someone you knew by name?"

"No, he and I were both bit players in one of many meetings I attended during my assignment in Tel Aviv. I didn't say anything to him at the restaurant because he was eating dinner with the other guy, and I didn't know if that meeting involved his business."

"Did the Mossad operative give any indication that he recognized you?"

"No. He glanced around the room every once in a while, but it was clear he didn't recognize me. He'd only seen me once. We'd never talked, and my hair was a different style and color back then."

"Can you describe the man with whom the Mossad officer was dining?"

"Yes. He was heavy set, and probably in his midfifties. He had light brown hair and light skin. In the heat of August, he was dressed in a light green polo shirt and khaki slacks. He was wearing nice brown loafers. On the basis of his attire and mannerisms, I'm fairly confident he was an American. They were speaking in English, but I wasn't close enough to hear the details of their conversation. The American seemed a bit nervous and ill at ease.

"One strange thing I observed shortly after I arrived was that the Mossad guy gave the American a cell phone - a smart phone. The American examined it for a minute, and then put it in his pocket. Then they kept talking.

"I felt the American was doing something improper, but I had no way of taking a picture or following them."

"Do you remember what time they left?"

---

[72] http://www.trattoriapontevecchio.com

"Yes. It was about nine thirty."

"Who paid?"

"The Mossad guy paid - cash."

"Do you have any idea where they went after dinner?"

"No, I don't. They were already in the middle of their meal when I arrived, and they finished and left well before I did. I would've aroused suspicions if I'd stopped eating, paid, and left when they did. After dinner, I wandered around the center of Florence for a couple of hours in the hope of running across them, but I didn't. The town is very lively until fairly late. I consoled myself by having some gelato at GROM, my favorite gelateria.

"When I got back to Rome, I reported the incident to the Chief of Station, but there was nothing we could do. I was pretty frustrated."

"If I showed you a picture of the other diner, would you recognize him?"

"Certo! - Of course. I can retrieve his image from the Florence sub-folder of the portion of my brain where I store my Italy photo folder."

"Thanks Kathy. That was incredibly helpful. Hopefully, I'll be able to tell you the background in a couple of months."

"Glad to help Farida. Now you owe me one - ha-ha! Talk to you soon."

Farida rushed backed to her office to tell Gianni. "You're not going to believe this, but I've got great news that falls into the 'It's a Small World' category. I just talked to a friend, Kathy Georgiadis, who returned from an assignment to our station in Rome last fall. Do you know her?"

"I've heard the name, but I don't know her."

"Well, she was in Florence on holiday in August of last year, during the time Congressman Haston was there. One evening, she was having dinner at a restaurant when she saw a Mossad guy having dinner with a probable American. The description sounds very much like that of the congressman. My friend said she'd recognize the American if I showed her a photo."

"How did she know one of the diners was a Mossad guy?"

"She'd seen him in a large bilateral meeting she'd attended when she was assigned to Tel Aviv. She has a photographic memory. She was not introduced to the Mossad guy at that meeting. He clearly didn't recognize her in Florence, probably because her hair style and color were very different from when she'd been in Tel Aviv."

"Wow! That's incredible! You've got to call Johnnie and ask him if you can show her a picture of the congressman."

"That's my next move. Then I've got to get a photo."

"No problem. I already have one in this folder."

"Fantastic!"

Farida phoned Johnnie and related Kathy's account of the dinner. She asked if she could show Kathy a photo of the congressman.

Johnnie told her to go ahead, but to ask Kathy to keep it confidential. He also asked Farida to call back after she'd shown Kathy the photo.

Farida thanked him. She called Kathy and asked if she could bring a photo. Kathy agreed.

Farida hurried to Kathy's office with the folder in an envelope. She pulled it out and showed it to Kathy.

"That's the guy," Kathy confirmed, "I'm positive."

Farida quickly slipped the photo back into the envelope and then gave Kathy a big hug of appreciation. "You've made an incredible difference. Please don't discuss this with anyone."

"No problem, my friend."

Farida effusively thanked Kathy again, and then headed back to share the news with Gianni and Johnnie.

On the one hand, they were delighted. On the other, the situation couldn't be more complicated - a congressman working with the Iranians and Mossad, and many, many unanswered questions.

Johnnie said he'd hurry to tell Director Pasquali who hadn't yet left for his meeting with the Speaker of the House. He asked Farida to inform CIA Director Rolph and the NSA guys.

Josh was delighted when Farida called. He couldn't believe their good fortune. It completely validated the work he and Daniel had done. He never ceased to be amazed at how often people encounter others whom they knew in the most unusual of circumstances, like Daniel and the HR guy running into each other in Amalfi.

As soon as Josh got off the phone, he passed the news to Daniel, and then to J.B. Next he phoned Sofie and requested a few minutes with the Director. She told him the Director would be unavailable until later in the day. She asked if the subject was time critical. Josh said it was important, but could wait a few hours unless the Director was scheduled to meet with the DNI. She said he wasn't.

When the Director was available, Sofie phoned Josh, and he and Daniel immediately went to see him.

"What's going on now, Josh?" the Director inquired.

"You're not going to believe this, sir, but it looks like the congressman is working for both the Iranians and Mossad. In fact, Mossad may be pulling the strings."

"How was that discovered, Josh?" the Admiral asked.

"It was only by chance that Farida, who is on our team and whom you met when the team visited, connected some dots. A CIA friend of hers mentioned to her a few months earlier that she'd seen a Mossad officer meeting with some unidentified American at a restaurant in Florence, Italy in August of last year. Farida's friend, who has a photographic memory, recognized the Mossad officer from seeing him once at a large bilateral meeting in Tel Aviv.

"When Farida saw that the congressman had been in Florence, she checked with her friend, and the dates matched. Then Farida showed the friend a picture of the congressman, and the friend identified the congressman as the individual she'd seen with the Mossad officer."

"That's quite a story, Josh. I'm really pleased that efforts you and Daniel have made resulted in probably uncovering the spy's identity. However, it's critical that you maintain the utmost secrecy, and that you spare no effort to ensure the accuracy of every detail of your analysis. That's important under any circumstance, but given the domestic political and foreign policy implications of this situation, it's even more critical."

The Director reflected to himself that he could never remember a case of a congressman involved in espionage. He also knew it was inconceivable that an intelligence service as professional as Mossad would undertake to involve a congressman without the express approval of the country's Prime Minister. The situation was further complicated by the fact that this espionage had been underway at the time of the Prime Minister's controversial speech to the Congress less than three months earlier.

The Director could envision that some in the Congress and among the public might attempt to justify the congressman's actions as in the best interests of the nation.

The road to wrapping up this case was likely to be very rocky, and filled with PIEDs (Political Improvised Explosive Devices). The political landscape of his job was by far the hardest to navigate. Too bad there wasn't a GPS system for that.

Shortly after Josh informed Admiral Saunders, FBI Director Pasquali began a private meeting with the Speaker of the House. It was very difficult for the Speaker to learn that a member of his own conference was involved in espionage, the first such case in the history of the Congress. This activity was quite surprising in view of the congressman's apparent devotion to country, his work ethic, and his love for his job. The Speaker had many tough questions for the Director, who was well prepared.

When the Speaker accepted the fact that Congressman Haston could be a spy, he asked what he could do to assist with the investigation. Director Pasquali said there was one important way the Speaker could help. It would be very useful to learn discreetly and as soon as possible if the congressman gained any new access to classified material about Iran, because the Bureau could be particularly alert for any attempt by the congressman to pass that information to the Iranians. The Speaker said there was a superb long-time staffer on the HPSCI, whom the Speaker could ask to let him know immediately and in confidence when any congressman requested and obtained access to intelligence about Iran. The Director expressed his gratitude and left.

Tuesday June 2

Minutes after he arrived at work, Josh learned there was a phone call from the Supreme Leader to Behrangi. It had been placed about two thirty in the afternoon Iran time. He immediately listened to the conversation, which was short, but very interesting.

"Mubarak, it is Sayyed. How are you?"

"Good afternoon, Sayyed. I am fine, inshallah, and you?"

"I am fine, inshallah. Where are you?"

"I am en route to Tabriz to go to my home town. Are there any problems?"

"No. I am calling to reassure you after our phone conversation last Friday evening."

"Ah. Thank you."

"We have confirmation that the one you called about is still with us. He gave us another gift on Saturday afternoon. The gift however, still concerns me that the other side is not sincere - that they are using us."

"I understand. I fear they cannot be trusted."

"I spoke again with Mojaezae (Foreign Minister Zarif). He continues to assure me that they are sincere. He believes that Shaejoka (the U.S. Secretary of State) is completely reliable. I will have to make some judgment before I decide whether or not to accept any deal."

"Hopefully, Allah will guide you."

"Yes. I pray for his guidance. At any rate, I just wanted to let you know that the one you called about is still in our hands."

"Allahu Akbar, Sayyed. I am grateful for your call."

"I wish you a pleasant visit with your family. We will talk soon."

"Thank you again, Sayyed."

Josh listened to the conversation again, and then translated it. He listened to the conversation several more times, and then finalized the translation. After that, he informed Daniel of the substance.

Next, he called Sofie to request some time with the Director ASAP. She expected he'd arrive in about fifteen minutes, but he'd only have a couple of minutes. She asked Josh to come to his office and await his arrival. Josh said he'd be right there. He printed the translation and took it to the Director's office.

When the Director arrived and saw Josh sitting outside his office, he smiled and greeted him in Persian. Then he said, "You again! I think you're turning into my shadow. Please come into my office."

Josh entered the office and explained what he had. He detailed what he thought were the most important points:

- The spy, D.H., probably Congressman Haston, had somehow provided the Iranians with information on Saturday, May 30.
- The information D.H. provided again suggested the U.S. was not sincere in its negotiations with the Iranians.
- The U.S. Secretary of State appeared to have been successful in convincing his Iranian counterpart of his sincerity.
- The Ayatollah was not convinced of American sincerity, and would have to make some judgment on that point before agreeing to any deal.

The Director thanked Josh and said he'd arrange to have the report sent immediately and "EYES ONLY" to the Secretary of State, the DNI, the FBI Director, and the CIA Director.

Josh returned to his office, and called Johnnie to update him. When Josh finished, Johnnie said he'd check with the leader of the FBI team that had surveilled the congressman on Saturday and Sunday to ask if anything they observed could involve the passing of information from the congressman to a contact.

Johnnie then told Josh that the Legal Attaché in Rome had answered Johnnie's query by reporting that the congressman had contacted the Embassy on the afternoon of Friday August 21, 2014, two days before his return to the U.S. He reported that he'd accidentally left his phone at a Persian restaurant called Kabab the night before. He went back to the restaurant, but the phone had disappeared. He said he'd purchased the phone in Florence, and it had an Italian SIM card and Italian phone number. It was cheaper than roaming with his U.S. phone. The Legal Attaché informed Johnnie that the phone had never been turned in to the Embassy.

Johnnie found a couple of interesting things in the Legal Attaché's response. First, he wondered why a traveler who was spending only three nights in Rome would go to a Persian restaurant rather than an Italian restaurant. Second, it was quite a coincidence that of all the types of non-Italian restaurants one could choose in Rome, the congressman chose a Persian restaurant. He could find those in the Washington, D.C. area.

Johnnie did know from friends who traveled to Europe that it made economic sense to buy an Italian SIM card for one's phone or to buy a disposable phone with an Italian SIM card. One could often get the SIM card for 10 or 20 Euros, and that included 10 Euros worth of talk time and often some data.

Johnnie did a quick Internet search for the restaurant Kabab. It didn't seem like the type of restaurant that would support the Iranian regime because it offered belly dancing with very revealing dress (or undress). From the TripAdvisor reviews, the place sounded great.

After finishing his conversation with Josh, Johnnie informed the other members of Team Triad about the Legal Attaché's report, as well as Johnnie's thoughts about the phone, and his research about Kabab.

When he told Gianni, he said he'd research the CIA's files to see if there'd ever been any reported connection between the restaurant and the MOIS. He'd also ask Farida to check with Kathy Georgiadis about the restaurant.

Gianni got back to Johnnie that afternoon with very interesting results. In early 2014, a senior official of an Italian intel service had informed the CIA station chief off the record that a waiter at the restaurant was initially a double agent for the MOIS and the Mossad. The waiter pretended to be working for the MOIS, but was actually controlled by Mossad. However, what neither Mossad nor the MOIS knew, was that the waiter was now a triple agent controlled by the Italians. The waiter was an Iranian of Jewish origin, but the MOIS didn't know about his Jewish heritage. He pretended to be a Muslim.

The Italians had discovered what the waiter was doing, and they brought him under their control. Gianni had found the information in CIA files, and Kathy Georgiadis had mentioned to Farida that she was aware of it. CIA had never informed Mossad because it could have severely damaged the relationship with the Italians.

Unfortunately, there was no way to ask the Italians if there was some connection between the waiter, the phone, and the congressman. Gianni surmised one possibility was that Mossad had loaded some data onto the phone and had the congressman deliberately leave the phone for the waiter to pass to the MOIS. Gianni then reminded Johnnie that a month earlier, Josh had told them that the Shaediha cryptogram had been created on October 1, 2014, suggesting that D.H. had started spying for the Iranians before that time. Gianni suggested a possible sequence of events:

18 August – Congressman Haston meets Mossad officer in Florence and receives phone, possibly preloaded with fake compromising info about the congressman.

20 August - Congressman "loses" phone in Persian restaurant and Iranian triple-agent waiter takes phone.

Soon after - Waiter provides phone to MOIS, which examines phone and finds scandalous info about congressman.

- Iranians contact congressman and blackmail him to spy for them.

- Congressman agrees.

- MOIS informs Ayatollah, who then shares info with Behrangi.

1 October - Behrangi creates Shaediha cryptogram.

Johnnie called the leader of the FBI team surveilling the congressman and asked if anyone had noticed anything unusual about the congressman's activities on Saturday - anything that might suggest he was transferring info to someone. The team leader said he'd check and call back.

He phoned back an hour later and told Johnnie that only one action was noted that might be relevant. After the congressman paid for his groceries, the man who bagged the groceries pushed the grocery cart, which had only one large reusable bag of groceries, to the congressman's 2015 Cadillac CTS sedan. Publix policy was for its baggers to ask each customer if the customer would like help taking groceries to the car.

The congressman and the bagger seemed to know each other very well. When the bagger finished putting the bag of groceries into the car's trunk, the congressman handed him something very small. The agent thought it might be a tip, even though Publix policy does not permit it baggers to accept tips. Publix did encourage its employees to get to know and greet individual customers in order to make its customers feel welcome and at home in its stores. It was also not surprising that a congressman would work at being friendly with constituents. So the agent had dismissed this action as unimportant. However, in view of the intel Josh had provided about info being turned over on Saturday, Johnnie asked the team leader to look into this bagger to see if he could find anything relevant.

In midafternoon, the Speaker of the House phoned the FBI Director to inform him that about nine that morning, Congressman Haston went to the HPSCI's secure information facility and asked to read the latest classified update on the nuclear negotiations with Iran. He had spent half an hour reading and rereading the document. Director Pasquali called Johnnie to let him know. He alerted the surveillance team.

Shortly thereafter, about three o'clock, the congressman slipped out of a House floor session and walked out of the Capitol Building. He started casually strolling around the Capitol grounds. At one point, near a couple of trees that seemed to block a view of the congressman from many angles, a man walking toward him came very close. When they were next to each other, the congressman discreetly passed something to the man. A surveillance agent used a concealed video camera to capture the transfer, as well as facial pictures of the contact. After the contact, the congressman reentered the Capitol.

Several agents attempted to follow the contact, but lost him at the L'Enfant Plaza Metro Station.

When the head of the team advised Johnnie of the contact and the video, Johnnie asked him to get the video to him immediately. As soon as Johnnie received it, he gave it to Shellie and asked her to check to see if the contact matched any members of the Israeli Embassy staff, and to see if the video revealed what the congressman had passed to the contact.

She took the video to an FBI colleague who specialized in identifying people in photos. Within an hour, he had the answer. The individual's name was Ariel Harel. He was ostensibly a low-level employee of the Israeli Embassy in Washington. However, the video did not reveal what the congressman had passed to Harel.

When Shellie took the ID to Johnnie, she laid out a scenario for the possible sequence of events involving the congressman, the Israelis, and the Iranians:

- The congressman read the intel paper in the HPSCI secure facility. Since he could not take notes or remove the paper from the facility, he memorized what he thought were the most important points.

- He returned to his office, typed up his notes, and loaded them onto a thumb drive.

- He took the thumb drive on his walk around the Capitol grounds, and passed the drive to Harel.

- Harel would take the drive to the Israeli Embassy, where Mossad operatives would examine the info on the drive and then add to it or alter it in whatever way they felt would meet their government's objectives. That might require them to get guidance from Tel Aviv.

- At some point, before the congressman went shopping at the Publix near his home in Florida, a Mossad contact, possibly Harel, would return the drive to the congressman.

- When the congressman did his shopping at Publix, he would transfer the thumb drive to the possible Iranian contact at Publix.

Shellie thought the contents of the thumb drive might be encrypted, perhaps with the type of system on the drive found in Rothstein's residence.

Johnnie complimented Shellie on the scenario she'd laid out. He thought it very plausible.

Johnnie alerted the head of the Washington surveillance team to be alert for any transfers to the congressman before the congressman departed Washington on Thursday afternoon after the House went into recess.

Then he called the head of the surveillance team in Florida and advised him to have the team look for a transfer to the Publix employee or some other contact after the congressman arrived in his home district. If they could detect a transfer to the congressman and then a transfer from the congressman to the possible Iranian contact, they could seize the thumb drive, and arrest the congressman and the Iranian contact. Johnnie said he'd fly down to Florida to be present with the team on Saturday afternoon in case it looked like they had an arrest opportunity.

Wednesday June 3

The leader of the surveillance team in the congressman's home district informed Johnnie that they'd identified the Publix employee who'd taken the congressman's groceries to his car. His name was Samir Mohsen. He'd been working at the congressman's Publix since October of 2014. He was married with two young children, had leased a decent home, and drove a late model Ford Escape SUV.

Johnnie thanked the team leader. He walked over to Shellie's desk and told her. He asked her to see what she could find out about Mohsen. She knew immediately that his name was Persian. She couldn't wait to see what she'd learn. Johnnie phoned Farida and Josh to let them know.

In the early afternoon, Shellie came to Johnnie and told him what she'd learned about Mohsen. He was an Iranian-American with U.S. citizenship. He was born in Iran and brought to the U.S. as a young child when his parents emigrated from Iran in the late 1980s. He grew up in Alexandria, VA. After high school, he attended Georgetown University's School of Foreign Service, where he received an undergraduate degree - a Bachelor of Science in Foreign Service - Culture and Politics. He continued on to obtain a Master of Arts in Arab Studies. His academic record at Georgetown was very good. After receiving his master's degree, he spent a year studying in Tehran.

When he returned from Iran, he obtained a job at a foreign policy think tank in Washington, where he specialized in Iranian affairs.

Strangely, in early October of 2014, he resigned from the think tank and moved from Alexandria to the congressman's home town, where he applied to work at the Publix store patronized by the congressman. The Publix employment seemed completely out of keeping with his education and employment history, and the pay was much lower than what he'd been earning at the think tank. He had no history of unlawful activity.

Johnnie phoned the head of the surveillance team in the congressman's home district to have the team initiate surveillance of Mohsen.

Thursday June 4

The House of Representatives adjourned about in the afternoon,. The congressman returned to his office in the Longworth House Office Building. He dropped off some work materials, discussed several business issues with his staff director, grabbed his rolling carry-on suitcase, and headed to the Capitol South Metro Station.

An agent surveilling the congressman got onto the same Blue Line subway car, pulling a small carry-on bag as if he was heading to the airport. The agent noticed an individual, whom he recognized as Ariel Harel, get onto the subway car and stand close to the congressman.

At the L'Enfant Plaza Metro Station, all three got off the subway and switched to the Yellow Line subway. All of them got onto the same subway car. A second agent also boarded the car. Neither agent stood near the congressman or near each other, but Ariel Harel stood very close to the congressman. At the next stop, the Pentagon Station, both agents noticed that while many passengers were getting on and off the subway, Harel unobtrusively slipped a small item into a partially opened pocket of the congressman's suitcase. One of the agents used a concealed camera to video tape the transfer.

Harel got off at the next subway station, Pentagon City. The second agent also got off and followed Harel out onto S. Hayes St., where Harel caught a cab. The agent managed to get a photo of Harel.

Just after the subway departed that station, the congressman leaned over and zipped the pocket shut. The way he did so clearly indicated that he had deliberately left it open for the transfer, and that he knew the transfer had occurred.

Both the congressman and the first agent exited the subway at the Reagan National Airport Metro Station. While the congressman was crossing to the concourse level of the airport via an enclosed pedestrian bridge, the agent phoned an agent at the security inspection point the congressman would probably be using. He let the agent know the congressman was coming. On the basis of the congressman's previous travels to his home district, they knew which airline and flight he'd probably use, so they knew which security check point he'd be passing through. A special TSA agent was in place to do a "routine search" of the congressman's luggage beyond the normal electronic scan of the bag.

The congressman appeared to be very nervous when his bag was being searched. It turned out there was a thumb drive in the pocket in question. There was a second thumb drive in the main compartment of the bag. The Bureau did not want to stop the congressman and take the transferred drive at this point. They hoped to catch him passing it to Mohsen. When Johnnie was told about the second drive, he guessed it might contain the encryption/decryption app and the keys. He figured that the Israelis had made a copy of that drive for themselves, and used it when appropriate.

After passing through the check point, the congressman headed to his departure gate. Another agent was at that gate. He would be on the congressman's flight. No other unusual activity was noted during the remainder of the day.

At the time the congressman was flying home, FBI Director Pasquali had a short meeting with the Speaker of the House, and informed him of the high probability that the congressman would be arrested on Saturday afternoon, if events played out as expected. The Director told the Speaker he would inform him immediately if the arrest took place.

Prior to the meeting with the Speaker, he had a conference call with the DNI and the Directors of the CIA and NSA, to describe the scenario he thought might unfold. They all offered the full support of their organizations. The CIA and NSA Directors had been kept fully informed by their staffs of the actions being taken by employees of each agency.

Friday June 5

The surveillance team noticed nothing unusual. In midmorning, the congressman held an open town hall meeting for his constituents. He handled every question he was asked, no matter how contentious, calmly and logically, on the basis of his own political beliefs and philosophy. Even those with opposite views liked his calm and sincere demeanor.

During the afternoon, he had individual meetings with constituents to discuss their specific problems and concerns.

In the evening, he went out to dinner at a steak house with a couple of his staffers. After dinner, he went directly home.

Thirty-five

Atop the Dome

Saturday June 6

Congressman Haston spent the morning in his district office, holding more meetings with individual constituents. He left at noon and went home.

He left home at three for his weekly Publix grocery shopping. He spent about fifteen minutes in the store, and then came out with Mohsen pushing his grocery cart, which contained a single bag of groceries. As Mohsen had done the preceding Saturday, he placed the grocery bag in the trunk of the congressman's Cadillac. Then the congressman handed him a small item, as an agent videotaped the whole event.

Before Mohsen could do anything with the item the congressman had given him, four agents, including Johnnie, approached the pair from four directions. The congressman and Mohsen at first appeared puzzled, and then seemed to understand what was happening, as puzzlement turned to deep concern.

"Excuse me, Congressman Haston and Mr. Mohsen, we are from the FBI. We are placing you both under arrest for espionage," Johnnie began.

"Let me see your credentials," the congressman replied.

Three of them, including Johnnie, showed their credentials. The fourth kept his eye on Mohsen, who tried to inconspicuously drop the small item under the congressman's car. Mohsen did not realize he was being videotaped by a fifth agent and that he was doing

370

exactly what the agents wanted. As a consequence of that action, the agents would not have to defend against charges that they had unlawfully taken possession of an item. An agent grabbed the small item, which turned out to be a thumb drive. They could use the videotape to show that Mohsen had deliberately tossed it away.

"You can't arrest me because I have congressional immunity," the congressman declared.

"That immunity does not apply to treason, sir," Johnnie responded.

"Nothing I was doing was treasonous," the congressman retorted. "Anything I did was in the best interests of my country. That's what I was elected to do."

"When you give classified U.S. information to foreign governments without authorization, that constitutes treason. In addition to impacting our negotiations with Iran, your actions have probably cost the lives of two highly placed Iranian assets, put the lives of Americans at risk, and caused serious national security damage."

"What evidence do you have to charge me with treason?" the congressman continued.

"We have some fairly well documented evidence, from your meeting in the restaurant in Florence, Italy last October through your actions of the past week. Much of that is on video. The contents of this thumb drive should seal the deal."

"That assumes you can read what's on the thumb drive," the congressman said.

"That shouldn't be a problem," Johnnie answered. "I believe we'll know the contents within a couple of hours." Johnnie had worked out a process with Daniel to securely transmit the data to NSA and have it rapidly analyzed by the same team of cryptanalysts who'd analyzed the encryption/decryption app and keys that Rothstein had used. The app might be the same, but the keys would likely be different. The data would be securely transmitted to NSA from the nearby FBI office. The team of cryptanalysts was standing by at

NSA. Garland Von Greif, the head of the cryptanalytic organization, was with them in order to arrange any additional support they might need.

Of course, the decryption would have been easier with the congressman's encryption/decryption keys. They would find the thumb drive with those keys a short while later when they searched the congressman's residence.

The interaction between the agents, the congressman, and Mohsen attracted the attention of Publix customers and a couple of Mohsen's coworkers who were in the parking lot assisting customers. One of the coworkers rushed into the store to inform the manager. He quickly walked up to the group to find out what was going on. As he approached, one of the agents stopped him and explained that they were from the FBI. He showed the manager his ID, and asked him to step back. The manager readily complied. He couldn't believe his eyes - that a congressman whom he deeply respected, and Mohsen, one of his solid, hard-working employees, were being arrested. He couldn't imagine what these good people had done.

While the congressman and Mohsen were being placed in separate vehicles to be taken to the nearby FBI office for questioning, Johnnie went to his vehicle to place a call to Director Pasquali to inform him of the arrests.

After Director Pasquali received the call, he immediately phoned the Speaker of the House. He then placed calls to the DNI, and to the NSA and CIA Directors. He told them that he would inform the White House Chief of Staff, and ask him to inform the President. The DNI said she would inform the Secretaries of State, Defense, and Energy.

The President instructed his Chief of Staff to arrange a meeting with key players such as the DNI and the Secretary of State to discuss how to deal with the Israelis. While he understood what motivated their actions, he found this operation particularly egregious.

Johnnie proceeded to the nearby FBI office and had the contents of the thumb drive sent to NSA via secure communications. The team of cryptanalysts received the data and loaded it onto a high-side supercomputer. One member of the team informed Daniel, who was at work with Josh to support the arrest operation.

Within an hour, the team had decrypted the file. It was a three-page document containing bullet points about the nuclear negotiations with Iran. They could tell from the file's properties that it had been created at 9:45 a.m., on June 2, within minutes after the congressman had finished reading the Iran intelligence document and left the HPSCI secure facility. They could see that the file had been modified the next afternoon at 5:30 p.m., while it was in the Israelis' possession.

Daniel phoned Johnnie with the details of the file's properties and the nature of the contents. He didn't discuss the specifics of the contents over the phone, because the info was classified. Johnnie used the fact of the drive's classified contents to provide the specifics of the charges against the congressman and Mohsen.

Johnnie phoned Director Pasquali to update him. The Director then followed up with the Speaker of the House, the President, the DNI, et al.

In the meantime, Josh phoned Admiral Saunders, who had come in to NSA HQ to provide any necessary guidance. Josh told the admiral what they'd learned. The Director thanked Josh and asked him to come to his office with Daniel and the team of cryptanalysts.

Josh told Daniel, who called the cryptanalysts, and all went to see the Director. The admiral complimented them on the great work they'd done in stopping the Iranian and Israeli espionage efforts, and thanked them for coming in on the weekend to do that. He explained to the cryptanalysts the highly sensitive nature of the situation.

Back in Florida, Johnnie and the other three agents who'd arrested the congressman met with him to see if he would respond to questions. Johnnie informed him that the Bureau now had the decrypted contents of the thumb drive. They revealed a document that had been created just after the congressman read the classified documents about Iran in the HPSCI secure facility on June 2, and that the document had been modified, probably by the Israelis, after the congressman had given them the thumb drive. The Bureau had video of the congressman giving the drive to Ariel Harel on June 2, receiving it back from him on June 4, and passing it to Mohsen on June 6. Johnnie did not say that they had no evidence that it was the same thumb drive that was changing hands in each instance.

Johnnie asked the congressman if he would like to cooperate and provide them with the details of his espionage activities. His cooperation would be taken into consideration when he was tried and would likely mitigate the sentence he would receive.

Congressman Haston adamantly reiterated his earlier claim that he had only acted in the best interests of the United States, and that he would have nothing further to say until he had consulted with his lawyer.

Johnnie replied that the law was unambiguous, and that what the congressman had done was clearly espionage. The Bureau would be able to provide compelling evidence of the congressman's actions and the resultant damage. Johnnie then provided the congressman with a phone he could use to contact a lawyer.

The congressman phoned Hiram Thompson, a longtime friend and talented local attorney who shared the congressman's political views. Thompson was taken aback by the call. After getting over his surprise, he informed the congressman that defending against espionage charges was beyond his area of expertise. However, he would immediately undertake a search to find a talented lawyer with the appropriate skill set. He would undoubtedly have to find someone in the Washington, D.C. area. The congressman asked Thompson to inform his oldest son, who would inform the rest of the family.

After the congressman got off the phone, Johnnie told him he would be placed in jail and formal charges would be brought against him in the next couple of days. While Johnnie was finishing, another agent opened the door and informed Johnnie that the Speaker of the House was on the phone and wanted to have a private conversation with the congressman. The call was transferred to the phone in the room where the congressman was being questioned. Johnnie handed him the phone, and the agents left the room.

When the congressman got on the phone, he apologized to the Speaker for any problem he might have caused, and said he felt he'd done nothing wrong. The Speaker replied that these accusations were extremely grave. The findings described to the Speaker by the FBI Director were very compelling, and the only such accusations ever made against a member of the House. The Speaker suggested that the congressman offer his full cooperation to the FBI, and do what he could to at least mitigate the damage to national security. The Speaker said that some of the facts were indisputable. For example, the Speaker had been informed by HPSCI staff of the congressman's access to intelligence on Iran in the secure HPSCI facility on the morning of June 2.

The congressman again apologized for any problems he might have created. The Speaker expressed his hope that the congressman would cooperate with the FBI, and that this issue would turn out ok for him. He then hung up.

After leaving the congressman to be placed in jail, Johnnie and the other three agents moved to the office where Mohsen was being held. There, they found a very different situation. Mohsen seemed at once depressed and relieved and apologetic. After they informed him of his rights, he appeared willing to cooperate immediately and without the presence of a lawyer.

Mohsen explained that during his post-graduate studies in Tehran, he lived with the family of his uncle - his father's older brother. Mohsen was very close to his uncle and the uncle's family.

One day, after Mohsen had been in Iran for about six months, the MOIS took him into custody, and accused him of conducting espionage for the CIA. Mohsen adamantly denied the charges because he hadn't been working for the CIA or any other intelligence agency. Although the MOIS had no proof, it did not drop the accusations. The MOIS informed Mohsen that if he didn't cooperate with them after he returned to the U.S., his uncle might suffer serious, unspecified harm.

So after Mohsen returned to the U.S. and began working at the think tank, he started to perform various activities for the MOIS, such as serving as a go-between to pass information. He was deeply troubled by what he was doing because he loved the U.S. and hated betraying his country, but he felt he had no choice in order to keep his uncle from harm.

Several years after his return to the U.S., his uncle in Iran died of natural causes, and the uncle's family moved to Turkey. However, the MOIS now blackmailed Mohsen with evidence that he had spied for them. Mohsen made a covert recording of one blackmail conversation with his MOIS handler. He had that recording at home.

In late September of 2014, the MOIS instructed him to move to Florida to serve as a contact with the congressman. So he left the think tank job he loved, and moved as directed.

The MOIS told him to try to get a job at a Publix supermarket near where the congressman lived. He applied to Publix and was hired as a bagger. He then asked the store manager to put him on a schedule that included Saturdays. The manager was very happy to have an employee who wanted to work on Saturdays.

The MOIS informed Mohsen of the time the congressman would come to the store on Saturdays. The very first Saturday that Mohsen was working, he saw the congressman and made sure to be the bagger at the checkout the congressman chose. He asked the congressman if he would like help taking his groceries to the car. The congressman said he would. While walking to the car, Mohsen let the congressman know he was the contact. The congressman had a thumb drive with him and passed it to Mohsen.

As of that Saturday, Mohsen helped the congressman take his groceries to his car every Saturday. Sometimes the congressman would give him a thumb drive and sometimes nothing. Whenever he received a thumb drive, he did one thing that the MOIS didn't know about - he made and kept copies of the files on the drive. The encrypted files were all unreadable, but he thought they might someday be useful.

Johnnie was ecstatic. He felt that NSA would be able to decrypt those files and then Team Triad could have various experts examine the data to see what U.S. info had been compromised and assess the resultant damage to U.S. national security. They would also be able to understand how the Israelis had modified the U.S. information.

Johnnie asked Mohsen how he passed the thumb drives to the MOIS.

Mohsen explained that he'd been given a key for a specific post office box. Some unidentified person, whom he had never seen, had the other key. The box was used for passing thumb drives in both directions and funds to Mohsen. Whenever he placed a thumb drive in the box, he would text the word, "ready" to a phone number he'd been given. If something was placed in the box for him, he would receive the same text msg.

Johnnie decided to take a shot at trying to lure the other user of the post office box to pick up the latest thumb drive. He thought it was a long shot because the arrests of the congressman and Mohsen were already on the news.

Johnnie asked Mohsen if he'd be willing to send the "ready" text. He said he'd be happy to. Johnnie had a special agent retrieve Mohsen's smart phone.

Johnnie asked Mohsen for the location of the post office box, the number of the box, and the key. Mohsen provided what Johnnie requested. Johnnie instructed a special agent to go to the location of the box and see if anyone showed up after Mohsen sent the text. When the agent was in place near the post office box, Mohsen sent the text. Unfortunately, no one ever came.

He asked another agent to look into the phone number used for the texts to see if its user and location could be identified. Nothing useful was found.

Johnnie then asked Mohsen if he'd be willing to cooperate and provide all the details of his work with the MOIS.

Mohsen said he'd be glad to.

Johnnie thanked him and said that his cooperation and the nature and circumstances of his work for the MOIS would go a long way toward minimizing any sentence he might receive for his espionage activities.

Mohsen asked if something could be done to protect his wife and children from the MOIS while he was in custody. Johnnie replied that as long as Mohsen was cooperating this way, the Bureau would safeguard Mohsen and his family in protective custody at an undisclosed location.

Mohsen thanked Johnnie and asked for permission to call his wife to let her know what was happening. Johnnie let Mohsen make the call and also instructed an agent to take the necessary action to arrange the protective custody.

Mohsen's wife was relieved to hear from him. As soon as news of his arrest had been reported, she'd been besieged by phone calls from the media, acquaintances, and strangers. She was under great stress and fretting about his well-being.

Mohsen cooperated fully with the Bureau and provided insights into MOIS operations that helped break up another MOIS espionage operation in the U.S. and one in Canada.

Sunday June 7

At about quarter to nine, just as Josh sat down on the couch with a cup of coffee and his Sunday *Washington Post*, he received a phone call from Kat. She informed him that there was something he might want to take a look at. Josh told Meihui he had to go into the office. He then poured his coffee into a thermal cup, took it to his car, and set out for the office.

When he arrived, he found a very interesting conversation between Behrangi, who had initiated the call, and the Supreme

Leader.

"Good afternoon, Sayyed. I hope you will forgive me for interrupting you."

"Good afternoon, Mubarak. It is never a problem when you call. I value what you have to say. I expect you are calling about Shaediha. I know that they have him now, but I have also learned the other dimension."

"You mean that he is really a toy of Shaeku[74]. That is quite surprising!"

"It does not surprise me. We see that Shaekubine[75] will do anything to stop us. So now I see why Mojaezae[76] insisted that Shaejoka[77] was serious, but the information from Shaediha said that they were deceiving us. So it turns out that Shaediha and Shaejoro were of absolutely no value to us - a complete waste of our resources. I am upset that our people could not validate these people. I have told them they must change their methods or I will change those who are in charge."

"I understand."

"So I interpret this event as perhaps a sign from Allah that we should complete the agreement. I will have to give this some thought before I make a final decision."

"I wish you the best in making such a decision. It seems very difficult."

From that point, the two switched their conversation to more mundane topics such as the weather and discussions about mutual friends.

Josh prepared a translation of the conversation. He decided to wait until the following day, a normal work day to inform the Director and Mac because he felt the info was of high value, but not

---

[73] Little Satan; i.e., Israel.
[74] The Israeli Prime Minister.
[75] The Iranian Foreign Minister
[76] The U.S. Secretary of State

time critical.

After finishing the preparation of the translation, Josh stopped to reflect on the implications of the congressman's espionage. It turned out there were both positive and negative aspects, not simply the negative. The key positive was that it might have moved the Ayatollah toward agreeing to the nuclear accord. The serious negatives were the loss of lives of the two Iranians who had been providing high-value HUMINT to the U.S., and the loss of an important NSA capability that provided far more than just intel about Iranian nuclear activities.

Josh felt it was too bad the congressman would never learn that he was a victim of the Law of Unintended Consequences and that his actions had the opposite impact of their intended objective. He had increased the likelihood of a nuclear accord. Because he'd lost his security clearance, he'd never know the bottom line of this conversation between the Supreme Leader and Behrangi.

Josh sent a high-side email to Sofie to let her know that he had something very interesting to pass to the Director in the morning. Then he shut down the office computers, locked the office and headed home.

That afternoon, the congressman's lawyer, Hiram Thompson, visited him in jail and informed him that he'd found a high-quality lawyer who defended people accused of espionage. It was Sean Chandler. Thompson explained all the cases in which Chandler had been involved, including the most recent one involving Rothstein. If the congressman approved the recommendation, Chandler would fly to Florida that evening and meet with the congressman the next day. The congressman approved.

Monday June 8

Sofie called Josh about seven thirty and said she'd read Josh's email, and had informed the Director that Josh had some interesting information. The Director wanted to see Josh right away. She also said the Director had asked her to arrange a nine thirty session with the Agency's senior leadership team, plus Josh, Daniel, J.B., Kat Marcus, Garland von Greif, the cryptanalysts who had come in on Saturday, and Josh's wife. She said she'd inform all those players except Daniel, whom Josh could tell.

Josh told Daniel and then headed to the Director's office with the translation of the important component of the conversation between the Ayatollah and Behrangi. When Josh arrived in the Director's office and explained the substance of the conversation, the Director was pleased. He told Josh that processing of conversations between the Ayatollah and Behrangi could now be handled differently because the Iranian and Israeli espionage efforts had been stopped. Any reporting on conversations not involving the espionage activities could be sent to a broader, but still limited distribution. Any conversations relating to the involvement of Rothstein and the congressman in espionage still had to be handled with great care because those items could be "discoverable" in the event of a trial, and could compromise sources and methods. The Director told Josh to wait until after the 9:30 session with the leadership team before taking any action.

At about 9:20 a.m., Josh and Daniel arrived in the Director's large conference room, where they were joined by all their colleagues who'd been involved in Meta and by Josh's wife, Meihui. Marilyn Carter had made seating arrangements for all of them.

"What's happening, Josh?" asked Meihui, who was seated on Josh's left. "This is very strange."

"Be patient, my dear," he chuckled. "You'll find out in a minute."

"Mais, oui!"

The Director arrived precisely at nine thirty. "Good morning," he greeted them. "I'd like to thank you all for coming on short notice. I've got some terrific news. Thanks to great work by Josh Shirazi, Daniel Dechado, J.B. Espèces, Kat Marcus, and Garland and his cryptanalysts, working closely with the FBI and CIA, we've been able to bring an end to damaging espionage operations directed at destroying the efforts of the U.S. and its partners to convince the Iranians to terminate their nuclear weapons program.

"Josh and Daniel developed and implemented an innovative strategy that enabled us to identify and stop two separate espionage efforts. They were assisted by Kat and J.B., and by our exceptional cryptanalysts. Each of the NSA people I mentioned made very important contributions. I'm convinced that without this innovation and teamwork, the espionage operations might have continued undiscovered for some time. This effort exemplifies the very best of our contributions to national security. There is no question in my mind that this only succeeded because it was a cooperative interagency effort. It would have failed without close collaboration between all the participants. No single agency could have succeeded in this venture by itself.

"I'd also like to make it clear that the Metanalysis project being conducted by Josh and Daniel was not simply a cover project. It is an undertaking that's very important to us; and I hope it will lead to significant improvements in our analytic capabilities. It will move faster now that Josh and Daniel can give it their full attention."

The Director did not express one thought he had. He imagined that on this day or within the next couple of days, there would be a very difficult private phone conversation between the President and his Israeli counterpart.

"And I imagine that you, Meihui," the Director continued, "could not figure out why your husband was working these strange hours on a project that did not seem time sensitive."

Meihui's face beamed as she learned what her husband had been doing. "You're right, Admiral," she said. "I was really puzzled. He never gave me the slightest hint as to why he'd get calls at strange hours and have to rush into work. Now I understand. Thank you very much for including me today. I'm so lucky to have the clearances to learn what he's been doing and so proud of him. Of course, a good deal of his success is due to my tutelage," she laughed.

"Mais, oui!" Josh said.

When the Director completed his comments, the Leadership Team spontaneously applauded. The Director then walked up to each of those who'd contributed to the mission's success, and personally thanked them. He also chatted with Meihui and told her what a terrific husband she had. He mentioned that Josh had described her exceptional talents. She thanked him profusely, and described how much Josh loved his work, and how he'd complimented the Director on his knowledge, guidance, and leadership.

After the Director left, members of the Leadership Team mingled with the analysts to compliment them and thank them.

When the Leadership Team left the conference room, the analysts and Meihui chatted with one another for a few minutes, and then returned to their offices. Before leaving, Meihui hugged Josh and told him how proud she was. He thanked her for being so supportive, and said he felt really lucky to have such a great friend and partner.

When Josh returned to his office, he picked up his translation of the Ayatollah-Behrangi conversation, placed it in an envelope, and took it to his former boss, Megan Volker, head of the Iran division. She welcomed him in Persian, and then invited him into her office. She asked him how things were going, and if there was anything she could do for him.

He proceeded to enlighten her about the counterespionage project and its outcome. He could see her mind switch from light, professional banter to a serious focus on substance. She asked many questions, and he provided detailed answers. When he was finished, she congratulated him, and asked if he'd be returning to the Iran division soon. He told her that he and Daniel first had to complete the Metanalysis project, which was a serious, high-value effort. He expected it would take another three to four months. She wished him success in that endeavor.

Josh then provided her with his translation of the conversation, and told her he'd arrange for the Iran division to get access to the audio of that conversation. He also informed her of the Director's guidance regarding the processing and distribution of this and future conversations.

After chatting with Megan a few more minutes, he returned to his office.

That morning, Sean Chandler met with Congressman Haston. After introducing himself, Chandler proceeded to describe his experiences with defending against charges of espionage. He also explained his terms of service. He asked the congressman if he would like to avail himself of Chandler's services. The congressman said he would.

Chandler described what Johnnie had told him about the evidence that the Bureau had of the congressman's purported espionage. Chandler asked if the congressman would dispute any of those details. The congressman said he wouldn't take issue with any of the details. However, his only motivation was to protect the national security of his country. He'd acted out of love of country and had taken no money for his actions. Chandler asked the congressman if he had any documented proof of his motivations. Haston did not.

Chandler explained what happened to Jonathan Pollard, who had also spied for Israel, one of America's closest allies. Pollard spent some thirty years in prison despite intensive efforts to gain his early release. Chandler said that, given the clear and unambiguous evidence and the damage that had been done, defending the congressman would be a major challenge. The most important factor in the congressman's favor was that he had a long history of honest and ethical behavior. Chandler then asked the congressman a number of questions. When he was finished, he said he'd return to Washington and begin to develop a defense. He'd be back in touch.

Epilogue

On July 14, Iran signed the Joint Comprehensive Plan of Action with the P5+1. The accord, which committed Iran to a series of actions that would forestall its acquisition of a nuclear weapons capability for at least a decade, was signed in Vienna. The accord blocked all four Iranian pathways to a nuclear weapon. In return for validated compliance and monitoring of Iran's commitments, nuclear-related sanctions on Iran would be lifted and Iran would receive an estimated $100 billion of its impounded funds that were held by other nations. Some Americans had the mistaken impression that these funds were all held by or controlled by the U.S. The reality was that a large percentage was in the hands of countries like China, India, and South Korea, and which were owed to Iran for the purchase of its oil. Those countries had only agreed to hold onto the money until certain conditions were met. Now that those conditions had been met, the U.S. could do nothing further to keep the money from being released to Iran. There were separate sanctions on Iran for other activities, such as missile development and terrorism. Those sanctions would not be lifted.

In early August, Congressman Haston and his lawyer reached a plea agreement in which the congressman would plead guilty and receive a fifteen-year prison sentence.

In late September, Josh and Daniel would complete the Metanalysis project and submit their recommendations to the Director. Many of those recommendations would be accepted and implemented.

The follow-on to the terrorist incident that Shellie had foiled would play out over a number of months. In late July, Johnnie discovered through the FBI's representative in Rome that several foreign women who'd been at Naples Airport at the time of the incident claimed credit for alerting the Italian security officer. In his report on the incident, the security officer stated that he only remembered a couple of things about the woman - he would never forget the material and buttons of her sweater. He saw them as he was looking at her hands when she pointed to the attacker. He also remembered exactly what she said to him when she warned about the attacker.

The Bureau informed the Italian Government in mid-August that an American woman told the Bureau that she was the one who alerted the security officer. However, she wished to remain anonymous to avoid coming to the attention of the terrorists. The Bureau included pictures of Shellie wearing the sweater and the words she remembered saying to alert the officer. Her face was not in the photos, only her upper torso. She had removed her wedding ring from her hand.

The Italian Government replied that the security officer confirmed that it was the sweater he remembered, and that the words of warning were exactly what he recalled. In early October, the Italian Government awarded her a medal for bravery, and asked the Bureau to present it to her. At about the same time, the Bureau also awarded her a medal. The President presented her with both medals in a ceremony attended only by Shellie, Director Pasquali, her husband, and her fellow Team Triad members.

Metanalysis Recommendations to the Director

Just before Christmas, Josh and Daniel provided the Director with a detailed report explaining their recommendations for improving the analytic capabilities of the entire U.S. SIGINT community. The most important of their recommendations are described below.

Education

A. Create classes, seminars, and/or lecture series:
1. To provide language analysts with deep insights into thought processes and cultural factors of foreign societies and organizations. Such classes would include the kind of probing, sophisticated interaction that Carolyn Rainier's tutor, Farhad Esfahani had used.
2. In which renowned investigative journalists, police detectives, FBI agents, and similar analytic experts would teach their analytic methodologies, techniques, and experiences.
3. In which the SIGINT community's best analysts would describe their analytic techniques, methodologies, best learning and developmental experiences, etc.
4. Which would describe major intelligence analysis failures.

B. Create a program to develop case studies on major SIGINT successes and failures, and ensure that those case studies be incorporated into education programs.

Organizational Structure

Require that any reorganization of analytic organizations, even those created by the Director, be reviewed by an independent panel of analysts two years after the reorganization to determine if the results were successful or flawed, and how the reorganization might be tweaked or changed to deal with any resultant problems.

Analytic Tools and Processes

Create a program to develop analytic techniques and methodologies with broad application. That project should include a bottom-up mechanism that would enable any analyst to suggest new types of analysis, new innovative analytic techniques, tools, and new types of training. The mechanism would insure that these suggestions were seriously considered by out-of-the-box thinkers and aggressively pursued. Josh suggested including his *Group Discovery and Affiliation Analysis* in this program.

Require that any project developing tools for analysts include at least one experienced analyst. If the analyst(s) on the team judged that the tool was flawed, the analyst(s) would have the power to have the development stopped and reviewed.

Create a process for identifying and dealing with analytic tools that were seriously flawed. Those in charge of creating the flawed tools should be held accountable.

Problems, Issues, and Challenges

Create an independent panel of analytic experts to address issues that trouble analysts or that could improve analyst career development and retention. The panel would present the Director with a quarterly report containing recommendations for dealing with issues that could not be resolved by the panel through discussions with appropriate parties.

Power Mentor

Establish a *Power Mentor Program* which would assign a high-level executive mentor to a select few young analysts determined to have exceptional potential and talent for analytic innovation. Analysts could apply to participate in the program by presenting examples of their analytic successes and innovation. This program would aim to:

- Help the analysts choose and move to the assignments best suited for improving their skills;

- Provide the support needed for analysts to overcome impediments to their innovation and development; and

- Enable NSA to easily and quickly identify the right analysts to deal with a new crisis situation.

Best Practices

Create a small group to identify and acquire best practices in analytic endeavors throughout the IC, the U.S. public and private sectors, and in foreign countries. Those best practices would include those of hostile foreign intelligence agencies.

Applicant Processing

Develop techniques, like those used by Levy Morris, to identify job applicants with exceptionally high innovation potential. Such techniques could be used for applicants seeking any type of job in which innovation plays an important role.

Character Index

Lexicon

With slang words like *comms* and *cryppie*, sometimes the full word is used and sometimes the abbreviation. It depends on the context.

- ASA – Army Security Agency
- CA – cryptanalysis – solving codes and ciphers
- CBP Officer – Customs and Border Protection Officer
- CIA – Central Intelligence Agency
- comms – communications.
- cryppie – slang for cryptanalyst
- cryptanalysis – the discipline of attacking encryption systems; i.e. codes and ciphers
- cryptogram – a text written in code or cipher
- cryptography – the creation and use of secure communications systems
- cryptology - communications secrecy, including both cryptanalysis and cryptography
- DF – Direction Finding. It can be used as an adjective, noun, or verb
- ditty bopper – a Morse-code collector
- DOE – Department of Energy
- DIA – Defense Intelligence Agency
- DNI – Director of National Intelligence
- encrypt – to use a code or cipher to protect text
- FBI – Federal Bureau of Investigation
- freq – slang for radio frequency
- GCHQ – (British) Government Communications HQ
- HF – high frequency portion of the radio spectrum

- HFDF – High Frequency Direction Finding
- HI – Hidden Influence
- high-side – refers to secure, classified telephone and computer networks or stand-alone computers that are not connected to any external network and can be used for classified information.
- HPSCI – House Permanent Select Committee on Intelligence
- HUMINT – Human Intelligence
- I-Brancher – an NSG language collector/analyst
- IAEA – International Atomic Energy Agency
- IC – Intelligence Community
- IMINT – Imagery Intelligence
- IRGC - Iranian Revolutionary Guard Corps
- Meta – counterespionage project
- Metanalysis – analysis improvement project
- MOIS – Iranian Ministry of Intelligence and Security
- NSA – National Security Agency – not to be confused with the President's National Security
 Advisor
- NSG – Naval Security Group, also known as NavSecGru
- op – slang for (communications) operator
- ops - slang for operations
- P5+1 - the five permanent members of the UN Security Council (China, France, Russia, the
 United Kingdom, and the United States), plus Germany
- R-Brancher an NSG Morse code collector
- Rev Guard - IRGC
- TA – traffic analysis
- target – a communicant or communications entity of interest
- SIGINT – Signals Intelligence
- SIGINTer – person who performs SIGINT
- SSCI – Senate Select Committee on Intelligence
- UHF – ultra high frequency portion of the radio spectrum
- VHF – very high frequency portion of the radio spectrum

End Notes

[i] A running key additive system is one in which the cipher is created by:

- Assigning a numerical value to each letter of the alphabet. In the A-Z Latin alphabet, the letters could be given values of 0-25.

- The key used to create the cipher could be the text of a book.

- An indicator at the start of the cipher indicates the page, paragraph, and line where the key begins; e.g., 340203 - page 34, paragraph 2, line 3.

- Using non carrying addition, the first letter of the key is added to the first letter of the plaintext to create the first letter of cipher; e.g., m of plaintext + f of key = R of cipher (12+5=17). If the sum is 26 or greater, 26 is subtracted from the sum; i.e., s of plaintext + m of key = e of cipher (18+12-26=4).

For example, the plaintext message, "Return to base now" encrypted with the key, "Once upon a time, he" would create the cipher, "FRVYL CHBBT AQRVA."

Key	o	n	c	e	u	p	o	n	a	t	i	m	e	h	e
Plaintext	r	e	t	u	r	n	t	o	b	a	s	e	n	o	w
Cipher	F	R	V	Y	L	C	H	B	B	T	A	Q	R	V	A

The message is deciphered by subtracting the key from the cipher; e.g., R of cipher - n of key = e of plaintext (17-13=4). If the cipher value is lower than the key value, 26 is added to the cipher value and then the key value is subtracted; e.g., F of cipher - o of key = r of plaintext (5+26-14=17).

[ii] This chapter title is enciphered with a simple encryption system known as uniliteral monoalphabetic substitution. The plaintext reads: Successful analysis can simply be a matter of looking at simple patterns

The cipher alphabet is an offset of one letter from the plaintext alphabet. It would have been much better to have had a cipher alphabet in a random sequence.

Plaintext	A	B	C	D	E	F	G	H	I	J	K	L	M
Cipher	Z	A	B	C	D	E	F	G	H	I	J	K	L

Continued:

Plaintext	N	O	P	Q	R	S	T	U	V	W	X	Y	Z
Cipher	M	N	O	P	Q	R	S	T	U	V	W	X	Y

[iii] Plaintext: The infidel crusader hates us but he tells us because we know his evil story and will tell it to his friends if he does not do as we say.

The plaintext is inscribed horizontally into a 10-column-wide x 11-row-deep transposition matrix. The letter x is arbitrarily used at the bottom right to finish filling the matrix.

1	2	3	4	5	6	7	8	9	10
T	H	E	I	N	F	I	D	E	L
C	R	U	S	A	D	E	R	H	A
T	E	S	U	S	B	U	T	H	E
T	E	L	L	S	U	S	B	E	C
A	U	S	E	W	E	K	N	O	W
H	I	S	E	V	I	L	S	T	O
R	Y	A	N	D	W	I	L	L	T
E	L	L	I	T	T	O	H	I	S
F	R	I	E	N	D	S	I	F	H
E	D	O	E	S	N	O	T	D	O
A	S	W	E	S	A	Y	X	X	X

The cipher is extracted vertically from the transposition matrix in the following column sequence 1, 3 5, 7, 9, 10. 8, 6, 4, 2:

```
 1  TCTTAHREFEA
 3  EUSLSSALIOW
 5  NASSWVDTNSS
 7  IEUSKLIOSOY
 9  EHHEOTLIFDX
10  LAECWOTSHOX
 8  DRTBNSLHITX
 6  FDBUEIWTDNA
 4  ISULEENIEEE
 2  HREEUIYLRDS
```

The cipher is reformatted into 25-character lines to conceal the column length:

```
TCTTAHREFEAEUSLSSALIOWNAS
SWVDTNSSIEUSKLIOSOYEHHEOT
LIFDXLAECWOTSHOXDRTBNSLHI
TXFDBUEIWTDNAISULEENIEEEH
REEUIYLRDS
```

[iv] Plaintext: This crusader covets money for his sinful life. It is his energy to sell us what we need. Now he is trapped.

The plaintext is first inscribed at an angle from left to right into a 10-column-wide x 10 row deep transposition matrix. Letters x, y, z, and a are arbitrarily used at the bottom right to finish filling the matrix.

1	2	3	4	5	6	7	8	9	10
T	I	R	D	V	N	I	L	I	S
H	C	A	O	O	H	L	H	O	T
S	S	C	M	R	U	S	T	A	O
U	R	S	O	F	I	Y	H	N	R
E	T	F	N	T	G	W	D	T	A
E	Y	I	I	R	S	E	S	R	W
E	S	E	E	U	E	I	T	D	X
S	F	N	L	N	E	Y	E	X	Y
I	E	L	E	H	L	P	X	Y	Z
S	E	W	W	U	P	X	Y	Z	A
10	1	4	7	2	5	8	3	6	9

The cipher is extracted from the matrix vertically in the following column sequence 10, 1, 4, 7, 2, 5, 8, 3, 6, 9:

```
ICSRTYSFEE
VORFTRUNHU
LHTHDSTEXY
RACSFIENLW
NHUIGSEELP
IOANTRDXYZ
DOMONIELEW
ILSYWEIYPX
STORAWXYZA
YHSUEEESIS
```

The cipher is reformatted into 25-character lines to conceal column length:

```
ICSRTYSFEEVORFTRUNHULHTHD
STEXYRACSFIENLWNHUIGSEELP
IOANTRDXYZDOMONIELEWILSYW
EIYPXSTORAWXYZAYHSUEEESIS
```

About the Author

Joseph E. Harb, Jr. has forty-four years' experience in the U.S Intelligence Community, with service in the Naval Security Group and at the National Security Agency. He has substantive experience with almost every aspect of the NSA intelligence production cycle - from user requirements, through collection, traffic analysis, cryptanalysis, foreign language analysis, intelligence analysis and reporting, dissemination, support to military operations, and crisis support. He studied eleven foreign languages, such as Lao and Amharic, from four different language families.

As an NSA executive, Mr. Harb managed large, complex intelligence analysis operations, was Director of the operational half of NSA's budget, and served as the NSA HR Director. He was awarded the National Intelligence Medal of Achievement, NSA's Exceptional Civilian Service Award, and two NSA Meritorious Civilian Service Awards.

He served five years' active duty as a Communications Technician (first R Branch, then I Branch) in the U.S. Naval Security Group, and another seven years in the Naval Reserve. His active service included one year aboard the USS Oxford off the coast of Vietnam during the Vietnam War.

In his spare time during a four-year assignment to Yokota Air Base, Japan, he authored *An Incomplete Guide to Japan*, which the Air Force distributed at no cost to U.S. military and civilian personnel.

His personal interests include international travel, cuisines, and wine, as reflected in his blog: http://viaggiviniecucine.blogspot.com.

"AN INTELLIGENT HORROR STORY,
A LITERARY CREEPSHOW.
IT WORMS ITS WAY UNDER YOUR SKIN
AND STAYS THERE."
—Darin Strauss, author of *Chang and Eng*

"[Gran's] detached and witty narration helps us believe, as she says, that 'what we think is impossible happens all the time.'" —*The New Yorker*

"I picked it up at 7 P.M. By 7:10 I was locked into the cold isolation chamber of Gran's prose. It was too late to get out." —*Daily Telegraph* (London)

"Hypnotic, disturbing . . . What begins as a sly fable about frustrated desire evolves into a genuinely scary novel about possession and insanity. Written with such unerring confidence you believe every word. *Come Closer* is one of the most precise and graceful pieces of fiction I've read in a long time." —Bret Easton Ellis

"Sara Gran has a talent for finding the uneasy areas in daily life and massaging them into outright horror. She tells the story simply and colloquially . . . which makes the transformation all the more terrifying."
—*The Charlotte Observer*

"I read *Come Closer* on the train, in a snowstorm, on a cold December night. It was the right atmosphere for this perfectly noirish tale of madness and love. Author Sara Gran writes with scalpel-like clarity, expertly blending tones to create a new kind of psychological thriller. Days after finishing it, it has not left my mind. I loved this book." —George Pelecanos

continued . . .

come closer

a novel

sara gran

BERKLEY BOOKS, NEW YORK

THE BERKLEY PUBLISHING GROUP
Published by the Penguin Group
Penguin Group (USA) Inc.
375 Hudson Street, New York, New York 10014, USA

Penguin Group (Canada), 90 Eglinton Avenue East, Suite 700, Toronto, Ontario M4P 2Y3, Canada
(a division of Pearson Penguin Canada Inc.)
Penguin Books Ltd., 80 Strand, London WC2R 0RL, England
Penguin Group Ireland, 25 St. Stephen's Green, Dublin 2, Ireland (a division of Penguin Books Ltd.)
Penguin Group (Australia), 250 Camberwell Road, Camberwell, Victoria 3124, Australia
(a division of Pearson Australia Group Pty. Ltd.)
Penguin Books India Pvt. Ltd., 11 Community Centre, Panchsheel Park, New Delhi—110 017, India
Penguin Group (NZ), 67 Apollo Drive, Rosedale, North Shore 0745, Auckland, New Zealand
(a division of Pearson New Zealand Ltd.)
Penguin Books (South Africa) (Pty.) Ltd., 24 Sturdee Avenue, Rosebank, Johannesburg 2196, South Africa

Penguin Books Ltd., Registered Offices: 80 Strand, London WC2R 0RL, England

This is a work of fiction. Names, characters, places, and incidents either are the product of the author's imagination or are used fictitiously, and any resemblance to actual persons, living or dead, business establishments, events, or locales is entirely coincidental. The publisher does not have any control over and does not assume any responsibility for author or third-party websites or their content.

COME CLOSER

A Berkley Book / published by arrangement with Soho Press, Inc.

PRINTING HISTORY
Soho hardcover edition / August 2003
Berkley trade paperback edition / May 2006
Berkley mass-market edition / July 2007

ISBN: 978-0-425-21647-7

BERKLEY®
Berkley Books are published by The Berkley Publishing Group,
a division of Penguin Group (USA) Inc.,
375 Hudson Street, New York, New York 10014.
BERKLEY is a registered trademark of Penguin Group (USA) Inc.
The "B" design is a trademark belonging to Penguin Group (USA) Inc.

PRINTED IN THE UNITED STATES OF AMERICA

10 9 8 7 6 5 4 3 2 1

For Warren and Suzanne Gran.
Thank you for everything.

in January I had a proposal due to my boss, Leon Fields, on a new project. We were renovating a clothing store in a strip mall outside the city. Nothing tremendous. I finished the proposal on a Friday morning and dropped it on his desk with a cheerful little note—"Let me know what you think!"—while he was in a meeting with a new client in the conference room.

Later that morning Leon threw open his office door with a bang.

"Amanda!" he called. "Come in here."

I rushed to his office. He picked up a handful of papers off his desk and stared at me, his flabby face white with anger.

"What the hell is this?"

"I don't know." It looked like my proposal—same heading, same format. My hands shook. I couldn't imagine what was wrong. Leon handed me the papers and I read the first line: *Leon Fields is a cocksucking faggot.*

"What is this?" I asked Leon.

He stared at me. "You tell me. You just dropped it on my desk."

My head spun. "What are you talking about? I put the proposal on your desk, not this, the proposal for the new job." I sifted through the papers on his desk for the proposal I had dropped off. "What is this, a joke?"

"Amanda," he said. "Three people said they saw you go to the printer, print this out, and bring it to my desk."

I felt like I had stepped into a bad dream. There was no logic, no reason anymore. "Wait," I said to Leon. I ran back to my desk, printed out the proposal, checked it, and brought it back to Leon's office. He had calmed down a little and was sitting in his big leather chair.

I handed it to him. "This is it. This is exactly what I put on your desk this morning."

He looked over the papers and then looked back up at me. "Then where did *that* come from?" He looked back at the fake proposal on the desk.

"How would I know?" I said. "Let me see it again."

I read the second line: *Leon Fields eats shit and likes it.*

"Disgusting," I said. "I don't know. Someone playing a trick on you, I guess. Someone thinks it's funny."

"Or playing a trick on *you*," he said. "Someone replaced your proposal with this. I'm sorry, I thought—" he looked around the office, embarrassed. In the three years I had worked for him I had never heard Leon Fields apologize to anyone, ever.

"It's okay," I told him. "What were you supposed to think?"

We looked at each other.

"I'll look over the proposal," he said. "I'll get back to you soon."

I left his office and went back to my own desk. I hadn't written the fake proposal, but I wished I knew who did. Because it was true; Leon Fields was a cocksucking faggot, and he did eat shit, and I had always suspected that he liked it very much.

that evening I was telling my husband, Ed, about the little mystery at work when we heard the tapping for the first time. We were sitting at the dinner table, just finishing a meal of take-out Vietnamese.

Tap-tap.

We looked at each other.

"Did you hear that?"

"I think so."

Again: tap-tap. It came in twos or fours, never just one—tap-tap—and the sound had a drag on it, almost a scratching behind it, like claws on a wood floor.

First Ed stood up, then me. At first, the sound seemed to be coming from the kitchen. So we walked to the kitchen and bent down to listen under the base of the refrigerator and look under the stove, but then it seemed to be coming from the bathroom. In the bathroom we checked under the sink and behind the shower curtain, and then we determined it was coming from the bedroom. So we walked to the bedroom, and then to the living room, and then back to the kitchen again. After we toured the apartment we gave up. It was the pipes, we decided, something to do with the water flow or the heating system. Or maybe a mouse, running around and around the apartment inside the walls. Ed was revolted by the idea but I thought it was kind of cute, a little mouse with the spunk to make it up four stories and live on our few crumbs. We both forgot about the story I had been telling, and I never told Ed about the practical joke at work.

the tapping went on for the rest of the winter. Not all the time, but for a few minutes every second or third night. Then at the end of the month I went to a conference on the West Coast for two days, and Ed noticed that he didn't hear it at all while I was gone. A few weeks later Ed went to a distant cousin's wedding up north for three days. The tapping went on all night, every night, while he was gone. I searched the apartment again, chasing the sound around and around. I examined the pipes, checked every faucet for drips, turned the heat on and off, and still the tapping continued. I cleaned the floors of any crumbs a rodent could eat, I even bought a carton of unpleasant little spring traps, and the sound was still there. I turned up the television, ran the dishwasher, spent hours on the phone with old, loud friends, and still I heard it.

Tap-tap.

I was starting to think this mouse wasn't so cute anymore.

the noise wasn't so unusual, really; our building was close to a hundred years old and one expected that kind of noise. It had been built as an aspirin factory when the city still had an industrial base. After the industry moved out, one developer after another had tried to do something with the neighborhood, full of abandoned factories and warehouses like ours, but the schemes never took off. It was too far from the city, too desolate, too cold at night. As far as I was concerned it was better that the development hadn't gone as planned. Our building was still only half full. I liked the peace and quiet.

The first time we saw the loft I was absolutely sure it was the home for us. Ed needed a little convincing.

"Think of the quiet!" I told Ed. "No neighbors!"

Conduits were in place for lighting and plumbing but they had never been utilized. We would have to do major renovation. "Think of the possibilities!" I cried. "We can build it from scratch!"

Six white columns held up the place. Heat was provided by an industrial blower hung from the ceiling. "It has character," I told Ed. "It has a personality!"

He relented, and we got the place at half of what we would have paid elsewhere. We spent the extra money on renovation. Ed gave me free rein to do as I pleased. I was an architect and now I could be my own dream client. I designed every detail myself, from the off-white color of the walls to the porcelain faucets on the kitchen sink to the installation of the fireplace along the south wall, which cost a fortune, but was worth the money.

The neighborhood, though, was sometimes difficult. No supermarkets, no restaurants, a few small grocery stores that specialized in beer and cigarettes. The edge of the closest commercial district for shopping was ten blocks away, and the nearest residential area was on the other side of that. But we adjusted quickly. We had a car to take us wherever we wanted on nights and weekends, and during the week we usually took the train to work. Our other concern when we first moved in was the crime, but soon enough we found out there was none. It was too desolate even for criminals. I did, however, come to be scared of the stray dogs that patrolled the neighborhood. The dogs kept their distance and I kept mine but I always felt it was an uneasy truce. I didn't trust the animals to keep their side of the bargain. Walking home from the train I would spot one lurking in a doorway or on a street corner, eyeing me with suspicion. I was sure I would have preferred a mugger, who at least would only want my money—I didn't know what these dogs wanted when they looked at me with their bloodshot eyes.

That fall I found out when a German shepherd mix followed me home from the train station one night. I thought running would only provoke him, so I continued to walk at a regular pace, faking nonchalance. The German shepherd trailed behind at an equally steady pace, also faking nonchalance. At the entrance to my building, a steel door up two wide steps, I put my key in the lock and thought I was home free—the dog stayed on the street. And then in one great leap he jumped up the two steps and attacked. With his front paws, as strong as human hands, he pushed me against the wall, ignoring my horrified screams, licked me right on my mouth and tried to seduce me. When I finally convinced him I wasn't interested, he sat down by my feet, panting with a big smile. I spent a few minutes scratching behind his ears and then sneaked through the door.

I would have forgotten about him except that the next day he was waiting for me at the train station again, and the day after that. Walking home with him became a routine. He knew a few simple commands ("sit," "stay," "no") and I was convinced he had started off life as somebody's pet. I even went to a pet store and bought a bag of nutritionally balanced dog biscuits for him. On our walks home from the train I used the biscuits to teach him a few more commands—walk, lie down, stop-trying-to-fuck-me (which we abbreviated as *Stop*). I hoped that if I got him into more civilized condition I could find a home for him. I would have liked to take him in myself but Edward was allergic; dogs, cats, hamsters, strawberries, angora, and certain types of mushrooms were

11

all hazardous materials, to be kept out of the apartment and handled with care.

But I was glad to have at least one friend in the neighborhood. And over the next few months it was my new friend, a nameless flea-ridden mutt, rather than Ed, who would be the first to see that I was not entirely myself.

not that Ed wasn't attentive, not that he didn't notice what was going on in my life. He just wasn't able to put the pieces together as quickly as the dog. Ed was my hero, my savior. Ed was the man who had imposed order on my chaotic life. When I was single, I'd eaten cereal for dinner and ice cream for lunch. I'd kept my tax records in a shopping bag in the closet. I'd spent Saturdays in a hungover fog, watching hours of old black-and-white movies. With Ed I spent Saturdays outdoors, doing the things I had always imagined I should do: flea markets, lunches, museums. He did our taxes, with itemized deductions, every January, and filed the records away in a real file cabinet. Here was a man who could finish any crossword puzzle, open any bottle, reach the top

12

shelf at the grocery store without strain. Here was stability, here was something I could rely on, my rock, day in and day out. Someone who loved me, who would never leave me alone. You can't blame this sophisticated, civilized man for not having the same instincts as a wild dog.

what we think is impossible happens all the time. Like the time Ed let himself into the apartment and then lost his keys, somewhere in the house, and never found them again. Like the Halloween morning where I opened a cabinet of dishes, all stacked in perfect order, and the stack of plates on the highest shelf came toppling down, one by one, to bounce off my shoulders and shatter on the floor. Or when my friend Marlene picked up the phone to call her grandmother and someone was already on the line; one of her cousins, calling to tell her her grandmother had died that morning.

We could devote our lives to making sense of the odd, the inexplicable, the coincidental, but most of us don't. And neither did I.

SOON after the tapping began, Ed and I started to fight. We didn't fight all the time, we didn't change all at once. It was just a little bickering at first, I thought it was just a phase. I didn't know it was a part of a pattern, because I didn't know there was a pattern to see. I didn't know that it would escalate. If I had to pinpoint when the phase began—the phase that turned out not to be a phase at all but the start of a steady decline—I would say Valentine's Day of that year.

Our plan that Valentine's Day was to avoid the crowded restaurants and have a romantic night at home. I got off work first so I was in charge of dinner. Ed, due home at seven-ish, was supposed to bring flowers and wine. By seven, I had cooked dinner—veal marsala and broccoli rabe—set the table, and had a store-bought chocolate soufflé in the oven. But then Ed called at 7:15 from the office and said he would be at least another hour or two. Some numbers had to be checked and rechecked and they couldn't wait until tomorrow. I watched the news on television, and then a few sitcoms. I ate a bag of pretzels watching a hospital drama. At eleven the news came on again. Not much had changed.

Well into the nighttime talk shows, Ed came strolling in the door with no flowers and no wine.

"Hi hon," he said, and walked across the loft to the sofa. He leaned in to give me a kiss. I pulled my head back. *How dare he,* I heard myself think.

"You're late," I said. *He's always late,* I thought. The tapping in the apartment was especially loud that night.

Tap-tap.

"I know, I'm sorry," he said with an exaggerated hound dog face. "Apology accepted?"

Tap-tap.

"No," I said. "Apology not fucking accepted."

"Oh honey, I—"

"It's VALENTINE'S DAY!" I yelled. "Where the fuck have you been?"

Tap-tap. Tap-tap.

"I called!" he yelled back. He walked into the bedroom to change into blue flannel pajamas and then yelled from there. "You knew I would be late!"

"You called four hours ago!"

16

Tap-tap. Tap-tap. Tap-tap. I was furious now. Nothing could make this okay.

"I'm sorry about dinner," he called, still in the bedroom. "I TOLD YOU I WAS SORRY!"

"You're always sorry!" I yelled back. "You and your FUCKING APOLOGIES!"

Tap-tap-tap-tap-tap—it reached a sort of crescendo and then stopped for the night.

Ed walked out of the bedroom and I walked in, slamming the door behind me. I lay in bed and in my mind reviewed every late night, every broken promise of my marriage. An hour later Ed came to bed and I pretended to be asleep.

that night I had an odd dream, which I remembered very clearly the next morning. A red ocean was rimmed with a shore of darker crimson sand. In the ocean a woman played in the waves. She was beautiful and had big dark eyes; her only flaw was her huge head of black hair, which was matted into dirty locks. I watched her from the shore. She walked out of the ocean and the red liquid rolled off her skin like mercury. Then we were lying next to each other on the sand. Her teeth were as pointy as fangs. I thought they were pretty.

"I like you," she said. She reached over and twirled a lock of my hair around her fingers. I blushed and looked down at the red sand.

"Can I stay with you?" she asked. With my index finger I spelled out YES in the crimson sand. Next to that she wrote her name: NAAMAH.

She put her arms around me and we hugged like sisters. I loved her so much, I wanted us to be to- gether always.

i was sure I had seen that woman before. She came in and out of my mind often the next few days, like a few notes of a song you just couldn't reconnect to the whole. Especially her lips, I was sure I had seen them before. It was a few days later that the name came back to me. Ed and I were at the kitchen table with our morning coffee and toast, talking about his friends Alex and Sophia. We hadn't exactly made up from the Valentine's Day fight but we had let it go, silently decided that it had never happened. I was half listening to a story about Alex's promotion, half thinking about what to wear that day, when her name flew back to me, unannounced.

"Pansy!" I called out. "I *knew* I knew her."

pansy had been an imaginary friend. I first thought of her when I was five or six. A mother substitute. I imagined her combing my hair, setting up for a tea party with me, tucking me into bed at night. My real mother had passed away when I was three— from a heart attack—and my father remarried very quickly, to a woman who had never wanted children. Noreen. Pansy wasn't another little girl, she was what I thought of as a grown-up, but she was really a teenager. She was modeled loosely on Tracy Berkowitz, a glamorous eighteen-year-old who lived down the block. But unlike Tracy, Pansy was wise and soothing and cared about me. I was not so lonely as to be deranged, to think that Pansy was real. There was no psychic break, no supernatural mischief. I was absolutely aware that I was real and Pansy was imaginary.

Until, one day, she wasn't. I was on my way home from school. The image that had loomed so large at six had, by the time I was nine, been relegated to a few minutes of attention before I went to sleep, where I imagined her kissing me good night. It was late spring, towards the end of the school year. The sun was bright and the hum of summer was already in the air, flies and crickets and the far-off sounds of Trans Ams and Camaros in town. I was walking home from school, down a block of neat white houses with patches of green lawn, each one almost identical to the next. I was walking slowly, not in a hurry to be home, or anywhere at all. The street was empty except for a woman at the end of the block, standing at the crossroads as if she was waiting for someone.

Without interest I noticed the woman on the corner. As I got closer she turned towards me and smiled. At first I thought she was Tracy Berkowitz. But no, I remembered, Tracy, unwed, had moved to the city months ago with her cop boyfriend. The move was a minor scandal on the block and there was no forgetting it.

The woman on the corner was looking right at me now. She had a mess of black hair and a pink pretty smile. I remember her skin, perfectly bisque with a soft translucent glow, like an airbrushed photo from a magazine.

It was Pansy.

My heart beat like a hummingbird in my chest. I went into a kind of panic, thoughts falling on top of each other with no order. It couldn't be her. But it was.

When I reached the corner she stepped in front of me, and I stopped. She bent down, leaning her hands on her thighs. The sun shone directly on her face, but she didn't blink or squint.

"Hi, Amanda," she said. Her voice had a clear, sweet tone like a violin. All my fears dissipated when I heard that voice.

"Can you see me, Amanda?" she asked.

Just then a growling Firebird sped by the cross street, honking its horn. Instinctively I blinked and turned towards it, for a half second or less. When I turned back, she was gone.

I was old enough to know that this was impossible, what had just happened, and that only crazy people believed in impossible events. I buried the memory so deeply it didn't resurface until the dreams began.

Incidentally, my father and Noreen died while I was in my second year of college. They were scuba diving off the coast of Jamaica and got caught in a coral reef and drowned.

* * *

I told Edward the whole story, about the woman I had seen as a child and the dreams I had had.

"So you saw a woman, when you were a girl, who looked like your imaginary friend, and last night you had a dream about her." Ed had a certain tone of voice, skeptical and a little condescending, which made him sound like a father whose daughter was late coming home from the prom. It wasn't one of his more attractive qualities.

"But who was that woman? Why did she know my name?"

"It was probably that Stacy woman."

"Tracy. But it wasn't Tracy. It was Pansy."

Ed sighed. "So it was Pansy," he said.

"Oh, forget it."

Edward put the paper down and reached across the table for my hand, which I reluctantly gave to him.

"Alex and Sophia said we·could use their beach house the last weekend in September. You want to go?"

"Sure."

Alex and Sophia were old friends of Ed's. A few times a year they gave us the keys to their beach house outside the city.

"We both need to relax," Ed said.

There was no more talk of Pansy or nightmares for the rest of the morning. Maybe Ed was right, I thought: Pansy never had pointy teeth, and I never saw her naked. Naamah had bigger eyes. Pansy was shorter. But as the day went on and their faces came in and out of my mind I was sure the two women were one and the same. Naamah could have been Pansy, only a few years older. Pansy could have been Naamah, dressed and made up for a costume party.

And besides, I was pleased with the dream, in a way. To see Pansy again was like a visit from an old friend. I was irked with Edward but I quickly got over it. He was right, after all. I was stressed, and we did need to relax. Somehow that explained away the strange dreams—stress. As for what I had seen on the street that day when I was nine, I told myself Ed was right. It must have been Tracy after all.

we could devote our lives to making sense of the odd, the inexplicable, the coincidental. But most of us don't, and I didn't either.

on the whole, Ed and I were happy—with each other, with the loft, with our careers. He worked in the financial department of a large women's wear corporation, I was an architect at a small firm, and we did quite well. We didn't lack anything. We loved each other, and it wasn't yet clear that the phase of fighting we were in had become a trend.

I was twenty-eight when I met Edward. I felt lucky to have found him. He was a man you could trust, a big-boned healthy blond. No skeletons in his closet. A large family of not-too-observant Catholics. All of his obvious and possibly problematic neuroses (mostly descended from growing up as a middle child, I thought, never receiving enough attention) were channeled into a desire for success, which I found appealing. He didn't like sports or late-night television, two big pluses. He had a good mind for details, a good memory, and a determination to follow through on his word: If he said he was going to call at three, he called at three. No surprises. That pretty much summed up Ed—no surprises. So when, after going out for two years, Ed said he wanted us to move in together, and if all went well, marry a year or two after that, I knew he meant what he said. I had been living in a little one bedroom downtown for three years. My apartment was cute and had its own charm, but it wasn't big enough for two. So I moved into Ed's place, a one bedroom in a modern apartment building near my office. Ed's place was a bit sterile, it had terrible cream-colored wall-to-wall carpeting and too much laminated furniture, but if all went well we planned to buy our own place within a few years.

Two years after we'd moved in together, we got married in a small private ceremony at city hall. It was either that or a huge blowout, which we both thought was a little tacky—Edward had five brothers and sisters and dozens of cousins, aunts, uncles, nieces and nephews, plus there were our friends, business associates, on and on. Rather than inviting them all, we invited no one. We went to city hall in the morning, got married, and went out to lunch at our favorite dim sum house with some friends afterwards. Soon after that we started looking for a home to buy, and found the loft.

of course, our life together wasn't always perfect. All couples argue and we were no different. There were a few things about Ed, small things, that drove me crazy. For instance he was almost compulsively neat—a scrap of paper on the coffee table for longer than a day or two would upset him. He was also given to a rigidity that could be slightly repulsive, like an elderly English bachelor—if there was no thin-sliced white bread for toast in the morning he could be thrown into a mood for hours. And he didn't take any deviation from a plan well—he wasn't one for getting lost in the countryside, or for long, aimless walks around the city. And the fact that when Ed chewed gum he would swallow it instead of spitting it out . . . for some indefinable reason that revolted me no end. And the toast, and the toothpaste cap that absolutely must be replaced immediately, and the shirts that had to be folded just so, and all the other little routines that had to be followed every day. Over six years, though, I had become accustomed to a certain amount of irritation, as I'm sure all spouses do, and these were small arguments and disappointments that didn't interrupt the steady flow of our marriage. When we started to argue a bit more than usual, when Ed's habits and rituals began to irritate me a bit more often, I was sure that it would pass.

she was subtle at first. It wasn't like everything went wrong all at once. Suppose you're looking at a bottle of whiskey. And one part of you says, Gee, I'd really like a sip of that whiskey. Then another part pipes in and says, Well, you shouldn't, you have to drive home, and you know whiskey's very fattening. And then a third part says, Just drink it. This mental voice is new, it's a sound you're not accustomed to hearing in your own head, but it's not

27

that different either, it's done a good job of imitating your own silent voice and you like what it's saying. Come on. Don't stop. Don't think. It'll be fun. Just drink it. Now.

You wouldn't guess that the third part wasn't you. You'd probably just drink the whiskey.

in March I started smoking again, which gave us more to fight about. I had quit when I first moved in with Ed. He said he was allergic to smoke. I thought he just never learned to appreciate the sharp bitter smell, like a smouldering fireplace, of a burning cigarette. But I knew it was for the best, and privately I was a little ashamed of myself for violating my body day in and day out. So I quit. Living in the new apartment helped. No ashtrays. No Formica kitchen table where I would sit and talk on the phone, cigarette in hand. A new apartment, a new life, new habits. I had a few sessions with an acupuncturist and it wasn't too hard, just sad, like an old friend moving out of town.

I started smoking again on a gray, drizzling Monday. I was on my lunch hour, eating a sandwich at a little coffee shop near my office. I had a newspaper open in front of me but I wasn't reading. Instead, I eavesdropped on the couple next to me. She was about my age, maybe a little younger, and had blonde hair pulled back into a knot. He was much older and looked out of place, more accustomed to the kind of restaurant that had a wine list and a maître d'. They talked about a trip to the Caribbean. When I stood up to leave my eyes caught hers. She gave me a sly little smile, almost a wink, and then lit a cigarette. The smoke rolled over the few inches to my table, and when the smell hit me I became weak. I watched the woman, her attention turned back to her partner, inhale deeply and then exhale, sending more of the woodsy smoke in my direction. She was clearly a longtime smoker; the cigarette fit into her hand, as natural and practical as a sixth digit. Like a starving woman looking at a steak, I wanted that cigarette. I imagined how easy it would be: *Excuse me, do you have another smoke? I'm sorry, can I bother you for a cigarette? Can I bum one of those? Do you have an extra? Give me one. Give it to me.*

I left the café, planning to distract myself with the change in scenery. But outside, where the rain came down in a thin, steady drizzle, it seemed every person

I passed had a cigarette in their hand, either lighting one or smoking one or putting one out. And the smokers looked so happy, so healthy, so satisfied with their smoking. How is it, I asked myself, that all this time I've thought smoking was dirty and toxic? Look at these people—they're glowing! The cigarette mottoes ran through my head. A thin woman in a black trench coat inhaled deeply from a long Waverly—The Smoker's Choice. A fit, middle-aged man in a three-piece suit lit a Texas straight—The Tasteful Smoke. I tried the breathing exercises the acupuncturist had taught me but with each inhalation I brought in the crisp taste of burning tobacco. I walked back to the cobblestone block where my office was, hoping for relief. It was even worse. In each doorway a person lingered with a cigarette, embers glowing in each direction. Kensington—The Mild Cigarette. Fairfax—The Refreshing Taste. Embassy Means Smoking Enjoyment. Lowes Means More Smoking Pleasure. I was almost at the office, and I knew that once inside the purified air I would be fine—but I had one more hurdle to jump. In the doorway of the building was a small, pale woman with long black hair in a tight black dress. She was smoking a Midwood Medium, my favorite. The Satisfying Smoke.

I stood in front of the woman with the black hair. It would be so easy to ask—but no, I wouldn't. I opened my mouth to say *Excuse me*, so I could press my way into the safety of my office. But when I opened my mouth and set my lips and tongue into motion, I found they were not my own at all. In my mind I made the *x* of *excuse me* at the top of my throat, but the tip of my tongue instead reached to the bony part of my upper palate to say, "Do you have another smoke?"

"Sure," said the woman with a smile. She reached into her purse for the pack and a book of matches, shook out a cigarette and held it out to me.

And so I started smoking again. I tried to convince myself with a circle of assumptions; I had asked for a cigarette, so I must have wanted a cigarette. Lack of willpower. My subconscious desires had overridden my superego. I circled around and around for a week before I just accepted the fact I was smoking again, and I would have to live with it or go through another long withdrawal. And Edward would have to live with it, too.

It took him a while to see that. When he first found a pack of cigarettes in my purse he was pure disappointment. It was my health, he said, he was so wor-

31

ried about my health. When that didn't work, it was the allergies, which I had long ago learned didn't need quite as much coddling as Ed led one to believe. His arguments fell on deaf ears. I was enjoying smoking again. I felt more like myself. I thought I might keep smoking for the rest of my life. Next his campaign picked up a little cruelty; I smelled bad, my teeth were turning yellow, smoking was filthy, low class. These weren't attributes that particularly bothered me, and I noticed they didn't bother most of the men I met, either. He pleaded, he yelled, finally, he gave up.

I felt wonderful, like my old friend was back in town. Sort of like seeing Pansy again, after all those years.

there was that tapping, and the fighting, and the smoking, and the dreams, and I never would have thought to link them if it hadn't been for a mistake, or what seemed like a mistake at the time. I had ordered a book from a small publisher out of state—*Design Issues Past and Present*—that I was hoping would inspire me a bit with a project at work. I came home to the loft one rainy April night pleased to find a package waiting by the door. But when I got upstairs and opened the box I saw they had sent the wrong book—*Demon Possession Past and Present*—instead. A disappointment, but nothing to cry about. I put the book on the coffee table, forgot about it, and went about making dinner.

After dinner was made I sat on the sofa. Ed was late again. Out of boredom I picked up the accidental book, *Demon Possession Past and Present*.

On the first page there was a little quiz:

Are YOU Possessed by a Demon?

1. I hear strange noises in my home, especially at night, which family members tell me only occur when I am present.

2. I have new activities and pastimes that seem "out of character," and I do things that I did not intend and do not understand.

3. I'm short and ill-tempered with my friends and loved ones.

4. I can understand languages I've never studied, and have the ability to know things I couldn't know through ordinary means.

5. I have blackouts not caused by drugs, alcohol, or a preexisting health condition.

6. I have unusual new thoughts, or hear voices in my head.

7. I've had visions or dreams of personalities who may be demons.

8. A psychic, minister, or other spiritualist has told me I'm possessed.

9. I have urges to hurt or kill animals and other people.

10. I have hurt or killed animals or people.

On the next page was an analysis of the quiz results. I had scored a four out of ten; there was the noise in our apartment, I had started smoking again, I had been fighting with Ed, and I had been having strange dreams.

0–3: You are probably not possessed. See a doctor or mental health professional for an evaluation.

3–6: You may be haunted, or in the early stages of possession. Do not be alarmed. Seek a spiritual counselor for assistance.

6–10: You are possessed. Consult with your spiritual counselor immediately. You may be a threat to the safety of yourself and your family.

Possession usually begins with a preliminary stage called "obsession"—the obsession of the demon with the victim. In this stage the victim is still alone in his body but all five senses, and in addition the memory and mind, can be manipulated and disturbed by the Entity. The victim may feel lust, envy, greed, or urges towards any of the sins with stronger force than ever before. It is common for the victim to hear the demon in the form of rapping, tapping, or scratching that seems to follow them around; also common is for the victim to have their dreams infiltrated by the Possessing Entity.

I put the book down and picked up a fat biography of Frank Lloyd Wright I had been meaning to read for months. But just a few pages in, as quiet as a mouse and loud as a gunshot, there it was again.

Tap-tap.

That same annoying noise. But it was clearer tonight. Now that I listened to it carefully I was sure it wasn't the pipes at all. And it was far too loud for a mouse.

Tap-tap. Tap-tap.

I was beginning to get uneasy. I stood up and walked around the apartment. Nothing. It was just like before; the sound was always close, but never exactly where I was looking. If I was in the kitchen, it was in the bedroom. If I went to the bedroom, it seemed to be coming from the bathroom. I gave up and went back to the sofa. I picked up a magazine from the coffee table. Miniskirts were coming back into style.

Tap-tap.

I was more and more uneasy. It had never been this loud before. The rain outside blew against the windows and I tried to tell myself the sound was just the rain, tapping on the glass. Or the pipes. Or a faucet.

Tap-tap. Tap-tap.

Alone in the quiet apartment, I now heard that it wasn't a tapping at all. More like a pitter-patter. It continued with a steady tattoo around and around the apartment. It sounded like footsteps, scratching steps like a dog or a cat running quickly over a wood floor, claws scraping on the wood.

Pitter-patter, pitter-patter.

Of course it wasn't footsteps. No one lived above us and there was obviously no one in the apartment with me. The sound got louder, closer. It couldn't be footsteps. As much as it sounded like footsteps there was no way, it was absolutely impossible, I shouldn't even let it cross my mind that the sound could be footsteps. I stared at the magazine. Slingbacks were the shoes to wear with the new miniskirts.

Pitter-patter, pitter-patter.

The sound that wasn't footsteps came closer. It circled around and around the sofa. I stopped pretending to read the magazine. It was in front of me, pacing back and forth in front of the sofa.

Pitter-patter, pitter-patter.

It stopped right in front of me. I couldn't move. I was sure I was hyperventilating. Just then I heard a noise to my left and I screamed.

Ed. Just Ed, coming home.

I saw her again in a dream that night. I was sitting on the sofa, listening to the tap-tapping, like I had been that evening. I looked down at the floor and I saw a pair of feet. Small, perfect white feet that seemed to materialize from thin air.

I looked up. Above me I saw a bright, black eye. She was standing right in front of me, and yet it was as if I was looking through a keyhole. I couldn't see her all at once. I saw a pert white nose, and then in a separate view the pink lips wrapped around pointed white teeth. If I looked down at her small white foot I lost sight of everything above the knee. If I looked at her hand all I saw was a hand, with long unpolished nails.

"Don't fight, Amanda," she said with her pink lips.

The room went black. I was falling, slipping down out of myself into a warm damp blackness. She took me to the crimson beach. We lay on the sand and watched the fish jump in and out of the ruby sea. Here I could see her clearly, as a whole.

"I choose you," she said.

"You'll never leave?" I asked.

"Never," she said. "Nothing can get me out."

She put her arms around me and pulled me tight against her. Our ribs crushed together and our hip-bones slammed and she pulled me tighter until I couldn't breathe, I was choking, and my spine met hers, vertebrae against vertebrae.

i didn't bother to read the rest of *Demon Possession Past and Present* right then. But I did put it on the bookshelf instead of returning it like I had planned. It was too late, I reasoned, for the other book to be useful now anyway—the project was due in a few days, and it would never get here on time. Besides, maybe someday it would be good for a laugh.

and another funny little thing I noticed. After that night, that dream, I never heard the tapping in the apartment again, and neither did Ed.

* * *

on Saturday morning we decided to drive downtown to run a few errands. Ed had run out of his allergy pills. He didn't need them every day, but they were important to have on hand in case he came across an errant cat or a renegade strawberry. I needed a bottle of hair conditioner and had also been thinking about a new toothbrush. We had been meaning to start checking prices on dishwashers—the old one left a thin layer of grime inside the coffee cups. And there was a Tibetan restaurant nearby where we liked to get lunch. In the car we bickered over which drugstore to go to. Like all couples we had developed our own language, a shorthand of associations and memories.

"Are we going to the Italian?"

"Too expensive. Want to go to the crazy lady place?"

"They don't have my conditioner there. How about the place with the socks?"

"I hate that place. How about the big place?"

"Which big place?"

"The new one, near the crappy French restaurant."

41

"Which crappy French restaurant?"

"The one where we went with Marlene, and she got the soup with the—"

"OH! Right, right, right. Near the Tibetan place."

"Right."

"Sure, let's go there."

In the big drugstore, a quarter of a city block, Ed waited on line to fill his prescription while I found my toothbrush and then my conditioner. With time to kill, I browsed the cosmetics section. I was looking at a cute red lipstick when Ed found me. He had his pills. We paid and left to go to the Tibetan restaurant for lunch.

On our way out of the drugstore we heard a rapid, high-pitched beep.

"Step back." A teenage security guard ordered us back through the alarm. Ed and I rolled our eyes at each other and stepped back into the store. After a nod from the security guard we stepped back out.

Beep-beep-beep.

The guard waved his hand for us to step back in. We stepped back in.

"Open your bags, please."

We rolled our eyes at each other again. Ed opened his bag, which held the pills, toothbrush, and conditioner, and fumbled in his pocket for the receipt. The guard nodded approval and then turned his attention to my purse. I held it open with an exaggerated sigh. He peered down into the bag and poked a hand in to rummage through the contents: wallet, keys, scraps of paper, change purse. After a quick minute he pulled his hand out, a black tube of lipstick held between his thumb and forefinger. It was sealed in clear plastic and had a wide white alarm strip wrapped around it.

"You have a receipt for this?"

I stared at him, shocked. "That's not mine."

"I'm going to ask you to come with me, ma'am." He put his hand on my arm to lead me towards the back of the store. I pulled my arm free.

"Get your fucking hands off me!"

The guard looked at Ed and me. "Do you want to tell me how this lipstick got in your purse?"

"I have no idea," I told him truthfully. "It must have fallen in. I was looking at it, but then I put it back. Seriously, I have no idea. Look—" I opened my wallet, which held a few hundred in twenties. "Do you think I would steal a four-dollar lipstick?"

"It's in your purse," he said.

"Listen," said Ed. "We'll pay for it. How's that?"

"But I don't even want it!" I protested.

Ed ignored me and looked at the guard, a come-on-we're-all-men-here look. "I'll pay for it."

After a dramatic pause the security guard nodded. He escorted us back to the cashier, where Ed paid for the lipstick, and then we left.

Outside the store we looked at each other in astonishment, shaking our heads as we walked towards the Tibetan restaurant. I lit a cigarette and for once Ed didn't scowl.

"I can't believe it," I said. I really couldn't. "I haven't stolen anything since seventh grade." When I was twelve and my stepmother said I was too young for makeup I went on a shoplifting spree, ending when I was caught red-handed with a contraband eyeliner.

"Maybe he put it there," said Ed. "Thought you wouldn't put up a fuss."

"Why would he want to do that?"

We were silent for a moment, contemplating the possible motivations of a rogue security guard.

Ed shrugged. "It must have fallen, like you said."

"Yeah. I guess when I put it back in the dispenser it fell back out."

"It must have."

"Must have."

"Yeah. It must have."

First Ed burst out laughing, then me. Almost arrested in the drugstore, over a four-dollar lipstick I hadn't even wanted! We told the story again and again to friends and coworkers, and even to Ed's mother, over the phone. It was too funny. Hysterical. And even funnier was that at the end I was glad to have the lipstick; it was a dark, brick red that I never would have bought, far from my usual neutral, pinkish brown, but for the rest of that summer and fall I wore the red lipstick almost every day and when it ran out, in mid-November, I went back to the same drugstore and stole another tube.

leaving work a few days later I walked by a hole-in-the-wall bar between my office and the train. I had walked by it a hundred times before without a second thought. Suddenly I wanted a drink. One drink, I thought. Just one. It had been years since I stopped into a bar, alone, for a drink. I stood in front of the door. It looked filthy inside. *One drink,* I thought. *Just one quick drink.*

An hour later I was on my third tequila, sitting at the bar with a man whose name I had instantly forgotten when he introduced himself to me. He was about my age, with short, scruffy black hair and an appealing, slightly wrinkled face. His arms were wrapped in tattoos; Japanese goldfish with bulging eyes and a mermaid with a sweet face and waves and waves of water in between. This was the kind of man I liked in my early twenties, before I met Ed.

"How about four," the bartender said. I nodded. The man I was sitting with smiled. He had a once-in-a-lifetime smile. The bartender gave us two more drinks.

I looked around the room. Mostly men, mostly tattooed like my drinking companion. A band was setting up or breaking down in one corner of the room.

"You can drink," the man said.

"I can," I answered, but I didn't feel drunk at all. Just happy to be out, having fun.

I got home late and Ed, naturally, was worried and angry in equal parts. I didn't bother to apologize, or even make up a very convincing lie.

"Worked late, hon."

Edward sulked, sitting on the sofa in boxer shorts and an undershirt. "I was worried. You could have called."

I ignored him and went to the bedroom to undress. In a red kimono I walked back to the bathroom and drew myself a bath, ignoring Edward again when I walked through the living room.

Let him worry, I told myself. Let him see what it's like, sitting alone, watching the clock, waiting for your spouse to come home. I lay down in the hot water and poured in half a bottle of lily of the valley bubble bath, a birthday gift from Ed I had been saving for a special occasion. My spine and neck relaxed in the soft hot water. I knew we would have a fight after I got out of the bathtub. Ed would ask what my problem was and I would say I didn't have a problem and he would say I was sure acting like I had a problem. Then I would say I guess the problem is that you think one member of the household can come and go as he pleases while the other has to account for every minute of her time. And he would say where the hell were you tonight. And I would say at the office, like I said. Call and check if you want. And he would look at the phone on its little desk by the book-cases, sitting there like a slug, and then look back at me. Forget it, he would say. Fine, I would say. Fine, he would say. We would go to bed chilly and wouldn't warm up again until the next morning, or the next evening over dinner.

two weeks later. Another night at home. Another takeout dinner, shared late. We had made up from the last blowout but there was still a chill between us, a polite caution that replaced affection. After dinner we sat on the sofa together and disappeared into our separate worlds. A documentary about World War II was on television. Summer had come on quickly and it was so hot in the loft that Ed, who dressed immaculately even at home, left his usual summer cotton pajamas in the dresser and wore just a clean pair of white-and-blue-striped boxer shorts and a white undershirt. I had on a thin camisole and another pair of his clean white-and-blue-striped boxers. Edward flipped through a magazine. I flipped through a book on midcentury furniture design.

I lit a cigarette. Edward gently rolled his eyes. We had made an agreement that I would keep smoking in the loft to a minimum, a concession to Ed's tragic allergies. I ignored him. I smoked and looked at my book, half listening to the television. The cigarette was in its usual place between the first and second fingers of my right hand.

I thought, *What if I stuck Edward with this cigarette?*

Everyone has thoughts like this from time to time: What if I burned my husband? What if I pushed him off this cliff? What if I jumped off this roof? The thought came into my head and then disappeared just as quickly. I lifted the cigarette to my lips for a last drag. Then, in my mind, I took it down to stub it out in the little white custard cup I used as an ashtray. Very nice, French, we had gotten a set of six as a wedding present, I don't remember from whom. I do know that I never before or after made a custard. In my mind my hand moved towards the table and snuffed out the cigarette in the little white cup. My fingers, with a chipped brown manicure, were at my lips, the brown filter suspended between the first and second fingers of my right hand. I took the last drag and then released my lips. I assumed my hand would move down to the table and put out the cigarette.

It didn't. Instead my hand made a quick turn to the right and stabbed the burning cigarette into Edward's leg, an inch above his left knee.

He screamed. I screamed. I ran into the kitchen for

ice and Edward kept screaming. He jumped up from the sofa screaming bloody murder.

"Shit! Fuck! What the fuck did you do that for? What the hell is wrong with you?"

I was speechless. Edward sat back down, still cursing. I sat next to him and held a bag of frozen peas over the burn. The screaming tapered off into a muttering, and then silence. He closed his eyes and leaned back.

"What happened?" he asked, after a few minutes. He wasn't really angry. Just shocked.

"I don't know," I told him. "I didn't mean to."

"Of course you didn't mean to," he said. "I know that."

"I don't know what happened. My arm just moved. I didn't mean to. How're you feeling?"

"Terrible," he answered. "It hurts like hell."

"I'm sorry."

"Don't be sorry." He reached over and ruffled the hair on top of my head. "It was an accident."

"I love you," I said.

"I love you, too," he answered.

"I don't know what happened. It's like it moved by itself."

"Maybe it's tendinitis. Julian's wife had it in her

shoulder and she couldn't even hold her arm up. It used to just flop all over the place."

"I don't think so," I told him. "My shoulder feels fine."

"You twitched," said Edward. "A spasm."

I knew it wasn't tendinitis. My arm hadn't flopped. It hadn't slipped, it hadn't twitched, it hadn't fallen. It had moved by itself. It had moved with a controlled movement away from the ashtray and towards Edward's leg.

Edward didn't say anything, and neither did I. There was nothing to say.

the day after I burned Edward, I took *Demon Possession Past and Present* down from the bookshelf and took the little quiz again. Not that I took it seriously. Not that I for a moment believed anything so ridiculous as that a demon or devil was influencing my life.

Are YOU Possessed by a Demon?

1. I hear strange noises in my home, especially at night, which family members tell me only occur when I am present.

2. I have new activities and pastimes that seem "out of character," and I do things that I did not intend and do not understand.

3. I'm short and ill-tempered with my friends and loved ones.

4. I can understand languages I've never studied, and have the ability to know things I couldn't know through ordinary means.

5. I have blackouts not caused by drugs, alcohol, or a preexisting health condition.

6. I have unusual new thoughts, or hear voices in my head.

7. I've had visions or dreams of personalities who may be demons.

8. A psychic, minister, or other spiritualist has told me I'm possessed.

9. I have urges to hurt or kill animals and other people.

10. I have hurt or killed animals or people.

This time I scored a five.

0–3: You are probably not possessed. See a doctor or mental health professional for an evaluation.

3–6: You may be haunted, or in the early stages of possession. Do not be alarmed. Seek a spiritual counselor for assistance.

6–10: You are possessed. Consult with your spiritual counselor immediately. You may be a threat to the safety of yourself and your family.

I read a bit more:

Some other signs of possession include a change in appearance and changes in personality that may be so subtle even those close to the victim may not be able to pinpoint the difference. Generally speaking, an overall increase in aggressive behavior is to be expected. However, until the very late stages of possession, the victim continues with his daily life largely intact . . . A sudden psychic ability is almost always present, and is in fact one of the first definite signs to look for when in doubt. Another common characteristic is the insatiable need to be desired by members of the opposite sex.

*   *   *

leaving my hairdresser's the next afternoon, I ran into a woman I knew. Bernadette Schwartz worked at Ed's company. She had been a model when she was younger and she still looked like one, tall and stunning with perfect long chestnut hair. I knew her a little, through company Christmas parties, and we stopped to say hello. She gave me a good hard look.

"What is it?" she asked. She peered at me with huge brown eyes, now ugly and accusatory.

"What's what?"

"You. Did you get work done?"

"Work?"

"An eye lift or something. Or maybe your teeth. You look different."

"Huh." I looked at myself in a mirror across from us. A mirror behind us was reflected into the first and I saw a fun-house, an infinite number of mirrors, each with a picture of me. I did look different; as if I had had a good night's sleep, or even a year's worth of good nights. My skin was bright and my eyes shiny. My whole face was plumped up, all the little lines of thirty-four smooth as satin.

"I know," said Bernadette, "you're *pregnant*!"

I rubbed my eyes and shook my head and then looked back at the mirror. My own true face, a little haggard, now looked back at me. Bernadette frowned.

"New haircut?" she ventured, less sure of herself now.

"Just a trim," I said. "Must be the weather. This humidity, it's always good for my skin."

when I got out of the train station that evening the German shepherd was waiting as usual, sitting quietly as I'd trained him to do. The routine was he wouldn't stand up to give me a kiss (the one untoward act I allowed him) until I had given him his first biscuit. I went to the corner where he sat waiting. Usually his tail would be wagging by now and there would be a big drooling smile on his face. But he sat, moping, as if I hadn't shown up at all. He looked away from me and then right through me. I took a biscuit, shaped like a cartoon bone, out of my purse and held it out to him.

He sniffed at the biscuit and looked up at me with

his big watery eyes, but he didn't take it. Instead he stiffened his back and shoulders and snarled at me, baring a row of yellow plaque-covered teeth. I dropped the biscuit and ran home.

When Ed got home I told him what had happened.

"Well," he said, "I told you not to mess around with strays."

Ed didn't believe that just because something was alive, that meant you had to love it.

i didn't obsess about the incident with the cigarette. I didn't make much of the book. Ed had forgotten easily enough. So I'd twitched. I'd slipped. I'd spasmed. It was summer and with the sun so bright it was hard to think about demons, hard to think about pain.

But two weeks later, at the Fitzgerald house, I had a little twitch again.

I had decided to become an architect when I was twenty. I had moved to the city when I was eighteen, to go to college, and I started with a major in art. I was in love—with my school, with the city, with the snow. I had come from a southern suburb where every star was brightly visible at night and the thermometer never dropped below fifty. I had spent eighteen years in continual boredom. Then when I was twenty my father and Noreen had died and left me nothing. Everything that could have and should have been mine had been eaten up by Noreen's fur coats and facial treatments. I went through the labyrinthine process of applying for financial aid and as part of the deal, got a job in the Department of Architecture office. One thing I noticed about the architects was that they dressed a hell of a lot better than the art professors. And they drove better cars. And they seemed a lot more likely to have spouses and even children, too. So I switched to the architecture program. After graduation I worked for one of my professors for a year, then moved to a big firm for a few years where I never even met three of the four partners, and then on to Fields & Carmine, where I had been for the past three years.

The Fitzgerald house was my largest project to date. I had high hopes; if all went according to plan I had a chance at an A.I.A. award and maybe a spread in *Design Monthly,* plus recommendations from the Fitzgeralds and their rich friends. If all went well, then the larger plan, to open my own firm, could be accelerated by years.

The job reminded me of Michelangelo's line about sculpting a block of stone; he chipped away everything that wasn't David. The Fitzgeralds, a nice millionaire couple my own age, had bought an old Victorian mansion in a run-down part of town. Even with an unlimited budget they couldn't find the space they wanted anywhere else. The huge Victorian had been converted first into three apartments, and then divided up further into a twelve-unit rooming house. You could get lost for hours imagining who had roomed there, but never mind. The task at hand was to turn the rooming house back into a mansion. I was working with a team of designers, decorators, plumbers, electricians, painters, air-conditioning specialists, woodworkers, and carpenters, and we would chip away all the divisions, additions, and ornaments that weren't the Fitzgeralds' house.

On a Wednesday morning I stopped by on my way to the office to see how the work was coming along. No one else was there. It was only eight-thirty and the workers wouldn't come in until nine or ten. The house was chilly inside. Only a few streaks of light filtered in through the shuttered windows. It was quiet and smelled like dust and plaster. I walked through the first floor. Half the rooming house partitions were torn down. They hadn't started to clean up yet and rubble was piled around empty door frames and steel beams. Eventually all the walls would come down and the first floor would be like a loft within the house—kitchen, dining room, living room, all in one open space.

I climbed the stairs, avoiding the thick dust on the mahogany bannisters. The house was filthy. My footsteps echoed off the endless yards of white drywall. Upstairs we would rebuild the original bedrooms, four of them, for a nice balance of openness and privacy. It would be great when they had kids. For now, each bedroom was still split into two lonely cubicles. A few odds and ends from the house's previous incarnations were still lying around: a yo-yo with a broken string sat in one corner; a stained brown tie hung over a hook on the wall; one worn black shoe lingered in a hallway.

Everything looked fine. I walked down to the first floor and was about to leave when I saw something I hadn't noticed before. A red glass doorknob on the living room door.

I could swear it hadn't been there earlier. In fact, I

could swear I had never seen one like it. I had noticed a few pretty, clear cut glass doorknobs around the house, and even one that was violet. Nothing special. But a smooth ruby red glass doorknob, without a scratch or a chip—I was sure I had never seen one like it before. In this sad white house here was a perfect round of red.

I *want it*, I thought. I took out the small tool kit I carried in my purse, released the tiny screws from the steel base, turned it out of its hole, and had the doorknob off in two minutes. I stuck it in my purse and left.

I didn't give it another thought until half an hour later. I was waiting for a train to take me to the office when I realized with horror that I had stolen a piece of my clients' house. What if I was found out? What if the Fitzgeralds noticed their doorknob missing? My career shot to hell over a doorknob. I thought about throwing it out. I knew I should bring it back.

But I did neither. I wanted it, and I kept it.

At home I installed my beautiful new ruby on the bathroom door. Ed came home later that evening, after I was in bed, and didn't see the new doorknob until the next morning. I told him I picked it up at a design showroom. We stood in front of the bathroom door, still in our underwear. He scrunched his brow.

"I don't know," he said. "Do you think it goes?"

"Yes," I said. "It goes perfectly."

He frowned. "It's *red*."

"I know. That's what I like about it."

"It's bright. Don't you think it's kind of bright?"

"We're keeping it," I said. Ed looked at me, a question written on his face. "We're keeping it," I said again, and went to the bedroom to dress.

i was on my way to work that morning when a black limousine, the size of two sedans, took a corner too close to the curb and splashed me with water from the gutter. Without thinking I walked up to the dark tinted driver's window of the car, now stopped behind a line of traffic, and tapped on the cold glass. No answer. I tapped again, hard enough this time to rattle the glass in its frame. A driver in a suit and plastic-brimmed cap rolled down the window. He had pink skin and copper hair pulled into a narrow ponytail, with a copper mustache to top it all off. He scowled at me.

"Yeah?"

"You should apologize," I said.

"What the fuck?" spat out the moustache.

"You should," I repeated, "apologize. Now." I leaned my face into the window and breathed in the leathery smell of the clean car. The driver had two choices now; apologize or push me out. He made a face and cursed under his breath.

"I'm sorry," he finally spat out, dripping with sarcasm. "I'm sincerely fucking sorry. Now get out of the car."

I stood back up, and he rolled the window closed. As the glass came up I saw my reflection. Distorted in the glass my hair looked longer and darker, my skin smoother, and my lips as red as the ruby doorknob.

we were on the crimson sand by the blood red sea. Her name was still spelled out in the sand.

"You're mine," she said. She licked my cheek with a tongue as stiff and wet as a snake.

I looked into her eyes. "You'll never leave?"

"Never." She wrapped her arms tighter around me. "Never never never."

"Why me?" I asked.

She didn't answer. Instead she smiled and licked my nose in a thin straight line from bottom to top.

When I woke up I could still feel the damp trace of her tongue on my face.

ed and I had another fight the next morning. Lately I hadn't been as neat and orderly around the house as usual, which drove him up the wall.

"Amanda, please," he said. He was looking at a pile of yesterday's clothes, left on the bedroom floor. He was standing in the middle of the bedroom in socks, underwear, and a pale blue oxford shirt, scowling at the clothes.

Usually I would have picked them up and put them in the hamper where, after all, they belonged. This morning, though, I didn't want to put the clothes away. No reason. I just didn't want to.

"Yes?" I said to Edward. I was still in bed—or rather back in bed, having woken up, gotten a cup of coffee, a cigarette, and an ashtray, and returned. So I would be a little late to work. Big deal.

"Amanda, these clothes!" He was clearly irritated

now, shifting his weight from one foot to another, torn between falling a minute or two behind schedule and dealing with the vital situation at hand.

"What about them?"

Ed scrunched his face and looked at me for a long anxious moment. He looked ridiculous, and it was hard to hold back a giggle.

"Oh, FORGET IT!" he said, and picked up the clothes himself. Not wanting to delay his schedule any further, he let the matter drop. I was sure it would be picked back up again when he came home that evening.

the connections slowly began to knit themselves together. One bright summer morning I was sitting at a conference table looking over plans for Linda Marcello's cottage for the umpteenth time. Linda Marcello was a longtime Fields & Carmine client. We were renovating her summer cottage upstate. Linda was difficult; she wanted light in the shade, she wanted a dark brown room to feel "airy," she wanted a terrace with no visible means of support. I was daydreaming about being outdoors, at the park or maybe the beach. My hand, moving to point out a walk-in closet, brushed against hers. When our skin touched

I saw Linda in her cottage, in the brown room that wasn't airy at all, sitting on the brown velvet sofa. I saw it as clearly as a movie rolling before my eyes. She sat on the sofa doing nothing, waiting for her husband to come home. He was due home hours ago. The boredom was excruciating. She looked around the room. What had she been thinking, with the brown? It could drive a person crazy, this room. She would have liked to go out but he wouldn't be happy if he came home and she wasn't there. Then the movie stopped and a new film started; I saw Linda again, ten years younger, in a cozy, cluttered white-walled apartment with two other young women. They were laughing and drinking wine—I couldn't make out all the words, but it was the kind of bonding/complaining conversation that young women have when they talk about men. They had all wanted to marry rich. Linda had.

The entire episode had taken only a second. Linda had no idea. Now I knew just the right thing to say.

"Did you see the paper today?" I asked. Linda shook her head. "The Marsha Merkon case finally closed. You know, the model, I mean former model, who was married to the head of Bluechip Securities."

"Oh really?" Linda turned around and looked at

me with great interest—the first time, I think, she ever looked at me at all. This was one of those big divorce cases with enough money and lurid accusations involved to make tabloid headlines on slow news days. I knew that Linda would have been following the case.

"Yep. She got twenty million. And you know she's not even fifty. Now she's got twenty million dollars and her whole life ahead of her. You know what she said?"

"What?" Linda asked.

"That she would have divorced him no matter what, even if she hadn't gotten anything. That she felt younger than she had in ten years."

"Huh," she said. She was smiling now, her eyes almost as bright as they had been back in that shabby little apartment with her girlfriends. "You know I met her a few times, at parties. She wasn't at all like the papers made her out to be. She was a very nice woman. In fact, we talked about having lunch sometime."

"Well, this is probably a good time to call her," I said. "You can take her out to celebrate."

"Or she can take me out, with her twenty million," Linda said, laughing.

The next evening, paying for two steaks, touching

the butcher's hand, I saw a clean, warm house where he lived with his wife and two young sons. The man who sold me my morning coffee, I saw a few days later, hated me. He hated all of us, going to our easy jobs in cushy offices while he got up at three in the morning to serve us our precious fucking coffee.

This new vision waxed and waned over the rest of the summer, and I was never sure what to make of it. More often than not, I ignored the snapshots that burst to life before my closed eyes, I dismissed them as fantasy—I had always daydreamed a lot.

I didn't tell Ed about it. He was a devout agnostic, and believed anything that smacked of metaphysics or the supernatural was mumbo jumbo.

the German shepherd continued to ignore me. Every night he sat outside the train station, waiting, and didn't recognize me when I arrived. Ed knew the dog too, and reported that when he came home each night, two or three hours after me, the dog was still waiting. Ed would stop and pet the big fellow and he recognized Ed as he always had—it was only me whom he didn't know anymore.

"**where** have you been?" It was James Cronin. A Monday afternoon at Fields & Carmine. James had the desk next to mine and we had never gotten along. With James everything was a competition; now he wanted to start about who took a shorter lunch.

"The coffee shop," I told him, "getting a hamburger."

"For two hours?" James asked, raising his eyebrows.

I rolled my eyes at him. "What two hours? I left at one and now it's—" I looked at my watch. Three o'clock. That couldn't be right. I bent down to look at the clock on James's desk. They jibed. Three o'clock.

My mind took a step backwards and then forwards, trying to make sense of the situation. I had gone to Pete's for a burger, then to the magazine stand on the corner, then back to work. I had looked at my watch on the way back and seen five to. One hour.

Impossible. But here I was. James was looking at me with his big gray eyes. I felt as if the ground underneath me was no longer stable but tilting, one way and then the other. My mind stopped to rearrange itself. I went into an emergency mode where the first thing was to deal with James Cronin.

"Oh, yeah, I did leave at one," I told James, as if I hadn't said it a moment before with an entirely different tone. "I had some errands."

I turned and sat down at my own desk. I went over the hour—no, two hours—in my mind again. First I had gone to the coffee shop for a hamburger. There was the usual waitress, the tired brunette. While I ate I read the newspaper, which I left in the coffee shop when I was done. Then I went to the magazine stand on the corner, down the block. I looked through a few women's magazines before I picked up *Architectural Record*. There was a little piece on my firm in the New and Noteworthy column. Of course we had a copy at the office but I wanted to show Ed. I checked my watch, twenty to two. Plenty of time. I flipped through a few women's magazines, a guilty pleasure. And then:

"Hey, hey. You can't read those here. Buy or don't buy. No reading."

I turned. It was the man running the shop.

"Well I AM buying, I'm getting this and I'm deciding about these others." I was angry but only for a second or two. Ridiculous man. How could people know what to buy if they didn't look first? I thought of the utter absurdity of the situation: a man who was talking customers out of shopping in his store. Probably went home every night wondering why he didn't sell more magazines.

And then again: "Buy or don't buy. Come on, lady." I would have walked out but I had been looking for that magazine for a week now, it was mostly sold by subscription and wasn't easy to find at a newsstand. I went to the counter.

"You know you're very rude, how is a person supposed to shop without looking around first?" I paid with five dollar bills and two quarters.

"You don't like it, get out. I don't need this."

I got angrier. All I wanted were a few magazines

and here was this abuse. "I am getting out, and I won't come back."

I turned and left. I heard him behind me: "Fucking bitch."

I ignored him. What a nut. How does a person like that come to run a business? I lit a cigarette and smoked a few drags. I was still angry, even though I was embarrassed about it. It should be beneath me, taking this moronic woman-hater seriously.

I checked my watch. Fifteen minutes left. If I walked the long way back to work, took the streets instead of the avenue, that would fill the time nicely. I could smoke another cigarette and relax. Stressful morning, trouble with the electricians at the Fitzgerald house, and now this ridiculous fight with a stranger. I was about to step into the street when a woman rushed by, or maybe a man with long hair, lightning fast, and almost knocked me down. I stumbled, and then caught myself. Fucking messengers.

And then a dip. I had closed my eyes for a second, a blink in anticipation of being hit by the messenger. I closed my eyes and there was a dip, a dip or a drop out of consciousness. I had a cigarette in my hand, the air smelled hot and dirty on the street corner, the messenger rushed by, I lost my balance, stumbled and then, I could just barely remember it, I saw black and lost the feeling of my feet on the ground.

It passed as quickly as it came, and there I was in front of the magazine store on the corner. The cigarette was gone. Of course you don't usually remember putting out a cigarette, not at a pack a day. That's twenty times a day you put out a cigarette.

Where was the magazine? I looked around my desk. Not there. In my mind I went back again to the magazine stand. After the messenger raced by I shook my head, took a second to get my bearings. Just a little moment of lightheadedness. I walked up the side streets back to work, smoked another cigarette, stopped to admire a beautiful red rose bush in a front yard. I stopped to check my watch before I came back into the building. Five to. What I expected. But I had only checked the long minute hand, not the short hour hand. So where was the magazine? I didn't have it on the way back to work. I remembered reaching into my purse for cigarettes and lighter and having both hands free. No cigarette, no magazine.

I mulled it over in my mind for a few minutes before I came up with an answer: I had fainted. That was the only possibility. When I thought I had only stumbled, avoiding the messenger, I had fainted. I had been out for an hour, righted myself, and then returned to work without knowing it had happened, drawing no attention from a single passerby, and then forgotten the whole thing. Sitting at my desk I weighed a visit to the emergency room. No, I was okay now.

It was just like people in this city not to stop and help. Of course the magazine dealer would have seen the whole thing through the door, but he certainly wouldn't have lifted a finger to help me. I called Edward at the office but he was out. The rest of the day went by without incident and at six I went home. There was a message from Ed on the answering machine saying he would be late again. I ate a bowl of cereal at the kitchen table and almost forgot about having fainted—until I went to the bedroom and started to undress, changing into pajamas for the evening. Underneath my jacket, on the left shoulder of my white shirt, was a spray of small brown dots.

It looked like blood. Enough so, in fact, that there was nothing it could be but blood. My mind flip-flopped again. Then I remembered lunch at the coffee shop—a rare hamburger. Mystery solved. The stain was from lunch. I had transmitted a fine spray of blood from a cooked hamburger around my jacket and onto the shoulder of the shirt underneath, then I had fainted, righted myself, and forgotten about it. As simple as that.

Edward came home at nine, with a bag of Mexican takeout for dinner and an armload of apologies. I told him what had happened and, shocked, he quizzed me with all the warmth of an emergency room doctor: What had I eaten? Was I getting my period? Had I slept well last night? How did I feel now?

"Why are you interrogating me?" I yelled. I felt fine, I looked fine, eventually I convinced him that I was fine.

It wasn't until a few days later that I happened to watch the television news. Ed was still at work. The sun had just gone down and a gray light was coming through the windows, meeting the blue from the television in the middle of the room. I was sitting on the sofa about to bite into another take-out dinner, pad thai and papaya salad.

A vaguely familiar face popped up on the television screen. Middle-aged, male, not at all attractive. Where did I know him from?

"Kareem Singh was buried today," a woman's voice said. Cut to a funeral in a crowded slum of the city. "The owner of a newsstand was killed with a box cutter on Monday afternoon in what police think was an attempted robbery."

Of course. The asshole from the magazine stand. Horrible. But I wasn't surprised, the way he'd acted. Probably said the wrong thing to the wrong person. And I had been there on Monday, it must have been right before—

For a very small moment, for a tiny sliver of time, the thought occurred to me. But as soon as the spark was lit it was put out again. Impossible. The television news moved on, cut-cut, and so did I.

It wasn't until months later that I would look back and realize that, most likely, I had killed the magazine dealer myself.

that weekend we went to the Asian Museum to see a rare display of Meiji Japanese furniture, Edward's favorite. After we walked through the exhibit we had an elegant lunch in the museum café, watercress salad and crustless salmon sandwiches—a little too elegant, I guess, because soon afterwards we were hungry again, and went for a walk in the park in search of hot dogs and pretzels.

In the park we ran into Alex and Sophia and their six-year-old daughter, Claire. I didn't like Alex and Sophia. All that could annoy me about Ed was amplified in Alex and Sophia. They worked in finance, in some capacity, and made tons of money. Their apartment was revoltingly spotless and bland with an absurd white carpet they paid a woman to come in and scrub twice a week.

Luckily they had Claire, so I had some entertainment when we met. While Ed and his friends talked about Alex's promotion, which was supposed to be interesting, Claire and I walked down to the lake to look at the swans. Swans were beautiful but could be dangerous, I explained to Claire as we walked. As long as they didn't feel threatened, I told her, they were fine. But if we were to get too close to the birds they would try to bite.

When we got to the water we stood there for a minute or two, watching four white swans pick each other's feathers clean with their hard orange beaks. Then Claire turned to me—not exactly to me but in my direction, a little to my left. She did this a few more times, and I looked around to see if anything interesting was going on. But I knew a little girl could find an unusual blade of grass or an out-of-place bottle cap fascinating, so I didn't give it too much thought.

Then Claire turned towards me again. "Are you sure?" she asked.

"Sure about what, honey?" I said.

She ignored me. "Okay," Claire said. And then she let go of my hand and ran to the water's edge and reached her hand out to the nearest swan. The bird bent its long neck towards Claire with a nasty look on its face. It all happened in the blink of an eye. I ran down after Claire, scooped her up, and jumped back. The bird waddled up the riverbank after us.

"Hey!" I yelled at the swan. "Fuck off!" It stopped and stared with its beady eyes. I ran with Claire in my arms like a sack of potatoes back up the embankment. After a few yards I put her down and we walked back towards her parents.

"Claire, why did you do that?"

She squeezed her eyebrows together and pouted. "She told me to!" she cried. "She said I could!"

"What are you talking about? No one told you to do anything."

"Her!" Claire said with frustration. She pointed to my left side, at about the same angle she had been looking earlier. "Your friend."

"Who, honey?"

"The lady who's always with you," she said. Claire pouted and looked at the ground.

When we got back to our little group I told Sophia that Claire had been telling lies.

that night I picked up *Demon Possession Past and Present* and took the quiz again. This time I scored a seven.

0–3: You are probably not possessed. See a doctor or mental health professional for an evaluation.

3–6: You may be haunted, or in the early stages of possession. Do not be alarmed. Seek a spiritual counselor for assistance.

6–10: You are possessed. Consult with your spiritual counselor immediately. You may be a threat to the safety of yourself and your family. See the RE-SOURCES page for a qualified professional in your area.

sister Maria, spiritual advisor, was the closest professional in my area. What could it hurt? I asked myself. I had always been curious to visit a psychic, just to see how they did it—the tricks they might use, the leading questions—because of course there was nothing to it. Of course I didn't believe in psychics or spiritualists or demons or devils. At the very best this Maria might be an intelligent person with strong intuition who could give me a little insight into the changes that I saw happening in myself the past few months. *Take some time to relax,* I imagined she would tell me. *Take some vitamin C.* At the worst, it would be good for a laugh. I used that phrase a lot that year, *good for a laugh*. And the word *curious*. That's what I would tell Ed if he found out that I wasn't at the Fitzgerald house that day, like I had told him—it was just for a laugh, I would tell him. I was curious.

In the northern tip of the city, where Sister Maria's shop or office or clinic was—I didn't know what to expect—the streets crunched with bottle caps and fast-food wrappers and used hypodermic needles. The windows in the run-down tenements were cracked, some missing and replaced with balsa wood or particleboard. But it wasn't wholly without charm: an elderly man sat on a folding chair in front of his doorway, hat in hand, and wished me a fine day. On a grocery store wall I noticed a small plaque from the Landmarks Commission; it had been the site of a famous jazz nightclub in the thirties. A slow wailing big band sound flowed through an open window. *Accompaneme,* the woman sang—come with me. A crowd of children played hopscotch in the middle of a street. Up the street a clique of teenage girls sat on a stoop and pretended to ignore the grandstanding teenage boys on the street around them.

At number 77 was a shop with a life-sized plaster Madonna in the window. She wore a black wig and a white dress, and at her feet was a bowl of water with coins at the bottom. The glass was clean and the street in front was well swept. A bell jangled when I opened the door. Inside was a neat little shop lined with shelves like a grocery store, except I wasn't quite sure what was on the shelves. Jars of herbs. Quarts of green and brown liquids labeled with numbers. Come-to-me oil, money-drawing soap, house-blessing spray, hot-foot powder, four thieves vinegar, Florida Water, St. Christopher oil. Candles in the shape of men, women, cats, and dogs. Lucite pyramids filled with lucky charms, and good old-fashioned crystal balls in various sizes. Behind a glass case of medallions and charms stood a teenage boy, a flaming queer in tight designer jeans with a silver ring through his bottom lip. He smiled and asked if he could help me.

"I'm here for, uh, to see Sister Maria."

He went to the back of the shop, opened a door, and called out in a language I had never heard before—Portuguese, maybe—but somehow I knew what it meant.

"A white woman's here to see you," he called. "I've never seen her before."

"Send her in right away," the woman called back. "Then lock up and go to lunch."

the back room was pretty much what I expected a low-rent reading room to look like; walls draped in deep red velveteen, a folding card table with more velveteen draped over it, anchored in place with a crystal ball, a cup for reading tea leaves, a pen and paper, and a deck of tarot cards. At the table sat a woman five or ten years older than me, with nutmeg skin and pretty features hidden behind cheap makeup. She wore blue jeans and a tight denim jacket. She gestured for me to sit in a folding chair across the table from hers. I sat down.

I was curious. It would be good for a laugh.

"What's you name?" she asked. I told her. She wrote it down on the paper and did a quick calculation.

"You number is seven," she said. She took the deck of tarot cards and laid seven of them out on the table. Death, The Tower, Queen of Pentacles, The Moon, Five of Swords, Eight of Swords, The Lovers. I had no idea what any of them meant. Maria looked at the cards for a few minutes, then back up to me with her eyebrows pushed together, then down at the cards again.

"Someone's watching you," she finally said. "She's right next to you. Beautiful, but black. Evil. Have you tried to get rid of her?"

This wasn't so good for a laugh. This was less funny by the moment. "Who is it?" I asked.

"It's not a who," Maria answered. "It's a what. A demon. I see her; she has long black hair and pointy teeth."

"Are you sure she's a demon?"

Maria nodded. "No one else has a black aura like that. So you haven't tried to get rid of it?"

I shook my head. "I didn't know."

"You really didn't know what that was?" Maria asked. Her voice was suspicious. I had a sick nervous feeling as she looked at me; it reminded me of being in school without having done my homework. I felt like I had been caught at something naughty.

"No," I told her. "How was I supposed to know?"

Maria looked at me crook-eyed again, like she wasn't quite buying my excuse. "You have to do exactly as I say, it's very important. I'm going to give you a wash. Number Five. For three nights in a row you pour it over yourself while you pray. Pray to God to help you. Then you stop for three days, then you use it again for three days. Use it until the bottle's all gone. It won't make her disappear but it will cleanse your spirit so you can fight her better. But the most important thing is that you never, ever give in. You give even an inch, she'll take a hundred miles."

"What if it doesn't work?" I asked.

"It always works."

"But what if it doesn't?"

"She'll possess you. She's probably already started. Not all at once. You won't lose yourself all at once. But a little bit at a time. That's why you have to do exactly as I say."

"I understand," I promised.

Maria stood up and I was clearly dismissed. Out in the store I settled the bill with the young man who had come back and was eyeing me curiously. He handed me a large jug of thin, greenish gray liquid in which floated a few leaves and twigs and some small berries that looked like peppercorns. On a white label with black letters was printed: "NUMBER #5: DEMON FIGHTING."

*   *   *

sister Maria had held me spellbound, but back at home it was easy for the whole matter to be *good for a laugh* again. Except I wasn't laughing, and I didn't tell anyone else about it, either. But I thought I might as well use the wash. I mean, it couldn't hurt. It's not like it would do anything, of course, but it wouldn't hurt. I rubbed off the neatly typed label with vegetable oil, so if Ed noticed the bottle I could tell him it was bubble bath. I stood in the bathtub, naked, and asked God to help me as I poured the liquid over my head. It smelled like licorice, and it stung slightly where it dripped into my eyes. I kept my mouth closed so I wouldn't swallow anything—I had forgotten to ask about that. I spread out my arms and let the wash trickle down my body, leaving a trail of goose bumps where it flowed.

Nothing happened. I wasn't sure if I was supposed to rinse afterwards or just let it dry on my skin, but it smelled strong and so I took a quick warm shower, and then dried off and put on pajamas and spent the rest of the night paying bills and watching television.

the German shepherd was waiting at the train station again a few days later, looking right through me. The idiot didn't even know who I was anymore.

"Go," I snapped. "Get out of here."

The dog looked at me and I looked back. I really hated him now, this stupid beast, staring at me with those big chocolate accusatory eyes.

"Go," I yelled again. I pointed towards the wasteland of our neighborhood, in the opposite direction from our house. Still holding my eyes, he pulled his shoulders down and his tail up, as if he were stretching his back. Then he leapt up to my outstretched hand and bit me.

I screamed, more from shock than pain. The skin on my hand was barely punctured, and it felt more like a book had been dropped on my hand than what I had imagined a dog bite would feel like. Then he lay down with his head between his paws and whimpered. Now, finally, the old adage had become true. He *was* more scared of me than I was of him.

"Fuck off!" I screamed. The idiot got up and ran away. I went home, washed my hand, wrapped it in a clean white dish towel, and called Ed, hoping he would drive me to the emergency room. He wasn't in, so I called a taxi to take me instead. By the time I got to the hospital it hurt at least as much as I had imagined a dog bite would. I tried Ed again. Still out. For three hours I sat in the waiting room and tried to guess what the other people waiting had wrong with them. Some were obvious—hacking coughs, swollen appendages—but most I had to guess. Finally I was ushered into a brightly lit little examination cubicle, where a doctor washed the wound and then asked if I knew the dog who had bit me.

"Why?" I asked.

"Because if you don't, you need to get two shots now, another in three days, another in seven, another in fourteen, and another in twenty-eight. Whenever there's a bite by an unknown dog, there's a chance of rabies."

"What if I'm really, really sure this dog doesn't have rabies?" I asked.

"If you don't know the dog," he said with irritation, "you're not really, really sure. The only way to avoid the shots is to get a brain sample from the dog. Now this is going to hurt."

The doctor gave me a shot with a thick needle in my right hand, near the bite, and then another shot in the upper arm. The shots hurt worse than the bite had.

It was obvious that a brain sample couldn't come from a living dog. *Good,* I thought at first, *serves the stupid fucker right.* Then I thought of that dumb old dog, the fellow who used to be my pal, my best buddy, how he never gave up trying to seduce me, even after I made it clear I was married. I couldn't. So on the third, seventh, fourteenth, and twenty-eighth day after the bite I went to the doctor's office for more painful shots, and I never saw the dog again.

ed was in a state when I got home at eleven that night, furious that I had let him worry. When I explained where I had been and showed him the ugly red puncture marks on my hand he relented and showed appropriate sympathy.

"Really, though," he said, after kissing my hand, "you should have called."

We were sitting on the sofa, curled up close. He gently held my bitten hand. For a few minutes we had been in love again. Friends again. And now this. *He wants an apology,* I thought. "I tried," I told him. "Twice."

"Still, hon, I was worried."

Where was he? I thought. "I tried," I said. "Where were you, anyway?"

Ed made a face. "What do you mean, where was I? Working, you know that."

"Just asking. You ought to get one of those cellular phones. In case of an emergency. You're out of the office so much these days."

Ed rolled his eyes. "I'm always out of the office a lot, Amanda, that's half my job. You know that."

Then why not get a phone? "Then why not get a phone?"

"Why, so you can keep tabs on me?"

"No, not so I can keep tabs on you. So if I get bitten by a rabid dog you can drive me to the emergency room."

Ed dropped my hand. "Do you plan on doing this often? Bothering stray animals and then getting rabies? Because if so, maybe we can get you vaccinated or something."

We sat stiffly on the sofa, side-by-side now. "Yes, Ed," I told him. "I plan on doing this often."

when I went to Dr. Flynn for my seventh-day rabies shot, the story about fainting a few weeks before at the magazine stand came out. Dr. Flynn was my age and blonde. She had been Ed's doctor for years. The first time I saw her, the day after my trip to the emergency room, I was immensely jealous. She wasn't who I would have picked to examine my naked husband. But my own doctor, Jeff Winston, had died of a stroke two months before, and Ed raved about Dr. Flynn.

She gave me a full physical, took blood for testing, and interrogated me for half an hour about the day I had fainted. What had I eaten? When had I eaten it? Did I have any strange food cravings? Strange dreams? Irrational thoughts? Had I been exposed to any toxic chemicals? On and on.

At the end of all the questions and tests and needles and samples she said I had low blood pressure and ought to eat more salt. I liked the sound of Dr. Flynn's diagnosis. Everything could be explained, my life could go on. All I needed was more salt.

I took the fact that Sister Maria's potion had done nothing as proof that there had never been anything wrong. Of course it had only been for a laugh, anyway. Just out of curiosity. But the dreams about a woman on a red beach continued just the same. And Ed and I continued to fight, and I kept doing things like snapping at cab drivers and occasionally going back for a drink to the bar where I had drunk all that tequila. A heat wave came over the city and everyone was on edge. Ed would come home each night and complain about the heat and I wanted to kill him. I knew it was hot. I didn't need to talk about it.

Occasionally I thought about how much I had changed over the past few months and I was able to take a step back and look at the situation and I was horrified. The old Amanda, the one I had chosen for myself and cultivated for years, would rear her head and scream.

Just when I was on the verge of seeing the truth, when the pieces would start to fall into place and I could almost see that the situation was horribly, drastically wrong, the demon's voice would step in and tell me No, I was the same Amanda I had always been. Only better.

then there was the Earmark Hotel party. The Earmark was a jet-set hotel downtown. Fields & Carmine had remodeled the lobby, restaurant, and bar, and we were all invited to the reopening party. Ed, naturally, had to work late that night, so I took a cab down with the other single people from the office.

I was planning to just stay for a few drinks, fulfill my obligations as a Fields & Carmine staff member, and then take off. But the party was swinging and the hotel was packed, and clearly there would be no quick in and out. The people I had come with drifted

away. I found myself talking to Tom and Bill Earmark, the brothers who owned the hotel. I barely
knew them—we had made a little small talk in the
office and I had sat in on a few meetings. But very
quickly Tom was taking me behind the bar for a mar-
tini he made himself, to avoid the line, and showing
me around the new space. He took my arm to lead
me through the crowd, and when he touched my arm
I had a flash of intuition—*He likes you, he always
has, from the first time he saw you in the office,
walking in the door with a sunburn across the bridge
of your nose and your hair down.*

Then everything got kind of blurry. I was talking
to Tom. His eyes, which had always been good, big
and clear and bluish gray, got better and better. We
drank martinis but I wasn't getting drunk. I was becoming less there. I was sliding away. I was talking to
Tom, I didn't know what we were talking about, and
his eyes were getting better and better, and so were
his cheekbones—irresistible, really—and I was talking, not just talking but flirting, horribly flirting, putting my hand on Tom's forearm and then on his
shoulders, tossing my head back when I laughed. But
I wasn't there. I was watching it all, I could see it,
but I wasn't inside of myself. It was all so muddled—

I caught snippets of conversation and odd sensations, like a strong smell of gin, the feel of the loud music pounding in my chest. I was watching a movie too late at night, half-asleep, not grasping the plot at all. We were talking and laughing, and then I got a tour of the empty kitchen, alone. Then we were getting into an elevator together. His arm was around my shoulders. I thought maybe I was here, in this elevator with Tom, but I could be in a different place. I could be a different person. I tried to get hold of the situation, to see for sure exactly who and where I was, but I couldn't get my hands around it, the situation kept slipping out from my grasp and I was left wondering, unsure.

We were in the penthouse. It was a great little space, separate bedroom off to one side, really modern and spare, all neutral colors, and of course, there was that great relaxing hotel anonymity. It was like looking at a photograph, seeing the room but not being in it. And then we were on the sofa with a bottle of wine and then we were in bed. Tom was beautiful without clothes. Tom screamed, he said my name, I saw red and heard a roar in my ears like an ocean, I didn't know who or where I was . . .

And then it was over. I was back solidly in my own body, completely present, sure of myself and my surroundings. I sat on the edge of the bed, naked and shivering. Tom lay on the bed, snoring a revolting drunken snort. I was disgusted. My stomach turned. How, I asked myself, how—how—how did this happen? A filthy horrible thing. The most filthy horrible thing I had ever done. As quickly as I could I put on my clothes and ran out to the street, where I vomited once in the gutter and then got a taxi to take me home.

wandering the aisles of a brightly lit supermarket in the city the next evening I couldn't get the night before off my mind. In the meat aisle I stopped and looked at the steaks. I would make Ed his favorite dinner tonight, steak with mushroom sauce, and I would start again, retrain myself to see him as my husband, the man I had chosen to love and respect for the rest of my life. All this nonsense had to end. We fought almost every day now. In a rare lucid moment I saw that we were dissolving as a couple, and if I didn't stop it now there would be nothing to save.

I was comparing prices on T-bones when the

demon slithered back into my thoughts. *Make dinner?* she said. *Hours in the kitchen and then he won't even come home on time and will never appreciate it. Besides, Ed hasn't cooked for you in ages, not since that horrible string bean mess he concocted months and months ago.*

I dropped the steak back into its bin, abandoned my cart, and left the supermarket. The rest of the evening was spent shopping for shoes. The demon loved to shop. Two or three times a week I would take out my credit card for little luxuries that later, at home, confused me. Why had I bought a leather jacket when I already had two in my closet? What made me think I needed a red cocktail dress?

I came home that night with three pairs of high-heeled pumps and nothing to eat. When Ed came home at eight, only one hour later than promised, we had a terrible fight over why I hadn't brought home dinner, which, he reminded me, I had said I would do.

the next day I went to a bookstore, a big multilevel place, airless and empty so early in the day. I browsed a few titles; psychic fine tuning, chakra realignment, aura cleansing.

"Can I help you?"

It was the voice of an adult woman, not the usual bookstore clerk squeak.

"No, thanks." I looked up with a smile. But no one was there. I turned in a circle and looked through the whole aisle. No one.

Back to the books. I looked at a few more titles. And then—

"Are you looking for something?"

I spun around as quickly as I could. No one. Over the top of the next shelf I saw the tip of a head, with thick dark hair, quickly darting through the next aisle.

Behind me I heard a bang. I screamed and jumped, turning around. The crash was just a book that had fallen down from a top shelf and onto the floor. Immediately I felt like an idiot. Just a book. Two young clerks came running over, a boy and a girl.

"Are you okay," squeaked the boy.

"Yes, I just—it fell. It surprised me. Sorry."

The girl bent down to pick up the book. *The Encyclopedia of Demons.*

"Actually," I said. "Can I—"

"Sure," the girl said. She handed me the book. I added it to the pile I already had, paid, and went home to pack; the next morning we were going away, to Alex and Sophia's beach house for the weekend, and Ed wanted to leave early to beat the traffic.

although it wasn't discussed, it was clear that Ed and I would both be on our best behavior this weekend, and get our relationship back on track. Saturday morning it seemed like it would be easy. It was a brilliant day, the sun was still summery yellow and warm, and we listened to a rock and roll marathon on the radio as we drove out. Ed sang along with the radio in a silly voice; I took off my shoes and rested my newly pedicured feet on the dashboard. We rolled down the windows and the sun shone into the car. When Ed's hand wasn't needed on the steering wheel, he put it in my lap.

Alex and Sophia's house was as bland as they were: lots of pale blue throw pillows and store-bought seashells scattered around. But it was neat and comfortable, and most important, it was steps from the beach. At the house I changed into a black one-piece swimsuit and Ed put on his loose khaki trunks that went almost to his knees. After a quick look around the house to check for necessities—soap, shampoo, towels, coffee—we walked down to the beach and settled in on a worn pink bedsheet we had brought from home. Ed took out a paperback novel, and after a few pages fell asleep, snoring on the sheet next to me. I lay down and tried to nap.

But I couldn't fall asleep. The sun was too hot, the small patch of sheet was confining, and Edward was annoying, snoring as he was. I was burning hot. I decided to go for a swim.

I stood up and walked towards the water. Officially, the season had ended. No lifeguards were out and swimming wasn't allowed but no one was there to stop the handful of us who bobbed in and out of the shallow water.

I swam up and down a few yards of the ocean, and then out a little further. The water was still shallow enough so that I could stand. I closed my eyes and felt the cold of the water and the heat of the sun. When I opened my eyes I saw a little girl, maybe five or six, a few feet away, between me and the shore. She shouldn't have been in the water alone at all, let alone out so far. Ordinarily I would have led her back to the shore. Today, though, I just watched her. She splashed happily around in the small waves, dunking her head in and out and letting her small body get tossed around by the gentle undertow. Her nutmeg skin was sunburned red on the shoulders. She saw me watching her and smiled. I smiled back.

"You shouldn't be out so deep," I said. She shrugged and dunked under again. A little wave came in and tossed her around. I saw the top of her head poke up from the water, then her tiny feet. When she finally righted herself and got her head above water she was coughing, maybe crying a little. Not hurt, but scared.

"I'll help you," I said. I swam towards her. While I was on my way another little wave came along, knocking her down again. I dove towards her and then reached out and grabbed her hair, as if to pull her head above water.

But I didn't. I grabbed her hair in my right hand and pulled down. Sickeningly I could feel the life drain from her as I held her under the water, feel the heat from her body trickle away. I saw her life before my eyes, most of it lived in a cramped railroad apartment. Just before she drowned I pulled her up and let her take some air, then pulled her back down again. It was a game. Up down, up down. The girl had a head on her shoulders though, and the next time up she started to scream. A fat middle-aged woman swimming near the shore perked her head up and looked around. I plunged the girl under one more time and dunked my own head too, as if we'd both been caught in an undercurrent, and then jumped back up with my arm around the girl's head.

"I think she's drowning," I called out to the woman, who was quickly walking through the water towards us. "Give me a hand." The strong woman grabbed the limp child out of my arms and ran with her towards the shore. I ran after her.

Back on the warm sand the child started crying, which was a good sign that no permanent damage had been done. The commotion woke up Ed and he came running down to where a small crowd had formed around the girl. She sat up, looked around, and threw up a stomach full of salt water—another good sign, the crowd agreed. The girl's mother came running, crying and screaming, as if she hadn't done worse to her daughter at home. I had seen it all.

"You saved my baby's life!" she cried to the older woman and me. The older woman looked at me oddly but said nothing. I could imagine her telling herself that of course I had been pulling her out, not pushing her in. That must have been what she saw. I must have been pulling her out. The girl herself was still in a mild shock. If she were ever to tell anyone that I had been trying to end her life, not save it, I was sure no one would believe her.

The older woman went off to the spot where her fat husband was waiting. The crying mother took her crying daughter back to their blanket. Edward took my hand and led me back to our own pink sheet, where we sat down and I started to cry myself.

"Shh." He wrapped his arms around me. "Everyone's fine. You must have been terrified, poor baby."

I looked up at the sky. A flock of birds was circling high above us, flying in and out of a V formation. One by one they left the V and then regrouped, flying into place one at a time to spell out a name, perfectly as a pen on paper.

NAAMAH.

*   *   *

back at the house Ed took the car and drove out to the bay to buy dinner, fresh steamer clams and corn on the cob, which he cooked himself. He asked me what I thought of dinner and if I was having a good time and I just kept saying "Mmm," which he took as a positive response.

After dinner we lay on the sofa. We had been planning on going back to the beach for the sunset but I needed to rest. After a few minutes Ed fell asleep again. I went to the bedroom and got out *The Encyclopedia of Demons,* which I had hidden in the bottom of my bag. With a sick feeling in my stomach I flipped through until I got to the N's. There she was, with a few pages in *The Encyclopedia of Demons* all to herself.

NAAMAH

The most famous stories of Naamah come from the Kabala, the Jewish mystical texts formerly available in full only to Jewish male scholars over the age of forty. Her name is thought to mean "charming" or "pleasant" in her native Aramaic, a reference to her desirability to men. Due to the occult nature of Kabalic wisdom, there may be much more attached to the name than we can know; especially one wonders about its origins and its numerological significance. Like most of her type, she is made stronger by water (especially salt water), sexual desire, and other impure thoughts.

Naamah's story begins at the beginning of time, as Adam's second wife: Adam's first wife was Lilith. While Adam was made from pure earth she was made from filth and sediment, and she could not be a mate for Adam. Adam wanted Lilith to be submissive, but Lilith refused, and she went to live by the Red Sea and became the mother of all demons. So God made a second wife, Naamah, and this one he made in front of Adam, starting from scratch, in order to meet Adam's specifications. He started with the bones, then the organs, then the muscles, blood, et cetera, and by the time God was done, Adam was so disgusted he would have nothing to do with her. And Naamah, along with Lilith, was banished to the banks of the Red Sea. In another story, Naamah's origins are vague but her purpose clearer. After Cain kills Abel, Adam is so horrified by his children that he refuses to sleep with Eve for over one hundred years. During this time, Naamah comes to him in his sleep and, preying on his dreams, impregnates herself with his semen. This is the source of the Jewish preference that men, especially rabbis and scholars, be married—unless a man made love to his wife regularly, what he thought was a simple nocturnal emission could really be a demon making love to him, impregnating herself with his seed. In Genesis, we see Naamah yet again. In this story she's the daughter of Lamach and Zillah. This Naamah wasn't a demon, just a human. But oddly enough, this Naamah married her brother, Tubal Cain, and then gave birth to a demon—Asmodeus, who we still know today. Hence her reputation as a fierce and proud mother, whose secondary goal—after seduction—is to eliminate any children that are not her own. In Kings 3:16, she appears again (along with Lilith), as one of the two harlots sent to test the wisdom of Solomon. Posing as two mothers arguing over the maternity of a child, the demons attempt to trick Solomon into making a foolish decision; instead, Solomon offers to cut the child in half, knowing the true mother will give up her claim. Defeated, the two demons go back to whence they came. As with all stories concerning Solomon, this myth figures in Freemasonry legend as well.

In addition to these, there are far more instances of Naamah's unfortunate influence throughout Christian and Jewish history.

The next morning I told Edward I didn't feel well—sun poisoning—and that I ought to stay home while he went to the beach. Once he was gone I read some more from the book:

If only the average person knew the early warning signs of possession, much heartbreak could be averted. The most common first sign is an unusual noise in the household, perhaps a scratching, a tapping, or footsteps . . . Once inside its victim the demon will usually start off with small mischief— petty theft, arguments, and the like. Its usual MO is to slowly work its way to a stronghold over the victim before revealing its true nature, thus insuring it will not be recognized and exorcised while its grip is still weak. Unfortunately, we see and hear of too many cases where, by the time the demon is discovered, the victim is so far under its control that he or she cannot be brought in for a voluntary exorcism. The chances of recovery from possession in these cases are small.

Ed came back from the beach that afternoon in a wonderful mood. He wanted us to drive out to a seafood restaurant on the bay that he had seen the day before.

"I still don't feel well," I told him. "I want to stay in bed."

He pouted. "Hon, come on, this is supposed to be our vacation."

"I don't want to," I said. "I feel like shit. Ed, I think I—"

Ed, I think I'm going crazy, I was going to say. *I think I'm possessed.* But he cut me off.

"Christ!" he said. "Can't we ever have any fun anymore? Can't we even have one fucking nice weekend at the beach?"

He scowled. The demon's voice screamed in my head, and the next thing I knew I was screaming at Ed.

"You want to have *fun*!" I shouted. "LOOK at me!"

"I just wanted—"

"YOU wanted! All you think about is yourself! Can't you see I'm sick, can't you see there's something WRONG WITH ME? YOU'RE SO FUCKING SELFISH!"

By now I was standing on top of the bed, and I caught sight of myself in the mirror on top of the bureau across the room. My arms were flailing like an animal's, my eyes were wide, my lips dark pink, and my hair in knots, almost dreadlocks.

I looked just like her.

Ed stood in the doorway, disgusted. He turned and walked out of the house.

I collapsed on the bed and started to sob. *You see,* the satiny voice told me, *this is how much he cares. This is the huge love you were so proud of. The one you thought would last forever.*

Ed, however, suffered from no confusion whatsoever. He came back late that night, hours after I had been pretending to be asleep, and went to bed on the sofa without even checking the bedroom to see if I was alive.

When I woke up the next morning he was already awake, sheepishly drinking a cup of coffee at the kitchen table. I sheepishly joined him.

"Hey."

"Hi."

"I love you." He said it first.

"I love you, too." I started to cry.

"Oh honey," he said. He scooted his chair closer to mine and put his arm around my shoulders. "Honey, did you ever think—I mean, you just seem so unhappy lately—maybe it's me, it just seems—I just think—well, maybe you could find someone to talk to. You know, like a therapist or something."

I looked up at Edward and saw his worried face and a strong love swelled in my belly and spread through me. For a moment the love eclipsed the demon's snaking thoughts. A therapist! I loved the idea. I wasn't possessed—I was insane! I would go to a shrink, maybe even to a mental institution for a while, but that was preferable to the alternative. A mental disorder I could handle. I could work with it, accept it, and eventually cure it.

"You're right," I told Ed with a smile. "I think I'm going crazy."

"No, honey, I didn't mean *crazy*, I just meant—"

"No, it's okay. You're right, call it whatever you want. I'll call Dr. Flynn tomorrow and get the name of a shrink."

Ed smiled. I smiled. There we were, husband and wife, one crazy, we thought, and one sane, as happy as happy could be.

the next morning I called Dr. Flynn first thing, and without giving her the details told her I needed an immediate visit with a psychiatrist. She gave me the phone number of Dr. Gerald Fenton, a personal friend of hers who, she assured me, was the best psychotherapist she knew.

"Tell him I sent you," she said before she hung up. "He's very selective. Booked for years. Tell him I sent you."

Dr. Fenton's receptionist told me he wouldn't have an appointment free for a new patient for at least a

117

month, and I almost gave up before I remembered the magic words.

"Dr. Flynn sent me," I told her.

"Well *that's* different," she said. "Let's see . . . Come in today."

"When?" I asked.

"Whatever," she said. "You can come right now, if you like."

I liked it, and I went right away.

Dr. Fenton's office was in a prewar apartment building in a quiet part of town near the park. The streets were lined with trees and women with baby carriages. I smiled at the babies. None smiled back. No living creature looked at me favorably anymore—babies scowled, dogs growled, cats hissed, even chipmunks and squirrels ran away. And other adult humans—well, forget about that. Yet here I was on my way to a psychiatrist's office, trying to convince myself that I had a regular psychological problem.

At Dr. Fenton's building I got buzzed in by a doorman and was then ushered into his office by a young, fashionable receptionist. I was told Dr. Fenton would be with me in a moment. The room looked like I had always imagined a psychiatrist's office would: a leather and wood Eames armchair for the doctor, a leather department store sofa where the patient could sit or recline. An oak bookshelf with psychiatric texts was interspersed with pre-Colombian reproductions and a few African masks propped up on stands. A nice botanical print, lavender, on the wall. A window that looked out to the apartment building across the street.

In a moment or two the doctor arrived with a smile and a warm handshake. Like the office, he fit well with my preconceived notions. Bearded, forty-ish, bifocals, plainly dressed in a beige cardigan, white button-down shirt, and black slacks.

"I'm Dr. Fenton."

"I'm Amanda."

He smiled. I smiled. We beamed at each other.

"So Amanda," he said. "Tell me about why you're here today."

I selectively told him about my strange behavior over the past two months. I told him about arguing with Ed, about the new voice in my head, about the messiness and the new attitude at work. I left out the part about the dog. I left out the part about burning Ed with the cigarette. I especially left out the part about the girl at the beach, which I had already convinced myself could not have happened. In my new, psychiatric world view, these were unrelated coincidences, with no relevance to the topic at hand. The doctor took notes on a yellow legal pad as I spoke.

"So," he said when I was done. "What's the problem?"

I looked at him. "Huh?"

"What is it about these changes that upsets you?"

"This isn't me. I mean of course it's *me*, it's not like it's someone else. What I mean is, it's not my usual personality. That's why I'm here."

"Well," he said, "it sounds to me like you're coming into your own. You're not a girl anymore, you're an adult woman and you need to become more assertive."

"But I fight with my husband," I said. "We're fighting all the time."

He gave me a slightly condescending look. "Fighting," he said, "is a part of any relationship. Fighting is a part of growth."

"But I'm not happy," I said. The snaky voice in my head agreed with the doctor. *Don't argue,* it said.

"That's a problem," the doctor said. "But maybe the problem is that you're resisting growth. The problem is that you're not being open to change."

"But what if I don't want to change like this? What if I don't like what I'm becoming?"

We're growing, the voice said. *We're becoming better and better.*

"You can't fight time," the doctor said. "Amanda, you're thirty-four years old. You're coming into your own."

"But I burned my husband," I blurted out.

"That was an accident," the doctor said. "You slipped. Maybe Edward's not what you think he is, maybe you need to reevaluate your relationship."

I hadn't told him about the incident with the cigarette. I also hadn't told him my age.

"How did you know?" I asked, getting nervous.

"Amanda, relax," he said. "Dr. Flynn sent over your records, it's all in here." He picked up an overstuffed manila folder from the table. "See?"

"I didn't tell Dr. Flynn about the cigarette."

He smiled. "Of course you did. It's right here in your file."

"Let me see that." I reached out my hand. The doctor pulled back.

"Confidential," he said.

"I never told her. Let me see that." My heart was racing.

The doctor scooted back in his chair. I stood up and reached for the file, but with his other hand he seized my wrist and held it, hard. I looked at his face. No smile. No friendly sparkling eyes. He was utterly, deathly serious. I stepped back and he eased his grasp on my wrist, not letting go completely until I was two steps away. I grabbed my coat and purse off the couch beside me and left the office.

later, though, as I walked around the streets of the tree-lined neighborhood, I thought maybe I had been foolish. After all, Dr. Flynn *could* have told him everything that I hadn't. There was no reason to assume anything out of the ordinary was going on. Still, I didn't like him. What was all that talk about becoming myself? He didn't think I was crazy, and if I wasn't crazy, I was possessed. The next day, I would ask Dr. Flynn for a different recommendation, or get one from a friend.

I walked through the park, embarrassed. The fact that I had run out of the doctor's office like a baby didn't exactly boost my self-esteem. What did I think, that the doctor was some kind of a voodoo priest? A satanist, maybe? Really, I was an idiot. I walked down a path that led into a little forest. How had I come to this? How had I—

I heard a rustle of leaves from the trees on my left. I looked around and realized I was deep in the little forest. I didn't see another soul. I shouldn't have been there but it was too late to turn back now. There was nothing to do but go on to the other side. I picked up my pace and walked farther. I heard another rustle— this time on my right. And then a laugh. A woman's laugh coming from the clump of trees on my left, and then again from the bushes on my right. I started to walk quickly, and then run. The rustling of the trees and the woman's laugh followed. I ran until I couldn't run any farther and I had to stop, panting, to catch my breath. I looked around—it didn't seem like I had moved forward at all. Had I been running in place? The trees shook around me and the laughter rolled off them like ripe fruit. The noise was deafening. A thin sweat saturated my clothes.

"Hello?" I said. "Hello?"

But I already knew who it was. I would fight her, I told myself. I would find a way to fight her off, destroy her if I had to, first thing when I got home I would tell Ed and—

The noise stopped. The forest was absolutely quiet, except for my own heavy breathing. The trees around me were perfectly still. My muscles burned. I could barely stand.

I felt a hand on top of my head. I felt it ruffle my hair and softly brush down my right cheek and back up again. It worked its fingers through my hair and massaged my scalp.

I started to cry. The hand started to push. It pushed me to my knees. Then it slid down to my lower back and shoved me onto my belly, grinding me into the rough concrete, until I moaned and gasped for air.

"Amanda," she whispered to me, "I really don't think Edward needs to know about this."

that evening, Ed still at the office, I consulted the RESOURCES section of *Demon Possession Past and Present* again. The second closest spiritual counselor was Dr. Ray Thomas, director and CEO of the Ray of Hope Fellowship.

"Located off Highway 55 North at Exit 12. Make a right at Domino's and then look for the Wendy's— The Ray of Hope Fellowship is in between Wendy's and Coconuts in the Newton Heritage Strip Mall," the book read.

The next morning I drove out to Highway 55, Exit 12, and looked for a Wendy's. The Ray of Hope Fellowship was a low one-story brick building recessed deep in the strip mall with a big sign in the lawn. WELCOME, the sign said. I parked in the lot out front and smoked a cigarette before I went in. It was a bright day and a group of boys were skateboarding in the Fellowship parking lot. MEGADEATH, their T-shirts said. METALLICA. ANTHRAX. I watched the boys and smoked for a few minutes before I got out of the car.

The doors to the Fellowship were open. Inside it looked vaguely like a church, although it just as easily could have been a corporate conference room. Rows of pews, or what could have been benches, faced an altar, or maybe a presentation stand. I walked up the center aisle. No one was around. Nothing seemed to be going on.

"Well, hey there."

I spun around. At the other end of the aisle was a man as nondescript as the building itself. His features were symmetrical and plain, not unattractive but not particularly engaging either.

"You startled me," I said. We walked towards

each other and met in the center. "I'm looking for Ray Thomas."

"That's me," he said, extending a hand. He wore a plain gray suit. We shook. "Let's have a seat." We each sat in a pew on either side of the aisle.

"So," he said loudly—the pews were a little too far apart for conversation. "Let me guess. You think you're possessed by a demon."

I smiled and nodded. His tone of voice put it all in perspective. So you think you're possessed, it said. Don't we all, from time to time.

"I suppose you took that quiz," he continued. I nodded again. "And you answered yes to a few questions, and you got a little spooked, and now you think you're involved in some sort of *spiritual warfare*." He said the last two words with a flourish of his hands that implied hocus-pocus, circus tricks, voodoo. "Let me tell you, publishing that quiz was the dumbest thing we've ever done. I had no idea how many people there were out there with mental health conditions until the calls started flooding in. Not that you're one of them," he added. "Did you bring the book with you?"

I reached into my purse and took out the book, folded open to the quiz page.

"Now let's take a look," Ray Thomas said. We were both smiling, almost chuckling. He took the book and read my marked-up quiz.

Are YOU Possessed by a Demon?

1. I hear strange noises in my home, especially at night, which family members tell me only occur when I am present. (I used to.)

2. I have new activities and pastimes that seem "out of character," and I do things that I did not intend and do not understand. (Yes.)

3. I'm short and ill-tempered with my friends and loved ones. (Yes.)

4. I can understand languages I've never studied, and have the ability to know things I couldn't know through ordinary means. (Yes.)

5. I have blackouts not caused by drugs, alcohol, or a preexisting health condition. (Yes.)

6. I have unusual new thoughts, or hear voices in my head. (All the time.)

7. I've had visions or dreams of personalities who may be demons. (Yes.)

8. A psychic, minister, or other spiritualist has told me I'm possessed. (Yes.)

9. I have urges to hurt or kill animals and other people. (Yes.)

10. I have hurt or killed animals or people. (Yes, definitely hurt, maybe killed.)

Ray Thomas wasn't smiling at all anymore. In fact he was frowning.

"What did you say your name was?" he asked.

"Amanda," I told him.

"Amanda, what we have here is a ninety to one hundred percent chance that you're plagued by an unwanted entity. At the very least we can be one hundred percent sure there's some entity interference going on here. How do you feel about a depossession?"

"Depossession?"

"We don't use the e-word around here," said Ray Thomas. "Fills people's heads with all kinds of ideas. Depossession is a simple process of visualization, separation, and healing. It's the most natural thing in the world."

"Does it work?" I asked.

Ray Thomas smiled again, and nodded his head. "We have over a ninety percent success rate with our depossession treatments here at Ray of Hope."

"What about the other ten percent?" I asked.

"Seven percent. Don't worry about that now."

ray Thomas took me to an office where I signed a release form saying that the procedure I was about to undergo was for entertainment purposes only. Then he led me into a small room behind the altar. The room was lit by fluorescent lights. There was a hospital-type bed made up with white linens and a blue blanket against one wall and a steel desk with a padded rolling desk chair against the opposite wall. He instructed me to lie on the bed. He sat in the rolling chair and scooted over to the bedside, then pulled a chain and turned out the overhead fluorescent.

"We start by visualizing a clean, pure space. Can you visualize a clean, pure space, Amanda?"

"Sure," I said. I stared at the ceiling and thought of an empty white room. The room had tall windows with sheer white curtains, billowing in a sunny summer breeze.

"We visualize with our eyes closed," he said.

"Oh." I closed my eyes and the white room became much clearer.

"You're in your clean, pure space," he said. "You're relaxing in your space. You're breathing deeply."

I was lying on a feather bed on the floor of the white room in a pair of white pajamas. A little sunlight bled in from behind the curtains. The room smelled like honey and flowers. I was somewhat relaxed.

"You're completely safe and secure and comfortable. Nothing can hurt you and you have no fears while you're in your space."

I felt moderately secure and relatively safe.

"Now imagine your unwanted entity. Remember, your space is a safe space, and the entity is there as your guest. You are in control. He or she cannot hurt you in your space."

I sat up from the feather bed. Someone was in the room with me. I turned around. Naamah was crouched on the floor behind me at the head of the bed. "Remember, you're in control here. This is your space, and you're in control of the situation."

Naamah laughed and scurried away, towards a corner of the room that had fallen dark. I couldn't see her but I knew she was there, in the shadows. I looked around the room. All the corners were dark now. She could be in any of them.

"Now imagine a thin silver cord connecting you to your entity."

I felt a yank in my stomach, a twisting like cramps. I looked down and saw a thick black cord, greasy and wet, extending from my pajamas and leading to the far corner of the room.

"In your hand you have a pair of scissors. These are very sharp scissors, and they can cut through anything you want them to."

In my hand I held a dull, old steak knife.

"And with your scissors you snip the cord. It's in your hands. You are now cutting the cord that connects you to your entity."

With the knife I tried to cut the cord, but the opposite happened—the cord cut the knife. The blade grew smaller and smaller until it fell away to nothing, and I was left with an empty plastic handle in my hand. The cord was swollen and hot where the knife rubbed against it.

"And now the cord is cut. I want you to see that the cord is cut, Amanda. I want you to see that you are now free from the entity."

Naamah leapt out of the corner towards me, stopping my heart. The darkness had spread from the corners and now only the center of the room had any light at all, and this a dull dim gray. I saw, without surprise, that the other end of the cord connected to her navel. It dragged on the floor between us.

"Be in your clean, pure space. Feel how good it feels to be free. Be aware of the space inside you where the invader was. We need to fill that hole with healing."

I was full of blood. It came out of my throat and dribbled down my chin. It dripped down onto the floor and slid across the room. The smell was overwhelming.

"And now you're full of the white light of healing. You're a strong, independent person and you can forgive your invader. You can send your entity love and forgiveness, and send it on towards the white light."

Naamah pushed me to the floor of the dark room, now slick with blood, and straddled me.

"Do you forgive me?" she asked.

"And now we're coming awake. We're coming out of our safe, secure place and back into the Ray of Hope Fellowship Headquarters."

My eyes popped open and I saw Ray Thomas standing above me.

"So how did we do, Amanda? Are we feeling free now?"

"Oh yes," I answered, without intent, without my own voice. "I'm so much freer now. This has all been a tremendous learning experience."

the demon wrote a check for $250 and drove back towards the city. Almost there, close to the airport, she stopped at a hotel lounge and made the $250 back having sex with a businessman in the hotel bathroom.

the next day I saw Dr. Flynn for my last checkup after the rabies shots. The first thing she said was, "How was the beach?"

I hadn't told her we were going to the beach. Nothing could be taken for granted anymore. No one could be trusted.

"You told me," I said, "to eat more salt." The book said that salt enhanced the demon's power.

She smiled. "Yes, how's that working for you?"

"I don't know," I answered. "How was it supposed to work?"

She ignored my question and gave me the shot, still smiling.

"And how was Dr. Fenton?" she asked. "Did he help you figure out your problem?"

"Go to hell," I told her. I got up off the table and walked out, leaving Dr. Flynn smirking behind me.

while waiting for a train to take me home from the doctor's office, I saw a quick movement, like a jackrabbit, just to my right. I thought I was seeing things. But then the quick white blur rushed by again. Then again and again, zigzagging back and forth. I was sure I was seeing things. No one else looked. But then a small white hand reached out from behind me to knock the book I was reading, *Demon Possession and You,* out of my hand and onto the tracks. I felt her cheek against mine and saw her black hair falling over my shoulder.

"Amanda, why do you make it so hard?"

*   *   *

i told Ed I didn't like Dr. Fenton, but would find another therapist soon. We were sitting at the breakfast table. Ed was reading the paper. "Fine," he said, nodding his head, and quickly went back to the paper. *This is how much you matter to him,* she told me, *a glance up from the paper, no hugs, no kisses, no questions.*

it all started to pick up speed. The joke was on me. Credit cards arrived for me in the mail, sometimes two or three a day. Not the usual schlock that you get, unasked for, like a virus, but high-end, mega-limit gold and platinum cards, a few I had even been rejected for in the past. When I first moved to the city as a teenager I had never even had a checking account before, and it took a few years and many mistakes before I learned how to handle money, which I now did very well. But those stains were still on my record, and as a result the best I could hack was a high-interest secured card with a thousand-dollar limit. Until now. I had no recollection of filling out the applications for these cards—let alone did I know why I had suddenly been approved—but the cards kept rolling in.

The cards were the kind of computer-generated error I could accept without too much trouble, and anyway, I was happy to have them. It was what she did with the cards that was disturbing: she used them. She wanted to shop. New items appeared in my closet daily, never anything I would have chosen myself, but nothing I was entirely unhappy with, either. Perfumes (she liked rich, heavy florals), a new Nepalese rug for the bedroom, crocodile pumps, and an alligator purse. My new credit cards went over their limit. She got more.

what she wanted most of all, even more than shopping or cigarettes, was men. The men she wanted were not those whom I would have picked. I had always looked for men with kind sympathy in their faces. Men with soft eyelashes who looked away and acted busy when you caught them staring. Men who didn't fidget with their wedding bands.

Naamah, naturally, liked men who hocked their wedding bands in pawnshops. Men who caught your eyes and held them—and then winked. Of course, I only saw them afterwards, when Naamah would leave and I would sink back into consciousness, naked and shivering, in bed with a man I had never seen before.

She didn't hesitate to deal with the men she didn't want, either. I was waiting for a train, on my way back from the Fitzgerald house. It was a little too late to be there, waiting alone for a train. The platform was empty except for myself and one other person, a man. I didn't like the look of him. He had the wrong expression on his face, and a mustache, and the wrong clothes—stained pants and a jacket that was cut-rate ten years ago. He was walking towards me. I wanted to turn around and leave, go back to the token booth and try to call a taxi, but I didn't. Instead I walked towards the man, meeting him halfway.

"Just miss a train?" I heard myself ask. He shrugged. I could not believe I was engaging this man in conversation. He was disgusting up close, with mottled, pitted skin and a shaggy grown-out haircut.

"I hate that," I said. "Especially at night. Espe-

137

cially at night when you're waiting for a train and there's someone there. And you never know. I mean, in the city you just never know who you're dealing with. They might have a knife, or a gun, or whatever. They might, I don't know, be the kind of person who hates men who hang out in train stations, waiting for women. She might be the kind of person who takes men like that and rips them limb from fucking limb with her bare hands."

The man left the station without a word, and the train took me home safe and sound.

in October Ed insisted on having Alex and Sophia over for dinner—a thank-you for the wonderful weekend at the beach. To tell you something about Sophia, I had never, in the six years that I knew her, not on one occasion, seen the soles of her feet. We had spent a week at the beach with them once, and first thing in the morning she slipped into satin wedge-heeled slippers. On the boardwalk she wore high-heel clogs; even in the water she wore cheap plastic thongs. She always wore a black suit, during the week, and always black high heels—strappy sandals in the summer, pumps in the spring and fall, tight curvy boots in the winter. Another thing about Sophia: she colored her hair (I could tell from the unchanging shade of baby blonde), but I never once saw her natural color, not even at the roots, not at her part, not even at the nape of her neck. I also never saw Sophia gain or lose a pound, never saw a wrinkle or a pimple or a pore on her skin, and never saw her sneeze, hiccup, burp, or fart—although she did occasionally release a dry cough from her throat. I couldn't stand her.

To tell you something about Alex, after six years I still knew nothing about him that didn't pertain to either his career or the fruits of that career—beach house, cars, Claire's private schools. I didn't know where he'd gone to high school, his favorite color, what books or movies or music he loved or hated. I was acutely aware, however, that he was a VP before he was forty and had 30 percent of his retirement income in stocks and the remainder in long-term bonds and real estate.

Ed and I had silently decided to put on a pleasant face for his friends and tell them nothing of our problems. Except that somehow Ed had gotten the idea that I would be cooking dinner, and was shocked, when he got home at six, to find out I had nothing prepared.

"I don't understand," he yelled. "You didn't make ANYTHING? We have people coming over in one hour and you don't even have a box of fucking rice in the house? What the hell am I supposed to serve, cereal and ice cream?"

"No, Ed," I told him. "You mean *you* didn't make anything, *you* don't even have a box of rice, and *you* have people coming over in one hour. And no, they can't have my ice cream."

For the first time I couldn't tell who was speaking, me or Naamah.

An hour would have been plenty of time to get something together but we easily killed it fighting and when they got to our place—complaining, as they did with every visit, of how hard our place was to find—we had nothing to serve. Ed confessed that there had been a little mix-up over dinner (he followed this with a revoltingly sycophantic little laugh), and that he'd have to run out and get something. I was beyond even pretending to be amused, and sat sullenly at the kitchen table while Ed babbled. Alex, good sport that he was, went along with Ed for the ride.

Sophia and I were left sitting around the dining table with a bottle of white wine. We both lit cigarettes, the first line of defense against silence and boredom.

"So," I asked her, "what's new?"

"Not much," she said. "We're moving the firm."

"Where are you moving?"

"Just across town. It's just a hassle, that's all. Missing files and everything."

"Moving's a drag."

"Yep."

We smoked and drank our wine. I looked at Sophia, and she was looking at me in an odd way.

"What's different?" she asked.

"What do you mean?"

"You look different. Did you gain a few pounds? It looks good on you. You look healthier."

"No, I don't think so." Of course I knew perfectly well what she was talking about.

"Huh. Well there's *something* different." Sophia was slouching a little in her chair in a typical businessman's posture, legs spread wide. In her right hand was a cigarette and in the other, a glass of wine. Now she put her cigarette out and straightened up in her chair into a stiff, nunlike position, and turned around so she was looking directly at me. I thought she was angry at me. In the corner of my eye I saw something scurry from behind the bedroom door to the bathroom. I was oddly comforted by knowing Naamah was in the room.

"I think," she said from this odd position, "I know what it is."

"What do you mean?"

Out of boredom I had been picking the label off the bottle of wine. Now I looked up at Sophia— and oh, what I saw. Her cheeks bulged out as if she had filled them with air. Her eyes opened wider, and then wider, until they popped almost out of the sockets. Her lips, now thick and en-gorged with blood, dropped apart to reveal black teeth that shrunk before my eyes into stubby little points.

I drew in a sharp breath with a tiny squeal and jumped out of my chair. In doing so I knocked over the bottle of wine. My eyes darted to the table at the sound of glass hitting wood, and then I blinked, and when I looked back up, Sophia was Sophia again. And she was laughing.

"All I meant," she said, "was that you're looking very good."

I stared at her, speechless.

"Oh, don't be silly," she said with a roll of her

eyes. "You're scared. Relax. Soon you'll have the world at your feet."

I said nothing, still frozen. I was just starting to see black, starting to feel myself fade away and the demon rise, when I heard keys rattling by the door. Ed and Alex were back with two shopping bags of take-out Japanese and the laughter of old friends. Naamah slinked back into the shadows, and the rest of the night went on without incident.

the horrible thing with Sophia had been so quick that the next day I thought I might have imagined it. Nothing could be taken for granted anymore. Nothing could be assumed.

So I didn't draw any conclusions from what had happened. But a week later another horrible thing happened: I was about to get into a taxi when a woman, a young redhead, appeared in front of me out of nowhere. She stepped right through the door I held open for myself and slammed it behind her. I stared at her through the window, streaked with rain and bright reflections of the streetlights around us. She looked back up at me, laughing, and rolled her eyes up and around in their sockets, revealing a black glistening hole between her eyelids.

Soon after that, during a meeting with a new client at Fields & Carmine, I bent under the table to get a pen that had somehow jumped out of my hand. There under the table, two seats to my right, was the upside-down face of the new client, also bent over, seemingly in search of his errant pen. He caught my eye. I smiled briefly and intended to straighten up again but the demon held me down as strongly as the client's eyes held mine. The client grinned widely, and then wider, stretching his lips across his entire face. He raised his eyebrows up into high pointy peaks until he resembled nothing so much as a clown. "I know you," he mouthed. His throat didn't make a sound but I heard his words clearly in a deep echoing baritone inside my head.

There were more incidents—an odd glance on line at the bank, a quick contorted face across the street—but none as direct as Sophia had been, and I learned nothing from these odd encounters except that there were others, and that I now had the misfortune of being able to see them. Naamah wasn't particularly interested in them, and I wasn't either. By now the most shocking truth wasn't that there

were more like her and me, or that her ability to manipulate me was growing so rapidly—it was that,
previously, I had been so stupid as to think I had any
understanding of the universe at all.

i went back to Sister Maria's. But Maria wouldn't let me in the door. When she saw me through the glass she ran out to the street and stopped me.

"Oh no," she said. "I have children here, my family lives in back. I can't let you in, not like this."

"Like what? What did I do?"

"Amanda, I can see her. She's stronger than ever. Go, get away from here. I tried to help you once already."

I started to cry. "But what am I going to do?" I pleaded.

"Wait here." Maria went back inside, locking the

door behind her. She came back with another large glass bottle like the one she had given me before. This one was labeled #17: DEMON BURNING EXTRA STRENGTH.

"And use it this time," she said, slipping it into a brown paper bag. "And there's a book that you need. *Possession,* by K. L. Walker. Now go!"

i stumbled away from the store. When I reached a particularly desolate street, lined on either side with weedy lots of burnt cars and old mattresses, I stopped and opened the bag Maria had given me. I opened the bottle and lifted it above my head. I tipped it just a little so that a thin stream trickled onto the crown of my head.

Just then the gray sky split open and fat drops of rain started to fall. I closed my eyes and continued to drip the liquid onto my head. It smelled like anise and musk and ginseng. Through my closed eyes I saw white lightning crack open the sky. My skin stung like a sunburn where the fluid had dripped on it. I opened my eyes to the filthy city street and then I heard laughter. Then I was laughing too, or rather, she was laughing through me. I laughed until I was lying on the filthy concrete, rolling around in yesterday's newspapers and used condoms. I dropped the bottle and it shattered, spilling the potion across the concrete. I rolled in the gutter, wet from rain and bloody from where my skin scraped the concrete and the broken glass. The corners of my mouth started to burn and then crack and bleed, but I kept laughing.

"Amanda," she said through her laughter, our laughter, "did you really think this would work?"

i kept searching for *Possession* by K. L. Walker, the book Maria had told me to read. Missing in every library, sold out in every bookstore. One afternoon I woke up from a blackout to find myself sitting on the floor in front of the mantel. I sat with my legs curled to the side and my face tilted towards the fireplace, as pristine as a girl in a Currier and Ives print. A fire was burning inside it; when my eyes focused and I looked closely I saw a little mountain of books, slowly burning away. As soon as I could, I ran into the kitchen for some water to put out the fire.

Five copies of *Possession*, all burned beyond

restoration, the letters of the title just barely visible on the spines.

I gave up on *Possession* and found another book that looked promising—*Demon Warfare Today*—but she knocked it from my hands again. I bought *Protecting Yourself from Evil* but it vanished between the bookstore and the loft. I had put it in my purse, but when I got home it just wasn't there. Soon I found myself unable to even set foot in a bookstore; I would start out with the best intentions and at the door I would find myself turning away, never able to open the door. I would end up getting an ice cream from a street vendor or stealing another lipstick from a drugstore. The same thing happened if I tried to enter a church, or a synagogue, or even the Society for Ethical Culture, as I tried one bright fall afternoon. Even if I had had the capacity to schedule and keep an appointment with a therapist, I wouldn't have gone. I was sure that there was no one I could trust.

The battle was all mine, and I was quickly, obviously, losing.

soon I didn't have a moment alone. When she wasn't inside me, I could see her scurrying around, looking over my shoulder, ready to jump in if necessary. In the apartment I would see a lock of dirty black hair or a small white foot hiding in the shadows out of the corner of my eye. At the office I would catch sight of her hand, with its long unpolished nails, scribbling alterations over my designs.

Blackouts became common. Ten minutes on the way home from work, an hour, then two or three, then whole days. Ed's birthday came and went and I didn't remember a moment of it. Apparently it didn't go well—the next day he wasn't speaking to me.

Most of the time I was in between the two extremes. I would start a thought—"I really ought to let this person merge in front of me"—and she would finish it—"but why should I?" Or she would start—"We won't go to work today. Instead, I think, we'll get dressed up and go back to that little bar where the bartender had those strong legs." I would scream and cry and beg and fight every way I could imagine, but she would always win. She was stronger, and so she always won.

my new psychic vision, which had seemed like nothing more than a clever parlor trick before, started to turn on me. In early November I was in the Fitzgerald house alone, double-checking the measurements of a wall where a closet would go. I was on the third floor, measuring, when I noticed a dark brown stain on the plaster, one big splash surrounded by an increasingly finer spray. It looked like blood. I tried to avoid the marks but while pulling a tape measure across the wall I couldn't help brushing the side of my hand lightly against a splatter of the stain. The dry skin on the side of my hand, under my smallest finger, barely brushed against the smallest dots of the stain.

When my hand met with the cold wall the world stopped. It all stopped and was instantly replaced with another world. Same room, but it was crowded with cheap, fading clothes. The air was hot and smelled like dirty laundry and cigarette butts. Summertime.

The room was quiet except for the grunts and footsteps of two men grappling in what looked like an equal struggle. The two were of similar size and shape and looked alike. Both were black, of medium build, and dressed in cheap pants and sweat-soaked shirts with wide collars. I couldn't see their faces clearly but their backs looked alike. They could have been brothers.

The man closer to me had something shiny in his right hand. I focused on his hand and my vision zoomed in, like a camera. It was a small knife, an open penknife with a black textured handle. In one lightning-quick motion he freed his right arm from the other man's grip, drew his arm back, and stabbed his brother in the side of the neck. The dying man fell against the wall, where his blood shot out against the plaster and sprayed to where my hand had touched . . .

And then it was over. I was back in the empty, quiet room. I let out a little yelp, ran out of the house, ran to my car, and drove away as quickly as I could.

It didn't end there. The Chinese vanity I had loved so much now had to go. Each time I touched it I was overwhelmed with a flood of sadness that the previous owner had left behind. He was a miserable little man, an antique dealer living alone in the back of his shop, whose main occupation was buying and reading porn. I traded the wardrobe for a plain Shaker-style dresser which carried no emotions at all, just a general sense of industry. A vintage yellow dress I had saved for special occasions now made me nauseated—its previous owner had been a drunk, and when I wore it I felt my liver burn with cirrhosis.

ON the first day of December I set out to buy Ed a Christmas present. Over the summer he had admired a little silver salt bowl in a ridiculously overpriced shop uptown, and I wanted to see if it was still there before I bought another blue sweater.

I was amazed at how quickly we'd fallen apart after the weekend at the beach. Even peaceful moments were glazed over with anger and resentment. No more laughing at bad movies. No more pet names. No more talking in our own secret code. Our time together was all very formal now.

"Are you going to the store?"

"Yep. You want something?"

"Can you pick me up some orange juice? The one—"

"Yeah, I know. Sure."

"Thank you."

"No problem."

I was walking down a quiet, tree-lined street on my way to the store. The air was cold and dry even though the sun was bright. On either side of me were the huge gingerbread limestone and marble houses that made the neighborhood famous. Most of them were apartment buildings now, or private schools. I walked and daydreamed. She would leave me, eventually. She would grow sick of me, get tired of the fighting, and leave me alone. I would finally be able to tell Ed the truth and he would have to forgive me.

A door to my right opened up and a crowd of girls

poured out, nine or ten years old, each seemed to have the same fine creamy skin, and thick hair held back in a ponytail. A few were wrapped in scarves and gloves and earmuffs, but most wore their coats open. I stopped to let them go. I wasn't in a hurry. I lit a cigarette and watched the girls pass. Behind the crowd were two women—teachers, I guessed. They looked at me pointedly. Just doing their jobs, I thought, the girls were their commodity, to be guarded with their lives. One of the girls was running in my direction, to catch a bus or an after-school dance class, and she turned her head around to call to a friend—"Call me tonight! Don't forget!"—and ran right into me. I grabbed her elbows to keep her from falling. She was momentarily stunned.

"I'm sorry!" she said. She was a brunette with a worried look on her little face. It was clear she expected a talking-to. I let go of her elbows and gave her a smile.

"Don't worry," I told her. "No harm done."

She smiled with relief and went running on her way. To my left I saw Naamah's shadow, standing behind me.

The crowd of girls thinned out and I went on. But further down the block I was hit again, this

time by a woman a little older than me, barreling
down the street in such a hurry I couldn't jump out
of her way quickly enough. She stumbled a bit
when she ran into me, and I took her arm to steady
her. Her blonde hair was crisply fluffed around her
face and over her forehead, arranged to hide her
wrinkles.

"Excuse *me*," she said, cold and sarcastic. She
tried to pull her arm back. I wanted to let go of her
wrist. I wasn't that angry. But my hand wouldn't
comply.

"You shouldn't talk to strangers," I told her. "You
should look both ways before you cross the street."
My eyes shifted out of focus and the world turned a
hazy black streaked with red as I heard myself
speak.

Finally the words slowed to a stop and the haze
cleared back into focus. The woman lay on the
ground, sobbing. I had snapped her wrist in two.

i tried to tell Edward. I tried to tell anyone who
would listen. But now, I found, it was too late. I
opened my mouth to speak and the wrong words

came out. *Edward, help me,* became *Edward, pass the salt. I'm possessed* turned into *I'm tired.*

I tried to catch her off guard, to scream out the truth at an unexpected moment. But you can't surprise a thing that lives inside you. The screams came out of my throat as long, dry coughs. *Help me,* I was screaming inside, *save me*—but all anyone heard was a long *ahem.*

Each day I would wake up and say to myself, Today, no more of this nonsense. Today, I am going to put all this craziness behind me and be a normal human being.

And she would answer: *But I love you, Amanda. I love you and I'm never leaving.*

Go! I would silently scream at her. *Get out!*

Oh no, she would answer, *I'm not going anywhere.* Then, first thing, she would start a fight with Ed. He would say "Good morning" and I would try to say "Good morning" back and nothing would come out. I would struggle and twist and try to use my vocal chords to speak and I couldn't. My throat was hers now. So I would say nothing at all. "Well *someone's* in a good mood," he would say, eyebrows raised. Or maybe after "Good morning" she would say "What's so fucking good about it?" or "Why isn't there more coffee?" or—and this was the worst—she would say "Good morning" back, the words so swampy with sarcasm that Ed would slam down his coffee and leave for work without saying good-bye.

every night now, after I fell asleep, she took me to the crimson beach by the red sea.

"Why," I asked her. "Why me?"

"Why not you," she answered. "Who would be better?"

I couldn't answer that. "I don't know what you want," I told her. "Tell me. I'll give you anything, whatever you want."

"All I want is you," she said. "I can't have fun without you."

"What do you want?" I begged. "What fun?"

"This."

* * *

we were back on solid ground, in a big glistening room with thousands of tiny lights. Chandeliers. A party. Black tie. The noise of the party was a steady, faraway roar.

I was standing by the bar, one finger tracing the neckline of my dress. It looked like me, it *was* me, but it was her. I was dressed perfectly. Black dress, sheer hose, shiny spike heels. I felt a thick coating of makeup on my face and a strain on my scalp where my hair was pulled into an upsweep.

There was a tap on my shoulder. I turned around; a man stood behind us, smiling. He was young and blond with a big smile. In his tuxedo he looked almost like a boy playing dress up.

"I thought you were meeting me on the dance floor," he said.

I shrugged. "I don't feel like dancing. Why don't we go for a walk instead?"

"Where to?"

"Around." I took his hand and led him across the big room to a little hallway hidden behind the dance floor. We walked; the hall got darker and the wallpaper ended and the carpet stopped. The sounds of the party were gone. We walked down a short flight of stairs to a concrete basement. The mechanisms supporting the party were hidden here—a walk-in freezer, a boiler, pipes that led from one mystery to another. The room was lit by a few bare bulbs.

"What are we doing here?" he finally asked. He smiled again but the smile was now a little nervous, a little forced. He was scared. I stepped towards him and kissed him, and he relaxed into my arms. While we kissed I began to take off his clothes: first the jacket, then the tie, then the shirt. The skin on his back was perfectly warm and smooth. I was lost in his skin and his lips, against the back of my eyes I saw a deep dark red. I was running my nails hard over his back, biting his lip, his tongue. He tried to push me away but he couldn't, I was too strong. Blood was trickling down his chin from his lip. He tried to scream but I muffled it with my mouth. I dug my nails deep into his back until the perfect skin was ripped. He tried to get hold of my arms, tried to do something, anything, but Naamah was stronger. She was bringing one hand up to his neck when we were interrupted.

"Hey!" we heard from the top of the stairs.

"Who's down there? Come back up, no one's allowed—"

I dropped him and ran.

we were back on the red beach. Crimson fish
jumped in and out of the ocean. The wind blew my
hair around my face.

"Why?" I asked her again.

"Why, why why?" She was making fun of me.
"You know why, Amanda. You let me in. You invited
me."

"You're LYING," I screamed. "I never wanted any
of this."

"Look!" She pointed to the horizon. Across the
sky a scene was played out. It was me and Ed in the
loft, the night I burned him with a cigarette. We sat
on the sofa. I moved my arm to put out my cigarette,
and just like I remembered, my right arm made a
quick turn to stick Ed in the leg with it. He screamed.
I screamed. And then the vision froze. In that split
second after the scream, a quick, small smile flashed
across my face. I was glad, glad because Ed deserved
it, that and worse.

"You made me!" I screamed. "You made me do it and you made me like it! All of it."

Naamah sighed, clearly impatient. "I never made you do anything," she said. "I only let you do what you wanted. I told you, Amanda, I can't have fun without you."

my performance at work started to slip. I came in late, I left early, I often skipped important meetings altogether. The work that I did do was creatively brilliant but technically sloppy. The demon had no mind for specifics—she didn't even care if a design was physically possible, for that matter, as long as it was pretty. My coworkers grumbled but I had been well liked before. Everyone, I imagined, wanted to give me another chance.

Everyone except James Cronin. He went to Leon Fields and John Carmine, ratted me out on the few shortcomings they hadn't yet noticed, and got himself placed in charge of the Fitzgerald house.

Nothing happened for the first week. And the second went off fine. But halfway through the third I was not surprised to find myself at the office late one night, asking him out for a drink.

We were alone in the office. James, Naamah, and me. He was sitting at his desk and I was standing next to him, unclear of how I had arranged for us to be there. Most of the lights were off. Only the one fluorescent fixture above his desk shone down on us, casting the room beyond into shadow.

"How about a drink?" I heard her ask.

"Huh?" James asked.

"Come on," she said. "One drink. I'm not ready to go home yet." I felt my lips turn up. One eyebrow arched and my head tilted slightly toward the right.

"Sure. Why not?" He stood up and reached for his coat. Then the edges of my vision turned darker and darker until I was seeing through a pinhole, and before we were out the door everything was black and I wasn't, I no longer was . . .

And then I was back. A horrible smell, years of urine and decay. Darkness. After a moment my eyes adjusted and I saw that I was outdoors, in an alley.

No, not an alley, but a tunnel. I turned around. The tunnel was about fifty feet long and ten feet wide, with a dim light at either end. Under the smell of piss was another smell, familiar, a mix of grass and dirt and shit. The park. I was in a tunnel under a hill in a city park.

I was standing above James Cronin's body. He was lying on his back. His neck was bent so his head was parallel to his shoulders and behind it I could see a thick pool of blood.

I stepped over James and walked ten feet south. Aside from my footsteps the tunnel was silent. Along the wall were the remains of an old water fountain, a stunning mosaic of Medusa, snakes coiling from her head; in better days water would have flowed from her mouth. Her eyes looked at me with complete understanding. I had always loved that fountain.

I walked back to where James lay and crouched down to look at him. Of course he hadn't moved. His jacket was open and the top of his pants was undone. He had probably been promised a little lurid semi-public fun. His face looked like it always did; even dead he looked smug.

There was nothing I could do. So I stood up,

walked out of the tunnel, walked through the park to the streets of the city, and then hailed a taxi to take me back home.

james, naturally, didn't come to work the next day or call in sick. At lunchtime a collective anxiety began to swell in the office. It wasn't like James not to show up. It wasn't like James not to call. A few people left messages on his answering machine. *James, we just want to know if you're okay. James, we're worried—please call the office.* The anxiety grew and by four o'clock we were asking each other, Does James have a girlfriend? Do you know any of his friends, relatives? Well, it's just one day, we reassured each other. Just a day. If he's not in tomorrow, we'll do something. No one knew what, exactly, we would do, but we were quite sure if he wasn't in tomorrow we would take action.

At lunchtime the next day Ginny McPhee called the police. Alex Levaux told her she was overreacting.

"I don't care," she said sharply. "It's wrong, to sit here and do nothing when James could be in the hospital or sick or something."

Two officers in blue uniforms came. Ginny gave them the general lowdown. They asked the questions you would expect, each one irrelevant. Was James a drug addict? Alcoholic? Gambler? Did he owe anyone money? I listened from my desk nearby.

The anxiety built to a crescendo when Ginny McPhee phoned the police again the next morning and was told that James was now officially missing. Fields & Carmine called his family in Ohio. Ginny checked in with the police every day. No leads, no evidence, no clues. Then something happened at Fields & Carmine I wouldn't have expected—we got used to it. We stopped talking about it. Stopped thinking about it. The office settled into a new pattern, a pattern where James was gone and that was that. Like the good stapler that was on your desk every morning for years, the best one that never jammed, and then one day it was gone. You spent a few days poking around for it and then you got a new one, and went on with your life, and accepted the disappearance as one of life's little mysteries, never solved. That's what we did with James.

Except Ginny McPhee. She cried at her desk. She talked about him all the time. She called the police every day until they finally had an answer, two weeks after his death: James had been mugged and killed in the park after leaving work on Tuesday. His body had been found the next morning but there had been a little mix-up with the ID. It was unlikely that the man who did it could be caught this long after the fact. So unlikely that the police made it perfectly clear it wasn't worth putting a lot of time and money into the thing. Fields & Carmine closed the office for the rest of the week and on Sunday we all cried at his funeral. Then on Monday we all went back to work and settled back into a new routine, a routine where one of our coworkers was dead, and that was the end of James Cronin.

SOON after that I stopped going to work. I don't know if I gave notice or just stopped going, only that I never found myself at Fields & Carmine anymore. Ed had no idea. In better days he had called me at work twice a day but it was months now since either of us had called just to hear the other's voice and say hello. By the time he even knew I had lost my job, it was the least of our concerns.

* * *

again, I found myself in the dark little bar around the corner from what used to be my office. Again, I was sitting with the same man—handsome, tattooed, drunk.

"Eric," I said. I didn't know how I had gotten here or how I knew his name, but here I was.

"Naamah," he said. "That's a weird one. What's that, Arabic?"

"Satanic," I answered.

"Huh?"

"Akashic."

"What's that, like Persian?"

"Oh yes."

"Huh. So, are we going?"

"Going?"

"For a ride. You said you wanted to go for a ride."

"Right," I said. "I'm coming. We're going."

christmas and New Year's came and went. I missed them entirely. The days were short and cold and the nights far too long. Ed stopped asking where I had been. No longer expected me home for dinner, no longer responded when Naamah tried to pick her little fights. He was at the end of his rope now. He had tried kindness, understanding, suggestions, attempts at therapy, he had yelled at me, he had pleaded, ignored, and now, finally, he was going on with his life.

The tables started to turn, and Edward was the one picking the fights. He was the one late for dinner, and then late for bed, and then home late, late, into the night.

The proof was a phone call. He thought I was out, not surprisingly. We'd given up keeping track of each other's whereabouts, and I wasn't usually home in the evenings anymore. But that night I was in the bedroom. The demon was doing something with the herbs she kept buried in my lingerie drawer. The little bundles of twigs and roots had started showing up a few weeks ago. What she did with them, I was never quite sure, but the time the demon spent at home was often spent with them, burning a little pile in an ashtray or rearranging the bundles into different combinations. Luckily the demon was interested in what Ed was saying and so she took me closer to the wall to listen. He was on the phone with someone.

"No. I don't know. I don't think she's going to the doctor anymore." A pause for the woman on the other end to answer. "I don't know what I'm going to do. No, not tonight, I'm already home. Tomorrow . . . Yeah, I know. It has to change . . . Of course I tried talking to her, I tried a million times. Look, just drop it, okay . . . No, I really don't want to talk about it. Tomorrow. Tomorrow . . . All right, good night . . . I love you, too."

Edward hung up the phone, and the demon went back to playing with her herbs.

SOON Ed was spending whole weekends out of the house. He made vague claims about business trips that neither of us pretended to believe. When he was home, he slept on the couch. We used chilly exaggerated "pleases" and "thank yous" with each other. If one of our limbs were to brush against the other person's it was immediately retracted and stiffened.

On his last day at home, Ed found me in bed with another man. The man had come to read the gas meter, apparently, and I couldn't say for sure what happened after that. When Ed came home, the man got up, got dressed, and scurried out of the building so quickly I didn't see him go.

Edward left me right then and there.

I lay on the bed, still naked, and cried silently to myself. Ed pulled out a brown leather suitcase I had never seen before and started packing. Even now I can't stop thinking about that suitcase. Was he waiting for this occasion? Did his girlfriend buy it for him?

He spoke the whole time that he packed, throwing as many clothes around the room as into the suitcase. Through the demon's filter I heard only snatches of words and phrases.

"I knew it . . . I fucking knew it . . . Bullshit . . . Responsibility . . . Refuse to take responsibility . . . Refuse to talk about it . . ."

Edward threw a shoe across the room. I felt my lips bend into a smile. I rolled back and forth on the bed and I heard myself laughing. The demon was hysterical, ecstatic. She wanted him gone. The last thing I remember from that day is Edward kneeling by the bed, trying to get me to focus on his words.

"Amanda, are you listening? Amanda this is TOO MUCH. I'm leaving. Amanda, do you hear me? I'M LEAVING!"

with Ed gone, time slipped away from me. I would wake up from a blackout thinking an hour or two had passed to find out days had gone by. Occasional slices of consciousness blended into each other and I was left with a string of non sequiturs.

I was in a bed, on a huge round mattress with the

softest sheets I've ever felt. The walls were sky blue with white rococo trim around the top. It reminded me of the Fitzgerald house. The room was huge, almost as big as the loft. It was maybe the biggest room I'd ever seen. I was naked and alone. And then the blackness drowned out my eyes and ears and the rest of me and I was gone.

Out of the blue room. Back in the loft. I was sitting in front of the fireplace, methodically burning each item of Ed's clothing. There was a knock at the door. No, a knock on *a* door. From the inside of the bathroom. The immense dining-room table had been moved in front of the bathroom to keep someone in.

"Please," a woman was crying out. "I'll do anything, just please let me out. I need a doctor. I've been hurt."

"Oh no," Naamah answered. "I don't think you're done yet."

Pink. Lots of pink. Slowly I saw I was in a woman's bedroom. No, a lingerie shop. Everything was pink and gold. The type of store found in every upscale mall and shopping district in the country. I could have been anywhere. Thin notes of classical music streamed through the aisles of wiry bras and flimsy negligees. I was walking down a long rack of bras, pulling out a lacy number every few feet. With a jagged, chipped fingernail on the index finger of my right hand I tore into the softest part of each little confection. *Rrrrrrrrrip* into white lace, red satin, black sheer nylon. *Rrrrrrrrrip*; a yellow underwire makes a particularly satisfying little sound. I walked the rest of the aisle and then back up the other side, singling out every fourth or fifth bra for a nice deep *rrrrip*.

Days later. All around me was grayness and a sour smell. On a train. The car was half full. A few men in sorry, sagging suits, women with too many children. I looked down; I was wearing a black dress I'd never seen before, buttoned down the front, very nice, and an equally mysterious pair of white leather pumps. Eyes. I felt a pair of furtive eyes darting up at us and then away, up and then away. I looked up; across the car I saw a dirty, rat-faced young woman, twenty at the oldest, watching me with a repulsive, knowing smirk. Greasy dark hair fell straight down from her scalp to the top of her shoulders. She wore a grimy denim jacket and underneath that a black top with the name of a death metal band on it. Her dishwater eyes shone. The rat face glanced around to make sure no one was watching and then turned back to give me her full attention. Then she stuck out her tongue, wide and flat, straight down to her chin. The top half of her body leaned backwards and her tongue slowly curled up towards her nose. For all the world she looked like a snake charmer with a wide, pink snake. The pink snake stretched to the tip of her nose, past the bridge, and then up to rest its tip in between her eyebrows. To my horror—and to Naamah's great amusement—the girl, with the blue underside of her tongue covering half of her face, leaned back even further, so her head was facing the ceiling, and her eyes rolled back to show only the whites.

From under her tongue came a little black cloud that smelled like blood. I watched in awe as the cloud floated towards my mouth. When it was close enough Naamah opened her mouth, leaned towards the cloud, and ate it right out of the air, as easy as a frog swallowing a fly.

I woke up on a street corner not far from home, vomiting into a trash can.

"Miss? Excuse me, miss."

I looked up to see a police officer standing in front of me, a burly mustached beefcake of a man trying to peek down my shirt. He offered me a ride home. I gratefully accepted. In the back of the squad car the doors didn't have latches. A thick divider of plastic separated the front seat from the back—or would have if the officer had shut it.

They always trust a pretty face.

And then the officer said, "The wife's got it, too. The stomach flu. Last week the kids had it, now my mother's coming down with it. It's a killer, this virus, it's a fucking killer and they all got it."

He paused and looked in the rearview mirror, where he saw me staring at him. He cleared his throat and adjusted his hat on his head.

"Excuse me," he said. "I apologize. What I mean is, the flu is a terrible thing."

We were back on the red beach by the crimson sea. Now I knew that the sea was blood, and it had stained the sand. She dipped in and out of the ocean, as sleek and happy as a dolphin.

I turned and tried to run. But it was as if I were the one who was underwater, I couldn't gather the momentum to move my arms and legs. And then she was right next to me, standing on the beach, smiling to show her small pointed teeth, watching me try to run.

"Amanda," she said, "stop trying. I love you. I'm never letting you go."

and then one day, during a long white snowstorm, Ed came home. The demon had brought me back to the apartment after days of her kind of fun and there he was, sitting on the sofa in a rumpled suit and tie, a little puddle of melted snow around his feet. For the first time in weeks I found my own voice.

"Ed," I cried. I ran to him, to his sad, aged face, and sat down close and put my arms around him. He stayed still and tense in his forward-facing position but I didn't mind. Just to see him again was more than I had hoped for. After a quick moment of having him in my arms he pulled away and stood up. He paced awkwardly in front of the sofa, looking out the windows, towards the door, anywhere but at me.

"I tried to call," he said. "I wrote. You never answered. I thought maybe you'd moved. I, I—"

He started to cry. He fought it at first, said "I" a few more times in a strangled, choked voice and then admitted he was crying, let his face crumple and tears pour down and his nose run as he paced. My heart leapt. Maybe there was a way, I thought, I could explain and—

"Oh Ed, I—" *I love you,* I wanted to say. *I love you and I miss you and I don't know why this happened. To us, out of everyone in the world. Remember the flowers you gave me on our third date? Remember the seagulls we laughed at on the beach last year? The horrible movie, the one with the subtitles, we made jokes about for weeks. Long Saturdays in the park. Sundays at the flea market. The Christmas party where we drank so much and got in a huge fight and almost killed each other, the next day it was so funny. The candy you bought me when you didn't come home. It's not fair. It's not fair.* But Naamah locked my throat closed and I sat poker-faced as he pulled himself together.

"I'm filing for a divorce," he said. "I want to get married again."

All the nights I waited. The nights you never called.

"I'm sure it's not a surprise. It's been over a year. She—well, I know you know. We both—there's no point in getting into it. I don't know why we could never talk about it, we could have done this so much sooner, we could have both gone on . . ."

The rooftop pool in California where we watched the sunset. All the take-out meals. The feel of your skin warm and dry against mine. Your mother's birthday parties. Your father's funeral. We were going to go to Hawaii someday, to Paris someday. We were going to buy a new dishwasher, a new car. Nothing's changed, I wanted to say, not for me, I'm still here, look at me, look at me—but when I tried to open my mouth I couldn't. I was falling, down into the thick red haze, an endless black well, I clung and grasped with all my might, I wanted to stay, but there was nothing to cling to, nothing to grab, and I fell and fell until I was gone.

I was lying on the crimson sand by the blood red sea. Naamah lay next to me. She smiled and in the sand she wrote two words with her left index finger: I WIN.

185

first was Lilith. She was Adam's first wife but she wasn't good enough at all, she wouldn't lie down and take it and she wouldn't do what she was asked or told. So I was made to order. Everything would be in place. Everything would be just so. There wouldn't be any mistakes, this time, and so on the new wild earth he watched while I was made from a handful of clean dust. First were the bones. He started with the feet and then up the legs to the hips, spine, and ribs, out for the arms, and then the white round skull on top. Next was what I needed to live—liver, spleen, bowels, uterus, heart and lungs, brain, eyes and *tongue, all made from dust before my partner's eyes. Then the muscles were layered on, then the fascia, the meridians, the tendons, and the veins. I was filled with blood, bile, mucus, tears. And then I was wrapped in skin and sprinkled with hair and the new lids on my eyes rolled up and the irises rolled down and, now complete and real, I saw my partner, alone in the world with me.*

My first sight was his face twisted with disgust, before he quickly turned away. He was disgusted by me, and begged never to have to look at me again. Because he had never known what was inside before. He had imagined a person was as sleek and neat on the inside as outside. He couldn't stand the mess, the chaos, the blood.

I wasn't needed. I wasn't wanted. But Lilith taught me a few tricks on the banks of the Red Sea. When Adam refused to sleep with Eve, horrified that Cain had killed Abel, I came to him in his sleep. He thought it was a dream, but he was the father of my first child.

They can't say no. All I need is a way in. A dream is the easy way but then they never know, they never even know I had them. I need someone like Amanda. She says she didn't know. She says she didn't want me. But I couldn't have gotten in if she didn't want me. Everyone wanted me. Each and every one.

Everyone except Ed.

then I was sitting on the sofa in our apartment. Through the windows I saw a wall of white snow falling down. People were everywhere, all of them moving, walking from one room to another and back again. Two were snapping photos, a few more were looking through the apartment, poking under the table and in the bookcases. A strange kind of party. A man took my picture; I shuddered at the bright light. When my eyes cleared I looked toward the open door of the bedroom. Where was Ed?

My hearing faded back in. At first all I heard was a general buzz, the chatter of the party, and then one voice singled itself out. A man was talking to me, yelling almost, right in my ear. I turned my head. The man was sitting next to me on the sofa, an older man with slicked back hair and a cheap suit, talking loudly at me.

"Why did you DO IT? Were you having AN AFFAIR? Did he GAMBLE? Did he DRINK?"

Shhh, I tried to tell him, you don't have to yell, but the words came out garbled and fuzzy; my mouth wasn't all mine again yet. I looked down and saw a stain on my dress, a big red wet stain on my abdomen. I'm bleeding, I tried to tell the man. He watched me carefully as I unbuttoned my jacket and then my shirt. Everyone was watching but if I was bleeding to death, I thought, I certainly ought to be able to see the wound. But after my shirt was undone and my stomach was bare there was no red. It wasn't me who was bleeding.

"Ed," I screamed. I jumped up off the sofa. "Edward!" Everyone in the room stopped moving and looked at me.

"Where is he?" I screamed.

No one answered. They stood still around me and watched as I ran to the bathroom, which was empty, then to the kitchen, also empty, and then to the bedroom.

In the bedroom, blood was everywhere. Splattered on the walls, smeared on the floor. The bed was soaked through with it. On the white cotton sheets we had picked out together last year. On the goose down pillows Ed's mother had given us two years ago for Christmas. On the black-and-white quilt we'd found at a flea market upstate, one beautiful sunny Saturday three years before. The smell was sickening. I closed my eyes and wished it all away, but when I opened them again nothing had changed. The man with slicked back hair stood next to me again.

"Why did you DO IT? Why did you KILL him?"

I moaned and vomited on the floor. When I held my head back up I saw, finger painted in browning crimson on the white wall above the bed:

I WIN.

someone in the building, I guess, called the police. His screams must have been unbearably loud—our nearest neighbor was two stories down. With the assistance of a public defender, who was obviously terrified of me, I pleaded to insanity and agreed to indefinite incarceration in a psychiatric hospital.

First I stabbed a girl with one of those homemade knives. I don't know why. Then, in solitary, I grew my nails long and attacked one of the guards. Lucky for her she wasn't pretty to begin with. So I got moved to high security.

She has a grand old time here, she has all the girls following her orders, she's sleeping with one of the guards and maybe one of the doctors. She's like a fox in a chicken coop here in the hospital.

When I have a rare moment to myself, I lay in bed and think about Edward. I try to think of the good times, about how beautiful he was, his blond hair falling over his eyes just so when he smiled. And our home, our great big beautiful loft. I try to hold on to every last inch of him; his hands with the always-perfect square nails, thin gold band around his third finger; the soft curve where his neck dipped into his chest, and then rose to meet his collarbone; the way he liked everything just so; he would be so pleased when the apartment was clean and everything was in its place.

But as much as I try, mostly what I remember is the bedroom filled with blood.

of course she fought at first. They all do. And then they see the possibilities and they're happy to go along. She could have gone on forever, in her small lonely life. But sometimes the door to a bigger life opens, and it isn't so easy to say No. You can't spend your whole life saying No. Sometimes you have to say Yes, and see where it takes you.

i'm hers all the time now, and when I see a small slice of the world it's through her eyes, which used to be mine. Once, some time ago, I caught sight of myself in a mirror. I looked so different, older, but really more beautiful. My hair was thick and it was longer than before, and my skin was creamy and smooth. At night she takes me to the crimson beach by the red sea and we lie down and she wraps her arms around me. She tells me I'm beautiful, that she still loves me as much as she ever did, that she still wants us to be friends.

"I'll never leave you," she tells me, and she jabs with her tongue. "I love you," she tells me, "I'll never leave you alone." And that's all I've ever wanted, really: someone to love me, and never leave me alone.

"josephine."

Maude said my name flatly, like I was dead or she wanted me to be. I sat across from her at a booth in the back of the bar, where the daylight never reached and the smell of stale beer and cigarettes never cleared. Maude had been the mistress of a gangster back in the thirties and he'd bought her this bar to set her up with something after he was gone. It was on the corner of Broadway and West Fourth, and if you'd never been there before it would take a minute to notice that there wasn't a girl in the place, other than Maude. And now me. It was a queer joint. She let the boys hang out here because it was good business—it's not like they had too many other places to go—and of course there was an even better business in keeping their secrets.

"Hiya Maude." She looked at me as if I were speaking another language. Pink lipstick was smeared on her lips, and she was squeezed into a gold strapless dress two sizes too small. Her hair was done up in a big blond pouf on top of her head.

I reached into my purse and pulled out a gold ring with a small diamond in a plain setting. An engagement ring. It was good. I'd boosted it from Tiffany's the day before.

I handed the ring to Maude. She grabbed it with her fat white hand, and then got out a magnifying glass from her pocketbook and looked the ring over, holding it up so it caught the yellow light coming from the bulb on the wall. She took her time. I didn't mind. Someone put a song on the jukebox. A few men started to dance with each other, but the bartender yelled at them to stop. They gave it up and went back to their seats. If the cops came in and saw dancing, everyone in the place would be locked up.

Maude looked the ring over a few more times and then looked up at me and said, "Fifty."

"I could do better in a pawnshop," I said. I couldn't hit Tiffany's every day and I wanted a good price. I wanted this ring to feed me for a month.

"Then do it," she said.

I held out my hand for the ring. She tapped it on the table, looking at me. We went through this every time.

"One hundred," she said.

I kept my hand where it was. She looked at the ring and fondled it a little. Black makeup spread out around her eyes when she blinked.

"One fifty," she finally said.

I nodded. She reached into her little gold pocket-book and counted out seven twenties and a ten and rolled them up tight. She handed the money to me under the table. I counted it and then put the roll in my purse.

"Thanks, Maude," I said.

She didn't say anything. I stood up to go, and then she said, "Hey. If you see Shelley, you can tell her not to show her face around here no more."

I looked at her and sat back down. "What's the problem?"

"I ain't got a problem," Maude said. "Not with you. But Shelley, she brought me a bracelet, swore up and down it had a real emerald in it. Later I found out it was paste. She ain't welcome here no more."

"She must have thought—"

"I don't care what she thought," Maude said. "It was paste. I don't care if the King of Siam gave it to her. If you see her, tell her I don't want to see her again."

I sighed. "All right," I said. "If I pay it off, you'll help her out the next time she's in a jam?"

Maude nodded. "I don't hold grudges, Josephine. You know that."

"Okay," I said, feeling heavy. "What'd she burn you for?"

"Two hundred," Maude said.

"You never gave anyone two hundred dollars in your life," I said. "Not even if it *was* the King of Siam." We haggled all over again for a while. Finally we agreed that one twenty-five would cover it, and I handed back over most of the money she'd just given me. I stood up and left. Ordinarily I would have stayed and played a bit of pool—some of the queers were good, and I liked to stay in practice—but I had an appointment downtown.

the bright sun outside was a shock after Maude's. It was one o'clock in the afternoon on May 14, 1950, in New York City. On Broadway I hailed a taxi to take me down to Fulton Street, and then I walked a few blocks until I found number 28. It was quite a place, a tall narrow building that looked like someone had poured it in between the two buildings on either side. The whole front of it was white stone carved up with clouds and faces and stars, and it came to a point at the top like a church. A doorman in a sharp blue uniform with gold braid opened the door for me with a big smile. Inside there were marble floors with clean red rugs and streams of people coming in and out, busy people in suits with briefcases and very important places to go. In the middle of the lobby was a big marble counter where a good-looking fellow in the same uniform sat guiding everyone on their busy way. But I already knew where I was going.

An elevator man in another blue suit and another big smile brought me up to five. On the fifth floor there were four mahogany doors set into mahogany paneling, each with a shiny brass doorknob and a frosted window with the name of the company painted in gold and outlined in black. Painted on the first door was *Jackson, Smith and Alexander, Attorneys-at-Law*. The next was *Beauclair, Johnson, White and Collins, Attorneys*. The third was *Piedmont, Taskman, Thompson, Burroughs, Black and Jackson, Law Office*.

The last door had nothing on it. That was the one I was looking for.

It was open. Inside was a waiting room with a pretty brunette girl in a white suit and black-rimmed eyeglasses sitting behind a desk. There was a beautiful red Persian rug on the floor and two ugly oil paintings of landscapes on the walls. Three oversized leather armchairs were set around a low wood table that had copies of *Forbes* magazine fanned out on it.

The girl smiled at me. I didn't smile back. I was tired of smiling.

"I'm here to see Mr. Nathaniel Nelson," I said. "We have an appointment. Josephine Flannigan."

"Certainly, Miss Flannigan."

She hopped up out of her chair and led me through a door behind her. On the other side was a corner office room about five times the size of the room I lived in. Here was an even bigger desk and a lot more leather furniture and a man and a woman. The man sat behind the desk. He was about forty-five, with silver hair and big brown eyes, and wore a dark gray suit that looked like it had been custom made for him. He looked tired, but had a strong jaw and a square face that looked like it wouldn't take no for an answer, like he had been the boss for so long he forgot he wasn't really the boss of anything at all.

I took a deep breath, and inhaled the smell of money.

The woman sat to the left of the desk. She was about forty and didn't look like much at all. She was pretty enough, if you didn't like personality in your women. She had blonde hair pulled back from her face in a plain, perfect chignon. She wore a black suit that showed nothing and didn't seem to be hiding much of anything at all, and too much makeup over a face that looked just this side of being alive.

"Mr. Nelson," I said. "How do you do. I'm Josephine Flannigan."

He stood up, leaned across the table, and shook my hand. He was taller than I thought he'd be, taller and wider. "How do you do, Miss Flannigan. This is my wife, Maybelline Nelson."

She stood up and I took her hand. It was limp.

The girl left and closed the door behind her and we all sat down. I took off my gloves and put them across my lap. Mrs. Nelson rested her eyes on something ten feet past me and over my left shoulder. Mr. Nelson looked at me and opened his mouth but I spoke first. I knew his type. If I let him take hold of the conversation, I'd never get it back.

"So, Mr. Nelson, who was it that gave you my phone number?"

"Nick Paganas," he said. I looked blank so he added: "I think you know him as Nick the Greek."

I smiled. I knew at least a dozen guys who went by Nick the Greek, but it wouldn't do any good to let him know that. "Sure, Nick," I said. "How do you know him?"

He looked down at the table and frowned. Then I knew how he knew Nick the Greek. But he told me anyway: "Mr. Paganas—he took me for quite a bit of money, Miss Flannigan."

"Stocks?" I guessed.

Mr. Nelson shook his head. "Real estate. He sold me fifty acres of land in Florida. Eventually I realized I had bought a nice chunk of the Atlantic Ocean."

"Sure," I said. I tried not to smile. "He's a professional, Mr. Nelson. He's fooled a lot of men of very high stature—you'd be surprised if I told you who." I didn't know who, exactly, we were talking about, but it was probably true. "What I mean is, you're in very good company."

Mrs. Nelson kept her eyes straight ahead, on whatever ghost she was staring at.

"Thank you, Miss Flannigan. That's a kind thing to say. Anyway, fortunately I realized this before Mr. Paganas left town, so I was able to recoup my losses. And something else. I told Mr. Paganas that I wouldn't report him to the police on one condition. If he would help me find my daughter."

"And he recommended me?"

"Yes. He recommended you," Mr. Nelson answered. "He said you no longer used drugs, that you were honest, that we could trust you. He said you knew—well, you knew the type of places where she might be. You see . . ." He paused and looked at his wife. She pulled her eyes out of the void and looked back at him. He turned to me again. "My daughter is on drugs, Miss Flannigan. My daughter is a . . . *a dope fiend.*"

I held back a laugh. I read the papers: every square in America these days thought their kid was a dope fiend. Mostly from what I gathered their kids smoked a little tea and cut school once in a while. And the paperback novels were full of them—kids who started off popping a benny and ended up on heroin, murdering a dozen of their neighbors with their bare hands. Kids from nice families who got lured in by evil pushers. On the book covers, the pushers always had mustaches.

I had never met an addict who came from a nice home. I'd met addicts who came from families that had money and nice houses. But never from a nice home. And I'd never met a dealer who had a mustache.

"Tell me about your daughter," I said.

He sighed. "Nadine. About a year ago—"

"How old is she now?" I asked.

"Eighteen."

"Nineteen," the mother cut in. She said it slowly, like it had only just occurred to her what was going on here.

"Yes, nineteen," Mr. Nelson continued. "About a year ago—"

"It started before that," Mrs. Nelson interrupted. She looked directly at me for the first time. "She started going into the city on the weekends with her friends."

"Where do you live?" I asked.

"Westchester."

"Ah."

She continued: "She started going into the city with her girlfriends every weekend. Didn't want to go to the club, didn't want to see her old friends anymore. Nothing so wrong with that. She was in her last year of high school."

Mr. Nelson picked up the story. "Except she started coming home—well, we thought she was drunk."

"Now, of course," Mrs. Nelson said, "we're not so sure."

"She started coming home later and later. Drunk or whatever she was."

"It seemed normal," Mrs. Nelson pointed out. "She was a young girl and she wanted to have fun. She wanted to spend some time in the city."

"She wanted to go to Barnard," Mr. Nelson said. "So she went to Barnard. We thought . . . You can imagine. We thought she'd get it out of her system after a few years of living in the city. Sow her wild oats and then get married or even start a career, whatever would make her happy."

"She always loved to draw," Mrs. Nelson said. "I thought she might like to work in fashion or advertising or something like that. It might be fun for her."

"But that didn't happen?" I asked.

"No," Mr. Nelson answered. "No. Instead we got complaints from the dorm mother, then from the dean. Nadine was coming home late, staying out, failing her classes."

"Even art," Mrs. Nelson pointed out.

"Even art," Mr. Nelson agreed. "And she was avoiding us. We hardly ever saw her anymore. Finally one night it all exploded. The dorm mother found something in her room—a kit for injecting drugs."

"*Shooting up,*" Mrs. Nelson clarified. I nodded solemnly.

"We wanted to take her to the doctor," Mr. Nelson continued. "But she refused. It turns out there wasn't anything the doctor could do for her anyway. . . . Well, I'm sure you know about that."

I nodded again.

"She promised to stop on her own," Mr. Nelson said. "But she didn't. She couldn't. This went on for months. Finally, they had to expel her from school."

"That was when she left," Mrs. Nelson cut in. "The day she had to leave the dorm. We went to go pick her up—"

"She was going to come home with us."

"But she wasn't there. She had left the night before. Just left, in the middle of the night."

"We haven't heard from her since."

"How long ago was that?" I asked.

"Three months ago," Mrs. Nelson answered.

"And you're just starting to look now?"

They looked at each other, annoyed. "We've *been* looking," Mrs. Nelson said. "First we called the police—"

"They didn't care. They said they would look into it."

"We never heard from them again," Mrs. Nelson continued. "That was the New York City police. Of course everyone in Westchester was very concerned, but there was nothing they could do. We tried looking around on our own, talking to her friends at school, trying to find out where—where people like that would be. But we got nowhere.

"So we hired a private investigator." Mrs. Nelson reached into her purse and pulled out a photograph. "He found out she was living with this man, Jerry McFall, in some little dump down on Eleventh Street. But by the time he told us about it, they were gone. He couldn't find them again."

She handed me the photo. A man and a girl were standing on Eleventh Street, near First Avenue. It was a sunny day. The girl was looking down at the ground. She had light hair and light eyes and small symmetrical features that didn't draw any attention. She was pretty, but only if you took the time to look. And there was nothing there to grab you and make you do that. Her hair was pulled back in a ponytail and she wore a tight black sweater with a black skirt and white high-heeled shoes. She looked like a cross between a college girl and a whore. And she didn't look happy.

The man didn't look happy, either. He wore a wide-brimmed hat and a fancy tweed suit. He looked like a pimp. He was thin and his face was long and narrow. I guessed he was a little younger than me, maybe thirty, give or take a few years. His eyes were dark and his hair was probably light brown. Not good-looking. Not ugly, either.

"What color are her eyes?" I asked.

"Blue," her mother answered. "Her hair is blonde, like mine."

"How tall is she?"

"Five feet three," Mrs. Nelson said.

That would put the man at a little under six feet. He looked like he wanted to smack the girl.

"The investigator took that," she said.

"We fired him," Mr. Nelson added. "That was all he came up with. I don't think he had the connections."

"*Underworld* connections," Mrs. Nelson explained.

"What we mean is, we need someone who knows about drug addicts, and girl drug addicts in particular. What concerns us the most is that Nadine doesn't have any money."

"This man, Nick the Greek, he said that you would

know where people like that go, how they make money and where they buy drugs and that sort of thing. You see, Nadine doesn't have any money—"

"We'd rather have her home, even as a drug addict, where we can keep our eyes on her and know that she's safe."

"We think you can find her," Mrs. Nelson said, looking at me. "We'd like to have her at home."

"We think you can find her, Miss Flannigan," Mr. Nelson repeated. "If you start looking today I'll give you a thousand dollars, cash, right now. And a thousand more if you find her. But that's to include all of your expenses, gasoline and meals and anything else you might incur—even travel."

A thousand dollars. Cash.

I looked from one to the other. They looked anxious and eager and hopeful. I knew they weren't telling me everything. Like I said, I'd never met a dope addict from a nice home. Maybe Mrs. Nelson hit the bottle, or maybe Mr. Nelson had a girl on the side, or five or ten girls. Maybe they spanked Nadine too much when she was a kid, or still did it, or gave her hell over her grades or were trying to get her to marry the guy from next door. Maybe the girl wasn't on drugs at all and just thought Westchester was a boring place to be and didn't want to go back there.

It didn't matter. With a thousand dollars up front, it didn't matter if I found her at all. If and when I found her I would worry about what to do with her.

I was walking out with a thousand dollars. That was what mattered.

"I have to be honest with you," I said. They already seemed ready to hand over the money but I figured it couldn't hurt to tighten the screws. "I've never done anything like this before. I'm not sure if I'm the right person for the job."

"I'm not sure, either," Mr. Nelson said. "Frankly, Miss Flannigan, all I know about you is that you live in New York City, you're . . . that you're in the same line of work as Mr. Paganas, and that you used to be a drug addict. But for now, you're our only hope."

I wasn't in the same line of work as Mr. Paganas, whoever he was, if he was selling real estate to Mr. Nelson. Not really. We'd probably started off in the same line of work, years ago, and while he moved up to selling real estate to people like Mr. Nelson, I'd moved down to boosting jewelry and pickpocketing. I figured he had recommended me because he didn't know any other dope addicts, and the whole business was probably not enough dough for anyone else he knew. I took in a deep breath and let it out slowly, looking from one to the other, like I was thinking.

"Okay," I said. "I'll do it."

They both looked like a weight had fallen off their shoulders. I told them the thousand would buy them a month. After that, if they wanted me to keep looking, they'd need to cough up more. I'd call them right away if I found anything, and if I didn't find anything I'd call them at the end of the week to check in. They agreed. Mr. Nelson handed me an envelope with ten hundred-dollar bills inside.

"So you'll call," Mrs. Nelson said again before I left, her eyes begging me. "You'll call right away if you find out anything at all."

"Of course," I told her. "You can trust me."